MAD BADGES

MAD BADGES

For Brad and Emily Cutright, two fine street cops.

a novel by

Dean Garrison

[signature]

ap
Aventine Prees LLC

The characters, events, organizations, and places in this book are fictional. Any resemblance to persons, living or dead, is purely coincidental.

Copyright © May 2003 by Dean Garrison
First Edition

Without limiting the rights under copyright reserved above, no part of this publication may be reproduced, stored in or introduced into a retrieval system, or transmitted, in any form or by any means (electronic, mechanical, photocopying, recording, or otherwise), without the prior written permission of both the copyright owner and the publisher of this book.

Published by Aventine Press, LLC
2208 Cabo Bahia
Chula Vista, CA 91914, USA

www.aventinepress.com

ISBN: 1-59330-045-X

Printed in the United States of America

ALL RIGHTS RESERVED

To John Kritschgau, Terry Hoatlin, Jim Billings, Mike Novakowski, Kenny K., Larry LeClair, Rudy Becker, John "Robbie" Robinson, Jerry Rauwerda, Tony Kruithoff, Pete Woodfield, Bob VanHouten, Krazy, Howie, and all the E.R. nurses at Saints, Butterworth, Metro, and Blodgett.

A lmost a year to the day before he helped kill Police Captain Maddox, Jack Pridemore was half-awake, late as usual, and struggling into his uniform in the filthy basement of the Mercer Heights Precinct locker room. The "Heights," as it was called, was a patrol sector that ran from the shitbox houses on Indianapolis Boulevard, down forty blocks on the east side of Bleeker Avenue's barrio to Cleveland Street, then east to the South Parkway, north for the 28 rotted industrial blocks of Bay Avenue, west for a dozen blocks on Belle River Boulevard, and north again on the Central Avenue corridor to Indianapolis again. The Heights was known as "The Depths" to police officers in the know. Pridemore had been there three months now, having come from a worse place, the famous South Precinct, after his long hospital stay.

Some of the standing water on the locker room floor was from the snow melting off of cops' boots. Some of it was leakage from various plumbing and heating problems in the ragged precinct building. Most of it, according to police lore, was the result of the downtown Command staff, with all of their computers and charts and inside cushy jobs, flushing their administrative toilets and shitting all over the average cop on the street. The walls in every locker room in the city had been painted a vague pink, the color of which was said to have a calming effect in a police management magazine that Chief Pearson had once read. The dents and dings and graffiti on the lockers had been hastily painted over by jail trustees using a thin tan city-purchased, low-bid enamel that barely covered the scrawled gang signs, obscene drawings, and various uses of the verb "fuck" that decorated the reachable surfaces. The cracked and peeling ceiling, its wire-framed light bulbs from a bygone era, had been left white and unwashed for years, the vents scarred with smoke from some ancient building fire. The old wooden benches were smooth and comfortable, having been burnished by the butts of a thousand sweating, spitting, and cursing police officers. Sometimes, after a long Watch, Pridemore simply sat there on the bench, gazing into his locker and massaging his scarred knee.

There were empty lockers, broken lockers, and lockers with neither locks nor doors. There were lockers with mummified rats inside. There were lockers that no one had been able to get into for years. There were lockers set aside for the visiting prosecutors, who seldom stopped by for their noontime fitness runs anymore. There was a locker, where the fat kid from the computer office kept his pocket protectors and his dirty magazines, and the locker reserved for the Federal guy who was on-loan to the Vice Unit, a Fed who was never there and who never changed clothes in The Heights. There were lockers for cops who changed at home and lockers for cops who had long since retired and lockers for dead cops that no one had ever bothered to clean out.

Pridemore tugged the sweat-stained bullet-resistant vest over his head, fastening it around his spreading, middle-aged belly. Somewhere there was a memo from the Equipment Office, instructing him to get fitted for a new vest. The memo, however, had been in error, because the new vests had never been ordered, and the budget for new equipment had run out the summer before, and any new vests would go to the captains, lieutenants, and building sergeants who left their new vests hanging in their new lockers anyway, and, besides, Pridemore had lost his copy of the memo. Sniffing a likely looking blue uniform shirt, that was neither too wrinkled nor too smelly, he struggled into it and covered the missing buttons with a frayed clip-on tie, the police union tie clip already in place. He stepped into the black fatigue pants, which per Command staff Order 04-871B were never to be worn with the blue uniform shirt and tie, which almost everyone ignored, because the striped-leg uniform slacks were commonly unavailable and looked silly anyway. The black clip-on tie, which almost every officer from Mercer Heights to Metro to South Precinct removed almost immediately upon hitting the street, was "the sign of a police professional," according to the Department's Manual of Procedure, and came in sizes Regular and Long. Badge 1659 was silver colored and, like the "J. Pridemore" nameplate, was polished down to a dull roar.

The shiny black gun belt was scuffed, gouged, and comfortable. It was a so-called "old style" belt from years before the Department had mandated basketweave style belts, which the Training Unit had deemed "less reflective in a tactical situation," or something equally as silly. Pridemore's belt, along with the three hash marks on his left sleeve, was a sign that he had been a cop for a long time. Eighteen years in all, seven on Afternoons in South; a year and a half in Property Crimes, the old Safe and Loft Squad, back when Linda wanted him to become a Detective, before the separation and eventual and inevitable divorce; nine odd years working Nights in the heart of darkness that was South Precinct; and now Nights again in Mercer Heights. They said, if you stood on your tiptoes on Belle River Boulevard and looked northward, you might actually catch sight of a human being, but then the South Precinct guys used to say the same thing about Cleveland Street at the bottom of Mercer Heights. The Department's recruiting officers liked to say, "It's not just a job, it's a career." The wise-asses said, "It's not just a career, it sucks, too." The boots were black and worn, stained with mud and road salt, with frayed laces that he would have to change any day now. He unholstered the .40 caliber, cleared it, checked it, changed magazines, and wished it were lighter, like the old 9mm Berettas or the old .38 Special Smiths. Glancing up and down the row of lockers briefly, he ran through a quick check of the spare, unauthorized, illegal, and highly irregular .380 Auto and slipped it into the pocket of his jacket. The black cloth gloves went in the other pocket. Pridemore grunted as he hefted the belt, snapped the keepers, and adjusted the cuff case and flashlight ring. Keys, baton ring, pepper spray, chewing gum. He checked the battered aluminum flashlight's bulb and slid the flashlight home. He ran a pocket comb through his thinning, grayish brown hair. The tattered leather briefcase that held a jumble of maps, memos, screwdrivers, lighters, pens, and assorted pain remedies fit under his arm. The uniform hat that he never wore but always carried was tucked atop the briefcase. Passing the cracked mirrors on the men's room walls without looking, he carried the whole mess across the hall into the muffled chaos of the Squad Room.

  Lieutenant Kenneth Berke was adjusting his pins and medals on today's freshly dry-cleaned shirt in the Commanders' Locker Room two floors above. He was not used to getting dressed this late, but had a special briefing to give the Night Shift troops this evening. He adjusted the polished silver collar bars and wiped some smears from the patent leather bill of his hat. Like any up and coming member of the Department's command staff, he wore the Department-issue whistle on a gold chain from his left epaulet. He maintained the creases of his immaculate uniform slacks as he removed them from the padded wooden hanger his wife had made him when he was promoted from Sergeant last year. His four years in Records Division and his two years in Personnel had taught him the look of success. They didn't call him "Jerky Berke" or "Berke Turkey" anymore, like they had back in his very short time on Patrol. He wished that his patent leather Oxfords made him look taller as he checked his image in the mirror. There were lighted mirrors at both ends of the short, carpeted row of tidy blue lockers in the Commanders' Room. He was only half listening to an Afternoon Watch Lieutenant who was gossiping about a female Lieutenant who had slept her way into a Captain's spot in Metro. Berke knew about the female Lieutenant in question and knew about others of that ilk who wiled their way into positions of responsibility and respect. He knew that he didn't have those advantages. He had earned his rank the hard way; he had produced when the Chief's Office wanted production; he had volunteered for work in Planning and Research. He had met the project deadlines and helped formulate the future directions of the Department. He was a team member and a go-getter. He was the pride of the Department, and he was going far in this organization, he knew. Lieutenant Kenneth Berke tapped a sheaf of Departmental memoranda and recent inter-agency updates into a neat stack for later perusal and headed downstairs to address the troops.

"Running late again, Mister Pridemore," remarked Sgt. Petty with a significant glance at the Squad Room's old wall clock. Petty was just passing out the night's stolen car lists, so Pridemore realized they hadn't actually begun yet. Pridemore grunted at Petty and put his stuff down by the wall.

In the back row of the room, a rookie who had just slid into a seat next to Buck Tyler, taking care not to scrape the chair. Tyler smoothed his enormous graying red moustache with his enormous right paw and said, "You don't want to sit there, Son."

"I'm sorry," said the rookie. "What?"

"I said, you don't want to sit there."

"Sure I do," said the rookie.

Buck Tyler hunched his great shoulders slowly, a sleeping bear roused from his nap. "No, Son, you *don't*." His voice was a low rumble.

The rookie glanced around for looks of support from other officers. Someone gave him a subtle head shake that told him to move. The rookie found a seat elsewhere.

Passing the small lesbian contingent that always sat in the front row, Pridemore made his way to the back, nodding at the cops he knew and ignoring the rookies, who in time would learn the routine and find their place in the squad room and their place in the Department. Sgt. Wheeler handed Pridemore a copy of the line-up as he passed. Sgt. Reed, whose case of "cruiser butt" had grown out of all proportion, gave Pridemore her brightest smile. She offered him a goldenrod copy of the list of rental cars that had somehow failed to return to the airport. There were two pages of finely printed car makes, models, and plates today. Pridemore politely declined his copy. Sgt. Lindsey, who had shaved his head again to disguise his baldness, looked up from the previous night's burglary list as Pridemore trudged by.

"The L. T. is coming in tonight," Lindsey warned. "Better button those cuffs."

"Uhhh, okay, thanks," replied Pridemore, doing nothing whatsoever about his appearance. He wound his way back through the chairs and tables to his spot beside Buck Tyler. James "Buck" Tyler pulled back the chair for him with one giant paw and let Pridemore sit down.

"You look tired," Buck said in a low whisper.

"You look like a red-headed closet queen," Pridemore replied, settling into his chair and adjusting his gun belt so that it wouldn't bite into his stomach.

Buck smoothed his moustache again and, without the trace of a smile, said, "But that doesn't make me a bad person, you know."

"No," Pridemore said thoughtfully. "No, it doesn't. Jack bad. Buck good."

At the front of the room, Sgt. Petty was saying something. The row of cops in the back row sat whispering among themselves, glazed eyes forward, ignoring the talking Sergeant. The cops in the middle rows, some of whom were working their way to the back, half listened to the speeches. The lesbian contingent down in front was always politely attentive. The rookies scattered throughout the ranks, sat next to their training officers and actually wrote things down. Petty ran the roll call, checking the names off his list. Everyone said "Here," except for two guys who said "Yo" and Jon Howard who always answered his name at roll call by saying, "Good night."

"Petty must be about the densest motherfucker ever to wear Sergeant's stripes," murmured Buck Tyler absently.

"You apparently don't remember Sgt. Sullivan very well."

"Hmmm, you're right. Sully was one spectacularly stupid fucker."

"Spelled his name wrong on the Sergeant's exam paper," Pridemore recalled, still whispering.

Finally, Buck smiled. To his left sat the tall Teddy Hoatlin, who was working a crossword, pretending to take notes.

"At least Sully had two testicles," Hoatlin said absently. "Sgt. Petty had one taken out last year."

"Cancer?" Pridemore asked.

"No, dipshit," sneered Buck Tyler. "He donated it to the Captain."

"So now they each have one?"

"Raisins. Little tiny things."

Hoatlin squirmed in his chair, adjusting his holster and running his fingers through his thick gray hair. "Well, I'm not for sure, but I think it was all those years Petty spent in Traffic, sleeping with a radar gun in his lap."

"But that doesn't explain how Petty got so dumb," noted Pridemore.

"He's a tool," said Hoatlin.

"A knob," Tyler added.

"And speaking of tools..." Hoatlin sat up in his chair. The room got quiet as Lt. Berke entered the room and Sgt. Petty fell silent. The whispering stopped. The Sergeants maintained their frozen smiles as Berke approached the podium with a handful of papers. The lesbian tribe perked up in the front row. The rookies sat at attention. Buck Tyler deftly snapped his tie back into place with two fingers.

"Good evening, People," the Lieutenant began. He gulped and shuffled his papers.

"I've got more time at the urinal than this little cocksucker's got on the street," Tyler observed quietly. Neither Pridemore nor Hoatlin cracked a smile. The line of dead eyes in the back row was as close to paying attention as they ever got.

The nervous little Lieutenant cleared his throat. "I have a memo here from Commander Jacobson downtown about our proactive policing of The Marble Room night club." Hoatlin's groan could only be heard by those seated near him. "There have been several complaints about officers responding to calls to keep the peace in the vicinity of The Marble Room. There's even some mention of both rudeness and even some of racial slurs."

"Oh my God," whispered Pridemore.

"Not surprising," noted Tyler, "as it's a nigger pimp bar."

"It is the assessment of Deputy Chief Forrest's planning team that a hands-off approach might be the best way to address this issue," Berke continued.

Connie Baldwin raised her hand in the front row.

"I'll entertain questions in a moment, please," Lt. Berke told her. The attentive lesbian put her hand down, trying to think of a follow-up question or two that would show her interest in the subject. Berke wondered if the dumpy, overweight female officer, in fact, had a crush on him.

"The Marble Room had, what, six murders in their parking lot last year?" Hoatlin whispered.

"Seven," Buck replied under his breath. "All misdemeanor murders."

"I asked Captain Maddox to ask Deputy Chief Forrest's office what exactly should be our stance with this hands-off policy," Berke continued.

"And what did Captain Maalox say?" Pridemore asked in a quiet singsong.

"It was explained to Captain Maddox that by hands-off, they meant, or rather, he meant. . ." His voice trailed off. "I mean, the decision of . . .uh . . .was reached." He glanced to his right, where Sgt. Petty smiled helpfully. "They don't want arrests for Disorderly Conduct or Excessive Noise at The Marble Room's two o'clock closing time."

"What about the fight calls there?" blurted out Connie Baldwin, having forgotten to raise her hand.

The little Lieutenant was perspiring now. He plucked at his tie. He was not very comfortable around patrol officers, especially Night Shift officers. "They're not . . .we're not saying *not* to make arrests for legitimate assault incidents that happen in our presence. Of course."

"Of course not," Buck chimed in helpfully.

"We're saying that our stance is to maintain the orderly flow off traffic to and from The Marble Room and its vehicle parking areas with a minimum of physical interference, short of the more confrontational methods that you may have employed in the past."

"In other words?" Hoatlin whispered.

"Maybe in English this time?" Pridemore suggested.

"In other words, let the colored guys shoot each other all night," Tyler concluded succinctly. "I like this plan."

Berke struggled onward. "So the club's owners have requested that we establish a presence in the proximity of The Marble Room . . ."

"That means, *be there*," Pridemore interpreted.

". . .but not to interfere with the orderly out-flow of patrons," Lt. Berke said.

"I figure that means, *do nothing*?" Hoatlin asked the members of the back row.

"Be there, but do nothing," nodded Pridemore. "Clever."

"We can do that," said an officer one row ahead of them.

"And let the niggers shoot each other all night," Buck Tyler concluded. "That sounds like a plan, don't it?"

Hoatlin nodded approvingly.

"So it's a containment plan?" Connie Baldwin asked encouragingly from the front row.

Berke considered the lesbian's assessment for a moment, wishing he could remember her name. "Well, yes, basically. It's peacekeeping at arm's length, so to speak." He was struggling to think of a better word than 'containment,' which he wished he had thought of. He would have to write that down for later. "Are there any questions that I can address?"

Off to the left a rookie started to raise his hand. His training officer snatched the rookie's elbow and brought it back down. The rookie said nothing. The lesson was learned. The roomful of police officers gazed blankly at the waiting Lieutenant, who was really sweating now.

Sgt. Petty spoke up. "We should start this plan this weekend?"

"Ummm, no," said Berke. "I think we can began implementing this plan immediately."

"Immediately?" cried Hoatlin in mock panic.

"We're late already," said Pridemore.

"I've been letting The Marble Room niggers shoot each other for two years now," Tyler announced proudly. "I'm way ahead of you guys."

Flex Sinclair, a black officer in the row ahead, turned and smiled. "That's *proactive* policing, Buck."

"Thank you, Brother," Tyler grinned.

"If there are no other questions or issues . . ." Lt. Berke started to say, preparing his escape from the Squad Room. His papers were in hand again as he swiveled toward the exit.

MAD BADGES

"I have a question about that notice we got last week on the bulletin board about overtime sign-up for parade duty in Metro," said a thin, freckle-faced officer in the second row. Sgt. Wheeler and Sgt. Reed glared at the offender. Sgt. Petty opened his mouth but closed it again as the Lieutenant began to speak.

"We know that situation has been confused," Berke said. "And downtown, they're developing a protocol to formulate a policy addressing that very issue."

The freckle-faced officer's mouth hung open. Sgt. Petty smiled. One of the lesbians started to raise her hand, but thought better of it and scratched her ear instead. Lt. Berke nodded with a reassuring smile and headed for the door.

"Slick white motherfucker," muttered Flex Sinclair.

"Raped again," said Hoatlin, adjusting his tall frame in the little chair.

"I kind of like it," Buck said.

"It's a grand plan," agreed Pridemore.

Lieutenant Berke made his escape from the Squad Room, down the corridor and up the stairs, ascending to the third floor where there were no grimy patrolmen or unshined shoes. He answered his telephone messages. He checked his email. Then he loosened his necktie, but only a little.

Captain Maddox's guts were aflame. It felt like last night's potato soup was racing this morning's soft-boiled egg in an acid reflux derby that might end up choking him to death. His stomach problems had begun when he left the radio car beat some twenty-seven years ago. With six months on the street he had been assigned to drive a District Commander's car, back when there were District Commanders and chauffeur-driven police vehicles. He had accompanied the Commander's alcoholic wife to museum openings and fund-raisers. He had kept his mouth shut and his nose clean, but had always listened carefully to the conversations in the backseat, be they political conferences or Department gossip. He had made Sergeant in the Data Processing Unit, when there was such a thing, and had patrolled a tiny three-man office for four years in the bowels of the old Headquarters building on 11th Street. When his promotion to Lieutenant had come, he was shifted to Administrative Vice, riding a desk once more and writing grants back when the Federal assistance money was plentiful and the Department's focus had been on the drug trade.

Captain Patrick Maddox had been invited to meetings back then, had seen the decision-making process first hand, and had witnessed the streams and eddies of ego and office politics as then-Chief Carmody had wielded power and budget. He had gone to the so-called "special meetings," where Carmody and his cronies had hatched public statements, damage control, and union contract negotiations. He had schmoozed with the City Commissioners and networked with the purse-strings administrators. He had liaisoned with Federal agency representatives and coordinated with other functionaries like himself, all of them looking for the leg-up, the opening, and the inside track. His guts had begun bleeding in earnest back then, what with the rubber chicken dinners, the diarrhea and hemorrhoids, and the constantly shifting insider politics. His ambitious wife, Sandra, had gone frigid in time for him to become impotent, while his juvenile delinquent teenage son was starting to impregnate trailer trash girls that had moved into his suburban hideaway. He knew how things worked, who to stroke this year and who to shun next year, when the timing of a budget request was ripe and when to hold your cards. But with every new lesson in his police administrative education, he had added an ulcer or a hairy mole that worried him in the shower or another clump of falling gray hair in the drain. By the time he had made his Captain's bars at forty-one, he looked like a fat, balding ulcerous sixty-year-old, though he didn't feel a day over fifty-five.

With the Captain's rank had come a Captain's responsibilities, namely supervisory, rather than administrative. They had kicked him out of the clean white tower of the downtown civic center, where memos came from, and dumped him in this ugly little ghetto precinct house, where memos ended up. After the first year in the Heights, it had slowly dawned on him why he had jumped at the chauffeur's job so long ago and with such eagerness: he disliked police work and, more specifically, police officers. He found that he and they had little in common. They didn't speak his language, and he didn't appreciate their humor, or what passed for humor. He hadn't minded writing the bid specs for the Department's Chevy cruisers in his downtown office, but he hated riding in one of them down here in the Heights. The smell and the grease and the uniforms and the attitudes all worked to undermine his digestive tract and ruin his erections. The other hard lesson that Captain Patrick Maddox was learning, too little and too late, was that his voice back at HQ was just one of many voices now and was frequently drowned out by the up and coming whiz kids in administration, the ones with master's degrees and computer savvy. They and their cell phones and teleconferencing palm machines were looking at Maddox and his little precinct and his miniscule budget as just another cop shop on the south side, no more a part of the grand strategy of the Police Department but simply a small box near the bottom of the ever-changing and rearranging organizational chart. That, along with the bile, had left a sour taste in his mouth.

The way out of this career plateau was, as always, up. The goal was to work his way somehow out of this pit of an office and back into the grace of Headquarters. He knew he couldn't do it by turning the Heights into a miniature model city or make its welfare-dependent drones into any sort of taxpayers. The Heights had been a dump since the 1970s, when the blacks and Hispanics had spilled from the Federal projects to the east and north in a flood of unprecedented baby-making. There wasn't much he could do about the citizenry down here. What he could do something about were the ragtag army of shiftless coppers who walked down these mean streets, these union-protected whiners who always looked for the short cut and always seemed to spoil the best intents of the civic center tower. If he could somehow turn these useless cops into models of police professionalism, Maddox thought, he might be able to escape the Heights and end his career, before it killed his stomach altogether, in some administrative spot in Internal Affairs or as a Deputy Chief.

The churning of the low-fat, low-sodium breakfast in his stomach and the bitter realities of a dog-eat-dog life in the Departmental hierarchy in his brain were working together to spoil his day. Which is why, when Jack Pridemore, rushing to end-of-shift, almost slid into Maddox's shiny Captain's Chevy with his filthy Ford patrol car in the Precinct's slush-covered parking lot, Patrick Maddox felt his options had started to spiral. He grimaced at Pridemore and the other cop in the cruiser. They smiled and waved and went to find a parking spot. Maddox would someday have to learn the names of some of these idiots. The next hour he spent in his private office bathroom, avoiding telephone calls and watching his pager flickering with trouble, trouble, and more trouble.

Edwin Suggs, black male, 23 years, dead of multiple gunshot wounds in the south parking lot of The Marble Room, 3260 South Cramer Avenue. A bouncer named Evan reported that Suggs had "a nine" at the time he was shot, but that some girl snatched it up and put it in her purse before the police arrived. A woman who did not want to give her name said "Bobo," reportedly a member of the Dudley Avenue Boys, was the shooter. Another bouncer said it was all over a girlfriend.

"I think she likes you, Bud."

Pridemore looked up from the Driving While Intoxicated Consent-to-Blood-Test Form that he was balancing on the corner of a linen cart and looked at the subject of Buck's comment. The homely little nurse with the funny little yellow eyeglasses and the acne scars was gliding past them again with another metal tray wrapped in blue. Her kinky reddish hair gave her a permanently shocked look. Her overbite, along with the way she inclined her head backward to keep the little yellow glasses perched on her prominent nose, worked together with her whiny, nasal tone to create a stupidly adolescent look, although she was easily past thirty. They had seen her before in Central Receiving's E.R., as they had seen most of the nurses and doctors and interns and surgeons and ambulance attendants before. And Nurse Yellow Glasses had seen Jack and Buck before. And hardly anyone knew anybody else's name. And nobody seemed to know Juan's name.

"Some days you're just a Big Little Boy, Buck," said Pridemore, chewing a toothpick and working his way down the checklist on the form.

Juan Doe #873 was a 250-pound Hispanic whose single remaining eye was probably brown. They couldn't tell for sure, because Juan's face was wrapped in bloody bandages. His other eye had probably been left in the windshield of the wrecked Toyota, along with his "Give Me Sex or Beer" baseball cap, but nobody had bothered to look for it. Juan was more concerned about his legs, both of which were broken at the thighs, than he was with his face, which had been thoroughly diced by the windshield. And they hadn't told him about the eyeball yet, as it was always better to give someone only one thing to be upset about at a time. And this was not the time.

"No," said the Pakistani intern, "I said I need a *Large* Laceration Tray." They were working on a stabbing victim behind the curtain in Bed 18. What troubled Buck Tyler about the Pakistani intern was that he did not speak with any traceable accent; his American English was flawless. He was even a bit of a smart ass.

"They don't *have* a Large Laceration Tray," replied Nurse Yellow Glasses defiantly. "They're *out.*"

"This tray doesn't have retractors," said the bald doctor whose right pinky was stuck into the stabbing victim's shoulder. "We're a centimeter and a half from the subclavian."

The black kid with the bald doctor's finger inside his shoulder was, of course, howling in pain. The beeps and chirps of various monitors, along with the singing and yammering of the drunks and drug cases strapped to their gurneys out in the hall, made for a symphony of barely controlled chaos, punctuated occasionally be a screaming crescendo from Juan Doe #873, who still refused to tell them his name.

"Would you like an Abdominal Tray then?" asked Nurse Yellow Glasses.

"Only if it has retractors," said the Pakistani intern.

"They usually *do.*"

"That would be fine then."

"I will *see* if they have any Abdominal Trays," Yellow Glasses huffed, sweeping away.

"Thank you, Nurse," called the bald doctor.

"See?" said Buck Tyler. "She likes you, man."

The fresh-faced intern, who was studying Juan Doe #873's X-rays with a doctor named Lew, was ignoring his pager. He looked at the caller's number and shut it off. Two minutes later, it hummed again. He checked it and pressed Delete once more, another busy young man with his love life in trouble.

"These films are fogged," said Dr. Lew.

"The patient didn't hold still," said Fresh Face.

"Get Radiology back up here to shoot this femur."

"Aaaaaahhh, my fucking leg!" cried Juan Doe #873.

"It fuggin hurts!" screamed the stabbing victim.

"I'm a little tea cup, short and stout," sang one of the drunks in the hallway.

"Oops," said Buck. "Here she comes again." This time he was not referring to Nurse Yellow Glasses but to the Impossibly Beautiful Blonde From X-Ray. The Impossibly Beautiful Blonde From X-ray never seemed to speak, never talked or made eye contact with the cops, and always looked composed and detached. She breezed in gracefully with three film plates clutched tightly to her warm little bosom, clicked her remote trigger, and gathered her plates. Then she was off again, the girl from Ipanema in green surgical scrubs, swaying gently and X-raying fractures. Dr. Lew looked at Fresh Face, and Fresh Face just shook his head. Buck Tyler simply exhaled. Even Pridemore dropped his toothpick and found he had checked a YES box incorrectly on the Consent-to-Blood-Test Form. No one seemed to notice or care that the Impossibly Beautiful Blonde From X-ray had X-rayed the wrong leg.

One of the druggies in the hallway made a grab at a passing ward clerk and scorned her as a bitch when she deftly avoided his filthy hand, which was strapped at the wrist to the rail of the gurney. The woman bent down gently to the druggie's head and soothingly whispered in his ear, "Your mother fucks Puerto Rican *dogs*." This sent the druggie into spasms of coughing and cursing, which the ward clerk ignored as she glided away.

"So listen, Paco," Buck said to Juan Doe #873. "Are you going to tell us your real name or what?"

"Fucking cops," spat Juan Doe #873.

"I'll take that as a No," said Pridemore.

"Your partner bailed out on you, Hombre," Buck tried again. They had found Juan Doe #873 hanging, half in and half out, on the hood of the Toyota on the passenger side, so they were pretty sure he wasn't the driver. Besides, the blood trail leaving from the driver's door had told them that Juan Doe #873 had not been driving. And yet he still wasn't going to give up his real name or the name of his escaped buddy. "It's up to you, Pedro."

"Fucking cops."

"You're probably gonna fucking die here tonight," Buck lied. Pridemore took a quick glance over at Fresh Face and Dr. Lew, who were huddled around the light box on the far wall. "You want us to get you a priest or something, Pedro?"

"Cocksucking cops."

"That's a definite No," said Pridemore, then to Juan Doe #873: "Do you have a wife or mother you'd like us to notify? We really should call someone, Man."

"You don't want to die alone, do you, Dude?" asked Buck.

"Come on, Man," Pridemore said, leaning closer. "For your mother's sake."

MAD BADGES 15

Juan Doe #873 started to cry beneath all the bandages. Gritting his broken teeth against the pain, he slowly worked out the word "Tony." His torn fists clenched and unclenched in the handcuffs. The next word was "Esteban."
"How do you spell that, Tony?" Pridemore asked.
Still no one had told him about the eyeball.

The Korean family that ran the East & West Café on the southwest corner of Unger and Market had decorated their bakery with old Bruce Lee posters, which confused Buck Tyler, who thought they were Japanese. At night, while they made the next day's cakes, cookies, and donuts, they fretted about the neighborhood blacks and, thus, were glad to have hungry police officers visit their shop. Everything cost a quarter if you had a badge. You could get a cup of tea for a quarter or three cups of coffee, two bagels with cream cheese, and a bear claw all for a quarter, so long as you kept the Africans at bay. The old man in charge nodded vigorously and smiled a lot, but understood no English. When the cops came in, he always spread his arms wide like he was going to hug them but always stopped just short of touching their uniforms with his flour-coated palms. The cruisers parked in back by the dumpsters, and the cops always slipped in through the side door, out of view of passing taxpayers and nosy Sergeants. They came in through the kitchen, where the crowd of Korean men and women of indeterminable age worked on their doughs and frostings. At the sight of a uniform, they always smiled but never seemed to be speaking, not even to each other. The cops stopped at the front counter for their orders, then sat in the back of the darkened dining room.
The cops called the old man "Mister Chi," although that wasn't his real name, and he didn't know why they called him that. Mister Chi had two daughters who emerged from the kitchen and changed the coffee pot. Magda was apparently the name of the tall, awkward one with the pitted face. She kept her hair long and wore T-shirts featuring the logos of American automobile manufacturers. Magda's crooked teeth detracted from her already unfortunate looks, but she was prompt and courteous and seemed to understand a little English. Lia was the name of the exquisitely beautiful second daughter who never spoke and never looked a cop in the eyes. Her teeth may have been crooked like her sister's, except that she never smiled or showed her teeth. Lia was

very tiny, wearing her black hair short and pulled back with a flowered ribbon. She wore an apron that said "Earl's Barbecue" on the front in large red letters and form-fitting blue jeans that clung to her flawless buttocks. Since Lia hardly ever came out from behind the counter, the cops seldom noticed her carefully red enameled toenails in her tiny wicker sandals. And, since none of the cops had ever slept with her, they had not seen the multitude of scars—from whatever Korean childhood bullshit they had been made—on her legs and back.

Most of the time it was the ugly Magda who served the cops their coffee and donuts. She never let on how much she understood their language, never even flinched at the mention of "pussy" or "Chink" or "crotch rot," although she understood them all. Magda secretly adored the long, tall Teddy Hoatlin and thought he was a funny sort of giant. But she never indicated as much, and he never knew. She had once heard Hoatlin telling a story about sex in his Chevy pickup back in his high school years, which is why she frequently wore a "Friends Don't Let Friends Drive Fords" T-shirt. But the message was lost on Teddy Hoatlin, who'd never had a thought for the gawky Korean coffee girl.

Street Sgt. Gibson was telling the story this time. Buck Tyler and Jack Pridemore had heard it before, but listened in silence as they sipped their coffee. Parnell and his rookie had never heard this particular war story about the career of Captain Patrick Maddox. Hoatlin was half-asleep with his boots up on a chair.

"So Maalox had just made Sergeant then, okay?" Gibson was saying. "He rode a desk in the Pin Maps and Pinheads Unit in Metro."

"I thought he was in the Huggies Squad then," Buck interrupted.

"Community Affairs," Parnell interpreted for his rookie. The rookie nodded in silence. Even Magda, who was arranging a tray of tarts across the room, understood about the Huggies Squad dimwits.

"Whatever," said Pridemore. "One of the Staple-Remover Unit assignments."

"Right," Gibson continued. "So Sergeant Maalox is getting a whole collection of Purple Heart ribbons for paper cuts downtown and he's watching the news one day. He sees Creepy Hal on the six o'clock news, and Channel 9 puts his name under it."

"Hal Griffith from Day Shift," Knolls told his rookie.

"So that fucking Maddox sees that Creepy Hal isn't wearing his uniform hat . . ."

"*With appropriate hat shield in proper alignment,*" Jack and Buck said in unison, quoting a line from the old Manual of Procedures.

"You guys remember that kind of B.S.?" asked Hoatlin.

"So nimrod Maddox sees a violation and writes it up and fires off a memo to Internal Affairs about how Creepy Hal was out of uniform and how it reflects badly on the professionalism of the Department and all that crap. And there's a copy of the I.A. slip that goes to Creepy Hal's Commander and a copy that goes to the I.A. Lieutenant, besides the original, which goes in the I.A. investigator's file. Creepy's commanding officer back then was Captain Terry..."

"Bless his soul, Captain Terry," Pridemore said reverently.

"Amen," intoned Buck Tyler.

"So now Captain Terry knows that the *reason* Creepy Hal was on the news that night was because he had just pulled this woman out of a burning car and saved her fucking life. So Captain Terry gets on the phone with the dildo from I.A. and explains it to him, how Creepy lost his hat and burned his fucking hands half off and saved this fucking woman from fucking burning to death. And he chews this I.A. guy a new asshole and wants to know the name of the little prick that beefed Creepy on this bullshit charge in the first place. And the I.A. fucking guy can't tell him, but he tells Captain Terry he'll straighten it out. So Terry lets it go at that."

"Get up and bring us some coffee, will you, son?" Buck Tyler said to the rookie. The rookie hesitates, glancing to Parnell for a clue.

"God, Buck, you're a lazy prick," says Pridemore. "Leave the kid alone. Just sit still, son. You're learning something there." He crossed the room, grabbed a toothpick from a little pink bowl on the counter, and brought back Magda's coffee pot, listening to the war story.

"So the fucking I.A. guy calls Maddox back and explains it to him. And Maddox is all embarrassed and shit. He withdraws the complaint and gets the charge slip back from the I.A. guy and burns it or something. And Captain Terry has ripped his copy to shreds the minute he got it, so that one's gone, too. So everything is fine and good in the world, and Creepy Hal doesn't know anything about it. He saved the woman's life, and he's a fucking hero. His fucking hands peeled for about six months after that, like he had a bad sunburn, and he had to wear gloves and grease and shit on his hands for about a year. But he's saved this cunt's life, and he's feeling pretty good about it. And we all know about it and everyone goes, like, 'Way to go, Creepy,' in the Squad Room and shit. And Captain Terry, rest his soul, wrote Creepy up for a medal for the thing, and he sends it up the line to HQ. Then Captain Terry retired."

"And two weeks later ate a fucking gun," mused Buck.

"Rest his soul," nodded Pridemore.

Gibson continued. "So the request goes up to Command, and the fucking guy in Command gets out Creepy's file and finds two slips from Internal Affairs in there from the prior year. One of them's for backing his cruiser into a fire hydrant or some shit. And the other is that fucking unfounded complaint from that asshole Maddox. You see, Maddox got back his copy of the I.A. slip, and Captain Terry had ripped up his copy, but there was still the third sheet of the charge that went to the Internal Affair Lieutenant. And he had signed it Approved, like those fuckers always do, and it gets shipped to HQ with all the other bullshit paperwork and gets stuck in Creepy's jacket at Headquarters. So, even though it's a completely unfounded complaint—in fact, it's a non-existent complaint that has technically been withdrawn—the fucking beef from that ass-wipe Maddox is now a permanent part of Creepy's file. Well, the building dweeb at Command doesn't know any of this. All he sees is that Creepy's got two I.A. raps for the past year, which means he's almost borderline to get fucking fired . . ."

"*A third such offense being punishable by the Department up to and including termination,*" Buck quoted the Manual aloud.

"Exactly," Gibson said to the mesmerized the rookie. "So the guy at Command doesn't know about the hat and the TV news and how that fuck-stick Maddox is really a worthless piece of shit, but he looks at the I.A. slips and refuses Captain Terry's request for the medal. And, by now, Captain Terry is gone..."

"Bless him," Buck murmured.

". . .and, to make a long story short . . ."

"Too late."

". . .Creepy Hal burns his hands half off and saves this woman's goddamn life, and he doesn't get a medal for it, not even a Letter of Commendation. He didn't get so much as a fucking Letter of Recognition for that thing. And it's all because of that bastard Maalox, who had just got his fucking sergeant's stripes and was looking to climb the ranks over the bodies of all the street cops he'd fucked over."

"On the other hand," said Hoatlin, who had suddenly come awake, "I once got a Letter of Recognition from the Chief's office for sitting in here." Even Magda knew this tale.

"In here?" asked the rookie, pointing at the floor.

"Right here."

"One of these lucky chairs, no doubt," added Pridemore.
"The dispatcher send me to a stolen car report while I'm sitting here eating a cupcake," Hoatlin explained. "And then she calls me back, that she forgot I was taking a 10-7, and she gives me a Disregard and gives the report to somebody else. So some other cop gets sent to take this stolen car report—I think it was Mick Benson from Afternoons—and he goes to the call. Well, the goofy guys that stole the car have stalled it around the corner, so when Benson is driving up, he just sees these two mopes and latches onto them. Two arrests for Auto Theft, and one of them's wanted on a homicide warrant out of Toledo or some place, and the guy gets his car back and—I don't remember who wrote him up for that bullshit—but, anyway, Benson gets a Letter of Recognition, which is worth two sheets of toilet paper. And I get a Letter, because the dispatcher left my name in the Call History on her computer. So I never budge from the East and West Café, but I get a Letter of Recognition."

"They call that 'recognizing excellence,'" Buck explained to the rookie.

"Well, you know, I figure I do an excellent job of sitting," Hoatlin stated proudly.

Magda scurried back to the storage room to chuckle quietly at Hoatlin's cleverness.

"It's because I'm gay," the complainant cried. "I just know it is. He just hates gay men."

"Who hates gay men, Mr. Bennett?" asked Pridemore, trying to write in the cramped little living room full of antique furniture.

"You can call me Charles."

"Mr. Bennett, who do you suspect did this?"

"He just a homophobic."

"Who's a homophobic?"

"Nelson's a homophobic."

"And who is Nelson, Mr. Bennett?"

"Donald Nelson is my landlord, and he just hates gay men. I know. Look! My God! He even broke Eunice the Unicorn."

Complainant Bennett's little apartment was a mess. It had been a tidy, if over-decorated little showroom of doilies and bric-a-brac, delirious wall hangings and handmade rugs. The tiny living room featured a wicker chair, a narrow rocking chair with embroidered pillows, a fireplace still hung with Christmas stockings, and dozens of shiny glass shelves. The shelves covered two and a half walls of the room from floor to eye level. Each shelf held twenty or more tiny little glass figures. There were small glass mastodons, glass giraffes, and glass poodles. There were itty-bitty glass pelicans, glass sea horses, and glass reindeer. There was even a little glass cobra. The ends of each shelf held a wine decanter or goblet of carved glass, each sporting an animal figure. Many of the items were now broken and scattered across the room. Pridemore had accidentally stepped on a shattered rooster, which he suspected was now stuck somewhere in the tread of his boot. And then there was the unicorn. Pridemore wrote "Eunice The Unicorn" into the burglary report under Missing Property, if only to amuse himself and the detectives who would be slogging through the Monday morning paperwork.

"Would you like some coffee, Officer?" Complainant Bennett purred.

"No, thank you."

"I'm sorry about this awful mess."

"It's not your fault."

"You're a dear to say so."

"Ummm, yes. Mr. Bennett, why do you suspect your landlord?"

"Well, there's no break-in anywhere."

"I noticed that, Mr. Bennett. I assume you locked everything up before you left?"

"I certainly did."

"And no one else has a key to your apartment."

"No . . .I mean . . .I don't . . .wait!" Bennett pondered the question, twirling a lock of hair by his right ear. "No. No, I don't think anybody else has the key. My mother has a key, but she lives in Palm Beach. She lives in a nursing home there."

Pridemore didn't ask why Bennett's mother in Palm Beach needed a key to Bennett's apartment on South Hawthorne Avenue. He didn't ask why a grown man collected little glass animals or why the man was wearing a crimson kimono covered with dainty elves. And Pridemore didn't even want to guess what the guy's green turban was all about. He wanted to get back out in the warm cruiser, where Buck was probably fast asleep by now.

MAD BADGES 21

"Does this guy, Nelson, live in the building?" he asked.

"Heavens, no!" the complainant replied. "He lives way out by Marionville somewhere. Nelson's a slumlord, he is."

"And he has a pass key?"

"Yes, he used his key just last month and came in while I was at work. He came in to fix the comfort station."

"Comfort station?" asked Pridemore.

"The crapper, dear," Bennett sighed. "It has never worked quite as it should."

"Do you have an address for Mr. Nelson?"

"Yes, of course. Somewhere. My, but this is a mess, isn't it?"

Pridemore nodded as Complainant Bennett whisked away to find his copy of the lease with Nelson's address on it. Pridemore took the opportunity to clear away some broken animals from the rug around him. He was writing "No sign of forced entry to the residence" when Bennett burst back into the living room, fluttering the lease.

"Here we are!" sang out Bennett, handing over the papers.

"This says the property owner is Beverly Nelson," Pridemore noted.

"His wife's name, no doubt."

"But you've mainly dealt with Donald Nelson?"

"Exactly. And he hates gay men."

"I see."

"Oh, my Lord!" cried Bennett, startling Pridemore. "There's blood on Munster Monkey!"

"Sure enough," Pridemore said, pretending to care about the clue.

"And here! And here, too! There's blood just everywhere!"

"Mmm-huh."

"It's a message," snapped Bennett. "My landlord hates gay men and alternative lifestyles and AIDS and everything. He's sending a message. The pig!"

Pridemore looked at the tiny flecks of blood. Sure enough, there was a minute trail of droplets across one of the shelves and down the side of the footstool by the rocking chair. The trail didn't seem to lead anywhere, which was fine with Pridemore, because he didn't want to follow clues anywhere on a night like this.

"And there's more over here!" Bennett shrieked, startling Pridemore again. "It's a hate crime. That's exactly what it is. It's a homophobic hate crime."

There was a box on the report form for "Hate Crime," which meant it would go in a special basket once it got downtown to the dicks. For some reason, the Department hated it when you checked the "Hate Crime" box and generated another entry for the City in the FBI's Index Crime list for the year. Pridemore had mistakenly checked the "Alcohol Involved" box on the report and was scratching that out to check the "Hate Crime" box, when Bennett screamed. Pridemore's right hand dropped reflexively to his holster.

"It's a rat!"

A small red squirrel dashed out from behind the rocking chair, paused on the fringe of the fake Persian rug, then darted across the room on his bleeding paw, and leaped up into the fireplace and out of sight.

"It's a red squirrel," said Pridemore, folding the Burglary report in half.

"How embarrassing," gasped Complainant Bennett, trying to catch his breath. He clutched at the kimono elves over his chest.

"You'd better close the flue on that chimney."

"I will. I will. Oh my!"

"You have a nice night now, Mr. Bennett." Pridemore zipped up his jacket as he opened the door to leave.

"Thank you, Officer," said Bennett. "Thank you sooo much."

"Don't mention it. That's what we're here for."

Back in the cruiser, Pridemore found Buck Tyler only half asleep. Buck scooted up straighter in the passenger seat and stretched.

"Routine B&E?" asked Tyler.

"Nope," Pridemore replied. "Lady just had a squirrel in her chimney."

"What the fuck's she want us to do about a squirrel in her chimney?"

"I dunno."

"D'you have to kill it?"

"No, it ran away. I got her all calmed down."

"Great," muttered Buck. "You're a fucking public relations dynamo, you are."

John Dennis Paul Doyle had been a good and relatively happy police officer for thirty years but had lived a miserable private life, marked by divorce, alcoholism, and suicide. The divorce part was actually three divorces, all the wives having left Denny. The alcoholism was what Denny had in common with two of his wives. The suicide was one of Denny's two sons. Denny's own slow death by liver disease, drunkenness, and a fall over a coffee table was not considered a suicide. He had simply not been able to handle retirement. But Denny had been a fine and happy cop, a street cop of the Old School. He had been a man in uniform you could respect, even though he had been made a Lieutenant in his final five years with the force.

There were two priests for the visitation at Lauder's Funeral Chapel that bitter cold evening. There was Father Price, of course, the Police Chaplain from St. Caimir's over on North Bleeker Avenue. Lenny Price was technically the Police Chaplain, even though he ministered to the both the cops and firefighters and even though he had a father, two uncles, two brothers, and a sister in the Fire Department. Father Price would have been Officer Price or Hook & Ladder Man Price if he had not been stepped on by a drunken horse in the St. Patrick's Day Parade on Boyd Avenue when he was fifteen. The other attending priest was Father Paul Doyle, Denny's surviving son, who had chosen the priesthood over his father's profession, having seen what the policeman's lot had done to his dad. The funeral itself was scheduled for the next afternoon at Queen of the Most Holy Rosary, Father Paul's church uptown. Everyone at Lauder's that night knew Father Price and Father Doyle and their stories, and everyone knew about Denny and the gin and the coffee table.

The only police officers above the rank of Sergeant present were those who had retired. They had come up through the ranks with Denny from the bricks to the desk, and many of them, like Denny, had their share of wives and bottles. Like Denny, many of them had seen a part of themselves die when they left the street. To them, Denny's physical death was the final episode in a line of Denny deaths. They knew that a part of Denny had died when his first marriage had ended and Joyce Doyle had packed and left with the children. Another part of Denny had died when his eldest son, Dwight, had jumped off the West Ferry overpass into traffic and left that hateful suicide note that the responding cops had torn up and burned. And then Denny had made Lieutenant six years ago and had been squeezed into a desk spot up in Third Shift Central, where he supervised two desk sergeants and fielded telephone calls from Command and drank from a pint bottle in his file cabinet. There had been a going-away party that rivaled most cops' retirement parties when Denny made L.T. and left the street. Many of the mourners at Lauder's that night had also been at the prior promotional wake. So, by the time of his actual retirement from the Department and the final revolt of his enlarged liver a year later, so much of Police Officer John Dennis Paul Doyle had died that there was not a lot left to cry about.

Pridemore was there, remembering the time the enormously fat mental had gone off on them in a hotel lobby over on Palace Avenue, before it had been renamed Antoine Fraiser Avenue. Denny had been a Sergeant then and Pridemore a rookie. Denny, not a large man by any stretch, had leapt onto the mental's neck, and they had all gone done in a whirling, slugging mess on the lobby floor. Rookie Pridemore had ridden the mental's beefy right arm, its fist clawing for his groin. The guy had obviously been going for their guns, they knew. Denny had choked the guy blue to no avail and had finally crashed a lamp into his cheek, ending the thing. Then Sgt. Denny had fixed all of the reports and the Use of Force narratives and the ambulance log. Denny had probably forgotten the whole thing long ago, of course, but it had made an impression on the rookie. You did what you had to do to get the job done and made sure everyone on your team went home alive.

Clark Daniels of Metro Days was there, recalling the irate wife with the scissors on that stairway on Vanderbilt; how Denny had spooked the woman with some chatter about voodoo and had literally pulled the rug out from under her. Bob Jensen, now in Vice, was there, thinking about how Denny had barked like a Canine Unit for a good fifteen minutes until the burglar came down from that attic on Neland Avenue. Lyle Parker, now a Traffic Unit investigator, was remembering the sweaty husband who had slipped out of their grasp and hit an air conditioner on the way down on a jumper case at the McLeary Gardens project. Lyle had felt really bad afterward and had not been able to eat for days; Denny had cheered him up with a cheese sandwich and a strange war story from his own rookie days. Big Dan Kritchgua and Big Don Klomparens were both there, giants in tight black suits, both of them having grown beards after their retirements. Yvonne Reynolds, a Records Unit clerk who had once soothed Denny between two of his divorces, did not recognize Liz Dunlop, a Juvenile Unit detective, who had similarly tended Denny's needs over much the same time period. Kimberly Hutchins, now a Homicide detective, had not been one of Denny's girlfriends. He had been her Training Officer way back when. As a young cop she had once tagged a 12-gauge sawed-off into Property with a 20-gauge shell still jammed deep inside the magazine.

When the inevitable nasty-gram came from the Property Room Supervisor, along with a complaint slip from I.A., Training Officer Doyle had stepped in and taken the hit, saving both her career and her reputation. Doug Quinn, who had been one of the officers on the scene at Denny's son's suicide, realized that Denny, whether in heaven or hell, now knew the contents of the note that his asshole son had left. When he had a moment alone beside Denny's closed casket, Quinn silently asked Denny's forgiveness in destroying that note.

Out in the foyer, between two huge wreaths, stood a large bulletin board covered with photographs of the living Denny Doyle. There was Denny, toasting Captain Terry at the latter's retirement party. There was a blurry picture of a blurry Denny, hoisting a cold one on a fishing trip. There were younger versions of Denny, Buck Tyler and Teddy Hoatlin around a keg after a touch football game. There was Denny in a tux, waving a champagne glass, at his daughter's first wedding. There was Denny with a beer stein at his second wedding reception. There was Denny with a tumbler of scotch, playing cards with the boys. There was a picture of Denny with Jack Pridemore and Judd Christian with drinks, of course, at some sort of police bash, all of them pleasingly shitfaced. Pridemore paused to study the picture and the undamaged face of his former partner, Christian.

"That must've been Denny's fortieth birthday party," said a whispery feminine voice behind him.

"Elaine, you made it," Pridemore smiled, giving her a hug. She held him for a few long seconds, searching his face. "I'm sorry I haven't been up to the hospital for a while. How's Judd?"

"Not much change," Elaine Christian replied. "How's your knee?"

"Better than it was. I hardly ever fall down now."

She let him go, but kept a loose hold on his sleeve. She pushed some thick black hair from her cheek with a slender hand and turned her huge dark eyes back to the pictures on the bulletin board. "Why the closed casket?"

"Ah, Denny, bless his heart, got drunk and fell over a coffee table," explained Pridemore, "but no one found him for a few days. Better this way."

"That's a shame." Elaine tightened her full lips into a grimace. "Denny went out with a glass in his hand."

"You still drinking?" she asked, bringing the subject back to him and them.

"Oh, a beer now and then," Pridemore lied gently. "They didn't let me have any while I was in Rehab for the leg." He massaged his right pant leg just above where the long scar started.

"Still hurt?" She looked down at the pant leg, remembering the exploded knee that had tangled in a cruiser's dashboard, the screaming in the emergency room, and the sight of her husband Judd with his lopsided head in bandages. They all still hurt, she knew.

"Mainly when it gets cold," Pridemore replied. "Is the Department still giving you trouble with the insurance?"

"They make us jump through hoops with the paperwork, but they're carrying us for now. Judd has to move to an Extended Care Facility later next month."

"A nursing home?" Pridemore asked, his anger rising.

"Well, they've given up on the therapy," she said in resignation. "It's now what they call a Maintenance Option."

"Maintenance." Pridemore turned the word over in his throat. He remembered the drunk in the van who had blown the stop sign and hit them; the guy had died at the scene. He remembered some of Judd Christian's brain on his sleeve as he tried to crawl over the steering wheel and out through the fractured windshield. He remembered the supervisor from Internal Affairs reporting that the speed of the cruiser, Pridemore's speed, had been eleven miles over the posted limit, thus, relieving the Department and the City of ultimate financial responsibility. He remembered Elaine Christian's long sad eyes, looking half again her thirty-some years, as she visited him in the hospital. She always told him how much better Judd was doing, improving day by day as the head injuries mended, but then he never got better. Jack remembered the first time he had gotten in a wheelchair and pumped his way down to Judd Christian's room, passing him in the first bed without recognizing him. They had had long talks, Pridemore making all the words and Judd's tubes and machines doing all the talking. Jack had cried and cursed. He had learned to walk again without a limp. He had used up his sick time, his vacation time, and his savings, and he had sold his house and car. He had gone home, knowing that his partner would never go home, and he had returned to work, only to be transferred to The Heights. "Maintenance," he said again.

Elaine's voice came back to him. "Would you like to go get a cup of coffee?"

"I've got to work tonight," Pridemore said, and he realized now he was holding her arm. She had leaned to support him. He could smell the scent in her still black hair. "I'm sorry."

"It's all right, Jack," she assured him.

"Maybe we could have lunch on Sunday," he suggested, brightening a little. "The three of us at the hospital."

"Why don't we meet at the hospital, eat first, and then go up to see him after." She had long tired of having a tray of food brought in for her, while the bags feeding the tube that ran from Judd's nose down into his stomach were changed and refilled.

"That's fine," said Pridemore. He kissed her forehead and held her for a second. Passers-by would have thought they were sharing a sad memory of Denny Doyle, but poor Denny had been dead a long time now.

Teddy Hoatlin and Pridemore were trying to write a report on a vacant gurney. Friday night madness was reigning at Mount Mercy E.R. as usual. An ambulance crew rushed in with a burn patient who was beyond screaming. A janitor with a bloody mop scooted past them.

A fat white lesbian had stabbed her fat black girlfriend with a pair of scissors and said she'd do it again, given the opportunity. She was on her way to jail. The black lesbian squirmed on a gurney, cursing the doctors and nurses and cops. There was a jagged gash in her enormous left breast, which one of the doctors was probing with a sterile swab, trying to determine if the chest cavity had been punctured. They could have more easily figured this out by listening to her chest sounds, but she wouldn't quit hollering.

"Ain't no motherfuckin' thang!" she yelled.

The doctors were trying to treat her and find out what symptoms she was experiencing, but she would have none of it.

"I don't need yo motherfuckin' hands on me, motherfuck!"

The nurses were trying to get some personal information from her, so they could contact her family and fill out forms and arrange for insurance coverage or whatever. She'd been in the trauma room for fifteen minutes and hadn't told them anything useful. The doctor with the sterile applicator asked her something in a low, calm voice.

"Of *course*, it motherfuckin' hurts!"

The nurses gave up and wrote her in as a Jane Doe. Teddy knew her as "Letisha," so she went down in the chart as "Letisha Doe." She spat at a male nurse who was trying to strap down her arm for an I.V. tube.

"They lyin'," she cried, denying everything. "Fuckin' *po*-lices is lyin'. Ain't nobody stabbed nobody here." She wriggled her huge body around, trying to get up. "I fell on them scissors! Didn't nobody motherfuckin' stab me!"

The hospital social worker, who had seen it all before, came into the triage room and checked with the cops. "What's on the menu for tonight?" he asked.

"Well, they were playing Paper-Scissors-Rock," said Pridemore, "and it got out of hand."

"I've warned these darn kids about running with scissors," Hoatlin said.

The social worker nodded. "Accidents happen, I guess."

"Motherfuckers!" wailed Letisha Doe.

Pumping, pumping, pumping.

Twenty-three, 24, and then 25 miles per hour. Simulated. With the stationary exercise bike's brake drag set to "Rigorous." Lt. Kenneth Berke would maintain the 25 miles per hour at Rigorous for twenty minutes, as he did every evening in the den of his sensible suburban home. On the bookstand in front of the handlebars was Wainright's "Management Strategies in the Modern Police Environment." Kenneth was reading the chapter called "The Percolator Model of Advancement." He knew that few, if any, of the other Lieutenants had studied Wainright, mainly because most of Wainright's theories had been dispelled by the more recent works of Siegel and Jennsen, particularly their book "Non-Linear Modeling in Police Theory and Organization." But Kenneth calculated that a well-rounded police manager should know such things. It didn't hurt to do one's homework. One never knew when a question might come up. One never knew when a six-year-old body of work like Wainright's might, just *might*, come back into style again for some unforeseen reason. In any case, Kenneth would be on top of things.

Pumping, pumping, pumping.

MAD BADGES

Priscilla Berke peeked through the slightly ajar door of her husband's study and watched his well-muscled back straining against the "Quantico Academy" sweatshirt. He hadn't actually attended the FBI Academy, but his heart was in the right place, she knew. She watched the sweat running down into his black bicycle shorts and marveled at the tight calves glistening on the bike pedal upswings.

"While the less proactive aspects of a specific law enforcement management matrix seldom impact a negative correlation of per capita index crimes, the ratio of all representational models to . . ." Kenneth was reading. He read it again. Dr. Wainright was so difficult to get through at times. Kenneth knew it was his own fault, his own shortcomings, that really prevented him from understanding Wainright. After all, Wainright's theories, among those conversant in community-oriented-policing-style management, had been criticized as overly simplistic. Berke vowed to try harder as he read the passage again. "While the less proactive . . ."

"Honey?" Priscilla called to him hesitantly from the partially closed doorway. She touched the edge of his door gingerly, as if it was hot. She called again, but he did not answer. No doubt, he was studying hard for the Captain's Examination, just as he had sweated through the Lieutenant's Exam before it and the Sergeant's Test before that. He always began studying for the next test immediately after attaining the rank he had been studying for since earning his last promotion. He was a driven man, Priscilla knew. That was one of the things she admired about him. She was proud of his drive and stamina. Her husband was a man who was really going places.

On the stationary bicycle, Kenneth was keeping the speed at only 23 miles per hour now and examining one of Wainright's negative correlation graphs. He did not hear the door creeping open behind him, nor his wife's timid voice. He glanced down at the timer between the handlebars. He had been at it for ten minutes now; he was halfway there already.

Priscilla had tucked Kenny, Jr. into bed after his bath and prayers. She had luxuriated for almost twelve minutes in a tub of hot water sprinkled with just a hint of generic brand scented bath salts. She had folded her warm and comfy flannel pajamas into the clothes hamper and had instead put on the blue pastel wild thing with the lace bodice, the plunging neckline, and the leg cutout. Priscilla had bent over the toilet, head down, brushing her mousy dishwater blonde hair with furious abandon, trying to achieve a lion's mane of wanton desire. She had checked the effect in the medicine cabinet mirror and saw that she only looked somewhat fuzzy and disheveled. She had rescued her look with a dangerously pink ribbon, which came to a reckless bow slightly to the right of the part in her hair. Darting to the bedroom dresser, she had tried on her daisy clip-on earrings, decided they were too much for the occasion, and opted for the tiny gold-colored clip-on hoops. Toying briefly with a black choker ribbon at her throat, she decided it made her look even paler than she was. She had applied just a mere touch of Tabu to her neck below her right ear and another to her left wrist. Priscilla Berke had skipped back into the bathroom, closing out the world, as she applied a third drop of perfume to the back of her left knee, and then—and then!—yet another drop higher up—*way* higher up!—on the inside of her thigh. Oh the joy! It had made her shiver, perking up her A-cup nipples against the cool blue fabric of the nightie. She had left the light on in the bathroom with the door slightly ajar, quietly switched off the reading lamp in the bedroom, and turned down the comforter and freshly laundered sheets.

"Honey," she called again, consciously lowering her voice. She didn't want to sound like she was merely calling him to empty the kitchen trash again. She opened the door to his study still wider and positioned her thin body so that he would see one naked leg and one inviting breast when he turned to her. "Kenneth?"

He made a sound like "hmmph." It might have been an acknowledgment. It might have been the unexpected peak in one of Dr. Wainright's convoluted graphs. It might have been frustration at the speedometer needle fluttering at only 21 miles per hour now. Priscilla abandoned her teasing pose in the doorway and padded across the sensible gray carpet to Kenneth and his stationary bike. She gently tapped his elbow, the sweat of his arm moistening the tip of her small index finger.

"Huh?" Kenneth finally said, turning to his wife. His eyes flickered up to the ribbon askew on her head, but not to the gaping bodice below.

"Kenneth, Honey?" she purred. "Are you about done?"

"I've got about eighteen pages left in this chapter," the Lieutenant replied.

"Are you sssure?" Priscilla asked, her uncertain fingers worrying the lace neckline.

"Well, it might be twenty pages." He turned back to the textbook as if he might actually tally up the remaining pages for her, ruining her efforts no matter what the number.

Priscilla parted the pastel nightie slightly. She wished she had closed the door on her way in. Leaning slightly forward, she thought of another tack. "If you have a few minutes," she whispered, wetting her thin pink lips, "I'd like to salute the Little Police Chief."

"Prissy...Honey...not now," Kenneth said, trying not to hurt her feelings with his evident disinterest. He stared through sweating brows at the dictums of Wainright, hoping she might think it over and leave him to his studies. Wiping his forehead with the fist of his right hand, he glanced down at the floor where her bare feet would be, but she was gone. Pumping, pumping, pumping. Kenneth Berke got the speedometer needle back to a rock solid 25 miles per hour and kept it there. He looked back over his shoulder for a moment and saw that Priscilla had already left the room and closed the door.

Deon Tolbert, black male, 19 years, dead of a gunshot wound to the head by the northeast corner of The Marble Room, 3260 South Cramer Avenue. According to witnesses, nobody saw nothing, nobody knew nothing. A woman said she had heard some noise earlier, but wasn't sure it was gunfire.

"What exactly is your *problem*, Mister Pridemore?" Sgt. Petty barked from across the gray metal desk. Petty often started conversations this way.

"I don't know. Is there a problem with me, *Sergeant*?" Pridemore's emphasis on the word *Sergeant* was unmistakable, even to Petty. There was a way that rookies said it that showed a sign of reverence. There was the way Command officers said it that was either belittling or endearing, depending on the tone. And, finally, there was the way that veteran police officers drummed out the word, as if you say, *You're in the way again, Little Man.* And that was the way Pridemore had said it. He couldn't even help it any longer. It just came out. *SARRRgeant.*

"There is certainly a problem with your stats for last month," snapped Petty.

"I see," said Pridemore, never asking what statistics Petty was talking about or what was wrong with them, either too low or too high, or even venturing a guess as to what was expected of him.

"You only made three traffic stops last month," Petty stabbed at the computer printout on the desk. As the Sergeant's voice rose, the police officer's jaw moved imperceptibly sideways and his eyelids relaxed into the game face that cops use for talking to mentally ill persons and irate taxpayers. Petty, too, knew the look, but continued talking anyway. "One of your traffic stops for December was an eleven year old in a stolen car."

"Yes?" nodded Pridemore, unperturbed.

"Yes what?"

"Yes, Sir?"

"No, Mr. Pridemore," Petty fumed, "I mean, is that *all* you have to say about it?"

"Well, Sergeant," Pridemore replied with that tone again, "the kid was too little to be driving. I had to arrest him."

"You *had* to?"

"No avoiding it."

"You *had* to arrest him?"

"That's correct."

"I'm sorry that the Department had to rouse you from your slumbers so that you actually *had to* go make a traffic stop and *had to* arrest somebody."

"That's all right, Sergeant. I was awake anyway."

Petty hated it when they froze him out like this. Pridemore, like most of the other patrol officers, knew this and used it when they could. What Pridemore didn't know was where this sudden interest in the Traffic Stop statistics was all coming from. From Command, probably, he figured, or from some middle management type who was trying to polish his unit's numbers with the chart-makers in Pinheads & Pin Maps.

"And your second momentous traffic stop for the month of December was a woman who actually ran into your cruiser, is that right?" demanded Petty.

"Backed right into me. Yup."

"In a Taco Bell parking lot?"

"Hmm, I thought it was a Burger King," said Pridemore.

"That's what you call a traffic stop?"

"It might have been a Taco Bell, but I'm pretty sure it's a Burger King."

"You're missing the point again, Officer Pridemore."

"No, I'm sure it was the Burger King. That's the one on Roxbury just south of Magnolia, right? Yup, that's the B. K. lot there."

Petty ignored him. "And your third and final traffic stop for the month was a man who ran into a train down on Sloan?"

"Yes," said Pridemore. "South Sloan Avenue, there where it crosses the railroad tracks."

"Really?"

"Truly, Sarge. I wouldn't kid you. That's where the train was."

"And you logged that as a traffic stop?" cried Petty, furiously.

"He was traffic, and he stopped. Yes."

"But *you* didn't stop him."

"Yes, I did."

"It says here that he ran into a locomotive."

"That's right."

"So who stopped him, you or the train?"

"Well, Sergeant," explained Pridemore, "the train stopped his car, and his car sort of bounced off, and then he tried to get out and run, and that's when I stopped him."

"And that's a traffic stop?"

"Yes."

"And you arrested him?"

"Yes, I had to. He was drunk."

"You *had* to?"

"Yes," Pridemore nodded. "I did."

"And you took the man to jail?"

"Well, I took him to Central Receiving first. He broke a bone in his foot."

"And after that, sometime, you eventually took him to jail."

"That's correct."

There was a long silence as Sgt. Petty glared down at the report in front of him. Officer Pridemore shifted his weight from one foot to the other. Sgt. Lindsey was straining to listen from the next room. Petty shuffled the sheets of paper and cleared his throat.

"Why exactly . . .?" He started again. "How exactly does a man crashing into a train constitute a Hate Crime, Mister Pridemore? Can you tell me that?"

"It's all there in the report, Sergeant. He'd had a fight with his wife at their apartment on Evers. He broke the TV and slapped her and spray-painted 'I HATE YOU, BITCH' on the hood of her car. Then he took off up South Sloan and, when he got to the railroad crossing, he . . ."

"I know all that!" interrupted Petty, rising from his chair. "But that's a domestic issue, not a Hate Crime."

"But he wrote 'I HATE YOU' on her car," said Pridemore.

"But that's not a Hate Crime. That's a vandalism crime or a domestic violence crime or a . . .a . . .a car crime, for Chrissakes! But it ain't no Hate Crime."

"The car crime, as you call it, was the Failure to Yield to a Railway Vehicle, which is why I made the traffic stop. It's right there in the report."

"And that is not what constitutes a legitimate traffic stop in this police department. A traffic stop is a moving violation for Driving While Intoxicated or Violation of the Basic Speed Law or Changing Lanes With Failure To Signal. It is not—I repeat *not!*—showing up after a guy has already hit a frigging train."

"But . . ."

"And spray-painting his wife's car is not—I repeat *not!*—a standardly indexed Hate Crime in this or any other police agency." Petty's telephone began to ring.

"But the guy wrote . . ."

"I don't *care* what they guy wrote on his wife's car door . . ."

"It was the hood." The phone rang again.

"Hood or door," continued Petty. "I don't care what he wrote or where he wrote it. Whatever it is, it isn't any sort of Hate Crime. And calling this other bullshit a legitimate traffic stop is also bullshit. In fact, all *three* of your traffic stops for the month of December are bullshit stops." The telephone rang again. Snatching it up, Petty barked: "What?" The voice of authority on the other end cowed the Sergeant's tone, as he responded with his name, rank, and a series of Yes-Sirs. Petty's face changed colors a couple times before he gently hung up the phone. He seemed to have lost track of what he was hollering about. His eyes rose to Pridemore as he tried to regain his focus.

"Was there anything else, Sarge?" Pridemore asked helpfully.

"From you," Sgt. Petty said slowly, "we need more traffic stops this month and less Hate Crimes. I want you to get approval in writing from a Sergeant before writing any more Hate Crime reports. Is that clear, Mister Pridemore?"

"Clear."

"And more Traffic Stops, legit ones. Is that also clear?"

"How many more?" asked Pridemore, knowing the answer.

"You know we can't dictate the number of traffic stops here."

It was a union issue. It was a public relations issue. The answer was always MORE, but never how many. What constituted ENOUGH was the decision of the supervisor, but there never was a quota, at least not one that anyone in Command would admit to. Pridemore knew it. Petty knew it. Everyone knew it. The trick was to make more Traffic Stops than the lowest cop on the shift and, thereby, avoid getting chewed out by the Sergeant. It was a game that everyone played. Everyone was secretly glad that Pridemore had quit playing the game and would be the one getting chewed out by the Sergeant at the end of every month. They respected Jacko for being the fall guy month after month. Frankly, Pridemore didn't care about the respect or the traffic stop statistics or the Hate Crime statistics. Sergeant Petty knew about the cops respecting Pridemore, and it pissed him off. Petty knew that Pridemore wouldn't make any more legitimate Traffic Stops this month than he had last month, and this too pissed him off. And Petty knew that Officer Pridemore didn't even care, and *this* was what pissed him off the most.

"Was that all, Sergeant?" Pridemore asked.

"That . . .is . . .all," Petty replied. After Pridemore left, Petty leaned back in the gray metal chair. The old chair groaned. Petty groaned. Sgt. Lindsey slipped into the room and headed for the coffee pot.

"Another heart-to-heart talk with Pridemore?" Lindsey asked brightly.

"That miserable fuck," groaned Sgt. Petty. He massaged his temples.

Sgt. Lindsey poured himself a cup of stale coffee and smiled to himself.

The wizened old Plymouth had made it out Belle River Boulevard to the madness of the 15 Extension and up to the crush of the 210 turn-off and west to the near suburbs, as it always did. At this time of the morning, all the heavy traffic was going the other way, in-bound to the downtown frenzy. The stationwagon was one of the few good things Linda had left him in the divorce that the medical bills hadn't also gobbled up. If you ignored the mismatched whitewall tires, the dented roof rack, and the missing trim, it was a fine old car. Old and ugly, but it always came through for you, Pridemore liked to think, like me. He stopped at the Shell station at Parkhurst and Annapolis for gas, a newspaper, and a frozen enchilada dinner. The parking lot at his apartment complex still hadn't been plowed and was slushy and gray. He backed into his parking space, an old policeman's habit, and got yesterday's mail. There was something from Linda's lawyer's office, a letter from his daughter, Jennifer, a postcard with a coupon from a carpet cleaning service, a larger envelope from the Police Union, and two offers for new credit cards. He juggled his packages, unlocking the door to 314-B and landed in the living room.

Mister Alp, his illegal roommate, glared at him from atop the television. Most cops were not cat people, Pridemore knew. Cats didn't do what you asked of them, so you never even bothered. Cats didn't care about you, but expected your utmost attention. Cats just needed an automatic can-opener and a source of heat; you could go piss up a rope for all they cared. But Pridemore had found Mister Alp out by the dumpster one day, after he had come home from physical therapy, and they had been together ever since. Where Teddy Hoatlin had his hunting dog and his pickup, not to mention his family of four, and Buck had his various student nurse pets and all his ex-wives, Pridemore had Mister Alp.

Before reading Jennifer's letter, Pridemore started the Enchilada Delight dinner in the microwave, cleaned up some Alp turds that had somehow missed the catbox in the kitchen, and stripped into his huge raspberry-colored bathrobe and limp black slippers. Mister Alp at first ignored the can of cat food, as he always did. Pridemore parted the heavy black-out drapes in the living room and cracked the window slightly to air out the place. The little apartment was bathed in a calculated dimness of 25-watt bulbs and dark lampshades; it seemed quieter somehow.

Jennifer was thinking of changing her major from History back to Journalism at Colorado State. She said she was getting serious about an architecture graduate, as the romance with the bass player just hadn't worked out. She said her work as a waitress was keeping her out of hock, which, Pridemore knew, meant that she needed some money. She said she missed him, which was not exactly true, and loved him, which was, in fact, the case. She had included a small photo, which Pridemore took into the brighter light of the kitchen to examine. A winsome little brunette in sweater and jeans on a porch somewhere, Jennifer Pridemore was a distant vision of her parents with her father's worried forehead and her mother's bright cheeks. Linda Pridemore's cheeks, of course, had filled out and filled out and filled out, until her features were but vague relief map in the putty of fat. Her thirties had not been kind to her, and she had fought back with chips and dips, coffee cake and ice cream, and a host of little snacks that bloated her almost beyond recognition. Then, at 38, she had found the real estate business more to her liking and had left the often irritable and sometimes drunk cop husband who could hardly even look at her anymore. That had been two years ago, and the lawyers were still sending envelopes back and forth. Tonight's letter, from Treeger, Treeger, and Helmstein, was a notice of change of insurance carrier or some such, and Pridemore placed it chronologically in the bursting brown folder called "Household" under the kitchen table. Mister Alp had added his own little touch by pissing on the folder once.

The letter from the Police Union legal staff told him they were appealing the City's position on his accident and sick time usage, which Pridemore knew already. He re-read the notice, making sure no action was required on his part, and filed it in a second folder marked "Knee." Eating his Enchilada Delight meal at the small kitchen table next to the unplugged telephone, he threw out the Sports and Business sections and read the national news about Republicans and Democrats, wars and rumors of war, toxic clean-ups and busloads of Filipinos driving off cliffs somewhere. There were crime stories from the city, which he generally ignored, and suburban news briefs about vandalism and car break-ins that he found amusingly trite. Mister Alp had by now finished half of his Tuna Surprise and trotted into the living room with Pridemore.

There was a tan sofa that Pridemore sometimes slept on, a coffee table that he would someday clear off, and a large television, which Mister Alp used as a lounge chair. Pridemore put a six-pack down on the brown carpet, found the remote, and sank into the worn out corduroy easy chair, heaving his slippered feet onto a battered footstool. The remote brought up the Hollywood Memories Channel, the way it always did, and Pridemore settled in for the day, popping open the first beer can and rubbing his scarred knee. Mister Alp was suddenly in Pridemore's lap, rubbing the top of his furry head against the man's chin. Bela Lugosi was upset about something again. He had concocted an aftershave lotion that he gave as a gift to his enemies. The scent of the lotion attracted Lugosi's giant killer bat, and the beast killed off all of Lugosi's enemies. After two beers, both Pridemore and Mister Alp were fast asleep.

In the dream this time, it was Judd who was driving, not Jack. He was trying to warn Judd about the eleven miles per hour, when the crash came, as it always did. The noise and the glass were about the same as usual. This time, it was Jack who was wrapped in bandages, looking up from the hospital bed and unable to speak. Judd and Elaine Christian came in and told him how good he looked. For some reason, Judd's face was always wrapped in bandages, too.

"How was your weekend, Good Son?" asked Hoatlin, cheerfully. By "weekend," he hadn't meant Saturday and Sunday, of course, but the last two days-off they had enjoyed, which this month was a Thursday-Friday weekend. The rest of the world was starting its weekend, while Hoatlin, Pridemore, and Tyler were beginning their work week.

"Swell," said Pridemore. He laced his boots.

"Do anything worthwhile?"

"I did the laundry."

"Is that all?"

"I folded it, too."

"Uh-huh," Hoatlin replied, nodding. There was locker room noise and conversation as Hoatlin adjusted his belt keepers and Pridemore pulled on his vest. Pridemore knew that the silence bothered Hoatlin, but he waited an extra few moments before launching the next part of their conversation.

"How was your weekend, Ted?" he asked finally.

There was junior high hockey and a trip to the mall and the game with Boston and the garage roof repair and something about a casserole that Ted's wife, Janet, had made but spilled in the kitchen. He had fixed the rattle in the transmission of his pickup and played cards with his buddy, Fred Ross, of Central Precinct; they had had some beers and some laughs, and Fred had told him about the problems they were having up there with their new Captain. It had been a busy and fruitful two days full of noisy children, trips to the hardware store, patient

MAD BADGES

wives, and band practice schedules. Teddy's home life was almost completely segregated from his patrolmen's lot. Pridemore would have felt envious, but he had already done the soccer mom and band practice routine once.

"Have you seen Judd Christian lately?" asked Buck Tyler, fighting with some uniform buttons.

"Yeah," Pridemore replied. "He's about the same."

"No improvement?"

"Nah. He's still hooked up to those machines."

"That's the shits," said Buck. He grunted his way into some longjohns. "Have you seen his wife lately?"

Pridemore waited a heartbeat. "Elaine? Yeah, we had lunch together." Without being asked, he quickly added: "She says the insurance people are still being assholes about the medical bills."

"Fucking City," said Buck.

"Back on the farm, we used to call them Cheap Bastards," Hoatlin agreed.

"Yeah, it's a raw deal," Pridemore said.

Tyler tucked a box of skinny cigars into his uniform jacket. "How's your deal going with the law suit?"

"The Union lawyers keep putting in the paperwork, but I don't know."

"Fucking Union," said Buck.

"Bunch a lazy bastards," Hoatlin agreed.

The line-up went as line-ups usually go. Sgt. Wheeler read off the car assignments and handed out the list of outstanding stolens. Sgt. Lindsey announced a sign-up list for a golf tournament with members of the Firefighters Union and passed out a flier for a wanted rapist. Sgt. Wheeler warned them about a smash-and-grab artist on Rhodes Street and about a biker conference at the Crocker Avenue Marauders M. C. Wheeler said he was holding the Afternoon Watch so that the Lieutenant could address the Nights line-up, thus alerting everybody to straighten up their hats and neckties and to hide their foodstuffs and drop guns.

Lt. Berke breezed into the Squad Room at just that moment with a large stack of papers. There was only one enthusiastic woman from the front row lesbian brigade today, but several attentive rookies. The Sergeants passed around blue sheets of paper that had a heading for Name, Precinct, and Date and were numbered Good 1-5 and Not Good

1-5. Hoatlin had already started his paper airplane folding, when Berke began.

"Good morning, People. Command wanted Captain Maddox and myself to pass on their appreciation of the good work you're accomplishing here in The Heights and asked that we distribute these questionnaires in an effort to facilitate your input into plans they have for the coming year's budget and Departmental Goals strategies."

Buck Tyler dutifully filled out his name and date, writing the word "Mars" where it asked for Precinct. Pridemore saw where the form said "Name (Optional)" and wrote "Optional" in the space. Flex Sinclair, who was sitting in the back row today, began drawing an artful rendition of a black man's lynching.

"Now you see before you a list of Good items," explained Berke to the few eyes that were actually pointed in his direction. "What we want you to put in there are the things that you, yourself, consider to be the good things that we are accomplishing here. Try to think of it as the What-we're-doing-right list."

Jack and Buck were already stumped. Hoatlin's aircraft design was improving moment by moment as he fashioned flaps and up-tilted wingtips. Flex Sinclair used the side of a pencil point to shade some trees in the background of his sketch and add texture to the hanging rope.

"Under that list you will find a Not Good list," Berke continued. "This doesn't mean necessarily bad. It just means that you should think of things that we all might do better, sort of a ways-we-can-improve-our-performance list, if you will."

"I thought not-good *meant* bad," whispered Buck.

"He wants us to write down better ways of not being good," explained Flex Sinclair, detailing the clouds in the picture he was drawing.

Somebody down in front asked the Lieutenant if he could use the back of the sheet, and Berke said, "Yes, by all means."

"By any means necessary," paraphrased Flex.

Buck Tyler was writing out the names of nurses he knew under the Good heading and the names of Command staff under the Not Good heading. Hoatlin had added a landing gear to his airplane and was working on a tiny cockpit with a little pilot inside.

Pridemore filled out his page quickly. "Good: 1 True, 2 Yes, 3 Blue, 4 False, and 5 Donuts." The Not Good list was: "1 No, 2 False, 3 Three, 4 You, and 5 The capitol of Illinois is Springfield." Flex Sinclair was signing his artwork with a flourish.

"The purpose of this exercise," Lt. Berke announced, "is to empower those of you who may sometimes feel that you don't have the opportunity to contribute to the goal-setting process. Command understands such feelings. They . . ."

"I'm starting to feel a bowel movement," Buck noted.

"They want you not only to share in the development process," explained the Lieutenant, "but to participate in addressing some of the issues that will be revealed by your own answers in the Not Good list."

Hoatlin carefully flattened his fully-fashioned fighter plane into the stack of questionnaires as it made its way to the aisle. Some of the forms came back wadded and some completely blank as Sgt. Wheeler took the stack down to the front. Making sure that at least one partially completed form was on top, Wheeler handed the stack back to the Lieutenant.

"Great," chirped Lt. Berke, taking the stack of input. "Command appreciates your time and consideration and will be reviewing your comments and suggestions with the utmost attention." He nodded to the Sergeants, waved goodbye to the troops, and left. The back row heaved a collective sigh of disgust.

"That's all for today, Crimefighters!" barked Sgt. Lindsey. "Have a quiet shift." The room filled with noise again as the chairs scraped on the floor and the equipment bundles were hoisted.

"I think I got a paper cut," Hoatlin complained.

"They'll make you a fucking Lieutenant if you keep that up," said Buck.

The phone attached to Patrick Maddox's belt was set to Vibrate instead of Ring. It lay on the bare floor of the restroom stall next to his pants, which were down around his ankles. The Captain's guts were not in good order this morning. With great effort, Maddox fished up the belt and the phone, checking the caller's number. It was Ruth Channing from Planning & Research. He could ignore that one. His head was killing him today, whole clumps of gray hair having come out in this morning's shower. He had taken two of the white ulcer tablets before taking the two blue headache pills in an effort to head off the stomach acid that the headache pills inevitably generated. He strained against his enlarged prostate and tangled intestines. No relief in sight.

The tiny telephone throbbed again. He checked the caller I.D. It was Captain Darcy from Training. Maddox could skip that one, too.

Darcy and his Training Unit had come up with that Federal grant to "develop a protocol for standards to measure the effectiveness" of the agency's SWAT team staffing. But they didn't call it "SWAT" anymore. Nobody called their SWAT team a SWAT team anymore. They were "Special Teams" or "Emergency Response Squads" or so-called "Tactical Units." And the grant money covered just the "protocol for standards," not even the standards themselves. And Darcy had his little Nazi Sergeants working on it full-time. Three little crew-cut tactical guys sat at their desks in carpeted offices downtown, wearing black fatigues and web holsters, typing reams of outlines, guidelines, and tables of content for grants and proposals. And all the time they knew that the funding would only last two years, after which they would rape the General Research budget to cover the additional cost of whatever goofy program they had gotten themselves locked into, which would by then be considered "absolutely vital" to the Department. And part of that budget would have to cover the combined salaries of the three little robots with their desks and web holsters. And Deputy Chief Griswold would approve any request that the little Nazis thought up, because he had been a web belted little robot himself back in the years when the Federal money was good. That had been his ticket to the top.

It was dog-eat-dog as the Darcy-Griswold faction tried to undermine Chief Pearson and Professor Lindstrum of the Crime Patterns Study Group, who were constantly jockeying for Department funding of their pet projects. And those factions regularly engaged in the Department's budget battle with the dweebs in Technical Services who were constantly whining about their ever-faster computers for Records and Communications, when none of it seemed to work properly anyway and the software updates had nothing to do with either better information services or better patrol communication. And those kind of budget demands always shorted the little guys, guys like Maddox, who had his own budget and had helped write his own grant for a study of patrol performance evaluations that would revolutionize the standardization of the supervisor's annual check-box system. Maddox knew what was important, how things worked, and where the money went. He didn't have the robots, the professors, or the techies to help him with his grants and budget requests. He also didn't have the energy to move his own plumbing today.

There were the forms for the calibration of the handheld alcohol breath-testing units, and there was the master schedule that laid out the months when the calibration forms had to be turned in. There were the forms for documenting sick-time usage, and a form that charted the Precinct's overall sick-time and vacation time usage to make it more digestible to the bigwig statisticians at HQ. Maddox had to take Lt. Berke off of his ongoing staffing study to address the problems in the Precinct's reporting report, that is, the log of reports as broken down by area and time-of-day and productivity ratio. These were not things one could ignore. Maddox had been forced to shift funds away from the new cruiser allocation to keep his sick-time usage evaluation project afloat. He had been doing this for years, in spite of interference from the police officers, their meddling Union, the filth and degradation of the neighborhood, and the continual budget battles with guys like Captain Darcy, Deputy Chief Griswold, Lindstrum, and the Police Chief himself.

The telephone started humming again. Maddox lifted it and checked the number. It was from the Deputy Chief Forrest's secretary. He *had* to take this one, he knew. The bile launched itself up into his throat. His rectum bled. His legs, which had long before fallen asleep on the toilet seat, prickled like a thousand needles. His eyes throbbed and head pounded as he mustered himself to answer the call.

"Maddox here."

"Captain Maddox?" asked the secretary's voice, as if she hadn't heard.

"Yes?"

"Apparently, Captain, you were not made aware of this morning's Command meeting," she said from the civic center's white tower.

"No. There's a meeting today?" He cringed, knowing someone somewhere at H.Q. had left him out of the loop again, ever eroding his position in the Department, a Department that was moving forward without him. Darcy and Griswold and that ilk, no doubt. "When is the meeting?"

"I'm afraid . . ." the woman's voice began, and Maddox knew immediately that he was in trouble. She paused for a moment. "I'm afraid the meeting has already begun. If you started now from your area . . ." Her tone made "your area" sound like "that pit in the animal kingdom." She continued: "Well, you would never make it on time anyway."

"I see," Maddox said, his voice calm but his brain raging. They didn't tell me there was a meeting, so I could miss it, so they could have Forrest's secretary call me and tell me how utterly screwed I am now, thought Maddox. Yes, that was basically it.

"Do you want me to send you a copy of the minutes then?" the secretary asked helpfully.

"Yes, that would be fine." He choked out a Thank You and was about to click the phone off when he thought of something. "Oh. My proposal for the sick-time usage study's budget. Did that get in?"

"I think your Lieutenant brought it with him," she said.

"My Lieutenant?" Ah yes, Maddox remembered, young Berke was delivering it. Good man, that Berke.

"And he's presenting it now, I believe."

"Presenting it?" Maddox asked, suspiciously.

"Yes, he laid it all out and explained it to the Command staff . . .in your absence."

"I see." Maddox's mind whirled, but his voice stayed level. That little prick Berke was wedging his way into Command staff meetings already, pushing him out of the way, making room for his race to the top. Devious bastard, that Berke. He'll either sabotage my budget proposal or, if they like it, he'll take credit for it. That evil sonofabitch. Those evil bastards! "Well, thank you, Miss . . .?"

"Miss Harper," she said. "Don't mention it, Captain." And the emphasis was on "Captain," as if to say: "I don't know how you ever made Captain, but you're sure as hell not going any higher in this man's police department." Maddox knew the tone.

"Thanks again, Miss Harper," he said and rang off. Bitch! Bastards! Darcy, Griswold, the Chief, that little prick Berke, and now Miss Screw-You-All Harper! Bunch of evil bastards, all of them. His stomach lurched. The bleeding, the burning, the oozing, and the throbbing all came to settle on him at the same time. Captain Maddox groaned in the john.

There were nights when you didn't feel like being attacked by a demented psycho wielding a ballpoint pen, and this was one of those nights. You just wanted peace and quiet, a leisurely donut and a couple of easy calls. You didn't want to get stuck in the cramped stairwell of a Bendix Avenue shitbox apartment house, wrestling with a madman. It hadn't even been their call, Pridemore and Hoatlin. They hadn't even been in that stairwell for the mental. It was a domestic across the hall that had brought them there. But Roger Lee LeBlanc had suddenly whipped open his cruddy apartment door and had leaped onto Hoatlin's back, and the fight was on. LeBlanc had the ballpoint, but the cops had the numbers. They had the guns and clubs, but he had the enthusiasm and the schizophrenia. They all went flying down the stairs in a pile of cursing and screaming just as Sgt. Lindsey entered the front door. Lindsey brought LeBlanc up short just inside the doorway and smacked him in the head with his flashlight. The madman went down on the floor, looking like a pile of bloody laundry.

Hoatlin was calling for an ambulance, his right sleeve ripped by the ballpoint pen. Pridemore was glad that it had been a Sergeant who had hit the man with his flashlight, because shots to the head with a metal flashlight were frowned upon by Internal Affairs, and Sgt. Lindsey would have to fix his own Use-of-Force report. Pridemore and Hoatlin, of course, would back him, no matter what the report said. That was how it went sometimes. Command said No to flashlight strikes, but they hadn't seen Roger Lee LeBlanc, lifetime mental and all-around Scary Guy. The Department had outlawed strikes to the head, but they hadn't been rolling down that dark and filthy stairway at 2 AM. Sgt. Lindsey was bitching, because he couldn't get his flashlight to work now, probably a broken bulb or push-button switch.

At the top of the stairs, Mr. Torres, who had been slapping his little wife, Rita, around their shitty apartment all evening, leaned out over the railing and shouted: "If you don't keep it down down there, I'm gonna call the cops!"

Hoatlin grinned, handcuffing the unconscious mental.

She was fumbling around with something, which made Pridemore nervous. She was brunette, what he could see of her, and about twenty-five. The Cadillac's plate came back to a dealership out in Pinecrest somewhere. It was 11 PM, and she was driving through the vacant landscape of the industrial park on Pritchard north of Dunham, a long way from suburban Pinecrest. Buck Tyler hadn't bothered to get out of the passenger seat, until he saw her fumbling around and noticed that Pridemore had paused. Buck lit her up with his flashlight from the right rear, his free hand near his holster. Pridemore stayed just to the rear of the driver's door and tapped on the window with his gloved hand. She turned toward the flashlight's glare and made a surrendering motion with her hands. The woman fiddled with the door and finally got it open. Pridemore relaxed a little, now that he could see both of her hands. Buck had moved up to the passenger side of the Cadillac to check the interior.

"I'm sorry," the pretty woman said. "It's not my car."

"Good evening," said Pridemore.

"My car's in the shop, and they gave me this one for the night, and I don't know where anything is in here." Her accent was a delightful German or Russian or Finnish or Swedish or Danish or something.

Pridemore reached the button on the inside of the driver's door, noting that the beam of Buck's flashlight was playing over the woman's knees. Once the window was rolled down, Pridemore closed the door for her. He had smelled no alcohol on her, and his adrenaline level was starting to return to normal.

"Thank you so much," she said through the open window.

"May I see your license?" Pridemore asked and was pleased to see that she found it right away and handed it over without a fuss. Her name was Michelle, and her license checked out. She was 29 and lived out in Glen Elgin, a suburb next to Pinecrest. He noted the make, model, and plate on his log under "Motorist Assist," not "Traffic Stop," and brought back her license. "Do you think you can work the window now?"

"Yes, thanks," Michelle said, running the window button up and down a bit to prove it. Buck Tyler's flashlight was still aimed at her skirt, which she luckily failed to notice. "I've got it now."

"And can you find the headlight switch okay?" Pridemore asked gently. She pointed to it, and he nodded. "Now if you push it all the way in, your headlights will come on, and you won't be driving around with just your parking lights, okay?"

"Oh, my goodness," she said, embarrassed. She blushed and switched on the Cadillac's headlights. "I'm sorry."

"You don't have to apologize to me," smiled Pridemore, "but you probably ought to learn your way around a Cadillac before you drive one."

"It's all different from my Volvo. I was trying to work the heater and missed my turn-off to the 15 West. I got off back there and got all turned around, and now I'm completely lost. I've never been down here before."

No doubt, thought Pridemore. He had her follow them out of the maze of factories to a South Parkway on-ramp.

"Tasty girl," said Buck, back in the cruiser.

"Did you hear that, Buck? She actually said 'my goodness.'"

"Amazing."

"Not 'motherfucker' or 'Don't you cops have anything better to do' or 'I've only had two drinks.' Just 'my goodness.'"

"And some nice legs," agreed Buck.

"And she said she was sorry."

"Holy shit, Jacko! Do you think maybe that was one of those human beings they're always telling us about?"

"Could be."

When they came to the on-ramp, Pridemore pulled over and waved her by. She pulled up along side and rolled down her passenger side window, demonstrating a newfound proficiency with the Cadillac's buttons. Buck tried to suck in his gut. Pridemore turned to the human being named Michelle.

"Thank you so much, Officers," she called out, waving. The Cadillac drove up the ramp and disappeared. Pridemore rolled up the window of the cruiser.

"Thank *you*, lady," Pridemore murmured.

"Thank you?" repeated Buck Tyler. "Where the fuck have we heard that before?"

"Someone said that just last year, I think."

"I didn't meet any human beings last year. Are you sure?"

"Maybe it was the year before," said Pridemore, though his memory was hazy.

"And she called you 'Officer.'"

"I know. I heard that."

"Amazing," whistled Buck.

"Amazing," said Pridemore.

"She likes you, Dude."

"Oh, shut up, Buck."

Timmy was cold. Pridemore stood in the archway between the little dining room and the tiny living room to make sure Timmy's three sisters stayed in the back bedroom and out of the way. Timmy's father, a factory rat from the hills of Kentucky or Tennessee or some other godawful hillbilly twilight zone, was in the bathroom just off the kitchen. The father was shaving, using a safety razor, Pridemore noticed, and not speaking at all any longer. He must have shaved four times by now. Timmy's mother was still at her night job. From the back bedroom came the occasional giggles and whispered questions of little girls who didn't understand why the police were inside their house at this hour of the morning. From the living room came the occasional sounds of heavy boots and the whispered questions of the cops and the morgue wagon people.

Little Timmy was curled up next to a long thin space heater on the worn brown shag carpet in the living room. He wore shoes with his pajamas and had pulled on his father's bathrobe. He had been dead four to eight hours, the field examiner from the ME's office had guessed. He had eaten some brightly colored capsules that he had found on the bathroom sink, antibiotics meant for his mother, and had vomited some of them up in his shabby little youth bed in the back. Timmy had gotten up and padded out to the living room, thinking he was just cold, not knowing that the approaching cold was his approaching death, having had no experience with such things. After all, he was only five. The field examiner looked up at Pridemore, who in turn checked that the little sisters were safely in the rear bedroom, then nodded the okay. The field examiner made a discrete incision and inserted a long slender thermometer. Pridemore looked away. Timmy's dad was still shaving. The sound of running water in the bathroom sink shielded him from the muffled noises in the living room.

The temperature was duly noted. Timmy was zipped up into a body bag for a future autopsy. The guy with the morgue wagon lifted the package easily and made his way out to the van at the curb, rather than risk bringing the wheeled cot up the icy front steps to the porch. It looked like nothing more than a man carrying a sack. The cops breathed a little easier, now that the body was out. One of them picked up scraps of paper from an EKG strip that the ambulance crew had run. Somebody turned down the room heater that had failed to keep Timmy warm. Father Price had arrived, there being no one else to call at this hour to smooth out what would be a rough morning for this family. Lenny Price was the guy you called when you didn't know what else to do or had no one else to call. These people had been in the city only a few months and had no local friends or family to contact. It had all been on the dad's shoulders that morning, and then the cops had come and taken over, and now it was up to Father Price. Pridemore warned the little sisters that they would have to stay put for a little while longer, then led the Chaplain back to the bathroom. Timmy's father paused his shaving and nodded at them in the mirror. He stood in a T-shirt and blue work pants, a white "Motel-6" towel around his neck. He had lathered for what must have been the sixth time, but had only shaved part of the soap away. Pridemore stepped into the tiny bathroom, close to the father.

"Mr. Egan, this is Father Price."

Timmy's father nodded absently, the right hand holding the safety razor paused in mid air on the way to his chin. The hot water steamed from the tap of the old sink.

"Mr. Egan," began the Chaplain in a low and reassuring voice, "my name is Lenny Price. They've taken Timmy with them now. Maybe we could sit in the other room and talk for a bit?"

With his left hand, Mr. Egan wiped away the shaving cream from his jaw. The flesh beneath was red and raw. "I knew my boy was dead when I touched him."

"I know," said Pridemore, gently plucking the safety razor from Egan's right hand. It was like taking something from a manikin—no reaction at all. Pridemore turned off the hot water faucet and guided Mr. Egan out of the bathroom, his large hand on the man's bony shoulder. The three of them came out to the dining room. Egan and the Chaplain sat at the dining room table. There was always a dining room table. They always seemed to do this at the table. Egan put his head in his hands. Father Price turned his chair so he could be closer to the man.

"Ruthie's at work," Egan voice said dully.

"We sent someone there to bring her home," Father Price explained softly. Egan's gaze faded into the middle distance as he started to weep.

The field examiner had told Pridemore that the ME would want the pillow that Timmy had vomited on, so Jack went to find it. Passing the three little sisters, who were only now becoming concerned, seeing their father crying softly in the dining room, Pridemore searched for Timmy's bed. They watched in awed silence as the giant policeman passed. Pridemore found the soiled pillow, folded it in half, and strode out of the bedroom with it under his arm. On the front porch, he turned the evidence over to the field examiner, who put the pillow in a paper sack marked "Office of the Medical Examiner." Both of them were glad to be out of the suffocating little house and in the fresh cold air.

"Thanks," said the field examiner, and he was gone.

Pridemore felt a tug on his sleeve and turned back toward the front door. One of the little sisters was there, huge eyes and tousled hair, her tiny flannel nightgown dragging on the floor. She stood in the open doorway, holding something out to him. Pridemore reached for it.

"This is Timmy's blanket," the child told him. "Sometimes he gets cold at night." She had seen Pridemore take the pillow, so it only made sense. Pridemore took the little blanket, not knowing what else to do, and thanked her. "Bye-bye," she said bravely.

Back in the cruiser, Flex Sinclair was working on the Incident Report. It was pretty simple really: Name of Deceased, DOB, times, addresses, Medical Examiner's name and arrival time, Autopsy Ordered, next-of-kin, Chaplain contacted, and so on. Not too complicated like a he-said, she-said report with its allegations and diversions. Flex looked over at his partner in the idling car. "You got a cold, man?"

"It's this goddamn weather," said Pridemore. "Plays havoc with my sinuses."

"Mine just give me headaches like a big dog," replied Flex, still writing.

"You want to get a donut after this?"

"No, I ate. Why? You hungry?"

"Nah," said Pridemore. "I just wanted to warm up."

Ten hours later, Pridemore sat at his own dining room table, nursing the first of several beers and scratching Mr. Alp's head. The cat played with the telephone cord. Jennifer Pridemore had been on her way out for a date when she stopped to answer the phone in her Colorado dorm room. They talked for a bit.

"So . . .you're getting along okay?"

"Yes, Dad, I'm fine."

"You need any money?"

"No, Dad, I'm all set. I could use a new pair of gloves though."

Pridemore wrote that down, Mr. Alp swiping at the pencil. "I won't keep you. I just wanted to check and see how you were doing."

"I'm fine. Is everything okay with you?"

"Sure," said Pridemore.

"Have you spoken with Mom?"

"Not recently. You?"

"She called me over Christmas break," said Jennifer, "just after I talked to you." There was a pause on the line, before she said: "You had another dead baby case today, didn't you, Dad?" It wasn't really a question. She had grown up a cop's kid.

"No, no," he lied quickly. "I just wanted to see how you're doing?"

"I'm fine, Daddy, but I've got to run."

"I love you, Jen."

"I love you, too, Dad. You really should retire some day."

"I will. You take care, Honey."

Pridemore hung up the phone and offered Mr. Alp some of his beer, but the cat just wanted more head scratching. Together they went into the living room, settled into the big chair, and watched Randolph Scott fighting a range war with rustlers. Mr. Alp curled up into a warm ball in Pridemore's lap.

There was a certain serenity to a Saturday night emergency room. Everything was well lighted, so there were no surprises to jump out at you from the evil darkness. The place was busy, but not frantic, because a nervous trauma center was a useless trauma center. And none of the bleeding, howling, drunken, or dying victims of accidents, stabbings, shootings, and beatings were related by blood or emotional attachment to the calm, cool, and professional, if not particularly warm and fuzzy, medical staff. So, basically, by not giving a shit whether you lived or died or how lousy you were feeling, the staff of the Mount Mercy E.R. remained detached and sensible enough to reason their way through your particular problem and save your life, your foot, your eye, or your infant. And if they lost your particular battle with The Grim Reaper—what the fuck?—there was always the next patient.

"So," said the freckle-faced nurse with the blue shoe covers, "are you still married?" She was talking to Buck Tyler and speaking from experience.

"No," said Tyler, "that was two wives ago."

She straightened the stack of rubber glove boxes she was carrying. Her blue eyes, sporting a bit too much eyeliner, flicked over to Pridemore, who was finishing a report, and then back to Buck. "You still do much . . . dancing?"

"I still like the occasional slow one."

"My husband . . ." she started. "My second husband after . . ." She began again. "Since . . . Well, I got married again. My husband doesn't dance at all."

"That's a shame," said Buck, trying desperately to read her upside-down name tag.

"Yes, it is," the nurse said. "I miss dancing once in a while." She sorted the glove boxes into racks marked "Medium" and "Large" and took her stack to the next curtained treatment room. "You behave now," she called back over her shoulder.

Watching her walk away, Buck Tyler studied the swaying of her behind, a slightly pigeon-toed walk that made her white uniform slacks glide back and forth across her hips. Been there, done that, he remembered. Not nearly as good as it looked, if he recalled. "Bye, Mindy."

She was pleased to know he remembered her name and gave him a sweet smile over her shoulder. Soon she had stocked all the glove racks in the row of treatment rooms and was off to the other corridor. She wished she could remember *his* name. She could remember the party where they had met and where they had first done it, how they were both pretty drunk at the time. She recalled being surprised when he had looked her up again and further surprised by her willingness to go a second time and then a third. But that had been quite a while back. They were both remarried now, he apparently more adept at marriage and divorce than she. Ah, cops, Mindy thought and smiled.

"Angels of fucking mercy," Buck remarked.

"You have a raging nurse fetish," said Pridemore.

"Gotta love 'em, dontcha?"

"Is it the tender loving care or the little white caps?"

"It's the uniform, Jacko. You and I both remember when nurses wore dresses with white nurse shoes and white stockings, fer chrissakes! Those were the days, Jack."

Pridemore nodded, vaguely remembering pretty nurses in slacks. The dresses had gone out of style a long time ago.

"Give me a nurse who can wrap those white stockings around me any day of the week," whispered Buck, "and I'll die a happy cop."

"You make them wear their outfits in the sack, too, I bet."

"It's like what you learn about cop groupies. They love the badge and the nightstick and shit, and they always want you to keep it on. Haven't you ever made it with a nurse, Jacko?"

"Not that I recall," Pridemore lied. He didn't want to go into it right then with Buck Tyler.

"Not even when you were laid up in the hospital all that time?" Buck prodded.

"Nope." That was true.

"Not even once?"

"They were busy helping me with bedpans and stuff," Pridemore remembered sourly. "It wasn't a romantic time."

"I'm not talking romance here . . ."

"You never are."

"I'm talking tonsil hockey in the linen closet," Tyler clarified. "Grab-ass in the O.R. Sausage slapping in the nurse's quarters."

"I get the point, Buck."

"Now *that's* romantic stuff. Me and two Swedish nursing students coated in melted butter. Good enough to eat."

"There's an image," Pridemore shuddered. He spotted a passing doctor whom he recognized and stepped into his path. "Do you know where our guy went?"

"Are you with the Cuban man beat with the mop handle on his kidneys or the kid with the corn rows who got his skull cracked with a lamp?" the doctor asked, smoothing his beard.

"The head injury."

"He went down to CT."

"Ah, CAT Scan," said Buck, "the Bermuda Triangle of hospitals from which no one ever returns."

"No, he should be back soon," said the doctor, not quite understanding. "I think it's mostly his jaw that's broken."

"So he's not gonna die?" asked Pridemore.

"Yes, he's going to die, I'm afraid," said the doctor mischievously. "We all are, you know. But, no, he's probably not going to die tonight of a fractured jaw." Buck groaned. The doctor grinned nastily and left. Pridemore noted the doctor's name for his report.

On their way out, they were passed by a little nurse with her red hair up in a large bun on her head. Buck turned to watch her slinky departure.

"Ouch! Ouch! Ouch!" he grinned.

Lateasa Combs, black female, 17 years, dead of a gunshot wound to abdomen near the west entrance of The Marble Room, 3260 South Cramer Avenue. Combs was apparently standing behind someone that Lionel Tolbert was shooting at. Tolbert, brother of the late Deon, was arrested leaving the scene. Several of Combs' family members and friends vowed revenge on Tolbert and his family. The Marble Room was fined for serving alcohol to minors.

Kilo was yelling at Neal Parnell's rookie. They had made the traffic stop, hauled out the irate driver, and spread him out on the hood of his car. Kilo was drunk and in an ugly mood. They had found a 40-ouncer on the front seat and a bag of weed in the console. Parnell had found a pistol in the waistband of the suspect's sweatsuit and had cuffed him. Kilo had cursed them both, claiming to be a cop. Every tenth asshole had a story like that. It was 3 o'clock in the morning on Denton south of Conklin, a whore corner or, as Command liked to call it, "an area of known prostitution activity." Parnell's rookie had just discovered Kilo's badge underneath the spare tire in the trunk of his red Ford Mustang, when Hoatlin and Pridemore rolled up.

"Stupid motherfucking rookie!" Kilo snarled.

"Ah, Sgt. Newly," said Hoatlin. "How are ya, Good Son?"

"I didn't know," the rookie said sheepishly. Parnell looked to Pridemore with an apologetic shrug. "I'm sorry, I didn't know." The kid felt awful.

"Motherfucker!" howled Vice Sgt. Ralph "Kilo" Newly, his words spitting out through his overgrown beard and moustache. "Don't you know who I am, fucking new boot?"

"Now, how could the kid know you if he's never met you, Sergeant?" asked Pridemore.

"Little prick shoulda known. I told him twice, the fucker!"

"Now, now," said Hoatlin, comfortingly, "let's calm down here."

"Get these fucking cuffs off me!" spat Kilo.

"In a minute, Ralph," said Pridemore. "In a minute."

"Cocksucker rookie!"

"Hey now," Hoatlin cautioned.

The rookie felt like shit. Parnell, whose job it was to guide the rookie through his second four weeks on the street, felt bad, too. Hoatlin was trying to be the voice of calm in the situation. They stood there, under a yellowed street lamp. The whore corner had cleared out in a hurry.

"Rookie motherfucker!" sneered the drunken Vice cop. He lurched at the kid.

MAD BADGES

Pridemore and Hoatlin reached out and grabbed Kilo, swinging him around, away from the rookie. They marched him over to their cruiser, his hands still cuffed behind him. Kilo was surprised when they bent him over their hood.

"Look, asshole," Pridemore said into Kilo's left ear, "the kid doesn't know you from Adam. His Training Officer doesn't even know you, Newly. That's how long you've been off the street. What the fuck do you expect him to do? You're shit-faced, and you look like a mope, and you smell like any other turd out here. So what exactly the fuck do you expect?" Kilo struggled against the cuffs.

Hoatlin, in his right ear, said: "You wanna dance, sonofabitch?" They both tightened their grip on his arms. Newly's shoulders tensed for a moment, then relaxed.

"That's better," Pridemore continued. "This is curbside, pal, and you don't mess with curbside." He shook Kilo's jacket to make the point. "You want to talk shit to a rookie? You want to an assault a P.O.? You want a Resisting to go with a DWI arrest? The Sergeant stripes don't work that way, especially not Vice stripes, okay?"

"You fuck around with us out here, Son," hissed Hoatlin, "and you'll find you can't badge your way out of it."

Kilo started to nod that he understood. "But . . ."

"But nothing, Sergeant," said Pridemore. "We can lose your shield and say we never found your I.D. and tell them you just looked like another shit-heel to us. They'll take you down to lock-up, where nobody knows who you are either, and start the paperwork. So, no matter which supervisor you find to cut you loose down there, you'll still have a jacket with I.A., and you'll still take it up the ass."

"I know," said Sgt. Newly. "I know."

"You've been inside too damn long," Hoatlin reminded him. "You've forgotten some basic rules. You've got the right to remain silent, and I figure you'd better start doing it now."

"I know."

"And you apologize to the kid," said Pridemore.

Kilo nodded his shaggy head.

"You say you're sorry, and we can talk about this thing. You shoot your fucking mouth off, and you're history."

"You'll be gone," added Hoatlin.

"I will," Kilo promised.

"We're all clear on that, Sergeant?" asked Pridemore.

"Clear."

They straightened him up and marched him back to Parnell's cruiser. The rookie opened his mouth to apologize, but Hoatlin shook his head. Parnell already had his handcuff key out.

"I'm sorry, Officer," the Vice Sergeant said. "I forgot who I was talking to."

Parnell and his rookie uncuffed him. They shook hands all around, Kilo apologizing again. He sat in the back of their cruiser, until Hoatlin could call a Vice Unit. A black guy with a doo-rag and a white guy with a pierced eyebrow showed up in a rusted Chevy Blazer. After a brief conference with Pridemore, during which he explained some unspoken rules of The Job and the curbside, they thanked him and took the drunken Sergeant with them. One of them drove Kilo's Mustang, while the other took the now-quiet Sergeant home in the Blazer. With no report to write, Parnell and his rookie turned their car around and pulled up beside Hoatlin and Pridemore.

"Thanks a lot," said the rookie.

"No problem," said Pridemore.

"I hope the Vice Unit doesn't hate us for this," Neal Parnell said.

"Who the fuck are they to hate us?" Hoatlin offered. "Truth be told, it's not like those fuckers are *real* cops anyway." All four of them nodded. Parnell and his rookie took off east on Conklin. Hoatlin and Pridemore left north on Denton. The whores would soon be back in force.

On the first day of March, Captain Maddox made a surprise visit to the Squad Room, just as Third Watch was about to be let out on the street. Sgt. Petty lined them all up at attention for inspection, as Maddox and Lt. Berke entered the room. The groans and foot shuffling stopped, and only the squeal of an old steam pipe could be heard. Maddox, his ulcers in high gear, was wearing a gray suit and a tie that was choking him. Berke was his usual spotless self in white uniform shirt with buttoned cuffs and a clipboard. They walked down the first line of officers, Maddox making comments and Berke writing them down.

"This man needs a reminder about regulation haircuts," the Captain said, and Berke made a notation. The notes were going directly onto warning slips for the Internal Affairs Unit. They moved down the line.

"This man doesn't seem to know where to find boot polish," Maddox said of Connie Baldwin, and no one corrected him. Berke had started to say something, but the Captain had already found Buck Tyler. When the Captain spoke, it was to Berke, not to the enormous police officer beside him. "We have improper footwear here." He was referring to Buck's rubber boots, which half hid the brown leather boots he was wearing today. "We have a tie with no tie clip. We have. . ."

"Sir," said Buck, "my tie clip was lost last night during an arrest." Pridemore in the second row shook his head, knowingly.

Maddox opened his mouth to speak, but Lt. Berke was already in Buck's face. "I don't think the Captain *asked* you anything, Officer." Sgt. Petty glared at Buck Tyler. The Captain moved up the line, a button here, a collar there, a scuffed holster or a missing name pin. It all went down on Berke's clipboard, right onto the Warning Slips for I.A. Flex Sinclair got beefed for no name pin on his shirt, and when he tried to explain that his name pin was on his jacket hung on a chair in the back of the room, Maddox told Berke to write him up for Conduct Unbecoming, which would never fly but could cause Flex trouble down the road. Hoatlin got written up for his sideburns, which Berke measured with a six-inch orange ruler. Every second officer got a slip for having a smudged hat bill, which Maddox called "a defaced uniform hat." Pridemore stood silent as the Captain pointed out his crooked name pin, missing tie clip, wrinkled shirt, and unpolished boots. Berke wrote it all down, a four-parter that would be harder to ignore at I.A. Captain Maddox had still not directly addressed any of the officers in the room.

"What I'm *not* seeing here, among other things, Sergeant, are decorations," the Captain said to Petty. "This Department presents awards to police officers on occasion, and the Manual of Conduct explicitly states that such decorations are to be worn at all times in the appropriate manner on the officer's uniform. I would suggest that you have this Watch return to this Squad Room in four minutes time with their uniforms and gear in proper order, including Departmental decorations." The Captain and Lieutenant made their way down to the front of the room, where they conferred about their list. Sgt. Petty barked the order, and the room cleared out.

When they returned with their hastily polished boots, mismatched name pins, and whatever Department-issued gear they could find, Sgt. Petty called them all to attention again. Maddox and Berke again inspected the line, finding that Hoatlin had actually trimmed his sideburns and Buck Tyler was wearing someone else's black boots. The Captain eyed the ribbons on Tyler's uniform shirt, noting that one of them was upside-down. They were not amused by the paper clip Flex Sinclair had fashioned into a tie clip, although Maddox referred to Connie Baldwin by her proper gender this time. Parnell caught it for his white socks, which they had missed the first time around, for not being the black or blue sock color specified by the Manual. Captain Maddox stopped suddenly in the second rank, and Berke, who was busy writing, almost ran into him. Together, they pondered Pridemore's uniform.

There was a tri-color, green, white, and gold, two-star ribbon, meaning five awards, for arresting an armed robbery suspect, arresting a rapist, arresting a burglar, delivering a baby, and arresting another burglar. There was a Distinguished Expert marksman pin with two tiny stars below it, meaning he had maintained his shooting record for at least ten years. There was a red, blue, and gold ribbon with a star, which meant he had worked in two Units, the Safe & Loft Squad and the South Precinct's Third Shift Watch, at the time that they were cited for a Unit Excellence Award. Then there were the Combat Stars, not one but two of them, one for the mental on East 35th Street who had stabbed Jack in the arm before he could be wrestled to the ground and the second for the junkie who had shot Officer Kyle Fredericks over in the McLeary Gardens projects only to be shot and killed by Pridemore in a dark stairwell. There were a throng of other arrests and wrestling matches, a second baby delivery, and a gunman on Commerce Avenue that Pridemore had run over with his car, but these did not appear as decorations on his uniform. In studying the awards on Pridemore's uniform, Captain Maddox and Lt. Berke almost missed his missing tie clip and wrinkled shirt. Captain Maddox did not know he had anyone so decorated in his Precinct. He wondered if, perhaps, this grubby officer with the "J. Pridemore" name pin perhaps had friends in high places within the Department. He would have to look that up sometime, he thought.

After they had finished harassing the "troops," Maddox and Berke spoke with the Sergeants briefly, then left. Sgt. Petty handed out Warning Slips to the officers who had not cleaned up their acts by the time of the second inspection. Pridemore got one for his missing tie clip.

"The Captain just hates niggers," Flex Sinclair complained, looking at his slip.

"Doesn't everybody?" Buck Tyler replied.

"The Captain just hates cops," said Pridemore.
"You got the wrong color skin," Neal Parnell said to Flex, "and I got the wrong color socks."
"You cheap shit," Buck told him. "Why don't you just go out and buy you some blue fucking socks."
Parnell grimaced, embarrassed about the Warning slip. Parnell's rookie was trying not to stare at the Combat Stars on Pridemore's shirt. When the rookie saw Buck and Jack later in the shift, he noticed that all the decorations were gone from Pridemore's uniform. He asked Parnell about it when they were alone.
"Only an asshole wears his ribbons out here on the street," Parnell explained to the kid. "Everybody out here knows what you're made of, whether you wear all your medals or not. Besides, imagine how long it would take him to get dressed every day if he wore all that bullshit?"

Gunderson from Forensics trudged through the back yard to the little house in the rear. It looked like a garage with windows. He opened the screen door with his flashlight, stepped inside, and found a clean end table on which to put his print kit and black canvas camera bag. He pulled out a handkerchief and cleaned his glasses.
"What have you got?"
"White male, 35 years," said Hoatlin. "He cut his wrists and ankles with a straight razor."
"Ankles, hmmm," said Gunderson. "Never hurts to be thorough. Where is he?"
"They transported to Central," Pridemore replied.
"He's not a K?"
"No," said Hoatlin. "They figure he'll make it."
"What the fuck do you need me for then?" asked the annoyed Gunderson.
"Sergeant Becker said we should get some photos. What took you so long? We've been here almost two hours."
Gunderson looked up slowly at Hoatlin from over the tops of his glasses. "Look, Pal, it's our *job* to get here too late. That's what we *do*. That's why they call it 'Forensics.' It's Latin for *show-up-after-it's-too-fucking-late-and-get-the-clues*. Christ! Didn't they teach you anything at the police academy?" Gunderson turned the evil eye away

from Hoatlin and took a small digital camera out of his canvas bag. "Okay, lead on."

They crossed the small living room to a kitchen. Gunderson paused in the threshold before stepping on the kitchen's tile floor. His practiced eye took it all in. There was blood on the sink. There was blood on a towel rack. There were smears on the doorway and light switch between the kitchen and the rear bedroom. There was a trail of drops from that doorway, crossing the kitchen, and a large puddle in front of the sink, where they guy had no doubt paused to bleed. Gunderson avoided the drops as he crossed the kitchen to the back bedroom.

In the bedroom was a wire cage containing a large Black Lab puppy that was wagging its tail at all the attention. They passed through the bedroom to a bathroom with a bloody shower stall. Gunderson pondered the mess. He raised the camera, just giving Pridemore and Hoatlin a chance to scoot out of the way. His first photo showed the whole shower stall with its bloody walls, bloody curtain, and the bloody trail that headed out to the kitchen. His second photo showed the stall with its floor solidly red. He took a close-up of the yellow-handled straight razor, still protruding from the drain, and a close-up of a message on the wall of the shower stall. The message, written in blood, read: "YOU DON'T CAR . . ." Gunderson looked at it sideways.

"What the fuck's that say?"

"I don't know for certain, but I think the guy was trying to write 'You don't care,' but he passed out," explained Hoatlin.

"He shoulda written 'I CAN'T SPELL,'" remarked Gunderson, disgustedly. He then became self-conscious and, looking around, said: "Nobody else here?"

"No, just us and the dog," said Pridemore.

"Cool." Gunderson relaxed. He found another angle that would take in the remainder of the bathroom and got another picture. When he came back out to the bedroom, he saw Hoatlin playing with the puppy through the wire cage. "Nice dog?"

"He's a sweetheart," said Hoatlin.

"The place isn't a toilet and doesn't stink," Gunderson commented, looking around. "Either the guy's a fag or he hasn't lived here very long."

"He's not a fag," said Pridemore. "We found his porno collection in the closet of the other bedroom."

"Anything good?" Gunderson asked absently.

"Nah," said Hoatlin.

"Why didn't he use *that*?" Gunderson wondered aloud, pointing at a bolt-action rifle leaning again the wall.

"He said he didn't have any ammunition," Pridemore explained.

"Loser. Probably would have shot at himself and missed anyway." Hoatlin nodded.

"That the happy family?" Gunderson asked, surveying a line of framed photos on the kitchen shelf. There were Christmas trees, Halloween parties, and a family at the beach. He looked at the pictures without touching them. He hadn't physically touched anything since he had been in the house and, God willing, he would get out of there without making any physical contact at all. He thought of petting the puppy but decided against it. "Wife is kinda young. How old did you say this loser is?"

"Thirty-five," answered Pridemore.

"Freshly divorced?"

"Last month."

"Yeah, I was depressed for about ten minutes after my first divorce," Gunderson remembered. "What a soulless predatory slut she was. Cut out my fucking heart and fed it to her new boyfriend, the bitch."

"We were *wondering* what happened to your heart," said Pridemore.

Gunderson looked hard at Pridemore. "The milk of my human compassion got curdled a long fucking time ago, Jack."

"So we'll tag the razor, okay?" asked Hoatlin.

"I sure as fuck don't need it," said Gunderson, packing his camera away. "Who's gonna feed the puppy?"

"He's got a friend that said he'll come by and take care of the dog while he's in the hospital," Pridemore said.

"This loser's got a friend?"

"Yeah," said Hoatlin. "The guy has a good dog, a good rifle, and a good friend, and he goes and tries to end it all. Go figure."

They all shook their heads.

"Funny how we all think of the dog's welfare first," mused Hoatlin.

"Ya gotta take your innocent victims as you find them," said Gunderson. "Sometimes it's only a fucking dog. Or a kid. But everyone else is just an asshole."

"A thought for the day," Pridemore smiled.

"I had an innocent homicide victim about two years ago," said Gunderson from the front doorway. "It was a kitten who got slammed against a wall in a domestic argument. The husband and wife were utter assholes. Only the fucking cat was innocent. And I can't remember any others right now offhand. Ninety-eight percent of all homicide victims are utter slimebuckets. Don't they teach you that at the academy anymore?"

"Thanks, Gunny," said Pridemore.

Gunderson pushed open the front door with his flashlight. "See ya at the next one, eh?"

"*Forensics* means warped-as-hell," said Hoatlin to Pridemore.

"I heard that, you lightweight motherfucker," came Gunderson's voice back through the screen door.

They almost missed the message on the screen of their Mobile Data Terminal, because Buck, half asleep in the passenger seat, had turned off the notification Beep. They were parked in a closed gas station parking lot at Jensen and Madison, when the message from Flex Sinclair appeared.

"Belle River/Houston," said the message.

Pridemore put the car in gear. They were only about ten blocks away. The car had traveled two blocks before Pridemore realized his headlights were still off. He switched on the headlights as they reached Belle River. Buck sat up to avoid any surprises. They could see the overheads on Flex Sinclair's cruiser as they crossed Boyd Avenue. Thirty-five, forty, forty-five, fifty, and then they were there. In the spotlight of Sinclair's cruiser, they could see Flex talking to the driver of a rusted out Toyota. There appeared to be only one subject in the vehicle. Pridemore flipped on his own overheads, and they both got out. Flex glanced over his shoulder and saw that his backup had arrived. Buck was starting toward the right rear of the subject vehicle. Flex walked back to them without keeping an eye on the driver, which Pridemore found strange. Flex had something in his hands as he motioned Buck and Jack over to his cruiser. They assembled by Flex's spotlight, keeping an eye on the stopped driver ahead.

"Look at this," said Flex Sinclair excitedly. "I gotta show you this."

He held the driver's paperwork in the spotlight.

"What've you got?" asked Buck Tyler.

"Look at this, man," said Flex Sinclair, waving the paperwork. "I got a nigger here with a valid license, current registration, *and* car insurance." Flex gave them an enormous grin. Buck and Jack shook their heads.

They only knew her as Wanda. She had been around for as long as anybody could remember. The only cops who knew her real name were the occasional uninformed rookie who would actually bother to arrest her or the occasional unfortunate turn-key down at lock-up who had to process her into jail. Wanda wore layers of coats, scarves, and hats, each rotting over the underlying strata of decay. Her pockets were stuffed with rotting dollar bills wrapped in month-old French fries and half-eaten things she had found in the trash. Her remaining four teeth were green and bothered her. Wanda shuffled from fast food dumpster to fast food dumpster, a walking zoo of body lice, fleas, and other unmentionable vermin. She had tuberculosis, long untreated syphilis, which is what made her insane, and arthritis, which was what made her a gimp. When she wasn't keeping up her constant conversation with voices of demons and long-dead relatives, she was shrieking at shopkeepers, cabbies, and cops. Just now, Wanda was dragging her bags, her diseased carcass, and a stolen Diet Pepsi across the parking lot.

"That lady stole a beverage, Officer," shouted the party store clerk, pointing at Wanda's retreating figure.

Pridemore, who was driving, considered putting the car in gear and roaring off, leaving the little man and his problems. The little clerk stood in the rain on the passenger side of the cruiser, where Teddy Hoatlin had the window down just a crack.

"She stole a jumbo cup!" cried the little man. "She does it every time she comes in here."

Teddy rolled his window down another three inches. "Then don't let her in your store next time, Son."

"But . . ."

Pridemore fished a dollar out of his pocket and handed it to Hoatlin. "But she . . ."

"Here's a dollar," Teddy told the clerk.

The nervous little man took the bill and looked down at it, as if Teddy had just handed him a lizard. Hoatlin started to roll the window up. The guy was wearing a tie with a short-sleeved striped shirt out there in the rain, for Chrissakes. Hoatlin and Pridemore could see that Wanda had made it up to the corner of Filmore and Pritchard.

"It was a dollar three," said the wet clerk.

Hoatlin rolled the window back down, so the clerk could get all the clues that his face had to offer. No one in their right mind ever arrested Wanda. The people at lock-up would laugh in your face. The motor equipment guy would curse your name for all the bugs Wanda had left in your cruiser. You would wonder what had possessed you to do it, as you scratched the lice that had invaded your uniform. Nobody screwed with Wanda the bag lady.

"A dollar and three cents," the clerk said again.

"Step away from the vehicle, Son," Hoatlin told him. When the clerk hesitated, Hoatlin's voice grew louder and sharper. "Go on. Get the hell outta here!"

Pridemore put it in gear. Wanda was out of sight by now. The cruiser tires screeched as they pulled out of the lot, heading the other way.

The form said: "PLEASE LIST BELOW, IN ORDER OF PREFERENCE, THE NAMES OF THREE MEMBERS OF THE DEPARTMENT OR OTHER PERSONS YOU WISH TO NOTIFY YOUR FAMILY IN THE EVENT OF YOUR ON-DUTY DEATH."

Pridemore looked down at the form. It had three spaces, numbered 1, 2, and 3, and had "Supplemental Personal Information #924-B" in the bottom left corner. There was a rustle of papers in the Squad Room.

"I didn't know there was going to be a quiz," said Teddy Hoatlin.

"Hmmm," agreed Pridemore, "it's a tough one."

"I always put Channel 5 in here somewhere," said Buck Tyler. "When I get killed, my ex-wives will want to get the news fast, so they can call the caterers for their parties." As superstitious as many old cops, Buck knew that, by saying *"when* I get killed," he was appeasing the Great Magnet that might someday pull him into or out of the path of a bullet.

"When you get whacked," added Flex Sinclair, "they're going to put up a granite penis memorial at the Mount Mercy nurses' lounge."

"Marble," said Buck. "Pink marble."

"And a magnifying glass so they can look at it," said Hoatlin.

Buck glared at Teddy. "Rock-hard marble."

"To scale, of course," added Pridemore.

"Three feet and six inches of stone-cold love," Buck mused aloud.
"One foot equals one inch?" asked Hoatlin.
Buck smoothed his graying red moustache with one huge paw. "Somebody's jealous."
"Maybe with a little chapel around it," said Flex. "Saint Tyler, Fucker of Nurses."
"Yeah," said Hoatlin, "so the nuns can hang their rosaries from it."
"A place for nuns to sit. Yeah." Buck liked the idea.
Sgt. Petty banged on the podium with a stapler. "Okay, crimefighters, let's get those forms done and passed to the front. We've got to get rolling here."
"Speaking of limp dicks . . ." Pridemore said.
Flex Sinclair wrote down the name of a black Sergeant he knew from South Precinct, Jack Pridemore's name, and finally "any non-white motherfucker below the rank of Lt."
Teddy Hoatlin, who had a brother in Metro and an uncle in the fire department, wrote their names in and added Father Price.
Jack Pridemore put down Father Price, Father Paul Doyle, and left the last space blank. In the past he had written Judd Christian's name, knowing that his old partner would handle anything that came up with Pridemore's wife and daughter. But his old partner was no more. Judd couldn't talk or walk or eat or sleep. He couldn't even breathe on his own now. Besides, thought Pridemore, he didn't really care who told his ex-wife that he was dead. Linda had moved on, making it clear that she didn't really care what happened to him in his silly job. Jennifer, on the other hand, would have to hear the news by phone or would get a knock on her door by two unlucky cops in Colorado who had drawn the notification duty that night. Either way, Pridemore didn't know how to fill in the last blank on the #924-B form.
Buck Tyler's choices were Father Price, Sgt. Lindsey, and "the weather bunny from Channel 5 with the big tits."

"Oh, no!" moaned Officer Becky Carpenter. "Not Seventeen-Ten."
"There must be something else," Pridemore said, hopefully, searching the wet parking lot for a working cruiser. They had been late getting out, because Becky had been delayed by Sgt. Wheeler, who had chewed her out about a domestic report she had written the night before. It had embarrassed her, getting reprimanded for some bullshit report error.

She just barely tolerated old guys like Sgt. Wheeler, Sgt. Petty, Teddy Hoatlin, and Jack Pridemore. And she absolutely despised Buck Tyler, the pig. At least Pridemore would keep his hands to himself.

The lot was filled with police cars. There were cruisers with "Out For Service" signs in their windshields and cruisers with only three wheels. There were red "BIOHAZARD!" signs on the cruisers with backseats recently stained by blood and/or vomit. There was an old Chevy missing a driver's door from an incident where one of the rookies had thrown it open without looking for passing cars. There was a green City pickup with a snowplow on its front bumper that someone had left there months ago. There were certain favorite cruisers that certain Day Shift cops had put "Out For Service" signs on, which were not broken at all. One of the newer Fords sported both a "BIOHAZARD!" sign and a missing battery. There was a burned cruiser on blocks under a tarp in the corner.

"I think we're screwed," said Pridemore.

"Shit!" snapped Becky Carpenter, loading her equipment bag into 1710's trunk.

Everybody knew about 1710. It was an old Dodge or Plymouth. You couldn't tell which, because the emblems had all been torn off. It had an old style light bar hanging off the roof, older than Carpenter's eight years on The Job. It had an old style radio with a "Squelch" knob and a "Gain" knob, neither of which made sense, and a volume knob than didn't seem to matter. The "Scan" button didn't work, which meant you either listened to South Dispatch or Citywide, but not both. It had Lincoln-Mercury wheel covers on the left side and no hubcaps on the right. The backseat was gone, just not there at all. Someone had covered over the rear seat floor brackets with a sheet of stained plywood and used it as a Canine Unit. Before it had been a dog car, 1710 had been a Sergeant's cruiser and, before that, a Captain's car. It still smelled like a Canine Unit, Carpenter thought. And the dog had been a cigar-smoker, too, it seemed. The screen between the civilized front seats and the madness of the space behind was an old style wire mesh, installed apparently in an age before suspects regularly spit at you from the backseat.

Pridemore settled into the driver's seat, its springs annihilated by the hulking cops of yesteryear. The seat seemed to tilt to the left, leaning Pridemore slightly toward the door. He inserted the shotgun into the riot gun bracket between the seats, noting that the bracket's electric lock was broken. Carpenter sank into the dilapidated passenger seat, wondering how many slimy old cops had slept, farted, and died of heart disease on its upholstery. Her five foot six inch frame allowed her to just peek out the window. She turned the window crank to vent some of the stale air. Pridemore fumbled with the key ring, which held a generic ignition key, a generic trunk key, a broken Trans Am key, and somebody's old house key.

Seventeen-ten roared to life in a never-say-die Dodge sort of way. Pridemore remembered that Buck Tyler had once been so frustrated with 1710 that he had taken it for a run up on the Parkway and thrown it into Park. Buck had told him how loud the noise had been as 1710 had swallowed its own transmission at 85. They had all been surprised when the old cruiser had shown back up from the City Garage three weeks later. With more than 115,000 miles on it, no one had wanted to do the paperwork necessary to sell it to one of the cab companies or take it for City auction or just junk it out. So 1710 kept coming back. It was the cruiser nobody wanted.

The "Yelp" button was the only working part of the siren board. Pridemore played it once briefly and ran the overhead lights. The old light bar didn't even have take-down lights in front or alley lights on the sides. There were two spotlights, however, and Becky was surprised to find that hers worked at all. She noticed that the glove box was held closed with a bent wire clothes hanger. The gas pedal seemed to work on a delay, which meant that when Pridemore's boot pushed on it, the engine hesitated, and then lurched. This will take some getting used to, thought Pridemore. At least the wipers worked. The worn-out shocks left them to bottom-out in a hail of sparks as 1710 swerved out onto Maynard and headed west. Pridemore's partner glared at him, but he didn't notice.

Becky Carpenter thought Pridemore was driving like an asshole. She didn't *need* this bullshit. She didn't *need* 1710 tonight. She didn't *want* to spend eight rainy hours with Jack Pridemore. She had brought a sandwich in a bag and, she decided, she would eat in the car. There was no need to meet up with one of Pridemore's demented old buddies for a greasy dinner somewhere. She had a tooth that was bothering her, which she also didn't need tonight. If Pridemore or one of those old bastards so much as mentioned the letters "PMS," Becky was going to shoot them on the spot.

"What a piece of shit," Becky grumbled.

Pridemore heard her only distantly. He was playing with the steering wheel, not certain if the car's fractured alignment was pulling to the right, or if the left leaning driver's seat was making it to seem so. They ground to a stop at Bryden and almost stalled out at the Hawthorne light. Pridemore checked the gas; the tank was full, because no one ever drove 1710 if they could help it. The headlights and the heater seemed to work for now.

Carpenter noticed that some disenfranchised soul had painted most of the dashboard with white correction fluid. Such childish shit. She looked out on the endless rows of shitbox houses cut up into shitbox apartments for shithead lowlifes that ran along the west side of Racine Avenue. The gates were broken, the windows were broken, the cars were broken, she noted; everything and everyone on Racine Avenue was a screwed up, broken down mess tonight. It looked even worse in the rain. She turned to the center console to type a "Calls Pending" search.

"Jesus! This car doesn't even have a computer!"

"Nope," Pridemore replied, absently. He was still fooling around with the steering wheel. It definitely pulled to the right, he had decided. They turned at Racine and Vanderbilt, where the old Jiffy Taco had burned down last year, and headed east.

"What an utter piece-of-shit car," muttered Carpenter.

"Used to be, police cars didn't even have computers," Pridemore said. He didn't really mind the absence of the Computer-Aided-Dispatch Mobile Data Terminal in 1710. It was, in fact, one of 1710's few redeeming qualities, he thought. You didn't know who was where and what they were doing, but Command couldn't very well keep track of where you were or what you were up to either. Of course, if you got yourself into a wrestling match with some puke, you'd have to call for back-up on the air. But that's how they had always done it in the past anyway. You didn't need a computer for that. Cops always screamed over their radios when they needed help. Most of the stuff that was supposed to come with the car computer software hadn't worked anyway, so you were basically on your own. Like it had always been, Pridemore remembered.

"Back in the day, huh, Pridemore?" Carpenter sighed.

Most of the cops in Mercer Heights thought Becky Carpenter was a lesbian, except, of course, the real lesbians in the Precinct, who knew better. She was a little bit muscular and a little bit plump, and her young face was a little too hardened for her years, but she was not a butch female cop. Pridemore, who had known her father, Sergeant Doug Carpenter, down in South Precinct, knew that little Becky had once wanted to be a pilot, that she had joined the Air Force, and had suffered a failed romance or two there. He knew about a failed romance with a patrol officer from Metro and how embittered she had become. Pridemore knew that Becky had only landed in police work after her dad had retired, dying of a stroke a few weeks later. He knew all this, but he didn't say anything. He was just another geezerly old cop to her.

They took a domestic on Scranton, where the father of the victim's children had thrown the victim through a window with surprisingly bloodless results. They had shooed a derelict away from the Pazazz Bar on Newton and called a cab for a drunk outside The Bendix Lounge on Bendix Avenue. They had taken an assault report on Evers just off of Trowbridge and found a wrecked stolen car behind a warehouse on east Rhodes. Carpenter had just finished writing the vehicle recovery report in a vacant factory lot on Cleveland, and they were off again.

"Check out this brain surgeon," Becky Carpenter murmured.

Pridemore looked to the right and saw a big white kid in an old Buick. He was sneering at their car and revving his engine. The Buick obviously had something bigger and newer under its hood than the original engine. Carpenter tried to look disinterested, but her door was vibrating from the sound. When Pridemore drove slower, Mr. Hot Rod hung back. When 1710 edged forward, the Buick roared up to keep pace. They both stopped for a flashing red at Unger Street. Pridemore pulled out, but hit the brakes in the middle of the intersection. The Buick got slightly ahead of them before it slowed.

"5BHV7F3," said Carpenter, catching the plate. She switched 1710's old radio to Wants & Warrants and checked the number. Mr. Hot Rod swerved right and took off down an alley.

"Good," said Pridemore.

"Prick," said Carpenter.

Passing under the South Parkway, they listened to the crackle of the radio. The Buick's plate came back, Not Stolen, to a suburban address. Just some white kid slumming or high on something he just purchased on Bleeker Avenue, thought Becky. There was a broadcast of a missing eight-year-old and a cancellation on a stolen Caddie. In the old industrial section of South Sloan Avenue, the Buick reappeared.

"Mr. Rocket Science is baaack," announced Carpenter. "I think he wants to race." The Buick swerved wildly, side to side, just missing Becky's door on the close passes and then kissing the curb on the right.

"Hmmm," said Pridemore. He threw 1710's transmission into Low and hurtled forward. They blew a stop sign at Magnolia and sped northbound, the old cruiser howling. Mr. Hot Rod had been taken by surprise, but he soon caught up, the Buick's huge engine drowning out the noise of the sick cruiser. Pridemore waved at the speeding white kid and flipped on the overheads to attract his attention. Mr. Hot Rod was snarling at the cops and down-shifting, when he ran out of road and hit the dumpster. The wrecked Buick rolled down into a gully of rain-wet trash. To Carpenter's surprise, Pridemore simply shut off the overheads and continued up Sloan to Pritchard, where he turned west. There was a moment of silence as 1710 caught its breath.

"We ought to check on him," Carpenter finally said.

"Fuck him," Pridemore replied. "He wants to race, he ought to learn how to drive."

Becky Carpenter considered this for a moment. "Maybe he's injured."

"Yeah? So?"

"We did run his plate," she said. "The tape will show that we made some sort of contact."

Pridemore sighed. It wasn't exactly like working with Buck or Teddy, of course. He rounded the block and came back to the wrecked Buick. Carpenter played her spotlight around the crash site but saw no one. Pridemore backed 1710 up so she could get a better look. The tapping on the right rear fender startled them both. Carpenter cranked down her window to see Mr. Hot Rod limping toward her. His shirt was torn, his face scratched, and his nose broken. In a daze he held up an apologetic hand.

"Satisfied?" asked Pridemore.

"Yes, indeed," Becky Carpenter said to Pridemore. She turned to the haggard Mr. Hot Rod, gave him The Finger, and snarled, "Numb Nuts!"

Raggedy old 1710 roared up Sloan Avenue and west on Conklin. Becky punched Pridemore lightly on the shoulder and laughed. They both laughed. Her tooth wasn't bothering her anymore, and neither was Pridemore or 1710. She wrote on her log: "Lost speeding Buick 5BHV7F3, Pritchard/Boyd area." She looked out at the rain-wet streets.

"You want to get a cup of coffee, Pridemore?" she asked suddenly.

"Sure," he replied, "I know a place."

Anita Gonzales was a pretty little woman. At least, she *had* been before somebody named "Lido" had knocked out her four front upper teeth. She sat on the plastic-covered sofa in the apartment's small living room, crying into a bloody towel. The other people in the room were apparently relatives and not suspects. It was hard to tell who was involved, because Anita spoke little English, and Pridemore and Parnell spoke very little Spanish. They were utilizing the translating skills of a little boy named Tino, who spoke Spanish at home and English at his grade school. Tino was somehow related to Anita, but was not her son. Anita bled and cried, the lap of her torn flower-print dress getting soggy with the mixture of liquids.

"So this Lido individual doesn't live here?" Parnell asked Tino. The boy said something to Anita, but a fat woman in stretch pants scolded him. A little bald man beside the fat woman rebuked her. Tino asked the bald man something and was scolded by a skinny teenage girl in a scarf.

Another bald little man shook his head and kept saying, "No. No. No."

Parnell had already made the mistake of asking the little translator who all these people were and had received a muddled history of the Gonzales-Perez-Vasquez family tree, which didn't help at all. But Tino was trying his best. Anita was apparently hard to understand, because Tino had to repeat and rephrase his questions over and over.

No, Lido did not live at 2263 South Cramer, Apartment C, upstairs back. Yes, Lido had lived there up until last Thursday. Yes, Lido had come back tonight. No, Lido did not pay rent and, therefore, was not the resident of record. Yes, he had moved out. Yes, he had relatives in the area. And Chocolate.

"Chocolate?" asked Parnell.

"What?" asked Pridemore.

"She said 'chocolate,' I think," said Parnell.

"I heard that. What about chocolate?"

"No, no, no," corrected Tino. "She means cocoa."

"Cocoa?" Parnell echoed. He wrote that down. "But not chocolate?"

"No, no," Tino said again. "Landro went to stay with his friend, Cocoa."

"Who's Landro?" asked Pridemore.

"Can you spell that?" asked Parnell. Only Parnell would have even tried to keep up with the actual transcription of this mess.

"Okay, Partner," Pridemore said to the kid translator. "Who is Cocoa?"

"He is Lido's friend who Lido has gone and stayed with," explained Tino. The kid started to say something further, but Pridemore hushed him. The small crowd at Tino's back was whispering among themselves.

"And who is this Landro?" Pridemore asked slowly.

"Landro, Lido, same, same," said Tino.

"Lido is his street name?"

"Street name?"

"His nickname," Parnell offered.

The kid still looked baffled. The crowd mumbled. Anita cried. Jesus wept from a portrait over the television.

"Lido is what you call him?" asked Pridemore.

"Si, yes," the kid nodded.

"But his real name is Landro?"

"Yes."

"How do you spell that?" asked Parnell, and the kid checked with Anita first before spelling it out for the cops.

"And his friend is Cocoa?" Pridemore asked the kid.

"Si, I mean, yes," replied Tino. "He live. . ."

"Wait, wait," Pridemore stopped him. "Do you know Cocoa's real name?"

The translator gave him a funny look. "That *is* his real name."

"Spell that," said Pridemore.

"Cocoa?"

"Yes."

Tino spelled the name. "K-O-K-O."

"Ahhh," said Parnell, scratching out the former spellings.

"Does Landro have a last name?"

"Yes," answered the kid patiently.

"And what is his last name?" asked Pridemore.

"Montez."

"M-O-N-T-E-Z?" asked Parnell.

"I think so," said Tino. He turned to ask the fat lady in the stretch pants, but she apparently wasn't sure of the spelling either.
"What is Koko's last name?" Pridemore asked.
"Vasquez."
"V-A-S-Q-U-E-Z?"
"Yes," said Tino. "Same as me."
"Koko's your brother?"
"My uncle," answered Tino Vasquez.
There was a short conference with the fat lady in stretch pants and the two little bald men. A bored ambulance crew came pounding up the back stairs, adding to the pack in the living room. They looked at Anita and gave her a bandage to bite on. She could not afford an ambulance or hospital, she said through Tino. She wanted to die. She wanted to know why Lido would do this to her. She was not suffering from double vision or dizziness. Yes, she had a headache, but it was probably from the broken teeth and nose. No, she had no insurance. Yes, she had a job. No, she still could not afford an ambulance. She would not sign the form where it said that she was refusing treatment, against medical advice. She would not sign anything, because she could not afford anything, she told Tino. Tino dutifully repeated it all. The ambulance crew shrugged and left, thumping back down the narrow steps.
"Okay, Partner," Pridemore began again. "Now Lido went to stay with Koko, right?" The kid nodded. "And where does Koko live?"
"Here," said Tino.
"Here?" asked Parnell.
"In this building?" asked Pridemore. The cops tensed up as the story changed.
"Downstairs," explained the kid.
"Is he here now?" asked Pridemore.
"He lives with his mother," Tino continued. He indicated the fat lady in the stretch pants. She nodded, terrified of the big policemen.
"Is he there now?" Pridemore asked again.
"No, he stay with Gloria, his girlfriend."
"Where is that?" asked Parnell. The kid checked with the fat lady, but Anita stopped her bleeding long enough to give them an address on Newton Avenue.
"Okay," summarized Pridemore. "So Landro Montez, who doesn't live here and doesn't pay rent here, but who stayed here until last

Thursday, came here tonight, and he got in an argument with Anita Gonzalez, and he hit her with his fist, and he left and went to a house on Newton Avenue, where his friend, Koko, stays with his girlfriend? Is that about it so far?"

Tino pondered it all for a moment. He then reviewed the facts with Anita, who nodded and cried. Pridemore noticed that she disagreed with one factual point, midway through the recitation. But on the rest of it, she concurred.

"That about right?" Parnell asked the kid.

"Anita say he not hit her with fist," explained Tino.

"Did he use a weapon?"

"Weapon?"

"What did Landro hit her with?" asked Pridemore. It made a difference in the report, whether it was a fist or a lamp or something, an Assault or a Felonious Assault.

"She say Lido hit her with his hands," Tino said.

"Hands, fists, whatever," said Parnell, scribbling. Pridemore stooped down to Anita as Parnell asked the kid some more questions. Anita's black hair and purple eyeshadow were a jumble of tears and blood. Her eyes were puffy from crying. Her nose was swollen and crooked. She had been pretty earlier that day, Pridemore could tell. He motioned for her to take the bloody towel away. Anita showed him her cut lips and red mouth. The upper four teeth were missing completely, not broken off. The holes glistened where the tooth roots had once been. Pridemore wondered how much that must hurt.

"How long ago did this happen?" Pridemore asked Tino, interrupting Parnell's questions. There was a conference between Tino, Anita, and the small crowd, which now featured a second skinny teenage girl. They all looked at the battery-operated clock on the wall beside the Jesus portrait over the TV.

They voted. "Twenty minutes ago," said Tino.

"Just twenty minutes?" asked Parnell. "We've been here fifteen minutes already."

"Twenty-five minutes then," Tino replied as if it were an auction of time.

"Was it more than an hour?" Pridemore asked Tino sternly. Tino checked around the room again. Everyone agreed the fight had been less than an hour ago.

"Okay, so roughly 2 AM then?" asked Parnell.

"Where are the teeth now?" Pridemore interrupted.

Tino shrugged. They all shrugged. Pridemore started looking around, afraid that the missing teeth were on the floor at his feet. Parnell and Tino were confused. Anita wailed with pain. One of the skinny teenage girls said something to Tino, who translated for the police.

"She say she threw them out, the teeth."

Pridemore whirled on the girl, startling her. "Where? Where did she throw them out?"

The alarmed girl pointed to the other room and said something to Tino.

"She say she put them in the kitchen," the kid explained. Parnell was getting nowhere with this report.

"Show me," barked Pridemore.

The skinny teenage girl led Tino and Pridemore into the apartment's tiny kitchen. She pointed to the kitchen table. There, in an ashtray, between a napkin holder and a salt shaker, lay Anita Gonzales' four teeth, roots and all. The red meat on the roots was still glistening amidst all the cigarette butts. There was no time for gloves. Pridemore gently picked out the teeth from the cigarette butts and took them over to the sink. "Get me some ice." No one moved.

"Ice?" asked Tino the translator.

"Get me some fucking ice!" snapped Pridemore. "And a baggie."

There was no ice in the apartment. One of the little bald men went downstairs to get some, but brought it back in a leaky paper sack. Pridemore glared at the man, who couldn't understand why the cops disliked what he had done. He was only trying to help. Pridemore pointed to a trash bag lining in a wastebasket in the corner, but no one could find a clean one. He hoisted the bag, dumped the garbage on the floor, and ripped out a bottom corner of the bag. Dumping the little bald man's ice into the makeshift plastic bag, Pridemore carefully placed Anita's teeth on top, added more ice, and tied the bag shut. He returned to the crowded living room. The fat lady, the teenage girls, the little bald men, and Parnell all backed out of Pridemore's way as he strode to the couch and bent down to Anita. Tino tried to translate, but was frightened of the big policeman now.

"These can be saved," Pridemore told Anita Gonzales, looking up from her bloody towel. "We have to get you to a hospital now."

But Anita would have none of it. Tino kept trying to explain what Pridemore was saying, but Anita shook her swollen face. She could not afford an ambulance, she told Tino. She could not pay for a hospital. Pridemore's face twisted in frustration. He squatted down to her eye level.

"Look!" he said firmly. "You're pretty. You are a *pretty* woman."

Tino translated, not sure if he was getting the words right. It didn't make much sense, but the policeman was talking slowly and clearly.

"You're a very pretty woman," Pridemore continued. "We can save these teeth. At the hospital, they can put them back in and save your lovely smile." He realized as he said it that he had never even seen her smile.

The kid translated.

"We can save your beautiful teeth, Anita," said Pridemore, and his use of her name caught her attention. She slowed her weeping and the shaking of her head, trying to understand what Tino was saying. "We must get you and the teeth to the hospital."

"No money," she tried to say, but it came out in bubbles of blood. She said something in Spanish to Tino.

"She say she has no money for an ambulance," said Tino.

"Fuck the ambulance! I'll take her. And you can pay the hospital later or not at all. Fuck it. Let's get going."

Parnell looked alarmed. Tino tried to translate without the bad words included, although everyone in the little room understood their meaning.

"You need your teeth, no?" asked Pridemore, right up to her face now. She started to nod as Tino translated. "You need to stay pretty like you were an hour ago. You need to keep that pretty smile. You need to look pretty...for...Lido."

"Jesus," murmured Parnell.

Anita Gonzales finally nodded.

"Alright, somebody get her a coat!" barked Pridemore. "Tino, you're coming, too."

With Tino, Anita, and her bloody bandage in the back seat, Pridemore roared off up Cramer toward Central Receiving Hospital. Parnell was on the radio, trying to get the dispatcher to get a Sergeant's permission to transport a female, non-emergency, to the hospital, but the dispatcher was having trouble finding a Sergeant to give such permission. Pridemore hit the siren to move a bus out of the way on St. Joseph, but just left it on until they reached the Emergency Only driveway behind Central Receiving.

"What have we here?" asked the first intern, startled that the cops were bringing someone in through the Ambulance Only area.

"Dental emergency," Pridemore told him, hustling Anita and Tino through the hall. "I've got the teeth with roots on ice in my pocket."

"We'll have to wake up an oral surgery resident for this," complained the intern.

"You'll fucking do that now, won't you?" asked Pridemore in a voice that needed no answer or discussion.

He lied to the nurse that Anita Gonzales was the victim of a traffic accident. He lied that her purse with its I.D. and credit cards had burned up in the wreck. He told them her name and said she had insurance. He lied and lied until they quit asking questions about the hospital bills and went to wake up an oral surgeon. They straightened Anita's broken nose and gave her something for the pain. They took the little makeshift bag of her teeth and moved them to a small tray of ice water. Before they wheeled her away to have her teeth put back in her mouth, Pridemore took Tino aside in the corridor. He told the kid that both of them should keep up the story about the traffic accident. They would be typically hazy about the details.

"Just tell them you're her son," Pridemore laid it out. "You're her son, and your Dad has a job and insurance, and she can sign any forms that they give her. She'll get out today or tomorrow, and you take her home in a cab." He gave the kid a ten. Tino said he understood. Pridemore scrambled the kid's hair and thanked him for all the translating.

"You talk a little fast and a little crazy," Tino told him.

"Yeah, sometimes I do," Pridemore replied. He realized he would probably never get to see Anita Gonzales' pretty smile, even if they managed to put it all back together again. Out at the car, Parnell was fretting.

"I finally got permission to transport from Sgt. Lindsey, but they know we were already enroute when I asked. They'll probably beef us to I.A. for it."

"Fuck 'em," said Pridemore.

"And you know she can't pay for the medical bills, Jack."

"Ahhh, fuck them, too."

"The good news is that Lido showed back up at the house," said Parnell, "and Flex arrested him with no trouble."

"Too bad he didn't fight us," replied Pridemore. "We could've bent that sonofabitch's teeth in." All in all, he was pleased. Fuck the

Sergeant. Fuck the Manual of Procedure. And fuck Internal Affairs, too.

Priscilla Berke knocked gently on her husband's door and then padded across the carpet, wearing nothing but one of his white uniform shirts and some perfume. She ran one sensibly unmanicured index finger along the front of his little desk, feeling the coolness of the wood. "Kenneth?"

Lt. Berke sat at his computer, frowning at the screen and trying to think of exactly the right search terms to type. He had been trying to formulate an argument that the community policing approach to the distribution of human resources—namely, putting the same foot beat officers in the same neighborhoods week after week—was less prone to the corruption of the individual officer than was the old style of policing, the "occupying army" effect of a faceless motor patrol in a hostile neighborhood environment. He was having trouble with the argument. The history of police corruption, it seemed, was a history of cops who were intimately familiar with their patrol area's merchants and criminals. It was the old beat cop who ate free apples and accepted free liquor from the Mom and Pop stores; it was the community officer, the one so familiar with neighborhood merchants, who could find a storeroom to sleep in on duty. For some reason, the "occupying army" of motor patrol never seemed to get cozy enough with their neighborhoods so that they accepted bribes or gratuities. It was an enigma of police work that the closer a friendly community came to its neighborhood officer, the more likely it was for them to corrupt him, compromise his effectiveness, and thus make him a criminal. This, of course, couldn't be right, Berke knew. He felt he must have missed something somewhere, which was why he was searching the World Wide Web for an answer.

Community-based policing and corruption.
Community policing and police brutality.
Community-oriented policing and bribery.
C.O.P. and corrupt.
Community policing, bribery, corruption, and scandal.
Road patrol and bribery.
Los Angeles Police Department, New York Police Department, and corruption.

Motor patrol, bribery, and community policing.

Berke had run across a web site that said the following: "An officer who cannot make the paradigm shift to community-oriented policing is unmotivated and prone to corruption." Berke wrote that one down for future reference. It was written by a professor from Minnesota who taught a course in "Re-Inventing the Future of Police Work in America." The phrase "paradigm shift" had always given Berke some problems, but he would try to work it into a sentence he could use next time he was at a Command meeting.

"Kenneth."

He tried another search engine with the word "corrupt" as a constant.

Corrupt plus community policing, Seattle, Washington, and failure.

Corrupt plus community policing, Tulsa, Oklahoma, and failure.

Corrupt plus community policing, University of Michigan, and failure.

Corrupt plus customer-based policing and community outreach.

Corrupt plus police, empowerment, and community affairs.

"Kenneth, Honey."

Berke whirled in his chair, startling his wife. "You shouldn't wear that shirt," was all he could think of saying. "You'll stain it."

"Stain it?" Priscilla repeated, puzzled.

"I just got that one back from the cleaners."

"I'll take it off if you like," Priscilla offered.

"And hang it up with the collar buttoned," he instructed, turning back to the computer. "I am kind of busy right now, Prissy."

Community policing and . . .and . . .

Alvin and Trudy Hoskins were fighting. Their second floor apartment on Converse Avenue was a mess. Both of them had been drinking. Alvin said Trudy was a whore and had stolen his paycheck. Trudy said Alvin was mean when he was drunk and had once broken her wrist. Pridemore and Tyler took Alvin to jail to sober up. When Trudy sobered up, she posted Alvin's bond.

Teddy Hoatlin had gotten himself a burglar. An old lady who couldn't sleep had peeked out her window to see a black guy inside her neighbor's car. He hadn't even bothered to pop out the dome light, so she had been able to see him pretty well. She had actually had telephone service, a rarity on Burris Avenue, and had thought the police ought to know about the crime-in-progress, a rarity verging on nonexistence for Burris Avenue citizens. The fact that anyone living on Burris had even *bothered* to call and report a crime had startled Buck Tyler, who had raced to the address in a white-knuckle ride up Alexander Street that almost made Pridemore sick. But Neal Parnell had gotten there first—he, too, being surprised at an actual *citizen* call from Burris Avenue—and had flushed the guy out from between two cars. The guy had run between some houses, over a fence, and had come to rest on the trunk of Hoatlin's cruiser. Teddy, who had not even been assigned to the call, had tippy-toed his cruiser, lights out, up the gravel alley at the rear of the address, simply curious at what an authentically reported crime looked like on Burris Avenue. None of them could remember such an event.

In any case, Hoatlin had turned the guy's pockets out, finding the usual coins, crack cocaine, keys, car stereo, and condoms, and had deposited him in the rear seat of his car. The guy had no I.D., but claimed he was Yuri Nelson, B/M, age 16. Hoatlin had looked at the guy's full goatee, the lines around his eyes and mouth, the general cast of his ex-con face, and told him he was lying.

"Who?" asked Buck.

"Yuri Nelson," Hoatlin replied.

"There ain't any black guys on this whole planet name Yuri Fucking Nelson."

"That's what I told him."

"What is he, Ukrainian?" asked Pridemore.

"Black Russian," said Hoatlin.

"He doesn't look 16 to me," added Parnell, looking through the rear window at the suspect. Parnell went to find out what vehicles had been broken into at the front of the Burris Avenue address.

The suspect thumped on the glass with his forehead. Hoatlin opened the door.

"These cuffs are too tight," the suspect moaned.

"Son, do you still want to be Yuri Nelson?" asked Hoatlin.

"My name is Yuri Nelson, and these cuffs are too tight."

MAD BADGES

"They're brand new handcuffs," Buck told him. "Give them some time to stretch out." Hoatlin closed the door again.

After a while, Teddy got tired of listening to the guy's wailing and whining about the cuffs, so he opened the door, turned the guy around, and eased up the handcuffs.

"You ever had a citizen call on Burris?" Pridemore asked Buck.

"I don't think so," said Buck. "I didn't know there was a working telephone on Burris Avenue."

Sgt. Lindsey showed up to see what a citizen complaint on Burris looked like. He checked out the suspect in Hoatlin's cruiser.

"That fucker's twenty if he's a day," said Lindsey.

Hoatlin yanked open the door where the handcuffed suspect was leaning. The guy half fell out of the seat. "You sure you still want to be Yuri Nelson?"

"My name is Yuri Nelson," the suspect pleaded, "and I'm 16 years old."

"There's an additional charge for giving a false name to a law enforcement officer," Sgt. Lindsey reminded him.

"We all would like to be 16 years old again," Pridemore told him, "but all of us here, including you, are *way* past that age."

The suspect started his usual refrain, but Hoatlin propped him back in the seat and slammed the door. Parnell brought back the vehicle information and the name of the insomniac who had eyeballed the crime. She had not only seen the crime, but had identified the guy arrested as the one who had broken into the car, and had volunteered her name, address, and telephone number. They were all amazed. Lindsey brought out his little yellow field test kit and tested one of the rocks of dope; the ample turned a pale purple, indicating positive, but weak, results for cocaine.

"The guy buys shitty dope," said Lindsey, tossing the little plastic test tube over a fence.

Hoatlin whipped open the back door and, again, the suspect sprawled to the ground. "You're absolutely, positively *sure* you want to remain Yuri Nelson?"

The guy looked up at Hoatlin's knees and repeated his name and age. Buck grabbed the guy's jacket and shoved him back inside. Hoatlin closed the door. The suspect, afraid of falling out again, was trying to scoot across the seat, when Hoatlin opened the door once again. Out he fell. With his head almost touching the ground, the suspect moaned out his name again.

"No, Dude," said Hoatlin. "I just want to know if you still wanted to be 16 years old." The suspect groaned. Buck snickered. Pridemore found an evidence bag for the car stereo and the suspect's belonging.

Two hours later, Jack and Buck and Becky Carpenter were having coffee at the East & West Café. Hoatlin, who had booked the suspect into lock-up, came in through the kitchen entrance, waved to Mister Chi and the adoring Magda, and settled into a chair. Magda came over with the coffee pot.

"Well," announced Hoatlin to the assembled cops, "there *is* one black guy on the planet named Yuri Nelson."

"No shit?" said Pridemore.

"No shit," answered Teddy. "Lock-up's got him on their books."

"Niggers sure work in mysterious ways," sighed Buck Tyler.

"But he isn't really 16, is he?" asked Pridemore.

"Nah," replied Hoatlin, smiling. "The mellonhead's 23 and on parole."

"Ahhh!" said Buck, comfortable with the familiarity of it all. "That makes sense."

"Let me guess," interjected Becky Carpenter. "He's on parole for breaking into cars."

"Yes," said Hoatlin, "that and a rape conviction."

"My, my," Pridemore said. "I wonder where he got that name."

"Niggers work in mysterious ways," said Buck.

"I just have a couple questions," said the defense attorney, rising from his seat. Peter Talbott was a skinny little guy in a large gray pinstripe polyester suit with a bold red tie. His shoes were athletic shoes, black all over, but still just tennis shoes. His hair spiked upward from his gaunt little face, making him look like a graying carrot. Talbott was an annoyance in the Criminal Courts building. He even annoyed other defense attorneys. Pridemore got along pretty well with defense attorneys, who were, all in all, a hard-working lot, who labored with varying degrees of enthusiasm, depending on the number of years they had practiced law. They were sort of like cops that way. And, like the ranks of police officers, they had their clueless few, like Talbott, who irritated everybody else. Pridemore, in fact, tended to like defense attorneys better than prosecuting attorneys, who were generally new lawyers with law school ideals, a self-righteous self-centeredness, and an endless zeal that was most annoying. But defense counsel Talbott was even more annoying than most anyone in the Criminal Courts building.

"Officer Pridemore . . .?" Talbott began. "It is just Officer Pridemore, not Sgt. Pridemore or Detective Pridemore?"

"That's correct."

"You said in your direct testimony that you were the one who took the accident report at the intersection of Chapman and Bryden on September 9th of last year, is that correct?"

"Yes."

"And you titled your report a 'Hit & Run' accident," said Talbott. "Am I stating that right, for the record?"

"That's right."

"And, if I understood your testimony correctly, you further stated that you followed a trail of some sort to my client's apartment building on Kendall Street. Isn't that so?"

Pridemore cleared his throat. The jurors looked at him expectantly. "I followed a trail of spilled engine fluid from the point-of-impact at Bryden and Chapman, three blocks to the west, south on Bendix, then west again on Kendall, to a damaged vehicle parked at 2353 Kendall Street." The jurors sat in rapt attention, never realizing what a Huge Nothing this case really was. They didn't know that Mr. Thomas Riley, the defendant, was simply fighting this case because it was his third offense. They didn't know how little the big sleepy cop cared about this Huge Nothing of a criminal case. They didn't know that Prosecutor Deborah Smith-Michaels was too green and too filled with prosecutorial holiness to simply offer Talbott and his shithead client a decent plea to get rid of the whole thing. They didn't realize that the judge was sound asleep.

"Now, by 'trail,'" asked Talbott, "do you mean a continuous trail."

"It was a fluid trail made of drops of apparent engine coolant."

"Did you get that analyzed?"

"No, I just followed the trail," Pridemore replied. Some of the jurors nodded at this, proud that they had understood the forensic implications of the evidence. Others of them were still baffled.

"So this 'trail,' as you called it, was not continuous?"

"It was made up of a series of drops of . . ."

"You said that," interrupted Talbott. "My question was, Was the trail continuous? Was it without interruption of any kind?"

Pridemore sat silently, watching the hyperactive prosecutor spring to her feet. "Your Honor, I would request that defense counsel be instructed not to interrupt the witness's answer."

There was silence. The court reporter coughed, discretely waking up the judge, who in turn pretended he had been awake all along. He asked the clerk to run back the last few questions on his computer screen. He pretended to study the transcript for a moment, having forgotten what this silly case was all about. The judge adjusted his glasses and squinted at his computer. The lawyers pretended that the judge had not been asleep. Only the jury was fooled.

"Ask the question again," the judge finally said. "And let's let the Officer here get out his answer. First the answer, then the objections."

"Thank you, Your Honor," said Deborah Smith-Michaels, who wanted someday to be a judge herself.

"Thank you, Your Honor," said Peter Talbott, who despised the judge almost as much as he despised his idiot client. Talbott much preferred his usual drug case clients, who paid him in cash, not checks, and who almost always took a plea.

"We have about ten minutes left until lunch," said the judge.

"Thank you, Your Honor," said the prosecutor.

"If it please the court," said Talbott, "I have only a couple more clarification questions to ask of this witness. If I may . . .?"

The judge nodded, thinking he would have French Onion soup for lunch.

Talbott turned back to Pridemore. "So you're saying that this so-called liquid stream was not continuous."

"I called it a 'fluid trail,'" Pridemore corrected him. *A liquid stream was something you pissed,* he thought.

"Okay, but this liquid trail was . . ."

"Fluid trail."

"This *fluid trail* was not continuous?"

Pridemore turned to the goofy collection of taxpayers, retirees, and assorted citizens in the jury box. "It was a series of drops that led to Mr. Riley's damaged car on Kendall Street."

Deborah Smith-Michaels liked this witness's style, even though she generally detested cops. She glanced at the jurors to see if they understood.

"But there were breaks in this fluid stream?" Talbott asked stubbornly.

"Fluid *trail*," replied Pridemore.

"There were breaks in this so-called *fluid trail*, is that correct?"

"It was like a series of footprint . . ."

"Objection!" interrupted Talbott, turning to the judge. "The witness's answer is unresponsive."

"Let him answer the question first," said the judge, who was now actually paying attention, now that it was almost time for lunch.

"Thank you, Your Honor," chimed in the prosecutor.

"You may answer the question, Officer," the judge told Pridemore.

"The fluid *trail* was a series of drops," Pridemore told the jury. "It is like following a series of footprints. There are breaks between the individual footprints, just as there are breaks between the individual drops of engine fluid in this case. But they *still* make a trail."

"But they still had breaks *between* the drops, correct?" asked Talbott, seething.

"Yes, of course," Pridemore answered in his most polite voice.

"No further questions," said Talbott, plunking down in his chair.

"Ms. Smith?" said the judge.

"I just have a couple questions left," piped up the prosecutor. Everybody always said that. Talbott squirmed in his seat.

"We're running short of time here."

"Thank you, Your Honor. I'll be brief." They always said that, too.

"Continue then, Ms. Smith."

"Just to clarify," the prosecutor addressed Pridemore, "the fluid on the road was engine fluid?"

"It appeared so, yes."

"It did not appear to be vomit?" she asked, tempting the objection.

"Your Honor," spat Talbott, not bothering to rise to his feet, "we've been over this material before."

"I'll allow it up to a point," said the judge, showing the defense attorney how much he disliked it when lawyers in his courtroom made Seated Objections.

"It did not appear to be a trail of vomit, is that correct, Officer Pridemore?" asked the prosecutor pointedly.

"No, the vomit was later," answered Pridemore.

"That was after you spoke with Mr. Riley on his porch on Kendall Street?"

"Correct."

"Or, rather, Mr. Riley spoke to you first."

"Yes," said Pridemore.

"And what did he say?" Deborah Smith-Michaels asked, again tempting the objection. Talbott sat still, too bored to object. He too wanted to go to lunch.

"Mr. Riley opened his front door and said, 'I'm an Irish devil,' and threw up on his shoes," Pridemore explained.

"No further questions," the prosecutor said brightly.

"Mr. Talbott? Have you anything further for this witness?"

"No, Your Honor," replied Peter Talbott.

"You are excused, Officer," said the judge, unable to recall the name of the witness. "We will break for lunch and be back here promptly at 1:30 then." He stood. They all stood. As the jury filed out, the prosecutor smoothed her black skirt over her thighs, pleased that she had left the jurors with a lasting image of the defendant to ponder on their lunch hour. The defense attorney straightened his loud red tie and ignored the whispers of his Irish Devil client. Pridemore was wondering where he could catch a nap.

The Captain's memo read:

IN AN EFFORT TO IMPROVE ON THE PROFESSIONAL STATURE OF THE OFFICERS ASSIGNED TO THE MERCER HEIGHTS PRECINCT, THE FOLLOWING RULES WILL BE ADHERED TO EFFECTIVE IMMEDIATELY:

OFFICERS *SHALL* STAND AT ATTENTION UPON THE ENTRANCE INTO THE SQUAD ROOM OF AN OFFICER OF THE RANK OF SERGEANT OR HIGHER. THIS POSTURE *SHALL* BE MAINTAINED BY THE AFFECTED PERSONNEL UNTIL SUCH TIME AS THE SERGEANT OR OTHER COMMANDING OFFICER INSTRUCTS OTHERWISE. (THIS PROVISION *SHALL* SUPERSEDE MANUAL OF PROCEDURES, CONDUCT, SECTION 12, PART IV, PARAGRAPH 2.)

"I suppose that is what passes for English," said Becky Carpenter, studying the bulletin board.

"Does this mean we have to stand when Sgt. *Petty* enters the room?" sneered Buck.

"No, Buck," said Flex Sinclair, "didn't you see the sub-section that says 'every Sergeant *except* Petty.'"

Parnell's new rookie spoke up. "So if, like, the Sergeant enters the room and, like, falls down with a heart attack, are we, like, supposed to keep standing at attention?"

Everyone looked at the rookie.

"Yes, son," explained Buck Tyler. "Remain standing until the Sergeant has stopped breathing."

Teddy Hoatlin chimed in. "Please remain standing until the Sergeant has come to a complete halt."

Pridemore, who was running late, burst out of the locker room door, a jumble of uniform parts and equipment. He stopped by the bulletin board to read the latest from Command. "Great. Police officer obedience school again."

Parnell's new rookie, who was adrift today because Parnell was out sick with the flu, spoke to Buck Tyler. "What if, like, you enter a room and a Sergeant is, like, already in there? What do you do then?"

"That's easy," Buck replied. "*Never* enter a room where there's a Sergeant."

"Good sound advice, son," said Teddy.

Parnell's new rookie nodded. They all filed into the Squad Room, where there were no Sergeants yet. They filled the back row quickly. The front rows, except for the lesbian contingent, were getting thin today, as more officers shied away from the head of the class.

Buck took Parnell's new rookie aside. "You had better sit down in front today, you know, since your Training Officer is out sick. You may want to ask the Sergeant a question or two. Shows your enthusiasm. Makes a good impression on them." The kid took Buck's advice and sat with the girls in front.

The assembled cops settled into silence and watched the clock.

"It's a test," said Pridemore.

"It's very suspenseful," Hoatlin agreed.

"I think I'm starting my period," said Buck Tyler.

There was a rustle down in front as Gladys, the black cleaning lady came into the Squad Room with her fresh trash bags. The whole Squad rose as one and snapped to attention, several of them saluting. The silence was remarkable, and Gladys turned slowly to see who had come in behind her.

"Whole buncha crazy motherfuckers," the cleaning lady murmured.

Buck was having a difficult time with the black ladies in the dining room. Pridemore was in the kitchen with Becky Carpenter and the retarded 16-year-old rape victim, Stacy. There had been a party upstairs. Stacy's cousin, Deshawn, and two of his friends had talked the retarded girl into an upstairs bedroom.

"They went pee on my bottom," was the way Stacy explained it. She had her pants back on now and was shivering inside a triple-fat Raiders jacket, looking smaller and smaller in the corner of the kitchen. Deshawn and one of his buddies were in the back of Neal Parnell's cruiser at the curb.

"You're Stacy's mother?" Buck Tyler asked the fat lady to his left. He was using his most gentle, most concerned and caring tone, what he called his "social worker voice."

"No," said the fat lady. "I just be her guardian."

"Her mama not here," said the birdlike woman with the tight cornrowed hair.

"Stacy doesn't live her?" Buck asked, smoothing his enormous reddish gray moustache and looking thoughtful.

"No, Sir," answered the third woman, who was oldest and obviously the sharpest of the trio, "this is my house. I am Deshawn's mother."

"I see."

"I am the one that called," the older woman added. It was a no-nonsense mother who would call the cops when it was her own son who was the suspect. Tyler was impressed.

He turned to the fat lady, who had said she was the retarded girl's guardian and who Buck was beginning to think was just a little bit slow herself. "We will be taking Stacy to Mount Mercy to have a doctor take a look at her, and we'll need a parent or guardian to go along."

"Oh, no," cried the fat guardian, worrying a handkerchief between her hands.

"I can go," volunteered the bird lady, "I'm her aunt."

An "aunt," Buck knew, was a complicated being in a case this, where a cousin had supposedly raped another cousin. He would rather have dealt with the no-nonsense mother, who seemed to have her shit together, except that she was the suspect's mother. "We really better have a parent or guardian go with us."

The retarded guardian moaned. The bird lady and the no-nonsense mother nodded that they understood. Buck turned toward the kitchen, where he could see Pridemore. Pridemore gave him a 10-4 look from where he stood, watching Carpenter interviewing the victim. Buck turned back to his trio of black ladies, his head barely missing the low-hanging brass chandelier, which wasn't quite centered over the glass-topped brass dining room table. There was an enormous African mask made of feathers on the wall to the right of him and a tall skinny black enameled grandfather clock to the left of him. Typical ghetto décor, thought Buck.

"Where are Stacy's clothes?" he asked them gently.

"She's wearing her clothes," the bird lady and the no-nonsense mother replied in unison. Their voices were soft and conspiratorial, as if they were confiding in the giant policeman. The three or four children in the adjoining living room were playing a video game and couldn't have cared less.

"No," said Buck, "I mean, where are her *other* clothes?"

"What other clothes?" asked the bird lady.

"The clothes she's not wearing now," Buck elaborated, a vision of patience and understanding.

"They're not here," said the no-nonsense mother. "Stacy don't live here."

"Right." Buck decided to talk more slowly and use his hands to emphasize the operative words. The fat guardian wept. The other two leaned toward Officer Tyler, listening intently like children hearing a ghost story. "But where does she keep her clothes."

"She's wearing her clothes," answered the bird lady, trying hard to follow the ghost story.

"Right," Buck said again, thinking he might have to shoot somebody pretty soon. "But we're looking for the clothes that Stacy's not wearing *right now*."

"Why?" asked the fat guardian through her handkerchief.

"Well," Buck explained, his hands making odd little cubes in the air, "we need to take Stacy to the hospital. We are going to need to keep those clothes that she's wearing right now. And when the doctors are done with her at the hospital, Stacy will need a change of clothes, so she has something to wear."

"Where?" asked the bird lady.

"Yes," answered Buck.

"At the hospital?" asked the fat guardian.

"Yes," Buck said again. He nodded and smiled, thinking maybe that would help.

"Why you taking Stacy's clothes?" the bird lady chirped.

"For evidence, Yvonne," said the no-nonsense mother. "They need Stacy's clothes for evidence. You and Shanika take my car and go get a change of clothes for Stacy. You come right back here, and I will take ya'll down to the hospital." Buck looked at her with awe. Not only was she a no-nonsense mother, she was a wizard of planning and organization.

"But Stacy will have to ride with us," he told them. "We'll need her guardian in the car, too. If someone wants to stop by Mount Mercy in an hour or two, they can give them a ride home." Everybody nodded all around. "Or we can drop them off afterward."

"An hour or two?" asked the bird lady. "What they gonna do with Stacy for an hour or two?"

"It's just an examination," Buck said, implying that it was nothing more than a brief check-up. He knew about the pages of questions that neither the retarded Stacy nor her borderline guardian could ever answer, and he knew about the spreaders and swabs and "morning after" capsules and the antibiotic shots and the stained panties in the paper bags. "Just a check-up by the doctors at Mercy."

"Mercy?" echoed the no-nonsense mother.

"Mount Mercy Hospital," Buck repeated with infinite patience. "Or we could go to Central Receiving Hospital, if you like."

"Oh, no," said the no-nonsense mother, shaking her head. "Mercy is fine." She went to get her coat. The fat guardian blew her nose. Buck's eyes came to rest on the bird lady, who was leaning toward him to say something. Maybe it was the end of this ghost story.

"Raylene don't like Central Receiving," the bird lady whispered to the big policeman. "Her man got stabbed here a couple years back, and he died in Central Receiving just waiting in the waiting room."

Buck nodded. He'd had the feeling he had been in this house before.

Alvin and Trudy Hoskins were fighting again. The television in their Converse Avenue apartment was busted. Trudy said Alvin had gotten drunk and kicked a hole in the TV. Alvin claimed that Trudy had thrown it at him. Hoatlin and Pridemore explained to them that there was no law against breaking your own television.

Parnell's new rookie was Jeff Something, and he was a little upset by the dead baby case they'd just had. The rookie and his wife had just had a baby themselves, and Jeff The Rookie was alarmed to see a dead infant not unlike his own. He had asked his Training Officer a question, which Parnell was still trying to answer when Pridemore came out of the East & West Café's kitchen and settled into a chair at the next table. When a rookie was having a heart-to-heart with his Training Officer, you didn't want to butt in, Pridemore knew. Parnell, however, kept talking to the kid, which he might not have done if Teddy or Buck had showed up.

"It's like the two-second delay on Monday Night Football," Parnell was telling Jeff The Rookie. "The television guys watch the show live, but we see it on tape a few seconds later. So when the quarterback yells something like "Oh Fuck!" they can bleep it out before it ever reaches the air. It's a delaying mechanism. That's what it's like. You learn to develop your own two-second delay."

"I see," said Jeff The Rookie, but it was plain he wasn't following it.

Pridemore was listening and making no secret about it, but he too was having a difficult time picking up the thread of the conversation. He nursed the cup of steaming coffee.

"It's kind of like driving school," Parnell tried again. "I don't mean the Pursuit Driving class you had at the Academy. I mean the Driver's Ed. course you took in high school. Anyway, do you remember how they taught you about when a deer or dog runs in front of your car, how you're supposed to drive through it without swerving?"

Jeff The Rookie nodded. His full coffee cup was growing cold in front of him.

Neal Parnell took a sip of his own coffee and continued. "Well, it's sort of like that. Your instinct, when you see a dog dart out in front of your car, is to steer out of the way or slam on the brakes or something. Now if you're on an icy road or crowded street, you'll probably lose control and crash or hit a child or something. So, in Driver's Ed. class, they teach you that following your natural instincts, swerving or hitting the brakes, will kill you, so they teach you to just drive through it. That's what we have here with the dead baby. That little kid was two months premature, so his lungs weren't worth a shit yet, and he died in his sleep, and his parents are upset as hell, and you're thinking about your own kid—I used to do the same thing when my kids were little—and it's all just a mess. Well, you see that crying Mom and that dead baby, and they're begging for your help. You can't do anything, and the paramedics can't do anything. No doctor in the world is going to bring that little baby back. It's gone. It's done. It's all over with. You and I stood in that kitchen and watched that little family shrivel up and die an hour ago, and we get through it by *not* following the normal instincts. We don't swerve, and we don't slam on the brakes. We drive right through it. Like they teach in Driver's Ed. class. By *not* following our instincts, we get through it. If we did the normal human thing and cried or threw up and hollered, we wouldn't be worth a damn to anybody. They'd have to call some really tough guy like Pridemore here to come and handle the situation for us."

The kid looked at Pridemore, who was smiling slightly, now that he understood where Parnell was going.

"Now we drive right through this little puppy in the road," Parnell continued, "because there's nothing we can do about it. It's some kind of bad shit, but we get through it. We got the neighbor to come over and stay with them. We call the M.E. and get the morgue guy to remove the body. We make some calls and take care of some shit that needs taking care of. We drive through it, see? And that ain't exactly normal, see? But if you're going to be a cop, you're going to have to develop that skill. It's like when you're afraid of a big, mean drunk, and all your instincts tell you to back up, to back away. Well, if you follow your instincts and back away, he'll kick your ass and eat your head. You've got to step *forward* when everything inside you tells you to step back. It's not about toughness and bravery and all that macho shit; it's about denying your gut instincts and driving right through it all. Mean drunk or dead baby or whatever the call is that Dispatch sent you to. And, after it's all over with, that's where the Monday Night Football two-second delay comes in."

Parnell took a break to sip his coffee. Pridemore was nodding slowly, glumly recognizing in himself the truth of Parnell's analogies. Jeff The Rookie was looking at the reflection of one of the East & West Café's ceiling fans in the blackness of his cold coffee.

"The two-second delay is sort of a coating, a buffer, between the bad word the quarterback said and the nice quiet families out there in television land. If there wasn't that coating, the words "Oh Fuck!" would bust out of their TVs and scare their little kids. They'd be shocked, and they'd be trying to cover their kids' ears, and then they would miss the next play. So the two-second delay protects that family. And our little built-in delay protects us from that bullshit mess with the dead baby. We can talk about it now, and we can deal with it. But, at the time it's really going on, there's no room to worry about your feelings or your own kids or any of that. So the delay in your feelings protects you from all that bullshit out there. Does that make sense?"

Jeff The Rookie nodded.

"The trick," said Parnell, winding up his fatherly speech, "is not to turn your two-second delay into a two-year delay or to make your drive-through-it reaction make you go home and drive right through your family and friends and your life. That's where you see your cop suicides and cop divorces and cop alcoholics. You gotta try to balance the whole thing."

"Neat trick," said Pridemore.

Parnell chucked Jeff The Rookie on the shoulder, rousing him from his reverie. The kid nodded and smiled. Just then, the kitchen door burst open as Teddy and Buck rolled in.

Parnell picked up his cup and the kid's cup to get some more coffee. "And speaking of heartless, insensitive bastards . . ."

"Somebody call my name?" grinned Buck Tyler.

"What was that baby call on Rhodes?" asked Hoatlin.

"SIDS death," replied Parnell.

"Sid who?" asked Buck. "Sid Wykowski? That squirrelly little guy that lives under the Parkway over Roxbury? I know that fuckin' guy."

Jeff The Rookie broke into a smile.

Buck took this as an affirmative as he plopped his bulk down in the chair beside Pridemore.

"Yeah, I know that little fucker. Smells like a fuckin' goat. Enough to gag a maggot. Fuckin' guy took a dump in the back seat of my car one time."

Lucas Trotter, black male, 20 years, dead of numerous gunshot wounds fired from two different caliber weapons inside his cousin's car in the south parking lot of The Marble Room, 3260 South Cramer Avenue. Witnesses reported that Trotter was arguing with two members of Tres-17s about some marijuana. Dalwyn "Bobo" Khalid was also wounded in the incident, but had nothing to say about the shooters or the reason for the shooting.

The Wednesday morning Command staff meeting had always been held in the big conference room just off the Chief's office, but there had been some sort of problem with the heating and cooling system, so this week's meeting was conducted in the Media Annex of the Civic Center, where the mayor usually talked to the press. The huge room had eggshell off-white walls, tall thin windows, and charcoal gray carpet. There was a lectern with a large crest of the City at the far end of the room. The horseshoe arrangement of linen-covered conference tables kept the participants, many of whom disliked each other intensely, at least eight feet apart. The 19 Captains, Deputy Chief Griswold, Deputy Chief Forrest, Chief Pearson, Chief Pearson's executive advisor, Professor Lindstrum of the Crime Patterns Study Group, and special guest, Assistant City Manager Rona Buckley, took their turns at the well-stocked breakfast buffet table against the left wall, the anorexic Buckley selecting a half-cup of tea. A tall elderly black man with a white jacket and a slight limp kept the donuts tidy and the coffee urns filled. Everyone called him "Gerald," but few of them knew that he was a disabled police officer from way back, who routinely fed the results of Command staff meetings to the Police Union, even if such information was rarely very helpful or interesting.

Captain Maddox looked forlornly at the pastry selection, passing over the tarts and bear claws in favor of a bran muffin. He knew that Chief Pearson's regular coffee was made with double the grounds that a normal human typically used, so he opted for a cup of decaf. There was a third urn of something called "Honeynut Song," which Maddox decided to skip. He balanced the fussy little coffee cup with the finger hole too small for an adult index finger and tried not to rattle the cup on its flower petal fringed saucer. The delicate tinkle of City logo-crested spoons and the clearing of manly throats seemed to echo around the immense room. The cream in the Media Annex was real cream, not the half-and-half that they served in the Police Department's conference room or the powdered creamer that Maddox had to endure in the Mercer Heights Precinct house, where the electricity powering the refrigerator was apt to go out unexpectedly at any time. He loaded his decaf with cream, which he knew he could scarcely afford with his Irritable Bowel Syndrome, discretely added a couple of tiny ice cubes, and found a white linen napkin.

"Thank you, Gerald."

"You're welcome, sir," replied the Police Union informant.

Maddox milled about with Captain Craig of the Two-Three Precinct, Captain Nettleton of Traffic, and Captain Jasper of Records. They hovered near the right leg of the horseshoe, exchanging pleasantries and Departmental gossip, while the enemy camp, made up of Captain Davis of the Detective Unit, Captain Brandt of Metro, and Captain Lockwood of the One-Eight gravitated to the left. The Captains with less seniority or political favor sat at the very feet of the two-pronged table. Captain Taylor, the token black commander from Community Affairs, sat next to Captain Zane, the lone female of the Command staff, who was seated next to Captain Torres, the token Hispanic captain, and acting-Captain Meredith, the other token black commander. Maddox noticed that there were several missing, either through illness, vacation, or other means. They all kept track of Chief Pearson's movements as he laughed at one of Deputy Chief Griswold's unfunny jokes, pumped Captain Darcy's beefy hand, and schmoozed with Assistant City Manager Buckley, all of them oozing across the carpet toward the head of the horseshoe. Deputy Chief Forrest, currently on the outs with the others because of a careless oversight in the Technology Services budget, was already seated. Deputy Griswold, who was on the inside track, because he had *always* been on the inside track, gently guided Rona Buckley to a chair beside Professor Lindstrum to the Chief's left. Captain Darcy, who had recently won an award from a national police officer training association and whose picture had appeared on the front page of both newspapers on Monday, was still chatting with the Chief.

Chief Pearson pretended to be surprised, as he always did, that everyone was waiting for him, and they all pretended to be patient, as they always had. He introduced the Assistant City Manager, whom he said needed no introduction. He "welcomed once again" the owl-like Professor Lindstrum who, he announced, had just published another article in the American Law and Law Enforcement Association's Journal. The Chief related a clever little story about a farmer and his chickens, which no one seemed to get, but which received a round of polite guffaws and hand claps. Griswold stood and delivered the issues to be discussed, several of them having to do with personnel budgets and shortages.

"You'd be surprised," began Captain Darcy, "what gains we are making in the inter-disciplinary skill development at the entry level." No one was surprised when Darcy took credit for all the Department's recent advances, of which there had been none, and none of the Department's recent embarrassments, of which there were several examples. He produced some examples, citing some of Captain Brandt's Lieutenants by name, of employees who were serving multiple functions in the areas of both community relations and employee development.

Professor Lindstrum cleared his throat and said, "We don't want to lose sight of the broader spectrum of administrative talent available within our ranks." There was a brief moment of silence as many of them scrambled to decipher what he had just said. Darcy, who despised the Professor and thought he had no business in this man's organization, noticed that the Chief was beginning to nod his head in agreement, so Darcy uttered an *A-men* aloud. Maddox gazed at an ice water pitcher on the table in front of him and realized the bran muffin he'd eaten was starting to eat him back. Soon all the Captains were nodding and agreeing with the wisdom of what Professor Lindstrum had said.

Several Captains on the other side of the horseshoe brought up "issues" they had with the Tech. Services Unit and its computer network. By citing several recent problems with the Detective Unit's computer system, Captain Davis gently heaped burning coals onto the head of Deputy Chief Forrest, whose oversight of the budget was generally regarded as the source of all equipment problems, even though the Chief and Deputy Griswold had hand-picked the Department computer system. Captain Brandt of Metro casually mentioned an incident in which 72 incident reports, including a downtown homicide file, had disappeared into the ether of the Department's network. On Maddox's side of the horseshoe, Captain Jasper of Records spoke up to divert any as-yet-unspoken accusations about his besieged domain. The flame slowly rose in Patrick Maddox's gut as the discussion ebbed and swayed, and he realized that he needed to pee. Captain Lockwood took this unrealized opportunity to pour himself a glass of ice water.

"And let's not lose sight of our Mission Statement as it impacts both community development and personnel administration," added Chief Pearson. Everyone nodded, including Captain Darcy, who thought that the phrase "mission statement" was a vaguely homosexual Jew-communist thing.

"That's correct," said Deputy Chief Griswold. "It's not all about computers that sometimes don't work or, for that matter, cars that don't work one hundred and ten percent of the time. I see these as mere glitches that will work themselves out with time and patience. I see several other problem areas, mainly in the interaction of some personnel with the informational resources we have in place." To Captain Darcy's surprise, Griswold had effectively rescued Deputy Chief Forrest from further criticism about the budget. Captain Lockwood of the One-Eight, who was one of Darcy's confidants and supporters, wondered if maybe there wasn't a very subtle power shift going on this morning. He gave Captain Davis a significant look, which the latter returned. Patrick Maddox caught the look but was too busy worrying about his growling stomach to afford it much thought.

"The issue here," said Assistant City Manager Rona Buckley, "is whether or not simple personnel multi-tasking alone can solve our problems."

"Yes, there are motivational considerations as well," agreed Professor Lindstrum.

"Exactly," added the Chief.

Rona Buckley was widely termed "that skinny cunt from the Civic Center" by members of the Department administration. Griswold and Darcy often referred to the City's highest ranking female as "Bony Rona" in private conversation. The Chief, who would never have allowed such language in his presence, saw her as a constant thorn in his side, always reducing personnel allotments and choking the fiscal planning that he and his staff worked so hard to justify. She and her sawed-off boss, City Manager Thomas "Elevator Shoes" Conrad, had no respect whatsoever for emergency services, although they tended to be even stingier with the Fire Department's budget.

"City Manager Conrad and I have recently been reading a book called 'Conscientious Discipline in Public Administration' by Dr. J. K. Fletcher," Buckley said, dropping her boss's name and bestowing a morsel of her hard-earned erudition on these lunkheads all at the same time. "Perhaps you've heard of it?" She looked around for a millisecond, knowing that she and Conrad had read an advanced reviewer's copy that no one else had seen. Professor and the Chief were pleased to see several members of the Command staff taking notes. Darcy scrawled "DUMB BITCH" on his notepad. Griswold scribbled "Fletcher?" on his ledger. Patrick Maddox wrote down the word "DISCIPLINE" and underlined it twice, his bran muffin, real cream, and decaf edging hotly up his gullet.

"That's sounds like a book we ought to be reading," lied Chief Pearson lamely. Darcy grimaced politely.

"I went through grad school at Northeastern with Fletcher," Lindstrum whispered to Griswold, never mentioning that he thought Fletcher was a pretentious tyrant of management theory academia. Deputy Chief Griswold nodded, as if he gave a dry fart about guys like Fletcher and Lindstrum.

Deputy Chief Forrest, who was just glad to be out of the spotlight for a while, asked: "Is that the same Fletcher who wrote 'Patterns of Disobedience' a couple years ago?" All eyes shifted to Forrest in blinking amazement. Forrest beamed. Darcy actually wrote the name "Fletcher" on his notepad now.

"Why, yes," said Bony Rona Buckley. "Have you read it?"

"Parts, yes," lied Forrest. "It's hard-hitting stuff." He had, in fact, seen the cover of "Patterns of Disobedience" once when an ambitious little Records Unit Sergeant named Berke had shown it to him some time ago. He had, of course, not read a word of it, but was pleased that he had remembered the author's name. And "hard-hitting stuff" seemed like a universally bullshit praise phrase. Forrest was pleased at having scored a point in this otherwise unproductive Command staff meeting.

"Fletcher knows his material," Lindstrum managed to gag out.

"Indeed he does," nodded Buckley. "There's a great deal to be learned about the inner workings of an organization and its personnel matrix from watching its patterns of disobedience."

"Sure sounds like it," the Chief added, having no idea what everybody was talking about.

Captain Patrick Maddox could stand it no more. He excused himself and left to find the men's room he had visited just before this meeting had started. Safely inside the restroom stall, he urinated first. Experience had taught him that vomiting first might cause him to piss himself slightly. He peed, flushed, and held the flush handle down to cover the noise as he lost his breakfast. He had to get out of The Heights. He had to get away from that ugly neighborhood, its ugly crime statistics, and its ugly cops. He had to get back to the Tower. At this point in his career, he would have given up one of his bars and gone back to being a lowly lieutenant, just to get into HQ. So long as I don't have to work for that bastard Darcy or that prick Griswold or those other scorpions, he thought. Damn Heights! Damn cops! Damn job! He flushed and flushed.

The top half of the driver was lying across a white line in the westbound lanes of South Parkway. It was still wearing most of a dark blue pullover sweater. The lower end of the sweater was just meat. Hoatlin said it looked like a male. Pridemore covered the thing with a yellow plastic emergency blanket, weighting down the corners with a dashboard ashtray, a shoe, a book of poetry, and a can of beer that had somehow come through the accident unharmed. The rain had lightened up to a slow drizzle.

"Fucking mess," said Sgt. Lindsey from under the bill of his uniform hat.

"Fucking rain," replied Pridemore. "You got Traffic Unit enroute?"

"Yeah. That one gonna go K on us, ya think?" He pointed to the ambulance, where three paramedics were working on the passenger.

"I don't know. Her hair's over there." Pridemore pointed to a surprisingly tidy blonde scalp by the guard wall. "She's fucked up good."

"This is all fucked up," spat Lindsey. "I was supposed to cut out two hours early tonight to go to a Father & Son breakfast at church. I guessed that's fucked up, too, now."

Hoatlin was shining his flashlight over the rail at the street below. It was a long drop. A cruiser was driving slowly up and down Cleveland Street, looking for the other half of the driver. Hoatlin was flashing his light so they would have an idea where on the expressway the thing had gone off. He leaned on the rail, careful to avoid the odd bits of human tissue that were stuck to it. The cruiser's spotlight played over the sidewalks and parked cars below. Somebody had already found a shoe on top of a wire fence, but they couldn't tell if it was part of the crash. Everything glistened with rainwater, making the search more difficult.

Pridemore trotted back up the lane to put down some more road flares so that some asshole drunk, ignoring all the lights from the fire engine, the ambulance, and the three cruisers, wouldn't crash into them while they were working. The two outside lanes were still backing up with drivers too stupid to change lanes and avoid the accident site. Pridemore hurled an unlit flare at an idiot who whizzed by at full speed in the inside lane, but it missed. When he got back, Hoatlin was pointing over the rail.

"They found a leg. See?"

All Pridemore could see were a bundle of flashlight beams down by the corner of Cleveland and Sloan.

"Charlie Three to Five," squealed their radios.

"Go ahead, Three," Hoatlin said on his portable.

"We just got the one. I don't see any more."

"Thanks, Charlie Three."

"It's a left, if that makes any difference."

"Ten-four," replied Hoatlin. "Thanks, Ron."

Hoatlin put his radio and flashlight away, stepping back from the rail.

"You think she'll make it?" Teddy looked up into the black rain.

"I don't know," Pridemore replied.

"Did you see her scalp over there?"

"Yeah."

"Pretty hair," said Teddy Hoatlin. "Blonde."

"Yeah...well..."

"So the Outreach Committee picked Sally and Fran MacKendricks and me to do the visitation duty next weekend," said Priscilla Berke. "Kenny, Jr. will go to my sister's for the day. We're taking the church van to a nursing home in Pollard, you know, the St. Bosco's Home with the big trees, the one that's behind the high school there?"

"I've got a Phillips head here, Honey," said Kenneth Berke from under his computer desk. "Hand me the other screwdriver."

"The one with the red handle?"

"I don't know. The straight-blade screwdriver."

Priscilla picked through the mismatched tools in the orange plastic toolbox. "There's a yellow one, but it's really tiny."

"Then let me have the red one, Hon." Kenneth's legs were all she could see of him. He was under there with a little flashlight that was dying fast, trying to install something amongst all the wires and cords on the back of his home computer. The computer and the maze of plugs and Kenneth and the toolbox would not all fit under the desk at the same time, so Kenneth had enlisted Prissy to serve as toolbox commander. She was glad to help. It gave them a chance to talk.

"Here," she said and tapped the red-handled screwdriver against his leg. His hand squirmed out of the dark space, felt in the air, and found the tool. "So we're taking some music tapes and Fran's Cocker Spaniel puppy to the St. Bosco's home, because Sally read that old people like dogs, especially puppies, because they aren't too big to handle, and they can't jump up and knock somebody down."

"At St. Boxo?"

"Bosco. St. Bosco. St. John Bosco."

"That's Catholic, right?" asked Kenneth's muted voice.

"What?"

"It's a Catholic old folks' home?"

"Well, yes, originally . . ."

"Why is a Methodist Church sending their ladies group to a Catholic old folks' home?"

"It's a nursing home," Priscilla reminded him.

"Nursing home, old folks' home, retirement village, whatever. It's still a Catholic place. Why are the Methodist ladies going there?" He grunted, twisting to reach something under the desk.

"It's not very Catholic anymore. That's just the name. They don't have nuns or anything weird like that. Besides, that's what the Outreach part means. We reach out to people in need. Why, next month, they're talking about sending three or four members to nursing homes in the City."

"Methodist Enrichment and Outreach for Women," chuckled Kenneth Berke. "I always get a kick out of that name, MEOW, in the Sunday bulletin. See if you can find me some needle-nose pliers up there."

Priscilla Berke knew that her husband didn't take the Outreach committee's work very seriously. He didn't take much of *anything* she did very seriously. Sometimes he couldn't even pretend to be interested in any of her outside activities, as few as they were. Her delicate fingers picked through the coarse and greasy tools in the toolbox. "The red ones?"

"They're like pliers," said her husband's muffled voice from beneath the computer table, "but they're real narrow at the tip."

Priscilla found a yellow-handled thing and tapped it on Kenneth's thigh. His hand fished out and grabbed the tool. "Cripes, Prissy, these are wire cutters." The yellow-handled thing came out again, and she went back to search the toolbox.

"So the MEOW ladies group is taking a dog to the Catholic old folks' home," Kenneth chuckled. "That's supposed to be a joke or what?"

"It's a puppy," she replied defensively. He always made her feel like she had to explain herself. She always felt that she had to justify what she did and where she went and with whom. She supposed that was how a good husband was. She supposed that was how he showed how much he cared. She found a second red-handled pliers-thing beneath the lift-out drawer of the little toolbox and handed it down to him. The lift-out drawer had oil or something on it, which smudged some dark stuff into the web of her palm. Priscilla dabbed at the smudge and lifted her slender finger to her nose. It smelled like a car engine. She rolled the stain around between her thumb and index finger, breathing in the sharp aroma. She decided against tasting it, as it was most likely a poison of some sort and would probably make her sick. She was glad Kenneth couldn't see her, because he would probably have something derogatory to say about her standing there, smelling her fingertips. "Sally read something about how it's good for older people to have something small to pet. It's the warmth or the fur or something. Anyway, it's good for them and makes them happy. That's why people with pets tend to live longer, I guess."

"Where did you read that?" Kenneth groaned from below the desk. "I really doubt there's any hard evidence of that."

"I don't know," Priscilla said, helplessly trying to explain herself again. "It's just something she was telling us. That's not important. What's important is that it seems to work and makes old people happy." She touched the tip of her stained finger to the tip of her tongue, before she could think about it anymore. It was tangy, but bitter, like metal or something. Yuck! But she didn't utter a word about it. "You can't take a kitten. Little kittens are nice and soft, but they have claws and can hurt the old people just by playing with them. Frannie said you can't de-claw a kitten until it's a couple months old, and by that time they're kind of too big, and you can't keep them still in your lap. It defeats the whole purpose, she told us."

"Cats are sneaky animals anyway," Kenneth Berke said. "You can't trust them at all." Priscilla was about to say something, but he continued: "Okay, Hon, take the cord with the square plug up there and plug it into the back of the scanner."

Priscilla wiped her fingers on a paper towel and bent across the desk, searching for the plug thingies. There were several cords behind the computer stuff. "The black one?"

"Yeah, it's black," he replied, his voice slightly tight with impatience. "Plug the black cord with the square plug into the back of the new scanner."

Priscilla hiked up her blue jeans a bit, putting one knee on the tabletop so she could lean out far enough to see what he was talking about. Her sandal came off and dropped onto Kenneth's shin.

"What was that?" he asked, alarmed.

"Just my shoe."

"Have you found the cord?"

"Yes, it's in. I hope it's not in upside-down."

"It only fits one way." He fiddled around with something under the desk. "This flashlight's about dead."

"Can I get down now?" asked Priscilla. The pressure of the hard desktop against her knee was starting to bother her.

"Just a second."

"Why do you need this new scan thing?" she asked. "What happened to your old one?"

"It's called a scanner, and I never *had* an old one."

"Then why do you need a scanner?" She didn't know much about it, but she imagined that expressing an interest in his computer stuff might please him. She slipped her other foot out of its little sandal and rested both knees on the top of the desk, taking the pressure off and allowing her to shift her weight.

"I need to be able to scan some of those forms up there into the computer," Kenneth explained. "That's it. The flashlight's dead. Turn on the desk lamp and bend it over to the side. I'm almost finished here."

She reached over and twisted on the high-intensity lamp, immediately feeling its warmth. "Why can't you just use a copy machine?"

"Because a copier makes paper copies, and a scanner takes the forms and puts them in computer files that we can use on our computers at work."

Priscilla's dishwater blonde hair was falling in her face as she turned her head to look at the stack of blue forms he was talking about. The sheets had taken a beating, some wrinkled and some folded, so that they made an uneven pile. They were numbered 1 through 5 for Good and 1 through 5 for Not Good, she saw. Taking care not to disturb their order, she turned the first few sheets over, reading the answers. Someone had written "Mickey Mouse" where it said NAME. Someone had drawn a picture of an African-American hanging from a tree. There was one that had obviously been folded into a paper airplane. Some of it was pretty crude. Some of it was silly. Priscilla knew that her husband would not find any of it very amusing. Someone had written that the capitol of Illinois was Springfield.

"Okay," Kenneth called up from beneath the desk. "I'm turning the computer on. Watch the screen and tell me what it says." There was a humming sound.

"It doesn't say anything yet." She blew some strands of hair away from her face. "What does this NOT GOOD stuff mean?"

"What?"

"These blue forms. What is all this GOOD and NOT GOOD stuff about?"

"It's a participatory management tool. Is the monitor doing anything?"

"It said boot-something, but now it's black again," she reported dutifully.

"We don't really care what they write down for the GOOD part. The Commanders already know what the police Department is doing good."

"So you're only interested in the bad stuff then?"

"No, the NOT GOOD list is hardly ever of any use to us in Command. It's more of a self-awareness exercise for the officers. If they sit down and think for a minute about what they're doing wrong, it might help them try to improve their performance. What does it say up there now?"

"It says it's configuring a list of numbers, and it says to Please Wait," Priscilla said, turning back to the pile of blue forms and blowing more hair away from her face.

"Good."

"It doesn't look like they took the self-awareness part very seriously," she ventured cautiously. As soon as she said it, she wished she hadn't. She shifted her weight a bit, because both of her knees were beginning to ache on the hard desk.

"I'm afraid, Prissy," Kenneth said flatly, "that many police officers in my Precinct have some pretty poor attitudes. Those poor attitudes are directly related to poor performance ratings." He paused for effect. "And poor performance ratings are directly related to high crime statistics. It's complicated stuff, Hon."

"It's showing that flag and badge picture now," Priscilla reported.

"Good. Now plug the gray power cord into the back of the scanner."

She did as she was told, hoping this project was about over.

"Got it?" Kenneth asked.

"It's in, I think."

"Make sure it's all the way in."

"It's in," she said again.

Kenneth Berke scooted out from beneath the computer desk with one handful of tools and an extra cord. He grunted as he stretched his arms and flexed his back. Brushing aside Priscilla's little sandals, he stood and dropped the tools back into the little orange plastic toolbox. He turned to see his wife, her little blue-jeaned rump up in the air, reading the blue forms. "You can get down now."

Priscilla clambered down off the desk as her husband went to get his swivel chair. She slipped back into her sandals. Kenneth was hunched over the desk already, studying the computer monitor.

"Are you going to use the scanner for little drawings they made on the forms?" she asked delicately.

"Some of them, yes," Kenneth replied. "I have hardly anything at all that I can turn in to Headquarters on this exercise, and they're going to wonder why I'm only turning in a handful of responses. I thought that they should see what I'm up against in my Precinct, the attitudes and the performance problems that I told you about."

"Some interesting artwork."

"Pretty immature, most of it. Sometimes, these employees act like a bunch of eighth graders. It all boils down to attitude and motivation." He pecked at the keyboard, and the scanner purred to life. "They don't seem to understand motivational guidance at all."

Priscilla reached out and turned over one of the blue sheets of paper. "That's pretty detailed." She was looking at the back of Connie Baldwin's answer form. On the page was a life-size pencil sketch of a hairless vagina with moist highlights and a dark center. Priscilla was surprised that it was a woman who had apparently drawn it.

"Oh, that," said Kenneth, glancing at the picture. "I don't get it either. I guess she just likes tulips."

Priscilla Berke took the little toolbox and put it away in the garage. Perhaps it was a picture of a flower, she thought. She supposed that made more sense.

This doesn't make any sense at all, Pridemore thought as he opened his eyes. He lay very still in his easy chair, gazing at a fine crack in the ceiling. Mister Alp stretched a little in his lap, but did not wake up. The television had shut itself off, as its self-timer was one of the reasons he had bought the thing in the first place. Everything was so very still, in fact, that Pridemore really wasn't sure if he was awake or sleeping. The crack in the ceiling had been there when he had moved in and had not changed much since. He had studied that crack before.

In the dream there were members of the Little Rascals, like Darla and Spanky and one of the little black kids—not Buckwheat, but another one—and there was the little sister of that dead kid, Timmy Something, over by Marion Street, the one who had handed him her dead brother's blanket. There was one of Flex Sinclair's sons, who Pridemore had seen one time when Flex came in for his paycheck. They were all running around yelling and jumping and playing in the intersection of South Bleeker Avenue and Hall Street, where Pridemore used to work in South Precinct. There was no traffic, but it still seemed like an unsafe situation. The drug dealers that usually hung out at the gas station on the corner were nowhere in sight for this particular dream. The Little Rascals' schoolteacher, Miss Crabapple or Appletree or something, was there, too, but she was of little help at all.

"Eighty-B," called the dispatcher's voice. "Car 80-B." That was his car number back when he had worked Property Crimes. He wondered if they really wanted him or if they wanted the detective who now had that call number. The dispatcher's voice repeated it over and over again with small pauses in between.

And he was trying to say something, but his voice was only a tiny, hoarse little sound, and his throat was dry. The words just wouldn't come out. So he was trying to get Timmy's little sister and the Little Rascals and their schoolteacher out of the intersection of Bleeker and Hall. But they just would not listen.

"Car 80-B," called the voice. "Car Eight-Zero B-Baker."

Now his daughter, Jennifer, was there. She was about six or seven, just the little bundle of energy as he remembered her. And dead Timmy was there, too, now. His eyes were blue, which surprised Pridemore, but then he'd never really seen Timmy's eyes before. And Spanky was holding Jennifer's hand. And Darla was holding Timmy's pillow. And Miss Crabtree—that was her name!—was holding hands with Flex

MAD BADGES

Sinclair's kid and that retarded girl who got raped by her cousins. They whirled in a circle, singing some sort of hymn or fairy tale song.

"Car 80-B. Badge 1659."

Now they were calling his badge number, so he knew they were looking for him, not some other guy who had the car number now. And he tried to answer, but his mouth wouldn't work. And he tried and tried to get everyone out of the road, but nobody was listening to him. And he realized somehow that there would be cruisers out looking for him, that they'd be looking for him at his last known location. Which was probably right here at South Bleeker and Hall. And he knew in his heart that they'd be coming Code. They'd be trying to reach him, but they would end up running over the children and Jennifer and dead Timmy, who had just come back to life.

"Badge 1659, come in. Car 80-B, Badge 1659."

But Jennifer, Flex Sinclair, Jr., Timmy's sister, and the Little Rascals kept dancing around. Pridemore struggled to get them all over to the curb. And the sirens were coming. The sirens were coming from South Precinct and The Heights and even Metro. They were a long way off, but he knew they were coming this way. And Miss Crabtree, the Little Rascals' school marm, had changed into Elaine Christian, but she was still wearing the schoolteacher's long white dress. And Elaine Christian strode up to him, her black hair blowing in a strange breeze and her dark eyes clear and sharp, and she stopped right in front of him.

"Come in, Car 80-B. Come in."

The sirens were getting closer, and the dispatcher's voice was more insistent. The kids all danced in a circle with Buckwheat now and Alfalfa, too. And Pridemore could see little Jennifer and Timmy holding hands and sitting over by the phone booth that the drug dealers used. And he wanted to tell Jennifer that Timmy was dead. He *had* to tell her. It might break her heart, but he felt it was really important to know when someone you were starting a friendship with was really a dead person. And now he could even see the blue lights of the first arriving cars way up Bleeker Avenue, coming down from Mercer Heights.

"It's raspberry sherbet," said Elaine Christian, still wearing Miss Crabtree's white dress. She poked him in the chest with her finger to get his full attention. The sirens were coming, but all the Little Rascals had disappeared somewhere. "You know, it's always been raspberry sherbet."

The dispatcher said: "Car 80-B. Come in, Car 80-B."

And Pridemore cried out: "Wait!"

This didn't make any sense at all. He looked at the crack in the ceiling and felt Mister Alp stir in his lap. Pridemore thought he was glad to be off South Bleeker Avenue and out of that mess. Mister Alp stood up on Pridemore's left thigh, stretched and made a little circle, then lay down again. Pridemore wondered why Elaine had said what she said about raspberry sherbet. He wondered why dead Timmy had blue eyes.

Alvin and Trudy Hoskins were still fighting. The door of their Converse Avenue apartment was broken off its hinges and lay against the sofa in the living room. Alvin said he had fallen against it when Trudy pushed him. Trudy said Alvin had been drunk again and couldn't find his key. Pridemore and Hoatlin warned them that the landlord might be filing vandalism charges later.

Crime Lab Supervisor Brigid Horrigan was a feisty little redheaded firebrand. She was 5' 1" and actually quite pretty, but one would never know that from the way she wore her hair in a tight bun atop her head or the way she buried her figure in pantsuits and oversized white lab coats. She wore very little makeup, not even to cover all the freckles. At 31, Horrigan had her Masters from Northwestern, was a past-President of the Midwestern Association For Forensic Science, had published articles in several international forensic journals, had been recognized by the courts as an expert in bloodstain pattern analysis and footwear impression identification, not to mention drug chemistry, and she was not about to take any crap from anybody. She had her tiny little legs with their tiny little all-white L.A. Gear shoes up on her desk. Also sitting in her glass-walled office was Crime Scene Technician Gunderson. They were discussing a certain Lt. Wilson from Homicide and what a complete moron he was.

"So he says he wants all homicide handguns fumed for prints," said Gunderson. "No matter what, he wants them fumed first."

"He said IMMEDIATELY, I think," Horrigan replied, waving the Lieutenant's memo. "What an excruciatingly ignorant jerk."

"It's like he's never heard of DNA or backspatter," said Gunderson. "He's fixated all of a sudden on print fuming. I told him that the blood work needs to be done first, but he didn't listen."

"Uh-oh," Horrigan said, straightening up in her chair. She indicated the reception window to the outside hall. "Who's this goof?"

Gunderson rose from his chair and, pretending to put away a journal on a bookshelf, glanced at the figure at the front counter. The receptionist was buzzing in the visitor.

"That would be Captain Maddox of Mercer Heights," Gunderson said, hardly moving his lips. "They call him 'Captain Maalox.'"

Horrigan pretended to point out something on the bookshelf. "Because he has ulcers or because he gives other people ulcers?"

"I'm not sure." Gunderson turned so that his back was to the door. "But he's a major asshole."

"Hmmm," murmured Horrigan, "Major, Captain, whatever. We've got 'em all here, don't we?" She moved toward the door, hoping to meet this Maalox person before he came inside her office. Opening the door to confront the visitor, Horrigan spoke to Gunderson conspicuously. "Have those small particle reagent studies to me by Thursday, Gunny." Gunderson played along and ducked out just as Captain Maddox came to rest at Horrigan's office. Horrigan was somewhat irritated with the receptionist for letting him in without a pass card. She drew herself up into the most imposing figure her 5' 1" frame could muster.

"May I help you?" Horrigan smiled.

A yellow paper sign on the door behind her read, "POOR PLANNING ON *YOUR* PART DOES NOT CONSTITUTE AN EMERGENCY ON *OUR* PART."

Maddox smiled. Or rather, Horrigan thought, he grimaced. He looked to her like yet another example of the Department's testosterone-based management style. Not the all-penis-no-brains of a Captain Darcy or the Deputy Chiefs, but more like one of their whipping boys, one of those wannabees who someday hoped to grow up to be a full-length member. Captain Prozac might be a better name for him. He took her hand without it being offered, but shook it as if he didn't want to damage its little fingers. She wished she had worn a glove; that always put them off.

"I am Captain Patrick Maddox," he announced. "You're in charge here, I understand?" It was more of an uttered doubt than a question.

"I am, indeed," answered Brigid Horrigan. "To what do we owe the honor?" He finally stopped pumping her hand and indicated a briefcase he was carrying. She would have to remember to wash that hand. The testosterone-based managers tended to play with themselves to excess. She hoped that her smile expressed some sort of interest.

He lowered his voice, glancing around for informants. "Maybe you can help me." Horrigan doubted it. She maintained her professional smile, wondering what this idiot wanted. He looked around for a place to put down the briefcase in private. Horrigan steered him away from her office door to a worktable off to the side. He put down the case and released the latches. "I need you to fingerprint a couple things."

Horrigan, hoping there wasn't an explosive device in the case, wondered what it was that had brought another slimy Captain into her domain. Drugs? Cash? Bombs? She reached over to a huge roll of brown butcher paper and expertly ripped off a large square to act as a drop sheet. The Captain removed two gallon-size plastic bags from his case. They were, Horrigan noted, not Department-issued bags or anything from the ATF or FBI. They were plastic freeze bags from a grocery store, probably something he had brought in from his own kitchen. They weren't even marked. Typical of the evidence-handling capabilities of the Command staff around here, she thought. One plastic bag contained a small paper liquor store bag wrapped around an empty half-pint bottle. She couldn't read the label. The second plastic bag contained a blue plastic cup with old cola stains, a banana peel, and a wadded up chip bag. Horrigan looked at the puffy, graying, and seemingly frightened fat little man and wondered why he hadn't already retired or died.

"What is all this?" she finally asked.

"I need you to dust these for prints," Captain Maddox said.

His use of the word "dust" told her worlds about his background. It was a hip, cop word from way back, so long ago, in fact, that its use on television cop shows was long past. If he had said, "powder these for prints," she might have listened further. If he had asked her to "process these for prints," she would have been pleasantly surprised. If he had requested that she "process these for latents," she would have become alarmed. There was also the fact that he had brought in the unlabeled items in plastic baggies. Only nice dry drugs and nice dry documents went in plastic bags, and then only in Department-issued, properly marked and dated, evidence bags, not some celery sack from some idiot's kitchen. Almost everything else in the world, from guns

MAD BADGES

to bloody clothing to tennis rackets, belonged in paper bags. Any numbskull knew that. Only television detectives played around with plastic bags.

"Have you got an Incident Number to go with this?" Horrigan asked.

"No, not yet," admitted the breathless Captain.

The Red Eyebrow of Doom began to arch above Brigid Horrigan's left eye. "I will get you a lab request form to fill out." She turned to a passing lab technician. "Denise, will you grab a 310 form for the Captain here?" The lab tech could tell that she was being warned about the presence of a Commanding Officer and, further, that the boss was running him through the hoops of bureaucracy.

"No, no," said Captain Maddox. "I just need you to dust these things. If there are no prints, we don't need a report."

"We *always* need an Incident Report number, Captain," Horrigan informed him. "That's the way things are done around here."

"But it's..."

"There is a crime, an incident number is generated, and that number goes with all items of evidence connected with the case."

"But there is no case," said Maddox. He waited until Denise had brought over the 310 form and left. "These are items found inside police cars. If there aren't any fingerprints on them, there isn't any case. So I won't need an Incident Report number."

"One *always* needs an Incident Report number," Horrigan stated boldly, although she realized she could douse all this crap with silver powder and send him on his way.

"How about this?" he suggested. "You dust these for prints. If there *are* no prints, we'll just throw them out. If there are some fingerprints, I will draw an Incident number."

"You'll have to draw it here and complete the 310 before you leave," she said, softening her stance on the matter. "This is not the way to do things. Especially, Internal Affairs things."

"I realize that," said Maddox.

She had him now. He was begging. This was good. He was backpedaling, like all those Feds who came barging in here all the time, all bluster and officialdom, no paperwork but a lot of demands. The little Irish redhead sent them all scurrying away with their FBI tails between their legs. Horrigan realized she could unload this problem in a jiffy with the right print brush.

"Denise," she called. Denise came over, wearing a plastic face shield and rubber gloves. "Could you dust that *bottle* for the Captain, please? I think just silver-black powder should do it." The lab tech also understood the term "dust" and its implications. She also understood that she was being instructed to use a less-than-ideal latent processing technique for this request. Denise brought back some powder and a fiberglass print brush. Horrigan snapped on a pair of bluish green rubber gloves and opened the plastic bag. She withdrew the half-pint bottle wrapped in the little paper sack. Neatly stripping the paper sack from the bottle, which they could now see was a brandy bottle, Horrigan tossed the sack aside and handed Denise the glass bottle. Captain Maddox followed the bottle, as Horrigan knew he would, the moron. "Let's see what that *bottle* tells us." With her left hand, Horrigan started to open the next plastic bag. With her right hand, she shoved the small liquor store sack and any latent prints it probably contained, into the trash barrel at the end of the worktable. Maddox was still watching the glass bottle, which happily yielded no fingerprints whatsoever.

Denise tried to hand the bottle back to Maddox or Horrigan, but Maddox said: "We don't need it now." Horrigan nodded to the lab tech, and the bottle followed the liquor store sack into the trash barrel.

"What else have we got here?" the Irish redhead mused aloud, removing the blue plastic cup, banana peel, and chip bag from Maddox's second store-bought kitchen bag. "No perishables allowed, Captain. That's in the M.O.P., you know." She tossed the banana peel away. Two more items yet to go in the trash and she'd be rid of this nitwit. While Denise gently applied the fingerprint brush to the sides of the blue plastic cup, Horrigan gently flattened the plastic chip bag, thoroughly smoothing away any possible fingerprints with her rubber gloves. Again, the Captain was watching the blue plastic cup and missing the evidence destruction going on under his nose.

"I think I've got part of a palm print," announced Denise to Horrigan's chagrin. She should have had Gunderson, not Denise, do it; he could make prints disappear on a clean porcelain platter. Horrigan could also have screwed up the prints herself, but that might have looked suspicious to the Captain.

"Now you need to draw that Incident Report number," Horrigan told the Captain, sliding the 310 form toward him.

"Certainly," he said. He started reading the form, which told them that he had never actually filled one out before. A dispatcher drew him a number over the phone.

Denise "dusted" the plastic chip bag and, of course, found nothing usable. She applied tape over the partial palm print on the side of the blue cup.

"Do you want to tag this, too?" Denise asked, waving the wilted chip bag.

"No, just the cup, I guess," said Maddox, struggling through the date, time, and Offense Description boxes on the form.

"Thanks, Denise," Horrigan said, when Denise had disposed of the chip bag. The lab tech searched her boss's face for some sign or sanction, but there were only those Irish freckles. Horrigan threw out the Captain's plastic kitchen bags and tore loose a proper paper evidence bag from a nearby rack. She had him write his initials on the lip of the cup and then stapled it away in the evidence bag. "You'll have to submit a list of suspects, you know."

"Oh," said Maddox, looking up from the 310 form. "Why?"

"Because it's a palm print," Horrigan explained. "The computer can't search for palm prints. Only fingerprints. You submit a list of suspects, and they are hand-checked against the recovered palmprint. It may take a while."

"But there are dozens of people who might have left that print."

"Be that as it may, you'll *still* have to submit names. And they'll have to have inked palmprints on file or it's no good." She was hoping he would simply give up and go away.

"Okay, I'll get a list to you."

"I assume this will be an Internal Affairs matter?" Horrigan asked.

"Uh...yes," Maddox replied.

"Then you will want to write a *dash-1* after the incident number."

He did as he was told, having investigated hardly anything in his career and having never fought his way through an evidence form. He initialed the evidence bag seal as he was told and kept the third copy back sheet as he was told. He thanked Horrigan and gave her his business card, which she promptly stapled to the evidence bag.

"You'll let me know then?" Maddox asked.

"First the suspect list, then the comparison," Horrigan smiled, "and *then* maybe an identification, and we'll call you."

"Thank you, Ms. Hornahan."

"Horrigan," said Horrigan, thinking *Captain Maalox*. She kept her smile until he had left the office. Gunderson reappeared in time to see her growling.

"What'd I tell you?" said Gunderson, grinning.

"Jerks with cruiser-littering cases," groaned Brigid Horrigan. "Like we don't have enough to do around here."

"Truth be told, the Command staff really *doesn't* have anything better to do."

"Don't I know it," Horrigan fumed. "This place would operate a lot better if those micro-managing pencil-pushers would just dry up and blow away."

"Now you're talking like a cop," said Gunderson.

Robert Lafnear, black male, 34 years, dead of a gunshot wound to the neck in the doorway of The Marble Room, 3260 South Cramer Avenue. Two witnesses who didn't want to be involved reported that Lafnear was shot by bouncers working for the bar. A search of the bouncers and The Marble Room turned up twelve knives, a box-cutter, and two handguns, neither of which was the caliber that shot Lafnear. A tipster later called to say that the Dudley Avenue Boys were involved.

The little Asian guy kept trying to sidestep Parnell. He was drunk or high or both, and he flailed his arms like he was shooing away flies. He was sort of staggering in place, a crablike movement of one step forward, one to the side, one half step back, a balancing heel down, and a planting of the foot forward again. It was sort of a Jack Daniels version of Tai Chi. He kept repeating something about the manager of the Black Juju Coffee House as he tried to get past Parnell.

"Get back!" snarled Parnell for the eighth time.

"He know me! That manager . . . he say . . ."

"Back up!"

A fight call at the Black Juju was a rare event. Most of the time, the place catered to vaguely suicidal suburban Goth teens, who dressed in black rags and even blacker makeup. They came to this late-night converted brick warehouse shop with its wire mesh windows and flat black walls usually to play chess, listen to poetry that they had written themselves, or simply to hit on the emotionally stunted Goth chicks, who drifted in and out and definitely looked better in the dark. There was spiky blonde hair, greasy black hair, nose rings, pierced nipples and penises, eyebrow rings, and cobra tattoos. There were crewcuts and pigtails, Kurt Cobain suicide T-shirts and Korn tank-tops. The punks had come and gone, the raves had come and gone, and there was nothing new under the sun, which is why they were out all night, sucking caffeine and gobbling sugar snacks. All that was left to them were the pimples, the bad teeth, and a slow death by suburban teen angst. So, usually, they were not a problem to the units patrolling South Antoine Fraiser Avenue.

"He do! I say, No! That man! He say I know!"

"I said back up!" barked Parnell.

"But you ask! He no say! I go here!"

"You *no* go here, pal!"

Nolan and Kibelewski were taking the assault report and losing control of the crowd that kept spilling out of the Black Juju onto the sidewalk, the techo beat thrumming out every time the door opened. The ambulance hadn't arrived yet. A tall skinny youth with spiked black hair, a nose stud, and black bicycle shorts kept yelling and pointing. The short, wiry Kibelewski was trying to keep him calm and out of the way, while keeping an eye on his cruiser door, which he had carelessly left open. The musclebound crewcut Nolan was trying to get some information from a kid with the cut-up face, who was sitting with his back against a light pole, his hands bleeding almost as much as his nose. A fat guy, who said he worked as a bouncer in a nearby tavern, kept saying something about people selling crack cocaine and marijuana inside the Juju. He was a pudgy cop wannabee, who was trying desperately to help out the cops, prove himself, and join the thin blue line of heroes. Every time Nolan or Kibelewski told him to go back inside, he disappeared for a while, only to show up again with another little informational tidbit.

"I said, stay back!" Parnell was growling at the Tai Chi guy. "You wanna go to jail?"

"I stay! I say! He not stay here!" Tai Chi kept up his crab dance, coming ever closer to Parnell's baton side, but never actually coming in contact with him. "You ask him! He tell me! I go there!"

"Get back!"

A fat Asian girl behind Tai Chi was pleading with him to go away with her, away from a fight with the police, and away from a certain trip to jail. A second Asian girl, wearing a gold metallic mini-dress, stood in the Black Juju's doorway, holding her cell phone by her ear. Parnell thought she had probably dialed her own answering machine to record all that was going on outside the coffee house, which was why he was being cautious about what he was saying aloud to Tai Chi. For reasons no one could fathom, Bicycle Pants and Cop Wannabee got into a shoving match beside the open door of Kibelewski's cruiser. Nolan was having little luck getting a straight story from the kid with the carved up face. Kibelewski broke away to secure his cruiser. Parnell was caught between the bleeding victim sitting on the sidewalk, the Asian guy doing the crab dance, and two couples of Goth kids pushing their way out of the Juju.

Pridemore and Hoatlin sized up the situation and parked diagonally, if not very gracefully, across the sidewalk. The door to the Black Juju slammed shut. The crowd parted in a ripple of black eyeshadow and torn jeans. The gold mini-dress girl held up her phone to catch the action but lost it in the rush. Pridemore backed up to Parnell, keeping Black Shorts at bay. Kibelewski hooked Cop Wannabee by his fat throat and handcuffed him to a parking meter. Hoatlin edged past the fat Asian girl and grabbed Tai Chi by the elbow, swinging him out and away from Parnell.

"But he say! I say!" And off he went. The momentum of Hoatlin's spin started a gentle sloshing motion in Tai Chi's inner ear fluid. The horizons of Antoine Fraiser Avenue went suddenly vertical as the internal wave crested and broke into a splash of Jack Daniels-flavored brain soup. Round and round he went, his arms trying to form wings, his feet twisting to make a landing gear. On the sidewalk he made almost three full loops. In his head, he made dozens, all of them in tilted slow motion. Tai Chi came to earth on the large chest of the fat Asian girl, his wings enfolding her as his puked all down the front of her dress.

"Do you want this goofball for something?" Hoatlin asked Parnell.

"He's got nothing to do with this mess, as far as I know," said Parnell.

"You need this one?" Hoatlin shouted to Nolan.

"No. He's not involved."

"What the hell? Nobody wants Mister Kung Fu here?" asked Hoatlin.

The ambulance finally arrived. Parnell, Pridemore, and Hoatlin stood with their backs to the assault complainant on the sidewalk and watched the crowd. The paramedics shined a flashlight in the kid's eyes, determined that he could walk, and helped him aboard the ambulance. Bicycle Pants was nowhere to be seen.

"I was just trying to help," cried the fat Cop Wannabee as Kibelewski uncuffed him.

"Get out of here," Nolan told him.

"Can I leave?" the fat boy asked.

"Yeah," Kibelewski told him. "You're un-arrested. Get going."

"I'm sorry. I was just trying to help."

"Get moving," Nolan warned him, and off trudged the fat kid.

The fat Asian girl and the cell phone girl helped Tai Chi into their car, vomit and all. The Goths were shrinking away into the night. Nolan, Kibelewski, Parnell, Hoatlin, and Pridemore stood on the sidewalk of South Antoine Fraiser Avenue and kept the peace. Arriving couples saw the bundle of law enforcement and quickly turned away. Someone opened the door of the Black Juju, letting out a metallic blast into the night air.

"Shut the fucking door!" the cops yelled in unison.

Lt. Jerry Crawford worked two days a month now. He had 37 years on the job, more than 4,000 hours of sick time to use or lose, and hardly any private life at all. At 61, he was nearing mandatory retirement, had survived three marriages, and had six grandchildren he had never seen. Crawford had been a Lieutenant back when his commanding officer, Captain Maddox had been a snot-nosed rookie. He had been on the job longer than his co-worker, Lt. Berke, had been on planet Earth. He had been a cop since Pridemore was a little kid. Crawford was a pre-Pearson command officer. He had been promoted to the rank of Lieutenant by the Chief who had been the Chief before the other Chief who Pearson had replaced. In all, Jerry Crawford had served seven Police Chiefs, not including the one Deputy Chief who had been made acting-Chief for two weeks, only to die of a stroke at his desk.

Crawford had come on in the Old School, back when men were the cops and women were the meter maids. Cops spat on Esposito and Miranda back then, wiped their asses with the Fourth Amendment, and counted on the Department to look the other way. There had been no Internal Affairs back then. There was no such thing as a Citizens

Review Board back then. There was no such thing as a Negro west of Boyd Avenue back then. People didn't yell or curse at cops back then, at least, not *sane* people. People did not throw bricks or bottles at police cars in those days. Back then, if you threw something at a policeman, they would wipe the street with your face. They would kick the living shit out of you in broad daylight, and no one would see a thing. And that was just for *throwing* the brick; if you had actually *hit* the cop you were throwing at, they would beat you like a circus monkey and throw you off the South Ferry Causeway. They called their batons "night sticks" and their shotguns "riot guns." Crawford had been shot twice, once in the shoulder and once in the ass. He had shot two or three guys, too, depending on whom he was telling the stories to, because only two of the shootings were "official." There was a one-legged Puerto Rican out there somewhere with Crawford's name on his stump. Those were the days.

But Crawford was not stuck completely in the past. The "good old days" were also pre-Union days, where the bosses could work you to death, overtime be damned. They told you to stand guard on the downtown museum steps, and you stood there in January. You got your promotion based on who you knew or who you were related to. You called in sick one time too many, and you could go find yourself another job. If you screwed with a Captain or Lieutenant, they would find a rat hole assignment for you and stick you there, and you were screwed good and plenty. When those guys fucked you, you *stayed* fucked. There were weasels like Lt. Berke back then, too, of course, not as slick or college-smart, but just as serpentine. There were psychotic rat-fuckers like Captain Maddox back then, too. Plenty of Maddoxes—Oh, yes!—and no Union to protect you from them either. In the first Manual of Procedures they had handed Crawford when he was a rookie, a 20-paged mimeographed thing that you had to keep in your locker, there were rules expressly forbidding union organizing or even *talking* about a police union. So Crawford remembered that the good old days hadn't always been that good and the new days were not always that bad. They were just different. You still protected the citizens from the assholes—although, it seemed sometimes it was just assholes and more assholes—and you still just tried to get home safely. And you still suffered with guys like Maddox and Berke.

So Lt. Crawford came in two days a month, both of them pay days, and called in sick the rest of the time, trying to use up his accumulated

MAD BADGES

sick time, which the City wouldn't pay you for unless you used it. His little bout with prostate cancer two years before and a friendly doctor with a pad of Excuse-From-Work slips kept the whole thing operating. He always came to work, completely out of touch with the day-to-day shenanigans of the Command staff, the shifting politics of the downtown tower, and the latest police management theories. Two days a month, Crawford signed vacation requests, checked the log books, threw away memos, and pretended to be confused by the old computer in the "Oh Three" office. The 0-3 office, sometimes called the O.D. office, for Officer of the Day, was a Desk Lieutenant's cubicle behind the Desk Sergeant's desk in the lobby on the Maynard Street side of the Precinct house. The "Oh Two" office was Berke's upstairs domain, and if you dialed "Oh One," you would get Captain Maddox's office. So Crawford ate peach yogurt at his desk in the 0-3 office and played solitaire on the old computer, pretending to be baffled by the new high-tech wizardry.

   In reality, Crawford's home computer, which he never discussed with anyone, was a top-of-the-line, ultra-fast machine packed with various motion pictures, sundry pornography, and outrageous space games. Crawford had started taking computer classes just for the hell of it when his third wife had left and his sick time usage had started. He used the name "Captain Crawdaddy" in Internet chat rooms, although he despised most Captains. He had learned that "data entry data entry" served as a universal password on most municipal databases. He had learned how to hack into Captain Darcy's downtown laptop and change his screensaver to say "CLOSET QUEEN." It had been Crawford who had swiped the text of Deputy Chief Griswold's confidential memos and sent it to the reporter from Channel 5. It had been Crawford who had completely erased a 200-page grant proposal from Deputy Chief Forrest's machine. The Department's computer network, like all the City's systems, was pretty well fucked up and low-bid to begin with, so they hardly noticed that some of these things were pranks from within. The key was not to tell anyone. The key was to enjoy it all by yourself. Crawford, the old geezer who could barely operate the antique computer in the 0-3 office, was enjoying his twilight years quietly.

   It was after five, and the lobby was pretty much cleared out. Lt. Crawford fumbled with a black queen on a black king on the computer screen until Sgt. Tuttle left the office. Alone, finally, Crawford logged into the System Administrator folder on the Department's Command

Network and typed in a Background Records query. He identified his computer as the machine up in Captain Maddox's office, now that Maddox was gone for the weekend, and asked for complete Criminal History requests to be sent to that computer. Crawford hummed as he typed the names.
    WASHINGTON.
    MONROE.
    JEFFERSON.
    GONZALES.
    MARTINEZ.
    PEREZ.
    SMITH.
    JONES.
    JOHNSON.
    GOREE.
    CARTER.
    MACINTOSH.
    HOLMES.
    POWELL.
    EZELL.
    JACKSON.
    ADAMS.
    FRANKLIN.
    WILLIAMS.
    KITCHEN.
    TORRES.
    MORENO.
    MARINO.
    POWERS.
    LAMONT_* (which meant any criminal with the first name of "Lamont.")
    DARRYL_*.
    KENISHA_*.
    TONY_*.
    DAVIS.
    CALDWELL.
    HARRISON.
    WILSON.
    PARKER.
    And for good measure, PEARSON.

When the Network asked Crawford how he wanted the 147, 603 Criminal Histories displayed, he selected PRINT. When it asked him if he wanted the printouts on Captain Maddox's old dot matrix printer in GOOD, BETTER, or BEST quality, Crawford selected GOOD. He wanted the ink to last as long as possible through this particular print job. After a brief software belch, the screen announced PRINTING BEGUN. Logging off of the System Administration Network, Crawford leaned back in his chair and got back to the boring solitaire game. There were some things you simply had to enjoy alone.

"I think this is going to be a bad summer," said Neal Parnell.

"You say that every fucking year," Buck Tyler replied. "Every fucking spring, you sniff the fucking air and say you think it's going to be a bad fucking summer."

"Well, I just have that feeling."

"You get that feeling every summer," said Pridemore, sipping his coffee.

"Every fucking summer," added Buck.

"There's just a lot of angry people out there, it seems to me," Parnell explained. "The mood just seems completely negative."

"It's the weather," said Pridemore.

"It's the niggers," said Buck. "They're multiplying."

"Maybe it's the heat," Jeff The Rookie suggested.

"And the spicks, who are multiplying even faster than the niggers."

"I wish it would rain," said Parnell.

"Rain would be good," nodded Pridemore.

"Keeps the niggers inside," agreed Buck. "They don't like showers."

"Jeez, Buck!" said Pridemore.

"Yeah," Parnell agreed, "give it a rest, will you?"

"What?" asked Buck.

Hoatlin finally put down his coffee cup. "What's with you, Buck? It's nigger-this and nigger-that and nigger, nigger, nigger tonight. Lighten up, okay?"

Buck Tyler looked surprised and almost hurt. "What'd I say now?"

"Just give it a rest, Buck," said Parnell.

"Please?" begged Pridemore.

They gazed wearily at the floor, avoiding each other's eyes. The ceiling fan's humming filled the silence.

"Then there's the greasers," Buck said from nowhere. "Is it okay to talk about the wetbacks tonight?"

"No," said Pridemore.

"Negative," agreed Parnell.

Hoatlin shook his head. "Well, all in all, I'd have to say it's too hot tonight."

Everyone but Buck nodded in agreement. It was late. The calls had been boring and long. The hours weren't moving fast enough for any of them. Jeff The Rookie brought over Magda's coffee pot and filled everyone's cup at the table.

"How about those white trash, banjo-playing motherfuckers on the second floor at 2401 Newton tonight?" Buck said with a grin. "Was that a convention of in-bred booger-eating morons or what?"

"Jeez!" said Hoatlin.

"Please!" said Parnell.

"Hopeless!" groaned Pridemore.

"What?" asked Buck. "What'd I say now? You guys are no fun at all sometimes, you know?"

"Too fucking hot tonight," said Jeff The Rookie, and they all looked at him.

The loud party was inside a little house that sat back from the line of shabby wood-framed homes on the south side of St. Joseph Street. Two neighbors had already called. Neal Parnell and Buck Tyler had already warned them once about the music and the breaking bottles. The resident was a white college kid who had mentioned to them that his dad was an attorney. He rented the place, he said, from one of his father's law partners, apparently another slumlord with a law degree. On the last visit, the crowd had been a mixture of white kids and black kids, about a third of them college girls. This trip, the crowd was about three fourths black males and one fourth white college girls, with the odd drunken white male passed out here and there among the destroyed furniture. There was a window broken out on the side of the little house. The foundation was trembling with deep bass backbeat. It was four in the morning.

"I gots to get up and go to work in the morning," called a woman in her bathrobe from the house on the left.

"Yes, ma'am," said Parnell.

"They turned it right back up the second you left outta here the lass time," called a man with a gray beard from the porch across the street.

"Yes, sir," replied Kibelewski. "Please go back inside, while we take care of this."

The house on the right side of the party address was an abandoned crack house, where no one lived or owned a telephone. Behind the party house was an overgrown alley and, behind that, was a metal-plating factory. There were probably only two working stiffs living in this whole block who had telephones, and this party was keeping both of them awake. St. Joseph Street was clogged with vans, purple compact cars, sport utilities, and assorted ghetto rides.

Kibelewski and Nolan were on the right. Buck Tyler and Parnell took the left. As they approached the dilapidated front porch, they could hear only music, the bass line rattling the house's siding.

"BITCH! YA WANNA BE MY?"

"I think we've got a violation here," said Nolan.

"There must be eighty people in there," said Parnell.

"I think we need a Sergeant," said Kibelewski.

"BITCH! BITCH! YA WANNA BE MY?"

Parnell took the point. He rapped on the steel front door with his flashlight. Nothing. He rapped again.

"Try it on the off-beat," suggested Buck.

"BITCHES! BITCHES! YA WANNA ALL BE?"

Parnell banged harder this time. Nolan applied his boot. The steel door didn't budge or open. Kibelewski shined his flashlight through the window at the living room ceiling, clicking it on and off. Nothing.

"BITCHES! BITCHES! YA'LL JUST BITCHES! BITCHES!"

"Fucker's are deaf!" said Buck.

"What?" asked Kibelewski over the noise.

They called for a couple more cars, but none were available. Parnell asked for a Sergeant, but was told there weren't any. The four cops moved off to the back yard of the crack house next door, where a children's broken swingset lay amid tires and broken boards. Now they could at least heard each other.

"BITCHES! BITCHES! YA'LL BE MY!"

"I say we wait until more cars are available," suggested Parnell.

"I think we should break a window and pepper spray them," offered Nolan.

The front door of the party house opened just long enough for someone to throw out an empty 40-ouncer, the glass shattering across the front steps. The jarring BUPP BUPP BUPP of the music blared out into the neighborhood. Kibelewski started toward the porch, but the door slammed shut again.

"Fucking Jig music," said Buck. He looked up to see a black child's face in a second floor window of the house on the left where the lady in the bathrobe lived. The child—Buck couldn't tell if it was a boy or girl—gazed impassively down at the nighttime activity. He waved. The child disappeared from the window.

"BITCHES! ALL OF YOU! BITCHES!"

"Maybe there's a back door," said Kibelewski hopefully.

"Nah, fuck it!" said Buck. "We'll back off and wait. Parnell's right. We'll wait for more cars." He gave Parnell a look like there was a plan. Parnell nodded.

"We can't just walk away," said Nolan.

"No, but we can't rush in there with that many drunks either," Kibelewski reasoned. "I say we wait."

"Parnell's right," said Buck. "We'll wait in the alley. You guys wait up the block." Buck gave Parnell a second knowing glance. Parnell was surprised to hear Buck say he, Parnell, was right about anything, much less say it twice.

"BITCHES! FUCKIN YOU BITCHES!"

So they backed off to their cruisers. Parnell asked Dispatch again for more cars and again was told there were no more cars available.

"Ain't you gonna do nothing about it?" cried the lady in the bathrobe.

"Please go back inside," Parnell told her.

"Ya'll juss gonna leave?" cried the man across the street.

"We're going to wait for backup," Nolan assured him.

"Shee-it," said the man disgustedly.

Nolan and Kibelewski walked down to their cruiser, drove up to the end of the block, and whipped around to watch the street. Buck Tyler had Parnell drive their cruiser, lights out, to the narrow alley at the rear of the party house. They could still hear the music clearly.

"THREE BITCHES! FOUR BITCHES! MORE BITCHES!"

"Pull up there a bit more," said Buck. He grabbed a large battered screwdriver out of his equipment bag. When they were past the rear of the nextdoor crackhouse, Buck opened his door. "Stay here. I'll be right back."

"Hey!" Parnell started to say, but Buck had already slipped out into the darkness.

The music pounded and pounded. Screams of joy, pain, or delirium pulsed from the little house. Bottles broke and girls shrieked. Parnell looked back at the glow of the party house, wondering if he should go find Buck. All of this made him very uneasy.

Then—POOF!—it was silent. No sound at all. Parnell looked back up the alley and saw that the party house was pitch black. Now what? There were shouts in the darkness as the party house began to empty out. Parnell started to open the driver's door, when Buck jumped into the passenger seat.

"Go!" snarled Buck Tyler.

Parnell closed his door and shifted into Drive, looking down at the electric company's glass power meter in Buck's lap.

"Fucking *go!*" Buck snapped at him. And off they went, lights still out, down the alley and out onto Dunham. They startled Nolan and Kibelewski, who promptly took off in the other direction. Parnell steered right one block, cut through a second alley, and came out onto Hayward, failing to stop for signs or rights-of-way. Buck rolled down his window and tossed out the electrical meter, which shattered and spun. Another left and they were out onto Houston Avenue. Buck rolled up his window.

"Better turn on the headlights now, don't you think?" said Buck.

"Oh." Parnell pulled the lights on.

"And maybe slow down, too. This ain't the fucking Indy 500 here."

Parnell slowed down. "It's illegal to tamper with the property of the power company, you know."

"Yeah," Buck replied. "It's a bitch, ain't it?"

The dispatcher came on and asked if they still needed more cars. Buck took the mike and said that the party had broken up peacefully. Nolan and Kibelewski cleared the call and were promptly sent on a domestic. Buck and Parnell stayed logged on the loud party complaint and went to get a donut.

"I wish you wouldn't do things like that," Parnell said, adding, "without at least warning me first."

"Let me guess," said Buck. "You wanted us to get our ass kicked in there?"

"Just tell me first next time."

"You wouldn't have gone along with it, man."

"Just let me know next time, okay?"
"Okay, next time," lied Buck Tyler. "Fuck it. I'm hungry."

The front door of the rented house on Scranton was painted shut or blocked by a bookcase or otherwise inaccessible, according to the little Vietnamese man who stuck his head out the window. Pridemore and Flex Sinclair walked around to the back and came in through the kitchen. The little man opened the back door and let them. Pridemore looked down at the array of forty or so pairs of shoes, neatly fanned out from the doorway and halfway across the kitchen floor. The room smelled of curry and heavy grease. The little man was wearing sandals. The pretty, black-haired girl at his side wore light blue socks. She covered her mouth and emitted a deep wet cough. Pridemore picked his way across the sea of shoes to the dining room. Flex hung back for a moment and spoke to Parnell and his new rookie, Mimi, on the back steps.

"We just came by for training purposes," explained Parnell. "The call history looked interesting." Flex Sinclair looked at Mimi, the fresh-faced rookie. She was wearing way too much makeup, he noticed.

"I think we've got some TB-infected gooks in here. Both Jack and me have tested positive before and taken the pills, but you might want to pass on this one."

"Affirmative," said Parnell.

"What pills?" asked Mimi The Rookie, brightly.

Flex Sinclair leaned toward her. "If someone with tuberculosis coughs on you, you get the germ in your lungs. Then you test positive for the TB skin test for the rest of your life. To make sure you don't actually come down with TB and infect the rest of the world, they put you on these big-ass pills that you have to swallow every goddamn day for six goddamn months. And the pills make you feel like puking every goddamn morning for the whole six months. So if you want to come in and catch TB from the gooks in here, come on in. But I've taken the pills, and I wouldn't advise it. Clear?"

"Clear," said Mimi The Rookie.

"Ten-four," said Parnell, and they left in a hurry.

Kien Thanh was the name of the complainant. He seemed to be the only one who spoke English. The coughing girl was named Tuyet

MAD BADGES

or something, and she stayed close to Thanh, who was her brother or father or husband, but definitely too old to be her son. Tuyet was pretty, but the useless rasping sounds told Pridemore that she was also very ill. As they walked up the hall to Thanh's room, Asian faces gazed from every door. Pridemore stood, writing on his pocket notebook as Thanh proudly displayed his driver's license, passport, and his old I.N.S. card with his tiny right index fingerprint in the corner. Pridemore used it to help him spell things as Thanh related the story.

It turned out not to be a burglary. It was Thanh's Pontiac that was missing. More importantly, it was the little purple cloth pull-string bag in the trunk of Thanh's Pontiac that was missing. There were jade stones in the little bag, Thanh said. The bag was worth more than the Pontiac, in fact. The bag was worth more than the house they were standing in, Thanh said. Tuyet turned away and coughed uselessly.

"So how many stones?" asked Pridemore.

"Four," replied Thanh.

"And jade is—what?—green?"

"No, no," Thanh told him. "White and butterfat. Better. Much better."

"What's butterfat?"

"A yellow. Not just yellow. Like yellow. Like...uh...butter."

Pridemore wrote "yellow" on his notepad. "I thought jade was green."

"Jade all colors," explained Thanh. "Red, white, purple, black, brown, blue, and Imperial."

"Oh," said Pridemore.

"Uh-huh," said Sinclair, who was standing in the hallway behind him, but staying away from the coughing girl.

"They're stones?" Pridemore asked the little Vietnamese man.

"Yes."

"I mean, they're like rocks or pebbles, round, flat what?"

"Saddles."

"Saddles?" said Flex.

"Yes."

Tuyet hacked quietly over by the closet.

"Like a saddle for a horse?" asked Pridemore.

"Elephant," answered Thanh. He handed Pridemore an old Polaroid that showed a tiny carved elephant and four tiny white and yellow elephant saddles. None of them, not even the elephant, was bigger than Pridemore's little finger. Pridemore handed it back through the doorway to Sinclair.

"How much would you estimate these little things are worth, Mr. Thanh?"

The man looked confused. "I Kien Thanh. That would be 'Mister Kien' in American, I think." He looked apologetic. Sinclair handed the elephant saddle picture back to Pridemore, who handed it back to Thanh, who put it into a shoebox of valuables.

"What are they worth?"

"About . . .uh . . .thirty thousand American dollars," said Thanh.

Pridemore tried not to look surprised. He wrote down the figure. Flex Sinclair gave out a low whistle. The coughing girl seemed to find this funny—Sinclair's whistle, not the thirty thousand dollars. Pridemore wrote down the vehicle information, the description of the cloth bag in its trunk, and the particulars of Kien Thanh and his employment.

Thanh worked in a sausage plant. The house was rented in his name. There were almost as many people living in the place as there were pairs of shoes on the kitchen floor. Some of these people were relatives of Thanh. Some were not. Some worked in the sausage factory. Others worked for a factory that sewed together ski pants and backpacks. Thirty-some people working 16-hour days at minimum wage, times six days a week, minus bus fare, groceries, and whatever the eleven hundred per month house rent was divided by thirty people; Flex Sinclair tried to calculate it. All of the profits from this beehive activity went to plane fare to get other relatives over here from the old country to work new beehives. Sinclair had to hand it to them as he looked around at the little floor mats where they slept, eight to a room, and smelled the foul odors from the kitchen where something was always cooking in a place like this. The sick girl coughed gently into her sleeve.

"You brought this jade from Vietnam?" asked Pridemore, conversationally.

"I buy with gold in San Francisco. I bring gold on boat from Vietnam. Trade for jades in California. Jades much easier. Lighter than gold."

"And you keep them in your car?"

"Sometimes. Sometime I keep here." Thanh pointed to the shoebox.

"Maybe you should keep them in a bank, eh, buddy?" suggested Flex Sinclair.

"No . . .ah . . .maybe." Thanh wasn't sure what the black police officer was saying. Where Thanh was from, the policemen were all soldiers. They dressed like soldiers and acted like soldiers. They took part or all of your money, as they wished. They took your daughter or wife, as they wished. The police where Thanh came from accepted bribes and expected bribes as a matter of course. Not like here. Police officers in the United States might be rude or nice or indifferent, but they were not soldiers. Thanh watched them on the TV all the time and marveled at the difference. But, like Vietnamese policemen, you didn't ask them to take off their boots before they entered your home. Thanh also could not grasp what the black policemen had said about the bank. Banks gave you paper and receipts and cards. Banks sometimes disappeared overnight and left you only worthless paper. Real money was gold or gems or something solid you could hold in your hand. You knew it was there. It was real. It was hard. You could not crunch it up like the paper the banks gave you. You knew where it was, unless of course someone stole your car with your life savings in the trunk. So Thanh nodded at the black police officer and hoped he was making the right gesture.

When Pridemore had what he needed for the report, Tuyet led them back down the hallway, through the dining room to the kitchen full of shoes. Kien Thanh excused himself to get ready for work.

"Always something cooking in a place like this," Flex Sinclair said to Pridemore as they tiptoed through the maze of shoes.

"Yup," agreed Pridemore.

"Smells like fried poodle to me." Flex opened the back door.

"It is lemongrass chicken with nuoc mam and coriander," whispered Tuyet. Pridemore studied her for a moment, not sure what she had said. Behind the voice, there was so little wind from her weakened lungs. "Would you like to stay for dinner?"

"No, but thank you," said Pridemore.

"No thanks," said Sinclair.

"Perhaps you have never been hungry enough to eat a dog," she said very gently. Her lips formed a slight smile as she spoke.

"I guess not," Flex replied.

"Thank you for helping my brother," Tuyet called after them. "He works very hard."

"I hope we can find his car," Pridemore said, waving.

After the door closed, they could hear more of the girl's worthless coughing. They were glad to be out in the fresh air again, at least as fresh as the air ever got down on Scranton Street. They sat in the cruiser, while Pridemore finished the stolen car report.

"I didn't know she could speak English," Flex Sinclair said suddenly.

"She won't be speaking anything for long, if she doesn't see a doctor soon," said Pridemore.

The problem was Captain Maddox's shoes and, of course, the hemorrhoids. The shoes were new wingtips; the hemorrhoids were old ones. The Average Mileage Per Precinct-Assigned Fleet Vehicle report was not done, and the downtown tower was already complaining about it. There was yet another union grievance about the sewer gas leaking into the locker room and another building inspector's complaint about the cracks in the walls of the lobby. Thank God, Sgt. Petty had steered that inspector away from the basement and the Squad Room. Maddox had to gas up his car at the fire station on Filmore, because the pumps were out again at the usual spot. The grubby firefighters in their slack shirts and partial uniforms just stared at him as he filled his own tank. Sandra Maddox had just announced a ridiculous new diet she was starting, which meant months of irritability at home that he didn't need and a refrigerator full of kiwi fruit and bean sprouts that he couldn't eat. His stomach turned over just thinking about it.

Bumping through the pot hole littered parking lot behind the Heights Precinct house, Maddox saw the Third Shift officers flowing out of his building. They were a ragtag bunch of immature men with no more pride than to wear blue jeans, sweatshirts, and tennis shoes. He waved and smiled, pretending to recognize at least some of them. Few of them even bothered to wave back, the louts. There was no pride left here, no pride and no respect. He had never asked for their friendship. It wasn't a popularity contest, he had been told when he got that first promotion. But he demanded some sort of respect around here. His Captain's bars earned him some measure of esteem in other parts of the City, but seldom any here. These slobs were almost as bad as the neighborhoods they patrolled and were just about as respectful.

He parked and locked his car. He said hello to Gladys, the cleaning lady, and greeted the Mexican guy from the motorpool. He barked at the ever-cheerful Lt. Berke, the little jerk, and ignored a rookie whom he didn't recognize. Maddox found his mail, junk, junk, and more junk mixed in with complimentary law enforcement equipment magazines and announcements for "Police Leadership" workshops. One of the typists from Records told him his secretary was out sick for the day, which Maddox thought was probably a lie, as he fumbled around with his office key. The door stuck as it usually did, and he had to put down his mail to play with the key in the lock. He unlocked the door, pushing it open with his hip, and discovered the rolls and mounds of dot matrix printer paper that covered the floor.

"Damnit!" Maddox shrieked. His guts lurched and burned, the breakfast oatmeal leaping into his throat. "Damn it all!" He dropped his mail and threw down his briefcase as the alarmed clerks from Records arrived to see what the shouting was about. Someone snickered as they surveyed the mess.

"There's nothing funny about a computer system that does things like this," he scolded them. Kicking away at the paper, he waded into the room and slammed the door in their faces. He tried to ignore the tittering outside his office. His desk phone buzzed, and he ignored that, too. Snatching up a section of the enormous snake of white paper that lay across his carpet, Maddox read the printout.

"LAMONT AVERY JACKSON, BLACK/MALE, DOB 10-18-84, 5 FT. 11 IN., 180 LBS., BLACK HAIR, BROWN EYES."

The rest of it was the same, criminal histories of Jacksons, Jeffersons, and Johnsons, a whole roomful of them. This computer system, thought Maddox, was a nightmare. This whole place was a nightmare. And it was killing his stomach. The printer's Out-of-Ink alarm was beeping.

"Damnit!" he roared again, grabbing his aching gut.

Antonio Middleberry, black male, 28 years, and Lisa Moore, white female, 19 years, both dead of gunshot wounds in the alley at the rear of The Marble Room, 3260 South Cramer Avenue. From the twelve casings found around the bodies, investigators knew they were shot with a 7.62 SKS assault rifle. Friends of Shanita Combs, Middleberry's former girlfriend, were reportedly involved in the murders. Everyone was reportedly inside the bar at the time and neither heard nor saw the shooting.

"I have here an incident report that you signed-off on dated the 29th of last month," said Lt. Berke, tapping his pen on the desk. "It appears to be a traffic pursuit that ended in a vehicle accident with injuries."

Sgt. Gibson tried to look at the report, but was blocked by Berke's hand. Gibson was still standing. Berke, seated comfortably at his desk, was going to make the Sergeant stand for a few moments more. It was Monday morning. This was going to be the Crisis-of-the-Day for Monday. At least the *first* one of the day, Gibson knew.

"First of all, are you aware of the Manual of Procedure directive regarding the reports of accidents resulting from pursuits with Department vehicles?"

"Yes, sir, I am." Gibson could see the M.O.P. book open on the desk next to Lt. Berke's left elbow.

"Maybe you could relate to me your understanding of the rules with regards the Manual of Procedure directive, Sergeant," said Berke.

"Well, sir, I believe..."

"Sit down, sit down, Sergeant," Berke interrupted. "You don't need to stand up for this."

For this? For what? Gibson wondered what the '*this*' was. You could never tell with a snake like Berke. Gibson was also having a hard time remembering what pursuit and accident they were talking about. Gibson sat in the hard plastic chair to his right.

"Now where were we?" Lt. Berke asked, as if he himself had not been the source of the interruption. "Ah, the directive, yes. You were going to explain your understanding of the directive."

Explain? Stand up for this? Gibson knew the Lieutenant enjoyed this game. The Sergeant tried not to let this power play crap rattle him, but it always did. He started to sweat.

"With regard to vehicular accidents that occur as a result of police pursuits, the Manual states that a Sergeant will be called to the scene; that the Sergeant will assign an officer to take the report who is not the officer involved in either the pursuit or the accident; and that, in the event of personal injury accidents, the on-scene Sergeant will advise the Patrol Lieutenant on duty, or other supervisor, so that the Traffic Unit can be notified," said Gibson in one long breath.

"And, in the event of a fatality," added Berke, "the supervisor shall notify the Internal Affairs Unit."

"Yes, sir." Gibson felt pretty certain that he had not worked a pursuit-related fatality in recent memory and, thus, was probably not in trouble here. But you could never tell with some of these Manual of Procedure types.

"So you feel that you're pretty clear on all that, Sergeant?"

"I think so, sir. Yes. Was there a question about one of my reports?" He could see the Lieutenant's fingers worrying the top corner of a report.

"Questions?" said Berke. "No questions, really. Not about the report." Dragging it out, making the subordinate twist in the breeze, relishing the pregnant pauses, all of it was Lt. Berke at his best, or worst, depending on which end you were on, thought Gibson. "The Captain and the Internal Affairs Unit asked me why it was that one of my Sergeant's would somehow fail to notify his supervisor in the event of a pursuit-related vehicle accident. They came to me with this issue, and I assured them that I would get your input on the matter. They seemed rather concerned, you see." In reality, it was only Captain Maddox who had complained about the incident. His stomach ulcers had been bothering him, so he had taken it out on Berke, using Gibson's report as an excuse. And the shit rolling downhill from Commanders to the troops never stopped for long on Lt. Berke's polished shoes.

"I understand," said Gibson. "Which incident were they concerned about?"

Berke stubbornly held onto the report, making the Sergeant wait for him to describe it. The wait was making Gibson's collar tighten.

"It seems there was a pursuit on the 29th, wherein Officer Kibelewski tried to make a traffic stop on a 2002 red Toyota pickup for a no-headlights violation. It further appears that the driver of the Toyota failed to stop for Officer Kibelewski's lights and sirens and, after a pursuit of approximately eight minutes, crashed into the front of a Holy Burrito restaurant at Central and Cleveland. You, it appears, were the Sergeant-of-record for the call, correct?"

"Yes, but . . ."

"And the driver of the Toyota sustained injuries to both his face and to his right arm. Isn't that also correct, Sergeant?"

"Correct," replied Gibson, relaxing a little, now that he remembered the incident and realized he had done nothing wrong.

"You're smiling for some reason, Sgt. Gibson. Is there something amusing about all this?"

"No, sir. I was just . . ."

"May I finish outlining the facts of the case here?" Lt. Berke asked. "You wouldn't want any of the facts overlooked, would you?"

"Sir," said Gibson, unsure if he should answer Yes or No.

Berke paused for dramatic effect, then continued. "You have a traffic pursuit which ends in a personal injury accident. You are the assigned supervisor on the scene, and yet somehow you fail to notify your Lieutenant, so that he or she might decide whether or not to order in an investigator from the Traffic Unit to look into the crash thoroughly, so that the City might lessen its possible exposure in a future civil action. Is that what we have here?"

"No."

"No?"

"It was not a pursuit-related crash," said Gibson.

"It says 'Pursuit' right here. Now, all of a sudden, it's not a pursuit? Didn't you check the report? Aren't those your initials at the bottom of this report?"

Gibson sidestepped the compound questions and tried to ignore Berke's rapid-fire delivery, the little prick.

"Kibelewski followed the Toyota, but lost it. He was not in pursuit at the time of the accident. The crash happened some time after Kibelewski had lost the pickup. It was, therefore, not a pursuit-related accident and didn't, therefore, require the notification of a supervisor. It was just a regular car-building accident . . .Lieutenant." Gibson felt he had made his case.

"So you took it upon yourself to fail to notify your supervisor, isn't that what you're saying?"

"The accident did not require such action, I felt."

"You *felt*," said Berke. "I see." He held that thought long enough to make Gibson feel uncomfortable again. "Do you *often* get the feeling that you're going to ignore Departmental policy or was this just a one-time whim with you?"

"The accident was some time after the pursuit had ended," Gibson restated, thinking maybe he had been unclear the first time. "It was not a result of the pursuit."

"So you have said, Sgt. Gibson. However, the Command staff asked me how you knew the pursuit had actually ended. They suggested that this was possibly an example of a lazy Sergeant who simply didn't want to follow through on the proper report writing and the proper notifications. I told them that Sgt. Gibson was a fine first-line supervisor and that I would look into it. But now that I'm looking into it further, well, I'm surprised at you . . ."

"The pursuit had been over at the time of the accident, as far as I could determine."

"Yes, but how do you know that?" Berke asked.

"I spoke with Kibelewski and reviewed the dispatch tape."

"And Officer Kibelewski allegedly said that he had broken off the pursuit? Is that what you're saying?"

"Yes, and the dispatch tape backed . . ."

"The officer told you this and you simply took his word for it?" interrupted Berke. "I see. And you listened to the tape, too? You based your whole report on that?"

"The dispatch tape backed it up. I was talking car-to-car with Kibelewski in a parking lot six blocks away when the alarm call came in from the Holy Burrito restaurant. There was no accident as a result of the chase."

"And you checked, of course, to see if any of your other people were out pursuing the vehicle?"

"No one called it out," replied Gibson defensively.

"I see." Berke tapped his pen some more. "That was good enough for you, I guess?"

"Yes." Gibson couldn't think of anything else to say. You were right one week and wrong the next, and you never knew why, and they always blamed you. Gibson hated this part of his job, the second-guessing, the nitpicking, and the Monday morning quarterbacks.

"What was the name of the dispatcher who took the alarm call?" Berke asked finally.

"I don't know," replied Gibson. "I suppose their I.D. number is on the tape."

"I don't see that anywhere here in your report." Berke pretended to shuffle through the report's two pages.

There was always something they could find missing from your reports. A determined Internal Affairs investigator or an ambitious supervisor or a floundering prosecutor could always dig down deeper and deeper into a written report to find one miniscule item that had been left out. If it wasn't the dispatch time, it was the dispatcher's name. If it wasn't the dispatcher's name, it was the dispatcher's badge number. Or the dispatcher's supervisor's name. Or the dispatcher's supervisor's badge number. Or the name of the alarm company's caller who had phoned the Police dispatcher. Or the time that the Holy Burrito restaurant normally opened in the morning. Or the mileage on the odometer of the wrecked red Toyota pickup. Or the mileage and Vehicle Identification Number of Kibelewski's cruiser. Or the Patient Number that Central Receiving assigned to the injured driver when he was brought into their emergency room. Or the names and numbers of the ambulance crew that responded to the scene. Or the length, in inches, of the Toyota pickup's skidmarks before it hit the store. Or the delay time between the moment the alarm came in and the moment that the alarm company phoned the police, which the alarm companies almost always lied about anyway. Or the name of the intern at Central Receiving Hospital who had first looked at the injured driver and determined that his right arm was broken. Or the name and telephone number of the Impossibly Beautiful Blonde From X-Ray at Central Receiving Hospital, which was actually the only morsel of trivia worth having. There was always something they could find that was not down there in black and white on your report. Gibson knew how the game was played, but it didn't make him feel any better.

"Well," Lt. Berke said finally, "I will pass on your version of the event to the Captain. We'll see where he goes with it from there." Captain Maddox, of course, had already forgotten about the incident. Internal Affairs had, in fact, never been advised that there even was a question about the report. And the Traffic Unit investigators—had they known about it at all—would have been thankful to Gibson for *not* calling them in the middle of the night to bother them with such chickenshit. But for now, it was Lt. Berke who was doing Sgt. Gibson a huge favor by representing Gibson's plea for mercy to the evil Captain and the demons of I.A. It was Sgt. Gibson who now owed Lt. Berke a favor. What had started out as a Huge Nothing was now a huge debt that this employee owed to his supervisor. It was a silly crash in the night, like hundreds of others, and meant nothing to anyone. But now it was Sgt. Gibson's whole future, his career, and his livelihood, all on the line with Captain Maddox. Gibson would owe Maddox, too, and they would never let him forget it. You were expected to overlook their shortcomings—always!—while they could remember your shortcomings and remind you of them and keep reminding you how you OWED them your job. That was how the game was played.

"Thank you, Lieutenant," replied Sgt. Gibson, his face stinging. That was also how the game was played. They sodomized you, and you thanked them for the torn anus. The more they pumped it up your butt, the more you called them "Sir." It was how guys like Lieutenant Berke, Captain Maddox, Deputy Chief Griswold, and Police Chief Pearson all operated. They were on top, and you were bent over. They did it to each other, and they all did it to you. It was how they had gotten to where they were in the pumping order.

"All right, Bob," said Lt. Berke. "I'm glad we had this little talk." He stood up and offered Gibson his hand, as if to say, I *told* you I would respect you in the morning. And Gibson shook the hand, confused as any other child raped by a father, and managed to squeeze out a smile. Berke led him to the door and thumped him on the shoulder. Just us boys. We all understand. You don't tell. We don't tell. It's how you get ahead in this man's police department, you know.

Gibson thanked him again and left. He took the stairs down to the first landing, but stopped to catch his breath. It hurt. It hurt so bad. Gibson was going to have that stupid Kibelewski's ass for this later.

Alvin and Trudy Hoskins were at it again. The kitchen of their Converse Avenue apartment was a shambles. Trudy said Alvin had deliberately broken a ceramic chicken that her mother had given her as a wedding gift. Alvin said Trudy was sleeping with his brother. Tyler took Alvin to Central Receiving for the broken nose and the cut on his forehead. Pridemore took Trudy to jail for domestic assault.

Junebug Terranova leaped out of bed and grabbed his gun. The door to his girlfriend's third floor apartment was rattling off its hinges as one of the cops outside yelled for him to open up. He could see shadows moving against the curtains in back. He could see flashlights on the side of the house. They shouted that they were the police and called him by name, Renaldo Guadelope Terranova.

"Fuck!" he spat and looked around for a way out. His small revolver didn't work, of course, and he had no ammunition for it anyway. Junebug didn't even know what kind of bullets fit the thing. He cringed at the pounding on the door and checked the side window again, only to see more flashlights. "Fuck!"

He cut through the kitchen, hunkered low to the floor, and kicked open the door to the back stairway. Looking at the gun in his hand, he pitched it into a pile of filthy laundry and charged down the steps. Below him he could hear the shouting cops, beating their way up the stairs.

"Fuck!" screamed Junebug Terranova as he flung himself through the window at the first landing. There was a crash of glass and more yelling from below, and then it all stopped.

"Dumbfuck," said Buck, looking down at Junebug.

Sgt. Lindsey walked over, looked at the bleeding mess, and said: "Ouch."

"That must hurt like a *bitch*," said Pridemore, flicking his shotgun's safety to the ON position.

Junebug Terranova groaned. His toes were next to his right eye now. The cement around his head was littered with glass and teeth.

"Has someone called an ambulance?" asked Lindsey. He looked around. Hoatlin shrugged. Parnell and Mimi The Rookie looked at each other. Pridemore shook his head. Lindsey got on his portable and called for an ambulance.

"You're supposed to land on the *top* of the car, Sport," Buck scolded the injured man. "Or, at least, the hood. You hit the roof off-center like this, and you're going to have fucking problems. See what it got you, landing like that? You left a grease spot all done the side of this nice lady's car, and you've got a sideview mirror sticking out of your ass."

"Graceless critter," added Hoatlin.

"Where'd you learn to dive like that, the cliffs of fucking Acapulco?"

"I think Houston, Texas is the center of the world car-diving championships," Pridemore told Buck.

"You might be right," Buck replied, "cause this little greaser's not worth a shit at car-diving."

Junebug Terranova hurt too much to speak.

"Don't look now, Son," said Hoatlin, "but I think you've wet your pants."

"No. I think his dick is over here by this tire. Or his thumb. One or the other. Hey, Junebug! Have you got a little flower tattoo on your thumb or your dick?"

"God, that's gotta hurt," Pridemore said, shaking his head.

"Your old lady's going to get herself a new rooster when she finds out you went and broke your back like this, Son," Hoatlin told Terranova, squatting down near his face.

"I think it's a finger," called Buck Tyler. "It's got what looks like a joint in it."

"What's this guy wanted for, anyway?" Parnell asked Sgt. Lindsey.

"Armed Robbery warrant out of Central," replied Lindsey.

Pridemore leaned against the car's front fender. "Some people collect stamps, and some people collect felony warrants."

Nolan stuck his head out of the broken window two and a half floors above them and yelled, "I found his gun."

"You want your gun, Pedro?" asked Buck.

Junebug just gurgled.

"He don't want his gun," Hoatlin said.

"He don't need it anymore!" Buck called up to Nolan.

"He wants his ear back though," said Hoatlin. "Son, you are one tore-up little mope."

The ambulance was arriving. Lights were on now in several of the surrounding windows. Mimi The Rookie directed the ambulance crew to back the rig halfway up the driveway. Parnell wrote down the license plate of the car Junebug had landed on, noting the crushed in roof edge, the missing mirror, and the broken windows. Nolan came down with the Junebug's rusty revolver in an evidence bag. The paramedics wrapped Terranova's neck in an orange C-collar, started an I.V. and tried to splint his legs. He made sounds like a dying puppy as they straightened the leg that was up by his ear.

"Spine?" asked Sgt. Lindsey.

"Yeah," said one of the paramedics. "He barely felt us move that leg. He's got nothing from the waist down. A permanent paraplegic, at least."

The other paramedic was looking up at the broken window. "That's about—what?—twenty feet?"

"Yeah," said Pridemore, "more or less."

They backboarded Junebug and hoisted him onto their cart. Hoatlin handcuffed the left wrist to the rail.

"Is that really necessary?" the paramedic asked, waving Junebug's other arm, which was flaccidly hanging off the cart.

"Regulations," said Pridemore.

The paramedic nodded. "You riding with us?"

"I'll go," said Teddy Hoatlin. "They're my cuffs."

They rolled him down the driveway to where Mimi The Rookie was holding open the rear doors of the ambulance. Buck Tyler leaned close to Junebug's ear.

"Flying Lessons, motherfucker. That's what you need."

It was easy for Gunderson to find the address of Los Herraduras, the Mexican cowboy store on Lexington. There were four cruisers in the parking lot. He didn't know exactly what he had. Parking the crime scene van on the sidewalk, Gunderson picked up his flashlight and camera and headed over to where Pridemore was standing by his cruiser.

"What have you got, Jack?" asked Gunderson.

"Dead guy stuck inside a ceiling vent," Pridemore replied.

"Did we put him there?"

"Nah."

"Cool."

"Hey," said Pridemore, "have you ever seen a $4,000 cowboy hat?"

"Can't say that I have."

"They've got a $4,000 cowboy hat in there."

"And a dead guy, too?" said Gunderson. "Cool. You're a wealth of fucking information."

Gunderson left him and walked across the little parking lot. He stopped outside the broken front door of Los Herraduras, put down his camera, and took some notes. Store name, address, storefront on the west side, connected to laundromat on the north and to an insurance office on the south, and the time was 0437 hours. He took a photo of the storefront and a close-up of the damaged door. He noted the heavy steel grates covering the rest of the display windows. You could tell what kind of neighborhood it was by the number of businesses with steel grates on their storefronts.

"Hey, Gunny," called Hoatlin, stooping out through the broken door. "How you doing?"

"Good, Teddy. And how are you this fine morning?"

"Great. Do you know what they've got in there?"

"Suppose you tell me."

"They've got this cowboy hat that sells for four grand."

"No shit? Is that why you called me out here?"

"Of course not," said Teddy Hoatlin. "There's a dead burglar who broke in through the roof and got jammed up inside the air vents."
"Been there long?"
"I don't know."
"Does he stink yet?" asked Gunderson.
"No, not too bad. But did you ever hear of such a thing? A $4,000 cowboy hat?"
"What's it made of, platinum?"
"The owner says it's got rare feathers and shit on it."
"I see." Gunderson had heard about enough of this overpriced, drugstore cowboy attire bullshit. He wanted to get in there, document the scene, and get the morgue detail to haul out the corpse. He wanted to get out of there and get back to the book he was reading, a biography of the Norwegian painter Edvard Munch. Gunderson generally disliked Mexican culture, Mexican food, and Mexican music. He especially disliked country music, country music people, country music bars, and country music clothing. "What the fuck does *Herraduras* mean?"
"Horseshoe," said Hoatlin.
"The Horse Shoe," sighed Gunderson. "Perfect. They sell overpriced cowboy hats and fucking horseshoes?"
"No horseshoes, but they've got some ostrich skin boots in there."
"With those little pointy toes for kicking rattlesnakes in the ass?"
"Yeah," said Hoatlin. "And they've got lots of different snakeskin cowboy boots."
"Cool," said Gunderson, thinking Jeez Louise!
He bent down, put his notepad on the carpet just inside the broken door, and laid the camera on top of the notepad. He nudged the doorframe with his flashlight to drop out any glass that might fall on him. Struggling under the horizontal push bar, Gunderson straighten himself up inside the store. He picked up his camera, took a close-up of the door's undamaged lock, and noted it on his pad.
"Hi, Gunny," said Parnell from over by the counter. Parnell's rookie, Mimi, was speaking in Spanish with the nervous little store owner. The place was relatively clean, Gunderson noticed, but extremely cluttered with merchandise. He looked at a rack of cowgirl shirts for a few moments before realizing there were eyes looking back at him from behind the rack. The store owner's wife and daughter gazed out at Gunderson blankly. The daughter smiled; the wife averted her gaze. Parnell met him halfway across the little shop.

"What have you got?" asked Gunderson. "And don't tell me the one about the $4,000 cowboy hat. I've heard it."

"Gee," said Parnell, "I was going to save that for later. Here, come look at it."

Gunderson allowed himself to be dragged across the store to a specially lighted neon display case, wherein sat the treasured hat. It looked like a plain off-white Stetson to Gunderson. The stitching was rather ornate. The hatband was beaded and snake-like. Two feathers with eye patterns sprouted from the right side of the hatband beside an American eagle medallion.

"Is that something or what?" Parnell said with awe.

"Yeah," replied Gunderson. "Okay now, I've seen the fucking hat. Where's the fucking dead burglar?" Mimi The Rookie looked up from her report pad. The store owner didn't seem to notice. Parnell led Gunderson along the back row of merchandise to an office door at the rear.

The place was packed wall-to-wall and ceiling-to-floor with cowboy shirts, boot-cut jeans, lace ties, rodeo jackets, denim vests, Stetsons, slouch hats, dusters, and boots of every variety. Before they reached the office door, Parnell stopped and pointed out the ostrich-skin cowboy boots. Gunderson agreed that they were the most glorious boots he had ever seen. Christ!

Gunderson shot a few pictures up the vent pipe, noting the upside-down burglar's reddened face, some photos of his stomach contents on the desk and chair below, and general interior views of the room. He copied down the name from the burglar's high school I.D. card and took a picture of the card, not that anybody really needed a photograph of the card, but because Gunderson was too lazy to copy down all the information. The detectives would look at Gunderson's pictures and would marvel at his thoroughness.

"You run this name?" he asked Parnell.

"Yeah, the guy's a hubcap artist from way back."

Gunderson shined his light up the vent pipe. "How old is he?"

"Eighteen."

"Looks embarrassed, doesn't he?" said Gunderson. "All red in the face."

"You'd be embarrassed, too."

"Is his ass sticking out of the roof?"

"No, just his shoes."

"Probably ought to get some pictures up there, too," sighed Gunderson. "Call the wagon yet?"

"They're on their way. I've got a ladder on the back wall."

"God, I hate ladders."

"Yeah, I know what you mean," said Parnell. "Ladders are for firemen."

"So how'd the front door get broken?"

"We thought maybe he had a partner."

"Nothing else disturbed?" asked Gunderson.

"Nope."

They made their way back through the forest of cowgirl lingerie, Texas belt buckles, and Jesse James dusters to the front door. Gunderson photographed the dead burglar's shoes protruding from the roof, fingerprinted an air conditioner that the guy had climbed on to gain access to the roof of The Horseshoe store, and took some general coverage shots of the place. While they waited for the Medical Examiner's team to haul the deceased out of the roof hole, Gunderson lit a cigarette in the front parking lot.

"Did you see the $4,000 hat?" asked Hoatlin.

"Yeah," replied Gunderson. "Looked like a fucking cowboy hat. Jeez-fuckin-Louise, Teddy. It's just a hat with a fucking feather in it from a fag fucking Mexican cross-dressing goat-roper's store."

"Yeah, but for $4,000?"

"Whatever . . ."

"Do you think that's what the burglar was after?" Hoatlin asked.

"Who knows? Who cares? One less fucking Male/Usual burglar. His mama will say he was looking for his lost keys or something."

"God, you're grumpy tonight, Gunny."

"I was asleep when they gave me this call," Gunderson lied. He wanted to get back to the Edvard Munch book. He took a full-body shot and a full-face close-up of the dead burglar once they had gotten him off the roof.

"We found a screwdriver inside the vent with him," said the M.E.'s field investigator. "You want it?"

"Nah," said Gunderson. "Positional asphyxiation on this one?"

"Yeah, looks like it."

Gunderson reconsidered. "Ah shit. I better take that screwdriver. The dicks will pitch a fit if we don't have a burglar tool of some sort."

After the morgue wagon was gone and the store owner had boarded up his broken door, Gunderson put away his camera and notebook and walked over to Pridemore at the curb.

"Hey, Jack. A heads-up for you. We've got a blue plastic cup downtown that your Captain brought in. The lab made your palmprint on it. There's no report yet, but it's coming in a day or so."

"A plastic cup?"

"Yeah, I guess Maddox found it in a cruiser and wants to know who's been leaving litter in their cars."

"No kidding," said Pridemore. "Amazing."

"Doesn't prove anything," Gunderson told him. "It's just a cup and just a palmprint. Doesn't mean you bought it. Doesn't mean you drank alcohol or human blood or liquid heroin from it or anything."

"It doesn't even mean I left it in the car."

"Exactly. Doesn't prove shit, but the Captain wanted it done anyway."

"Maddox is *that* kind of Captain."

"They all are. Just thought you'd want to know."

"Thanks, Gunny."

"No problem. It don't prove fuck-all."

"I hope not," replied Pridemore. "Hey, did you get to see that $4,000 hat in there?"

"Yeah. Great hat." Jeez!

The middle-aged woman in the fluffy lilac dress and the white canvas shoes was squirming around on the hard plastic chair. Her groin was full of The Grunge, of course, and it made her itch and twitch. The Grunge, along with the herpes, the gonorrhea, and the heroin addiction, made Cynthia Jester unable to sit still in the prosecutor's waiting room. Her coarse black hair, pulled back in a ponytail and tied with a scarf, seemed to fit her little girl outfit. Her wildly crooked front teeth and her enormous breasts, pushing out the lilac fabric in all directions, made the whole effect rather comic. It was the best that Prosecutor Don Van Dorn had been able to come up with on such short notice. Pridemore knew all about Cynthia and kept his distance at the far end of the row of chairs. He tried to entertain himself with an old *People* magazine, having found little else of interest in the stack of hockey, home decorating, and health magazines on the little table in the corner.

MAD BADGES

Cynthia, whose birth name was Bad Orange Hair, was a half-blooded Abnaki Indian who always told people she was Cherokee, because no one had ever heard of the Abnaki tribe. She was named after her mother, a Canadian prostitute who had tried to dye her hair red with mixed results, and had later taken the name of one of her mom's boyfriends. The name "Cynthia" was her mother's attempt at whitening her daughter's lineage after their move to Nashville, Tennessee, but the daughter had found that pretending to be a Cherokee woman had its selling points. She had dropped out of a junior high school in Baltimore and had struck out on her own with a black pimp named Lawrence Whitehouse. She had worked the Kansas City-Phoenix-San Diego-Syracuse circuit with Whitehouse and three of his Chinese girls, until the night he got shot to death by a crazy nigger in Evansville, Indiana. After several changes in pimps, one of whom was actually white, Cynthia had landed at the corner of Denton Avenue and Perez, where she had worked ever since.

She religiously utilized lubricated condoms with customers. The problem, of course, had been all the unprotected sex with all the pimps, who flatly refused to wear condoms, and all their friends and gambling buddies and dealers and cousins. And their orchestra. Cynthia had the clap, crabs, yeast, and lice. She knew about her H.I.V. infection but not about the hepatitis or the breast cancer. She drank wine when she couldn't find marijuana and smoked marijuana when she couldn't find crack cocaine and smoked crack when she couldn't afford the heroin, which was most of the time now. Cynthia had been beaten with wire hangers, burned with cigarettes, and raped by scores of angry psychotics. With all of that, her teeth bothered her most of the time and her ass bled regularly. So Cynthia Jester squirmed in the hard chair, uneasy in the lilac dress, and was the oldest looking 19-year-old that Pridemore had ever seen.

Cynthia had been in custody as a material witness for two weeks now, and she thought she was fat. She had always gained weight in jail, mainly due to the fact that she never ate anything more that Cheese Crispies and Red Pop when she was out on her own. So she was embarrassed by the silly-ass outfit they had made her wear as well as her weight gain. Cynthia did not know if the cop was there to watch her or what his role was in this case. Mr. Van Dorn, that bald, bearded prick from the Prosecutor's Office, had been pretty secretive about the whole thing. All he needed from her, he had said, was for her to testify—*truthfully*, he had emphasized—that a certain Michael Siranthony

Stovall had been her pimp for a few months three summers ago. That was it, he had assured her. That was all he needed. In exchange for her testimony, Van Dorn promised that he would speak on her behalf at her seventh drug possession trial.

Stovall was a five-time loser who was serving 20-to-30 for stabbing a crackhead to death in the July before last. This week, Prosecutor Van Dorn was trying Stovall for the three-year-old murder of a pizza delivery driver. He needed Cynthia Jester to place Stovall in the area of Denton Avenue and Magnolia in the month of the murder and needed Pridemore to testify about a .32 caliber pistol he had taken off of Stovall on a traffic stop a year later. Pridemore, who could barely remember the Stovall traffic stop or the gun involved, was studying a copy of his written report. Van Dorn's other witnesses were as shaky as Cynthia.

"You're my best witness here, Officer," Van Dorn had told Pridemore, once he had gotten him into his office and out of Cynthia Jester's earshot.

"I'll have this report up there on the stand?" asked Pridemore.

"You bet!" said the enthusiastic attorney. "You can't read from it unless the defense attorney asks you to, but you can use it to refresh your memory."

"Great report, too, Pridemore," said the detective who was leaning against the bookshelf behind Van Dorn's desk. "We couldn't swing it without that report."

Pridemore knew all about Van Dorn. He was a bald and confused and one of the most irritatingly hyperactive members of the Prosecutor's Office. He always told you that you were his best witness. He told everybody that. Every case was a hugely dramatic undertaking. Van Dorn was always the star, no matter how muddled the case. Pridemore knew that, as soon as he left the office, Van Dorn would tell the detective what a worthless witness he was. He glad-handed you into his office, bum-rushed you out of his office, and belittled your contribution to *his* great case afterward. Everybody was a lousy witness and all the evidence was shaky as hell on a Van Dorn case. A Don Van Dorn criminal case was always won, not by his crappy witnesses and his rotten evidence, but by his sheer talent as a prosecuting attorney. What Pridemore realized about Van Dorn, that the breathlessly eager detective didn't yet know, was that Van Dorn would even ridicule the detective's contribution to the case, once the thing was over. If Van

MAD BADGES

Dorn won, it was *his* win. If he lost, it was *your* fault. There was no real winning when Van Dorn was in charge.

"Yes," agreed Van Dorn, "it's a very thorough report. Very crucial to this case."

"Good," said Pridemore, "because I don't remember this guy at all."

"Not a problem!" cried Van Dorn.

"No problem at all," the detective assured him, bobbing his head.

"The arrest record and the jail print card tell us who you arrested that night," explained Van Dorn. "No big deal." Pridemore knew it would only become a big deal later, if Van Dorn lost this case. Then it would be the patrol officer's fault for not remembering the name and face of a man he had arrested on a traffic stop years before. It would be Pridemore's fault then. Actually, Pridemore didn't care very much who won the case, so long as he could get home and get some sleep.

"You're still working Nights?" the detective asked sympathetically, knowing full well that they had dragged Pridemore out of bed to testify.

"Yeah."

"That's rough," agreed Van Dorn. "We'll try to get you on and off in ten minutes tops."

"Good," said Pridemore, knowing that Van Dorn had pulled that ten-minute figure out of his ass.

"I've got a lady-of-the-evening to put on the stand just before you," winked Van Dorn.

"Fine," Pridemore replied wearily.

"In fact, I've got to go ask her something. I'll be back in a sec." The prosecutor snatched up some papers and left the room.

Pridemore rubbed his eyes and looked at his old report again.

"You know," began the detective, apparently uncomfortable with the silence between them, "we're not actually *after* Stovall." He left that startling announcement to hang in the air momentarily for emphasis. When the uniformed cop failed to either ask a question or show any interest, the detective continued. "Stovall is already doing a 20-to-30 rap downstate for one murder. We want him to tell us about a gang shooting at Isabel and Franklin from six years ago. He refuses to cooperate on that thing, so we brought up this case to give us a little leverage on that one. If we can get a conviction here, we can offer a reduced sentence for his testimony in the gang murder. That's why this case today is important." The detective was still waiting for even a glimmer of interest on Pridemore's face. "Maybe you remember the double murder at the Bernardo's Chicken place on Franklin?" Pridemore massaged his temples, his eyes shut to the office's dead fluorescent lights.

"I really don't give a *fuck* about your little murder case, either this one or the old one, son," Pridemore said finally. "Some day, when you've got a little more time on The Job, you'll understand that none of this means shit to a tree."

"But..."

"Not a damn thing. One civic improvement homicide, more or less. No sense getting your panties in a bunch over a routine drug murder. It'll wear on your soul."

The detective was thinking of worn out shoe soles.

"Just keep that Sherlock Holmes B.S. to yourself," said Pridemore. He got up and walked out, leaving behind an enthusiastic detective who couldn't understand this lack of interest. This was, after all, a Murder Case.

Out in the waiting area, Van Dorn was huddled with Cynthia Jester, going over some fine points of her invaluable testimony. She was nodding listlessly. Van Dorn was sitting leg-to-leg with her, pointing at an Incident Report as he spoke, apparently unaware of The Grunge, the lice, the hepatitis, and all the rest.

"I'm going out to stretch my legs in the hall," Pridemore told them. Cynthia looked up at the old cop.

"Good! Fine! Uh, great!" Van Dorn's hand made a waving gesture. "But don't go too far. When we need you, we'll *really* need you here."

Pridemore looked back. The old cop and the old whore smiled briefly at each other.

"So it's three o'clock in the morning," Buck was saying, "and these two cops from South find this dead nigger on the sidewalk."

Pridemore and Hoatlin had heard this particular cop legend, so they sat quietly drinking their East & West Café coffee. They had even heard Buck Tyler's version of this legend before. Pridemore had heard it as "dead Mexican in an alley," "dead nigger on the corner," and even "dead Puerto Rican pimp in a phone booth." Hoatlin, too, had heard it any number of ways, but Buck always started it with "dead nigger on the sidewalk." Parnell had heard it once or twice before and was vague on the details. Parnell's rookie, Mimi, had never heard The Legend of the South Parkway Overpass before. She sat in rapt attention, like all rookies do, and tried to grasp the special meaning of every word, as rookies try to do with all war stories. She tried to absorb every nuance and inflection in her brain sponge, as all rookies tried to do with parables. And she let her coffee get cold. Rookies searched for the moral in every story, that critical morsel of truth that might someday save their lives. They had spent so much time getting yelled at and chewed out in the Academy, and so much time being grilled and tested during their training phases, that their sensory reception was in Ultra Highly Tuned Mode by the time they hit the streets. Which was why Buck was telling the story now. He had free rein with Mimi The Rookie's brain cells. He could shape her whole future with a swipe of his brush on the blank canvas of her mind. She would never forget what she heard here tonight, they all knew. They had all heard one version or another of the tale when they were rookies, and none of them had ever forgotten it. The moral of the story was debatable, of course. Some received it as a Sermon on the Mount, while others heard it as a long, rambling joke. The real key was what you did with the information once you had received it, how you incorporated it into your wealth of knowledge or your collection of bad cop jokes. That was the key to all war stories. The key to telling a parable as blatantly illegal as The Legend of the South Parkway Overpass was to forget the names of the participants and wait until the statute of limitations had run out. That way no one ever got in trouble for it, and you could change the details to fit your particular audience. Had Mimi The Rookie been a black female, Buck might have begun the whole thing with two cops finding "a dead Mexican on the sidewalk." It was not a story set in concrete. Or perhaps it was.

"So it's really late, and these guys aren't in the mood to take a D.O.A. report with the detectives around and supervisors and everything. They talk it over. Nobody around. No windows looking down on them or anything. They decide they don't want to deal with this bullshit on their shift, right?"

Mimi nodded. Hoatlin grinned.

Buck continued, on a roll. "So they look around and see that no one's watching, and they grab this fucking guy and throw him in their trunk. And they take off with this dead nigger in their cruiser."

Hoatlin had once heard the story told with a frozen corpse in place of the usual "dead nigger on the sidewalk." Pridemore had once heard it with a headless body, probably in a Halloween retelling of the tale.

When Parnell had first heard it as a rookie, the story was pretty much the same as it was now, mainly because it had been Buck Tyler telling it the earlier time, too.

"So they can't exactly bury the fucking thing, and they don't want to jam another cop in the Department with all the paperwork, so they drive out to Berwyndale, out by the old airport, and they find this nice quiet factory. They look around. It's all clear. They open the trunk and drag out this dead nigger and drop him behind this dumpster. They shut the trunk and take off like a raped ape back to town. The problem is—see?—that there's these two Berwyndale patrolmen sleeping in their car behind the next building. They see this City cruiser go back there, lights out and shit, and they wonder, you know, what the fuck is this? So the Berwyndale coppers go back to the dumpster and they find the dead nigger right where our guys dropped him. Now—ya know how much those guys in Berwyndale hate fucking niggers—they were mad as hell. They called a supervisor, and he says, 'Let the City take care of their own nigger bodies,' and orders his guys to take it back. So these Berwyndale fuckers load up this dead nigger in their back seat and drive back into South Precinct and fucking throw him out down by South Bryden and Lattimore somewhere, just dump it in the fucking street."

Pridemore had thrown out Mimi The Rookie's cold coffee and brought her a fresh cup. Magda, who always paid attention when Teddy Hoatlin was in the place, listened to the story from behind the kitchen door. She, too, had heard the story before, but she couldn't judge its meaning.

"So now it's like five in the fucking morning. This South Precinct Sergeant is just about to go home when he comes across this dead nigger in the middle of the fucking road there. He doesn't really want to deal with the fucking thing either, so he calls one of his two-man cars over to take the thing down to West Ferry and slide it in the river. Well, one of the guys in the car that shows up already *knows* about the other City guys who found the dead nigger in the first place, the guys who dumped him in Berwyndale, see? So he calls them down, and they come over to Lattimore and Bryden and see their dead nigger in the middle of the street, and they're shitting bricks, thinking their ass is grass with the Sergeant and I.A. and shit. Well, once the South Sergeant has told them all how he doesn't want to deal with this dead body so late on his Watch, they come clean and tell him how they originally found the body on *our* side and dumped it in Berwyndale, and how somehow those fuckers in Berwyndale found it and brought the goddamn thing back into town."

Parnell liked the part about the Sergeant's involvement. It was one of the few stories with a supervisor portrayed as a stand-up guy.

"Well, the Sergeant is pissed Big Time now. He doesn't like the Ramp Rangers from the fucking State Police and he can't stand the County Mounties with their fag white cruisers. But this Sergeant really, really, absolutely *hates* the fucking small time cops from fucking Berwyndale, who gave his wife a speeding ticket for five miles over the limit one time or some shit. So it's like about 5:30 now. They put the dead nigger back in their car and they all get up on the South Parkway and head west, the Sergeant included. They get way out to Berwyndale again, where South Parkway ends and turns into the West 53, okay?"

Mimi The Rookie nodded, even though she had no idea where West 53 was.

"Out by the old airport," said Parnell helpfully.

"No, past that," said Buck. "It's where the Parkway goes high over the Beltline and is coming down, so it's like five stories high at that point. Well this is right over downtown fucking Berwyndale. Their main street there. It's called Main or Elm or some shit."

"Pasqual Avenue," said Pridemore.

"Right, that's it. So these South guys, Sergeant and all, stop on the South Parkway overpass that's like four stories high over sleepy fucking Berwyndale. No one's around, okay? Fucking small-town cops are all asleep and shit. So the City guys get this dead fucking nigger out of their trunk again and—all together now!—they heave this stiff motherfucker off the overpass. So it's four stories down, right? Fucker hits the center line in the middle of fucking Pasqual Avenue and blows up like a fucking jelly donut. Brain, blood, guts and shit everywhere. And the South Precinct Sergeant says, 'Let 'em try to bring *that* shit back onto our side of the line!' And they all get the fuck out of there and back to the City. So the fucking Berwyndale cops find this mess on their main street when the sun comes up, and there's not much they can do about it, see? They can't exactly say they saw the City cops dump it in the first place. What are they gonna say? They saw it and took it back to the City, but those mean City guys brought it back? So they say nothing, right? The Berwyndale detectives put it on their books as an unsolved or a suicide jumper or some shit. But no one talks, and the South Sergeant and his guys get home on time, and that's the name of that tune." Buck grinned at all the cops at the table.

Mimi smiled, too, although she had been waiting for a different kind of ending to the parable. Like a moral to the story or something. It showed—What?—the value of teamwork or the difference between City cops and suburban cops? She sipped her newly cold coffee and speculated. Maybe it was about Getting Out On Time. Or how to be resourceful when faced with a recurring problem situation. Or the correct response to finding a dead black male subject in your patrol area. Or how some Sergeants could actually be trusted to come up with the right answer once in a while. Or how to solve a problem so it didn't come back to bug you all shift. Mimi wasn't sure. She would have to turn that one over in her fresh rookie brain and sort it out. In any case, it had been an entertaining tale, she thought.

Later she would talk to Training Officer Parnell in their cruiser and ask him: "What was that story all about?"

And he would say, "What do you *think* it's about?"

She hated when they answered a question with another question. All rookies hated that.

It was all about Paperwork Reduction. As the fresh air of springtime settled into the foul heat of summer, the officers of The Height Night Watch shifted their paperwork reduction efforts into high gear. It wasn't a matter of cutting corners; it was a matter of survival. You couldn't spend half your shift on some chickenshit call when the City was falling down all around you. Some things you just had to let slide.

Hoatlin and Pridemore had a Disorderly Person call first thing out of the box. They rolled up on The Four Corners Tavern at Filmore and Evers. There was a drunk Mexican in the doorway, arguing with a bartender. The bartender, seeing that help had arrived, started getting surlier with the drunk. Hoatlin told the bartender to go inside.

"What's your first name, Son?" Pridemore asked the drunk. He had left his report pad in the car. Hoatlin had even left the cruiser running. It was paperwork reduction night.

"I don't gotta tell you my name," the drunk said.

"Just your first name."

"I don't have to tell you SSShit." There was a spray of beer spit.

"Okay, then I'll call you Poindexter," said Pridemore. Teddy Hoatlin, who was now one step above the drunk on the steps of The Four Corners, was sizing up Poindexter for a blow to the kidneys.

"I don't gotta tell you fuckin' cops jack shit!"
"I know that, Poindexter."
"My name's not Poin-dogger," said the drunk.
"Then what is your first name?" Pridemore asked, polite as hell.
"Jerry. But I don't have to tell you shit-else."
"That's fine," said Pridemore. He leaned into the drunk, crowding him to the edge of the steps. "Listen, Jerry. Hey, Jerry, are you listening to me?"
"I can hear ya," said Jerry The Drunk.
"Hey, Jerry, I've got a message for you, man."
"I can hear good. You're pushing me."
"We're not pushing you *yet*, Jerry," Hoatlin said from behind the drunk.
"Listen, Jerry," Pridemore told him, leaning closer. "I've got a message for you. Are you listening, Jerry?"
"I'm listening!"
"Here's the message, Jerry. GET THE FUCK OUTTA HERE NOW."
"Did you hear that okay, Jerry?" asked Hoatlin close to the drunk's ear. "Did you understand that message?"
"Uhhh . . ."
"Let's review, shall we, Jerry?" said Pridemore. "Here it is once more. GET THE FUCK OUTTA HERE NOW."
"I don't have to . . ."
"That's it. That's the whole message. We're done."
"Maybe he didn't understand the message," said Hoatlin. They were so close to him now that Jerry couldn't even raise his arms.
"You can't arrest me. I ain't done nothing."
"We're not going to arrest you, Jerry," Pridemore explained. "If you don't get out of here in the next four seconds, we're going to beat you down like a rented mule and stuff you into that fucking trash barrel over there."
"But you can't . . ."
"Just watch us," Hoatlin interrupted.
"Three, two, one . . ."
Jerry The Drunk lurched off the step. He looked for the trash barrel that the cop had mentioned, but couldn't see it. He saw the cops coming down the steps toward him and moved up the sidewalk. At the corner, he mustered up enough courage to shout something back

at them, but promptly fell on his ass. Rising with difficulty Jerry The Drunk staggered away into the night.

No report. No nothing. Clear.

Next drunk. First name: Eddie. Pueblo Lounge on South Hawthorne. Barmaid said he pinched her. Doctor Hoatlin examined the injury and determined that she would live to serve another beer. Eddie didn't want to go. Eddie didn't understand the message they had for him. They put him in the car. Eddie didn't want to go home and wouldn't tell them his last name. Eighteen blocks up Newton to Market, and they stopped in the parking lot of a closed hardware store. New message: GET OUT. Eddie didn't understand the new message. They hauled him out and left him sitting in the dark.

No report. No nothing. Clear.

Next drunk. They knew his first name was "Lloyd," so they didn't have to ask. Bobbery Bar at Alexander and Racine. He got the message right away, having heard it before. He'd been inside a trash barrel before. Had once woken up in the middle of a golf course out in the suburbs. Lloyd said: "Thank you, Officers. Have a nice night." He left in a hurry.

No report. No nothing. Clear.

Next drunk. First name: Gary. Brixton Bar on Brixton. Gary seemed both drunk and high. The bartender said Gary had broken a potted plant. The bartender said he wanted to press charges. Hoatlin suggested that multiple trips down to the courthouse might not be worth his time. Gary didn't get the message. They took him to the same hardware store parking lot and kicked him out next to Eddie, who is now fast asleep.

No report. No nothing. Clear again.

Next drunk. First name: Maxine. Back at The Four Corners on Filmore and Evers. Maxine didn't get the message, too drunk to hear and too drunk to walk. They found her I.D., drove her to her apartment on Vanderbilt, and left her with her husband. He thanked them.

No report. No nothing. Clear for the next.

Next drunk. First name: Unknown. He had fallen asleep while waiting for the light to change at Kendall and Dudley. They positioned the cruiser's push bumpers against the front of the drunk's Lincoln, so that it wouldn't take off when they dislodged him from the brake pedal. He was a fat guy and was sleeping soundly. Pridemore nudged him over to the passenger side and parked the Lincoln at the curb.

Pridemore popped the trunk, locked the doors, dropped the guy's car keys in the trunk, slammed the lid, and drove off.
No report. No nothing. Clear again.
Next drunk. First name: Unknown. He had been trying to get into a closed party store on Cleveland Street. Zero message reception. Sgt. Gibson stopped by and helped them put him in the trash barrel. When he came out, he was in a much better mood and walked away quietly.
No report. No nothing. Clear.
"You guys really ought to *write* something once in a while," Sgt. Gibson told them, brushing off his uniform pants. "Your stats are gonna be too low at the end of the month."
"We will," Hoatlin promised.
"Thanks, Sarge," said Pridemore.
Next drunk. First name: Ernesto. Squeeze Inn bar at 1551 Conklin.

Deshawn McKenzie, black male, 23 years, dead of a single stab wound to the back, east of the main dance floor, The Marble Room, 3260 South Cramer Avenue. Everyone was reportedly outside of the bar except for The Marble Room employees, none of whom reportedly saw anything.

For two weeks in the summer, it was like old times again. The Department's Computer-Aided Dispatch system and the Mobile Date Terminal system in all the cruisers collapsed one Wednesday evening for no apparent reason. The Tech. Services people and the Communications people scrambled to save the whole thing. The hardware people blamed the software people. The software people said the hardware people weren't maintaining the system properly. The Police Union claimed the initial purchase of the C.A.D. software was irregular and that the City's Purchasing Department was receiving kickbacks for buying an inferior program. Someone said that parts had to be ordered from Egypt or Israel; they weren't sure which. Someone from the software company suggested that the dispatchers were typing too fast. It was the Crisis of the Month in the Tower.
On the street, you could tell the men from the boys. Anyone with twelve or more years on the job could remember a time without police

car computers. They had done it all with voice on the air back then. You never looked at a computer screen back then. The dispatcher told you to go to a Man-With-A-Gun call on Vanderbilt Street, and you just drove there and handled it. If the psychotic woman on the first floor of the Vanderbilt address was likely to cause you trouble, someone would warn you on the air about her and might even remember her name. You went where you had to go and did what you had to do, and you wrote it up only if you felt it needed to be written up, and there weren't any computer-generated call numbers to make you do otherwise. Cops with less than twelve years on the Department were frequently baffled. Where were the call-encoding boxes? Where were the log entry auto features? Where were the patrol sector designators? How could you route a follow-up incident report to a specified investigator? The young cops were lost without their auto-mapping displays. The old cops thought it was rich.

"We don't need no stinking computers!" was how Buck Tyler had expressed it.

"We used to do it all with our voice," Pridemore explained to a rookie. "You knew everybody in the Precinct and everybody in the surrounding Precincts by their voices. Someone could get on the air in South Precinct and say 'Hey, Jack. Watch out for that dog in the back yard on Newton Avenue.' You could tell by the tone of a Dispatcher's voice if she thought the call was bullshit or worthwhile. It was always like that before computers."

"I remember one time that Big Mark Rayburn called for back-up on a traffic arrest," said Hoatlin. "And his voice sounded worried. Well, that scared the shit out of everybody, because Big Mark was a giant. Muscles out to here. Tough as nails, an old ass-kicker from way back. So when a guy like that calls for help, your first thought is, Oh Shit, we're in for a brawl. People came flying in from three Precincts. It turned out, Rayburn had gotten a little guy out of a car, who had dope and a gun on him, and the guy started shouting about racism and white cops and shit, and a crowd formed. When it got to be about twenty upset people with poor attitudes, Big Mark called for help. Must have been about 14 cars there when I pulled up. The crowd went away, and Big Mark hooked up the bad guy with no problem. But cruisers kept showing up from all over the south end, just to see what kind of call would make Big Mark Rayburn's voice sound worried. It was like that back then. You did it with your voice."

It wasn't as if the Department's computers worked very well when they *were* working. Messages got sent or they didn't get sent. One day the Confirm Warrant button might not work. The next day the Vehicle Want button wouldn't work. Sometimes the whole system would work flawlessly for days at a time, then suddenly quit for no reason for a couple of hours, just to make you appreciate it. So the old timers spent the system's downtime enjoying the break, and the younger cops spent the time waiting anxiously for their screens to light up again.

When the rookie got lost on Sunday morning, it was a scary time for everyone. He started to call out a Traffic Stop, then shouted and went silent.

"Unit calling?" the Dispatcher asked after she had listened to dead air for a few moments.

"--three!" cried the rookie, jumping his mike.

"Unit calling?"

There was silence.

"Unit calling, what's your 20?"

Silence.

"Unit calling, what's your location?"

"I'm east," yelled the kid. "East of . . ."

Silence.

Pridemore thought it sounded like the new guy from Metro. Becky Carpenter thought it was one of Parnell's rookies. No one was sure.

"Unit calling, please identify."

The frustrating silence continued.

The Dispatcher was cool and calm, listening and thinking perfectly, her words brief but patient. She waited for a reply. They all waited. The whole South end was silent.

"Unit calling, what's your location?"

The words were garbled. The kid said something about "three at gunpoint." The tension ratcheted up another notch.

"Unit calling, please identify."

"David Three!" moaned the kid. Which meant he was a Metro car on the wrong channel. The Metro Units headed south. The Mercer Heights cars drifted east. The South cars headed north and east. They rolled down their windows to listen for sirens. The inexperienced ones started racing to the undisclosed location, confusing the experienced ones who were listening for the kid's siren. They looked for his overheads. They cranked up the volume on their radios.

"David Three," asked the Dispatcher calmly, "what's your location?"

More silence.

The guy could be hamburger by now, thought Hoatlin.

"David Three, copy?"

Silence.

"David Three, Badge 921?" called the Dispatcher. They had looked up his name and badge number. The Metro Units were crawling all over his Patrol Area, shining spotlights up and down alleys.

"David Three, repeat your 20."

Nothing.

"David Three, repeat your location."

Silence from the kid.

"David Three, what's--"

"Eastern!" the rookie cried. "Bay!"

Every cop on the South end tried to decipher it. Eastern and Bay ran parallel. Both were north-south avenues. Bay was the easternmost avenue in Mercer Heights. If he was east of Bay, he was in his own area, Metro, or in the upper section of South Precinct. It was hard to tell. The South Precinct units started combing the alleys and side streets north from 67th Street. A couple Downtown units joined the Metro Precinct search. Some diehards from Central raced all the way through Mercer Heights to Metro.

"David Three, state your location, please." A slightly pleading edge came into the Dispatcher's voice.

"I'm in an alley," the kid yelled. "I can see a barrel factory."

Minds raced. There was a barrel factory in South Precinct, H & W Containers, something like that. There was a barrel and canister sealant plant on Cleveland. Two Dispatchers searched the Yellow Pages. Veteran cops searched their memories. Other rookies thought about how their Training Officers had stressed geography. It wasn't a joke now. They were glad it wasn't them.

"David Three, repeat your location."

Nothing.

"David Three, repeat your 20."

There was an unintelligible squawk, then silence.

"Can you see the freeway?" asked a Metro Sergeant in frustration.

"East of . . ." The kid was cut off.

Silence. Terror. Hadn't he said that he had three suspects at gunpoint?

"David Three, please clarify."
Another squawk, more silence.
"I see an orange water tower!" cried the rookie.
Minds raced, headaches and memories.
Pridemore floored it. Carpenter banged her head on the roof as the cruiser leaped across the railroad crossing at South Sloan. The car launched out onto Evers and squealed diagonally across a parking lot to Boyd.
"He means the storage place on Boyd!" shouted Pridemore.
"DeVille Storage?" Becky knew the place.
"Yeah!"
"What the fuck's he doing over there?"
"We'll ask him if we find him," snarled Pridemore over the whine of the engine.
They screamed up Boyd to Carmicle and found DeVille Packing and Storage. The south entrance was dark and locked. Pridemore swung the cruiser around the back to an open gate on Dunham. They spotted the kid's parking lights between a warehouse and an overgrown hurricane fence.
"Over here! Over here!" The rookie was screaming and waving his flashlight, the gun in his right hand. He had three nervous Puerto Rican males on the ground, one wearing a pair of handcuffs hooked to his left wrist.
"You relax now, hear?" Pridemore said to the first one, nudging his pistol into the guy's nose. Pridemore snapped the loose cuff from the first suspect's wrist to the second suspect's ankle. Becky Carpenter handcuffed the wrist of the third suspect to the fence.
"One of them got away," said the rookie.
"You look like shit," Carpenter told him, looking at his torn sleeve and muddy pants.
"Three Charlie Nine," called Pridemore.
"Go ahead, Charlie Nine," said the Dispatcher.
"He's at Carmicle and Boyd. DeVille Packing and Storage. Entrance is from the east on Dunham. Everything is ten-four. Three in custody. One still out on foot."
"Ten-four, Charlie Nine," replied the Dispatcher. "Carmicle and Boyd."
They patted down the suspects for weapons and looked in their old Buick. Pridemore told the rookie to put his gun away. Becky backed

up their cruiser and switched on the overheads so that the other units could find them.

"I thought I was on Bay," the rookie said weakly.

"You're on Boyd, kid," said Pridemore. "In The Heights. Is something wrong with your radio?"

"Is something wrong with your fucking goddamn brain?" Becky Carpenter asked the kid.

Pridemore knew there would be time for that. "You all right, son?"

"I fucked up," said the rookie.

Pridemore nodded. "You fucked up. But are you okay?"

"Yeah, I think so."

"Think so?" said Becky. She was unimpressed. "*Think* so. Shit!"

The other cruisers started arriving in droves. The kid's Sergeant told the Dispatcher that no more cars were needed, but they kept coming anyway. The fourth suspect was long gone, but there were cruisers out to find him and kick his ass anyway. The Metro cops apologized to the Heights cops and the South cops. In the spotlights and strobes, Pridemore recognized a Central officer he hadn't seen in years, and they got to chatting. When the Metro Sergeant was done chewing out the rookie for his fuck-up, the other veterans started in.

What the fuck was he doing in The Heights?

What the fuck was he making a stop for with four assholes in the car all by himself?

What the fuck was he thinking?

What the fuck was he using for a fucking brain?

Where the fuck did he learn about radio traffic?

Why the fuck didn't he know his geography?

What the fuck kind of cowboy did he think he was?

Who the fuck taught him to handcuff prisoners?

Who the fuck makes a traffic stop behind a fucking factory?

Why the fuck didn't he call for back-up?

Where the fuck had he learned to jump his mike like that?

Where the fuck was his common sense?

The arrested Puerto Ricans got bounced around a little harder than normal, until the tension passed. Once a translator arrived, they were able to identify themselves and even the one who got away. This information was broadcast for the other units.

A Metro Lieutenant arrived and thanked Jack and Becky for finding his rookie. Soon the Lieutenant was chewing out the kid, too. Across

MAD BADGES 161

the whole South end, rookies huddled with their map books, studying the streets and avenues, glad someone else had stepped in it so badly.

"If the computers were working . . ." a young cop started to say.

"Computers don't help you if you don't know where you ass is," snapped Becky Carpenter.

"But they're talking about putting Global Positioning devices on the cruisers," said the Metro Sergeant.

"That's just so they can keep track of how many of us are at the donut shop," replied Pridemore.

"Still don't help you if you can't find your ass!" said Carpenter.

"Friggin rookies," said the Sergeant.

Alvin and Trudy Hoskins were trying to kill each other. Having been kicked out of their Converse Avenue apartment by the landlord, they were starting to destroy their new apartment on Summit Avenue four blocks away. The crime statistics for Converse dropped off suddenly as the call volume for Summit increased. Alvin said Trudy had thrown him out and had broken a lamp. Trudy said Alvin had taken her welfare check and spent it on beer. Tyler told Trudy to go to bed and sleep it off. Carpenter told Alvin to find another place to stay for the night.

Richard "Dix" Sherwin was an extraordinary loser. He had telephoned his ex-wife to tell her he was going to kill himself, but she hadn't been home. So he told his eight-year-old son, Patrick, to pass on the message for him. Patrick had cried when he relayed the message to his mother, and she had called the cops. Buck and Sgt. Wheeler had banged on the second floor apartment door for a long time before kicking it in. Pridemore had found the guy hanging in the bathroom doorway, his feet just touching the floor. He was wearing cut-off jeans. His chest and beer gut, a maze of inter-connecting Satanic tattoos and blue panthers, was exposed. His feet were full of blood and coated with the dried stool that had loosened from his bowels. Photographs of his wife and kids from happier days were neatly wrapped in plastic lunch bags and protruded from the waistline of his shorts. Dix had killed off all of his beer, smoked up all of his dope, and had found himself an orange extension cord from the bed of his pickup parked out back. His eyes were closed and his head was tilted sharply to the right.

The flash from Gunderson's camera lit up the dingy apartment. "You say this fucker called his kid first and told him he was committing suicide?"

"Yeah," replied Pridemore.

"What a complete ASShole," said Gunderson.

"Father of the fucking Year," added Buck Tyler.

"He looks a little taller than the picture on his driver's license," commented Mimi The Rookie.

"He *is* a little taller now, Dear," explained Gunderson.

Two items crossed Edith Huckabee's desk on the same morning. They had been carefully paper-clipped together when they had arrived on the City mail cart, but had become separated somehow in the mail sorting processed. Edith was Deputy Chief Griswold's executive assistant and prided herself with the efficient dissemination of the Department's mail, memos, and minutiae both into and out of Griswold's domain. Normally, none of the morning's mail would have presented a problem to Ms. Huckabee, but that morning, Edith was having hot flashes, and her son-in-law had lost his third job in a year, and she suspected she was being replaced by a mere Office Assistant 3 from the Administrative Services secretarial pool. So Edith couldn't really be blamed for the mix-up.

The first item was a copy of a letter from a citizen addressed to the Chief of Police. Such letters were known in administrative circles as "Cit. Comps," which stood for both "citizen complaint" and "citizen compliment." They were almost always addressed to Chief Pearson's office, but they almost never made it there. All Cit-Comps went through the desk of one Beth Anne Delano, an assistant to one of the Assistants on Chief Pearson's staff. It was Beth Anne's job to decipher a Cit-Comp, determine if it was a complaint or a compliment, mail back a generic letter of concern or thanks from the Office of The Chief of Police, and to figure out what officer or officers were involved in the problem or the wonderful police work. The back of such a letter was date-stamped, assigned a Cit-Comp number, and marked with the Precinct name, officers' names, and badge numbers. The envelope containing the letter was attached to the back, so as not to cover up the officer information, and a two-sided copy was made. This method provided documentation of the letter's postmark and recorded the envelope's return address for those citizens too stupid to write their return addresses on the face of the letter itself. Beth Anne would then file the original letter and envelope in the Cit-Comp file and send the copy on to the appropriate Precinct Captain for verification and documentation.

The Cit-Comps arriving in Beth Anne's in-box were about evenly split between compliment and complaints. The favorable Cit-Comps were generally written by upstanding citizens who genuinely appreciated something that a member of the Department had done for them. This might be finding someone's dog or daughter, changing someone's flat tire, generally frowned upon but tolerated by City leaders who saw it as a possible exposure to liability, or some other kindness. The negative Cit-Comps were generally routine claims of racism, brutality, rudeness, or harassment and often contained phrases like "fascist police," "corrupt cops," or "filthy bastards." It was the prevailing opinion in the Department that negative Cit-Comps would far outnumber positive ones if more of the people doing the griping knew how to write or could afford a postage stamp. There were, of course, the letters so torturously composed that not even Beth Anne Delano could figure out whether they were negatives or positives. And there were always the meticulously lettered missives, sent by the obviously insane, that spoke of aliens in police uniforms, cops poisoning the water supply, and other international and intergalactic conspiracies, like the one from the guy who claimed to have been "teleported into a garbage can by your Gestapo Martians." Hundreds of such letters arrived each month on Beth Anne Delano's desk. She had written "J. Pridemore, Badge 1659, Mercer Heights" on the backside of this particular Cit-Comp.

The letter had arrived in a pink greeting card envelope. There was a return address of 2263 South Cramer in Mercer Heights. The block letters were drawn in a third-grader's scrawl, many of them in upper case. The message was from a Mexican woman named Anita Gonzales, who wanted to thank a police officer whose name she misspelled as "J. Pridemare." Officer "Pridemare" had apparently saved her from some kind of beating, had found some teeth that had somehow been knocked out of her head, and had taken her to a hospital in his police car to get the teeth put back into her head, and she had wanted the Police Chief to know how very much she appreciated this act of kindness. She said she had not known that teeth could be put back once they were knocked out. She said her teeth were fine now. She said her cousin was helping her write this letter, because her English was no good. She said she was moving to an apartment in the suburbs to get out of her bad neighborhood, but just wanted to say thanks before she left. Beth Anne Delano had figured it sounded like a favorable letter, which was a rarity for the outgoing bin for Mercer Heights Precinct, and had sent it on to Captain Maddox.

The two-part letter that had come back up the pipeline from Mercer Heights included the Captain's initials and the original Incident Report number for the Anita Gonzales call. Paper-clipped to the copy of the favorable Cit-Comp was an Internal Affairs complaint by Captain Maddox about the officer's Unauthorized Use Of A Department Vehicle to transport a female subject, which violated the Department's Manual of Procedure, Section 12, Part B, Subsection IV, as regards "Proper Use and Permission to Use City-Owned and Operated Vehicles." The Captain had, in fact, circled and underlined the sentence in Anita Gonzales's letter that mentioned Pridemore taking her to a hospital in his patrol car. Attached to the back of the Captain's I.A. complaint was a copy of the original Incident Report.

So, by the time the paper clip came off in Edith Huckabee's in-box, there was no way that she could have known that the complimentary Cit-Comp with the Captain's initials on it and the Internal Affairs with Captain Maddox's signature under it were supposed to be all one package. Edith initialed the favorable letter and sent it on to the Department's Awards Committee, which was not actually a committee at all, but a Clerk Typist on the Chief's staff. Edith was feeling a hot flash coming on as she picked up the Internal Affairs complaint from Captain Maddox. It was Deputy Chief Griswold's standing order that Edith Huckabee sign his name to all Internal Affairs complaints, okaying them for investigation, no matter how unfounded or bizarre. Edith signed Griswold's name to the complaint form, Incident Report attached, and sent it on to the Internal Affairs Unit. Then she made herself a cup of herbal tea.

Evan Hodges, black male, 25 years, dead of multiple gunshot wounds to the chest, near the west entrance of The Marble Room, 3260 South Cramer Avenue. Hodges had been a bouncer at the bar for almost a year. Barry Hodges, brother of the deceased, thought that Hodges was killed in retaliation for an earlier shooting in which Evan killed a subject named Robert Lafnear in self-defense. Another bouncer reported having heard the shots, but said he didn't see anything.

There was a reason that rookies were never assigned to ride with Buck Tyler. Almost never. Actually, there were numerous reasons, of course, but chiefly among them was that Buck himself hated the kinds of questions that rookies tended to ask. Like, Why didn't we arrest that man we saw Urinating-in-Public in Bendix Park? Or, Why did we start a shoving match with the guy who only sassed us in the Fraiser Projects? How did you know the woman in the red bathrobe was lying about the sexual assault? Or, How could you tell that the burned Chrysler was not really a stolen car but at all, but had been traded for dope by the registered owner? Why did you throw that drunk driver's car keys into the weeds on Conklin?
Sergeants Gibson, Reed, Wheeler, and especially Sgt. Petty understood what havoc Buck could wreak on the psyche of an impressionable rookie officer. One eight-hour shift with Tyler could set a rookie back months in his training, virtually destroying his esprit de corps, and render him useless as a promotable resource. Rookies mistakenly assigned to Buck's care, either through oversight or lack of personnel, were frequently scarred for life, their enthusiasm for a police career in tatters.
So when Sgt. Petty told Buck to quit bitching about the Department's vehicles and take what was left and Sgt. Reed told a rookie named Steve to quit whining about his Training Officer being

out sick for the night and find himself a patrolmen, Buck Tyler became a temporary Training Officer. The kid had barely got his door closed, when Buck floored the cruiser and roared out of the parking lot.

"What about our vehicle checklist?" Steve The Rookie cried out in alarm.

"Checklist?"

"The pre-patrol vehicle checklist."

"You can do that later," Buck told him.

"It's supposed to be done before we start operating the vehicle."

"Whatever. Son, checklists are for *fags*!"

"Oh," said the rookie.

Buck turned north on Central, cut off a pickup in the right lane, and veered off to the left. He took Central up to Belle River Boulevard and swung the cruiser east again.

"Don't you ever complete a pre-patrol checklist?" Steve The Rookie asked gently.

"Nah. I got all my shit. You got all your shit, right? Badge, gun, flares, whistle, condoms, right?"

The rookie mentally ticked off the items. "I don't know if we have a full supply of road flares in the trunk, sir."

"We'll have to wing it. And quit calling me 'Sir.' I work for a living." Buck swerved south on Sloan, waiting for that first call and wondering where to eat lunch.

"I don't have a Recruit Evaluation form for you," Steve The Rookie said apologetically. "My usual Training Officer is Officer Parnell, and he usually brings the evaluations."

"No, I don't have one either."

"Oh...okay."

"That's a checklist sort of thing, right?"

"Well, kind of, yes."

"And checklists are for *fags*, right?"

"Okay."

"Do I look like a fag to you, Son?" Buck asked.

"No, sir."

"Didn't I already tell you not to call me 'Sir'?"

"Yes, sir. I mean..."

"There you go again. You're not a fag, are you, Son?"

"No," said Steve The Rookie evenly, leaving off the 'Sir.'

"Good," said Buck. "If you keep talking about evaluations and checklists, everybody out here's gonna think you're a fag."

"Okay."

They took a fight call, which Buck used the siren for, scaring all of the participants away before they even got there. They took a domestic, where Buck told the live-in boyfriend to go away for eight hours or Buck and Steve The Rookie were going to beat his ass. They talked car-to-car with Teddy Hoatlin in a dark parking lot behind a church for twenty minutes. They still hadn't written anything but addresses on their Logs.

After half an hour of silence, Steve The Rookie asked: "So, how long have you worked for the Police Department?"

"All fucking day," Buck replied. It was the definitive conversation killer.

The rookie didn't speak again until 4 AM. Buck had just turned onto Antoine Fraiser Avenue from Indianapolis, when Steve The Rookie said: "I'll bet you've had a lot of calls on this street."

"Well, yes, I suppose I have," replied Buck Tyler in a suddenly expansive mood. He drove slowly. There was hardly any traffic. "Had a drunk guy leave a baby in a car in that parking lot to freeze to death, but she survived somehow. Used to be a shitload of burglaries at that shoe store over there before they put the grillwork up. Had a third floor jumper from that building on your side, broke both of her fucking ankles, the dumb bitch. Misdemeanor murder or two every summer at that bar on the corner or in the gas station lot across the street. Had a woman who got mad about something. She threw some gasoline in that stairway over there and cooked a family in that second floor apartment. Woman and two little kids. Didn't even know them. Stupid bitch had the wrong address. Had a burglar fall through the fucking ceiling of that clothing store. Guy beat another guy to death with a fucking paint can in that fix-it shop once. One morning we found a couple carved to ribbons on the corner. There's no house there now, because it burned down. Never solved that one. That bar there used to have regular fights and killings. This one on the right used to account for two or three bodies a year until it went Mexican and calmed down. Pulled a woman out of a burning apartment up here on the left once. Had a fat whore overdose and fall out of a parked car just the other side of that tree. This chicken place on the right had a murder in the parking lot last year. The other chicken place up here on the left and the gas station lot on the corner kills three or four every year. Had a guy get his eye gouged out with a screwdriver on that sidewalk there.

See that window, second floor right? Had a guy get in a tug-of-war with his girlfriend over a shotgun, blew his fucking face off. Another old guy got beat to death with a wrench inside that used car place on the left. This Mexican place on my side doesn't have a lot of murders, but the drunks seem to run out in traffic a lot along here and get killed at bar time. You gotta watch out for them if you're running Code to a call down here. The place on the corner used to get robbed a lot until the owner whacked a robber. A drunk Indian fell on his head from the porch roof there. Lots of fatal accidents at this next corner. Murders behind that bar there all the time, summer or winter. Usually it's the bouncers killing gang guys or the gang guys shooting the bouncers. Burglaries at that cash place on your side. Always make a huge mess, but never get anything. This little shitbox hotel on the left. They have an annual whore-tossing contest off that third balcony."

"That sounds like a lot of interesting calls," said Steve The Rookie.

"Not really," said Buck. "Not more than five of them were even worth fucking going to."

Captain Maddox hated vacations. At one time, when his son was still small and his wife was still attractive, they had all gone to Florida for a week. It had rained every single morning. It had broiled every afternoon. Their rental car had broken down in alligator country. The locals had robbed them blind. The car repair place had gouged them almost as much as the seedy motel. Sandra had managed to come home with a wonderful bronze tan. Patrick had suffered the worst sunburn of his life. His head, balding even then, had become red and blistered. His son had stepped on a jellyfish, and they had spent some time in a hospital. The Florida hospital had gouged them, too. It had taken Maddox almost two years to pay for that "budget" vacation. He had never been to Florida again.

One summer, when he was a Sergeant in the old Data Processing Unit, he had been coaxed into a camping trip in Michigan's Upper Peninsula. He had rented an overpriced motorhome that got three miles to the gallon and had parked it in a campground. While his wife and son frolicked in the nearby lake, happily consumed by insects, Maddox had sat at the motorhome's dinner table, working out the number designations of all the blocks in Metro Precinct for the new Computer-Aided Dispatch system. It had been a favor to his supervisor, then-Lieutenant Griswold. Griswold had thanked him for all the hard work, but had later taken credit for it at a Command Staff meeting. After the motorhome broke down, Maddox vowed to spend the rest of his vacations working at home. So, this summer, with Sandra away at her sister's house in Maine and his son painting houses and smoking dope in Kentucky, Maddox was free to pad around his own air-conditioned suburban house and work on his revolutionary grant proposal for so-called Community Coordination Officers, which budgeted salaries for sixteen C.C.O.'s, two Sergeants, one Lieutenant, a civilian liaison person, and a Captain to be named later. Maddox, as author of the grant, would be the natural selection for the Unit Commander's spot. He was using all the keystone words, the "proactive policing," the "community enrichment," the "citizen empowerment," and so on that the Feds loved to hear. He had garnered the support of Inter-Urban Council Chairman Reverend Roy Bramble by promising that the Community Coordination Officers would be seventy percent black. Bramble didn't really have much use for the plan at first, but Maddox had assured him that it would improve the plight of the African-American community. Maddox had reached out to Familia Urbano leader Encarnacion Ortega by promising that sixty percent of the Community Coordination Officer would be Latino and eighty percent of them bilingual. He had even received the blessing of the Mercer Heights Outreach Ministries by implying that at least one Community Coordination Officer would speak to at least one church congregation a week in the inner city. To juggle all these cutthroat tasks, Maddox would need an ambitious Lieutenant for the day-to-day schmoozing with community warlords. Berke might be up to the job, but Maddox wasn't sure. He also wasn't sure if Berke could be trusted, so he hadn't run it by him yet. Maddox would need Sergeants who were true believers, and he had his eye on a clean-cut black Sergeant from Community Affairs and a bilingual white kid from Technical Services. If he could fund the project, housing it in perhaps an abandoned gymnasium or church, he was confident he could wrangle a Commander's office in the downtown tower, whence he could coordinate the community coordinators. It was a bold stroke, he knew. He had been slaving over it day and night, on-duty and off, weekends and vacation days, since the start of the year. Now that he had a whole week to himself, Maddox planned on finalizing the presentation. But first he was going to see his doctor about these hemorrhoids.

Alvin and Trudy Hoskins were still trying to murder each other. Their whole apartment building on Summit Avenue was in an uproar. Trudy had broken the windshield of Alvin's Honda with a brick. Alvin had taken the clothes out of Trudy's closet and burned them in a pile in the alley out back. Flex Sinclair took Alvin to jail for arson. Hoatlin took Trudy for vandalism.

Police work in July was all just a matter of bodily fluids, Parnell decided. There was those adrenaline rushes as you ran Code to a Man-with-a-gun call. There were semen stains in the panties of the rape victims. There was that awful black syrup that leaked out of the old ladies who had fallen dead in their little apartments, not to be found for two weeks. There was the carrots and hotdog vomit from the dead children hit by cars. There was the barbecued chicken wings and malt liquor vomit from the shooting victims on Evers Street. There was the enchilada and beer vomit from the stabbing victims on Bendix Avenue.
There was the wet shit that filled the shorts of the car crash victims. There was the vitreous eye fluid from the crash victims who had neglected their seat belts. There was the brain glop sprayed behind the chair where the headless man sat with his shotgun on Trowbridge Avenue. There was the urine from the drunks who could no longer hold it and let it all go in the back seat of your cruiser. There was all the spit they left on the inside of the cruiser's rear windows. There was puss from the whores and gay hustlers, who raged with exotic diseases and skin lesions. There was the snot that filled the noses of those who could no longer breathe in the burning houses. There were tears everywhere.
There was blood, of course. There were bloody steak knife blades and bloody box-cutter handles. There were blood-soaked Metallica T-shirts, blood-streaked pantyhose, and bloodstained blue jeans. There

were bloodstains on the walls and doors, the toilets and bumpers, the curtains and headlights, the towels and boots. There was blood pooled on the floors of taxicabs. There were bags of good blood hanging from poles in the emergency rooms and bad blood smeared all over the floors of those same rooms. The dead when you found them always seemed surprised at the amount of their own blood. There was blood on baseball bats that had never seen an inning of baseball. There was blood in the alley, blood on the crib, blood on the telephone, blood in her ears, blood in their hair, blood in the sink, and blood on the light switches.

There was sweat, sweat, and more sweat. There was sweat under your vest. There was the sweat when the guilty were about to confess but hadn't yet. There was sweat and pain and grunting as you helped the firefighters and the morgue wagon guys drag a fat man down a tight stairway. There was sweat in every broiling second floor shitbox apartment from Yonker Street all the way down to Cleveland Street. The fans didn't work, the air didn't move, and sweating people killed other sweating people just for changing the TV channel wrong. Sweat was everywhere. You breathed sweat in July. Parnell sweated out his uniform shirt and hated it all.

"They done stole all my shit," said Jamal Fullerton, shaking his head. "That is some fucked-up shit, man."

"Do you have renter's insurance?" asked Pridemore, knowing the answer already but needing the information for the burglary report.

"Say what?"

"Renter's insurance? Insurance for people who live in apartments?"

"Nah. Shit. I ain't got no assurance."

Pridemore wrote down a NO. "Do you have the makes, models, and serial numbers for the missing items?"

"No. Yeah. Wait. Sure. That shit's in the rental papers. I got 'em here somewhere." Jamal took out a pile of unopened bills, welfare office documents, and parole hearing notices.

"Is all stuff that missing rented?" asked Pridemore.

"Yeah. I got all this shit from Rent Town or Rent City or some shit."

Pridemore looked at the broken door of Jamal's little apartment. The door was splintered and lying on the brownish carpet. The burglar or burglars had trashed Jamal's living room, destroying his black enameled entertainment center to break free the cords and plugs of his giant TV, stereo system, electronic game center, and speakers. Jamal's woman was watching the cop from the kitchen doorway. She had nothing to say. It was three in the morning, and she wanted to get to bed. The story was, she and Jamal had been out late, had come home to find all their shit gone, and had called the police.

One of three things was true. Either it was a real burglary where the thieves had taken only the rented items and not even searched the rest of the apartment for cash, jewelry, or dope. Or—and this seemed more likely—Jamal had taken all of the rental equipment that he could no longer afford over to a cousin's house, kicked in his own door, and was making a false report to cover it up. Or the rental place had gotten tired of waiting for Jamal's payments and had come in and repossessed the stuff.

"Here it is." Jamal handed over the nine-page, fine-print rental agreement.

"I just need to write down some numbers," Pridemore said. He risked sitting down on Jamal's flea-bitten couch and smoothed out the crumpled documents on the coffee table. The rental company had given Jamal one enormous television, one powerful Japanese stereo system, one combination DVD/VCR system with amplifier, and a state-of-the-art electronic gaming console. It was about $1,600 worth of stuff, Pridemore figured. According to the agreement, Jamal had paid $300 down and was scheduled to pay "Only $199.95 per month" for the next six years. Part of this was insurance, but most of it was interest. So, basically, Jamal had signed himself up to pay about $15,000 for $1,600 of stuff that he wouldn't even own in the end. He had never read the fine print, which the rental company knew he wouldn't read. He would never pay it, of course, because he didn't have a job. He had known that when he signed the agreement. The rental place had even known he wouldn't pay it, which is why the first down payment went to insurance against the loss that would inevitably happen. In the end, Jamal was expected to move without leaving a forwarding address. The stuff would disappear one way or another. And Jamal's credit rating would go in the toilet until he got a new girlfriend under whose name he could rent and purchase things. Jamal knew it. Pridemore knew it. The rental place knew it. And the mob that provided insurance to the rental place knew it. The organized crime outfit that owned the insurance company that covered the rental company's losses would write it off as a loss and not have to pay taxes on any of it or on any other money they happened to be laundering through this complicated business. According to the receipts, Jamal had managed to keep up with the payments for five months, or about $1,000, but hadn't made a payment in three months. It had apparently come time to cut and run. Either all of Jamal's rental shit was at Jamal's cousin's house or the repo guys had made a visit. Pridemore wrote down the serial numbers of the equipment. He gave Jamal an Incident Report number and left.

The downstairs apartment didn't answer Pridemore's knock. He banged on the door of the house to the south. He pounded on the door of the house across the street. Finally, he got an answer at the house to the north. He asked the old man there if he had seen anything unusual at Jamal's house.

"You mean them niggers carrying all that shit outta there?" the witness inquired.

Sounded to Pridemore like Jamal's cousins. He asked: "What did they do?"

"They came around ten in the morning," the old man explained. "Made a whole lotta racket. Sounded like they was tearing the place down."

"Did they have a vehicle?"

"Yes, oh, yes. Big old van. Brand new. White, a plain white van, and brand new. Three niggers in orange coveralls and a fat white man driving."

Repo team, thought Pridemore. Not Jamal's cousins after all.

"No markings on the van?"

"Nope. Just plain white."

"And this was at around ten this morning?"

"Yes," said the old man. "I seen them niggers in orange, and I figured somebody tried to fuck the rental boys."

"You're probably right," said Pridemore. "Thank you."

"I woulda called the po-lice, but I got no phone."

"Thanks again."

"Niggers stealing from niggers to pay the white man," said the old man. "No offense intended, Officer."

"Hard to figure, isn't it," said Pridemore.

"Least them niggers got a job."

"Yes. Thanks again."

Mystery solved, thought Pridemore. As he walked back to his cruiser, he could see curtains move in two of the houses where no one had answered his knock.

At the peak of the summer heat, the City's sanitation workers went on strike. Rotting garbage piled up for two weeks on sidewalks, alleys, and stairwells all over town. The papers were filled with the story. The evening news featured interviews with citizens whose noses were offended. The Mayor was making noises about declaring a State of Emergency.

"This town is beginning to smell like a fucking science project," said Buck, reading his newspaper in the passenger seat.

"The problem," said Pridemore, waiting for the light to change, "is that the rest of the city is starting to smell just like The Heights."

Buck nodded. "Exactly."

The Crisis of the Day for the last Monday in July lasted almost four days and occupied much of the waking hours of Captains, Lieutenants, and even Sergeants throughout the City. This law enforcement crisis did not involve a major crime, a criminal conspiracy, or a violent breach of the peace. Monday's Crisis of the Day was the heart attack that Deputy Chief Forrest had reportedly suffered over the weekend. Sunday night, he had complained of indigestion, they said. He had gone to bed early that night, they said. His wife had found him shaken and nearly unresponsive on the floor of their bedroom, they said, and she had called for an ambulance. He had been admitted to a suburban hospital room for observation, they said.

Lt. Vargas from Central had heard that the Deputy Chief was on a ventilator and had already been visited by a priest. Forrest was not expected to live out the night, they said. Lt. Ramsey from Vice had heard that Forrest had a history of heart problems and had suffered his attack while engaged in intercourse with his wife. Captain Brandt of Metro, who had it first hand that the Deputy and his wife hadn't had sex in years, told Deputy Chief Griswold that the story was bullshit. Griswold had told several people that the story about the priest was bullshit, because Deputy Chief Forrest was a Lutheran, not a Catholic.

Griswold did, however, tell Captain Darcy from Training that he had heard Forrest had one foot in the grave. One of Captain Jasper's people from Records had heard that Forrest was actually banging his girlfriend, a secretary in the Human Resources Department, at the time of the heart attack. Someone else claimed it wasn't a heart attack at all, but a stroke. Captain Craig of the Two-Three had heard from Lt. Nickels, one of Captain Nettleton's people, that Chief Pearson had telephoned Nettleton that Deputy Chief Forrest was paralyzed and on a breathing machine.

The significance of Pearson having told this personally only to Captain Nettleton from Traffic was not lost on the other aspiring Deputy Chiefs in the Department. Many thought that the open spot would automatically go to Captain Darcy. Deputy Chief Griswold would be pulling for him, as Darcy had ridden Griswold's coattails up the promotional trail thus far. Others were certain that Captain Davis of the Detective Unit was an equally likely contender, as Chief Pearson himself chummed around with the man; they were members of the same country club, in fact, and often played golf together, it was said. Davis had the Chief's ear, they said. Nettleton, might be the better of two evils, others argued, because he had an IN with both Chief Pearson and Deputy Chief Griswold, something neither Captain Darcy nor Captain Davis had. Someone said that Chief Pearson's driver had personally told someone that the Chief would be going outside the Department for a new Deputy Chief. Furthermore, Professor Lindstrum had advised the Chief months ago that a minority candidate from outside the Department was essential to the new "diversity culture" within the Command staff. Others said that one of the three minority Captains was a shoe-in for the empty spot.

The death of Deputy Chief Forrest would mean to Captain Maddox that a way out of Mercer Heights might be opening up. He did not expect that Chief Pearson or Deputy Chief Griswold would look kindly on his promotion to Forrest's job. No, that was too much to hope for. Maddox wasn't thinking that way. He considered instead that, if Captain Darcy got the Deputy Chief's position, there would be an empty place in the Training Unit, which Maddox might be in line for, or at least a strong contender for. This was, of course, assuming that Captain Darcy's pull with Deputy Chief Griswold's people was as reliable as rumored. Should Chief Pearson override Griswold's nomination of Captain Darcy to Deputy Chief Forrest's empty position and appoint Nettleton to the post, Maddox might still be in line for a lateral move to Nettleton's former desk in Traffic, as Nettleton's chief Lieutenant was close to retirement age. If, as some said, Chief Pearson went outside the department to replace the deceased Deputy Chief, the whole promotional structure would be clogged up, and Maddox would have no hope of getting out of The Heights. On the other hand, there were the rumors that Professor Lindstrum and Chief Pearson had been talking for weeks now about creating a *third* Deputy Chief's position, a minority spot, no doubt, but a spot that might free up several lines of promotion. Maddox was on the telephone for two days with both Captain Craig and Captain Jasper about the possibilities.

Lt. Berke, like many of the administrative Lieutenants within the Department, was monitoring the situation by phone and email. Berke had heard from one of Deputy Forrest's Sergeants that minority Captain Taylor, the token black commander from Community Affairs, was guaranteed a promotion to the Deputy Chief's job. The beauty of this situation was that Taylor would undoubtedly be taking his black female Admin. Lieutenant with him, leaving an empty Lieutenant's spot in Community Affairs, which Berke would surely be considered for. If, on the other hand, they plugged acting-Captain Meredith, the other token black commander, into either the empty Deputy Chief's spot or Captain Taylor's post, once Taylor had been promoted to Forrest's job, he, Berke, would still have a promotional path open to him. Berke knew that Captain Taylor was making a mess of Community Affairs; Berke knew this from his friend, Lt. Hatfield, in Records, which had office space next to Community Affairs. Furthermore, Berke knew that acting-Captain Meredith's Precinct was in open revolt with his handling of staffing, discipline, and equipment; Meredith's area had some of the worst stats in the whole Department. So, if Meredith was incapable of handing his Precinct, they might just pull him inside to Taylor's spot, and there would still be an opening. Berke knew that neither Taylor nor Meredith nor, for that matter, Captain Zane, the lone female of the Command staff, was able to compose a legible press release or articulate the smallest sound byte. There would, therefore, still be an opening for an articulate Administrative Lieutenant somewhere in the food chain, even if he was white. So the impending death of Deputy Chief Forrest opened up several possible avenues of promotion or lateral transfer that might get Lt. Berke out from under Captain Maddox and away from Mercer Heights.

Flowers and cards flowed from the downtown Tower to the suburban hospital room where Deputy Forrest lay. They telephoned his wife and sent a Sergeant to chauffeur her from home to the hospital and back again. Chief Pearson's people talked to the hospital people, leaking information back and forth. One of Griswold's people had a brother on the hospital staff who was trying to keep them up-to-date with the doctors' latest findings. After Chief Pearson's visit to the hospital Monday afternoon, he had a scheduled appointment with Professor Lindstrum, which was duly leaked to Captain Darcy's office. By Monday night, rumor had it that Chief Pearson had appointed Captain Zane as acting-Deputy Chief, the first female to hold that position. One of the Lieutenants from Technical Services had it from a good source that Zane was going to be promoted to Deputy Chief, not just acting-Deputy, at a Wednesday morning press conference. Upon hearing this news, Captain Maddox became depressed about his chances for promotion or transfer, as Zane's empty spot was no better than the command at Mercer Heights.

Lt. Berke, on the other hand, thought that the rumors of Zane's promotion increased the likelihood that he could escape both Maddox and the Heights. It was all up in the air on Tuesday with phone calls and emails racing around the Department, and Lieutenants contacting Captains they hardly knew, if only to touch base with them. The scramble was in full gear Tuesday evening, when one of Captain Meredith's people heard that Deputy Chief Forrest had suffered a second heart attack. This, combined with a story from Metro that Chief Pearson was simply going to eliminate Forrest's position entirely, sent the Command staff and their administrative Lieutenants into rumor overdrive. There was a brief panic when someone heard that Forrest had died early Wednesday morning, but the story didn't check out. The cell phone on Captain Maddox's belt was buzzing all morning. Deputy Chief Griswold's line was tied up all day. Lt. Berke found dozens of frantic email messages on his computer after lunch. The place was in an uproar. Everyone waited for Chief Pearson to announce Captain Zane's promotion to acting-Deputy Chief on Wednesday, but 5 P.M. passed without a word. Lt. Berke spent Wednesday night on his telephone with his contacts in Tech. Services, Community Affairs, and even Traffic, trying to learn the fate of the dying Forrest.

The final crushing blow came on Thursday. Deputy Chief Forrest arrived at his office bright and early, explaining to his secretary how painful it had been to pass a kidney stone. The doctor had put him on a low-sodium, low-calcium diet, and he couldn't drink any more coffee. Deputy Chief Griswold and Captain Darcy arrived later in the morning to welcome him back. They told him how glad they were that he was in good health, both wishing he were dead. Forrest thanked them for the flowers and wondered what all the commotion was about. Captain Maddox took Friday off as a sick day.

The so-called "Father" sat in his legless armchair, which was so low to the filthy living room floor that, in his drunken state, he found it impossible to stand up. So he sneered at the four police officers in his shabby little house.

"Fuck you! You got no right to come in here!"

"We have the right," explained Sgt. Gibson, "because we've had a child welfare complaint."

"You got no fucking right!" shrieked the "father." His name was Merl Poleski, and he was shitfaced, and he wasn't taking any crap from anybody tonight. His six-year-old daughter, Kendra, was scurrying around the house, packing up the baby's things and preparing to leave. The baby, four month old Andrew, was sleeping through all the screaming, having no doubt slept through fights before. Poleski's wife, Janet, was away at work, having left her drunken husband in charge of the children. From the looks of the house, Pridemore didn't think much of Janet's housekeeping or mothering skills. "Get the fuck out of my house! Fucking pig cops!"

Becky Carpenter wanted to beat him to a pulp. Pridemore stood looking down at Merl Poleski in blind rage, which he was trying to hide from the busy little Kendra. Hoatlin stood in the kitchen doorway in silent anger. Sgt. Gibson had explained over and over again, how they were removing the children from this obviously unfit home, how they had the right to do so under the Child Protection laws, and how Janet and Merl Poleski would both have to come down and appear before a judge to prove themselves worthy parents before they could get their children back. Kendra had bundled up the baby in a pink and yellow blanket. She found him a clean bottle from the vile kitchen and fixed him a bottle of warm sugar water.

"I'll have your fucking badge, you asshole cop!" Merl threatened the Sergeant.

"I would appreciate it if you didn't use that kind of language around the children," Gibson said evenly.

"They're my fucking children. I can say what I damn well please. What's your badge number, you asshole?"

"My badge number is 405," Sgt. Gibson told him for perhaps the fifth time.

Becky Carpenter took the Sergeant's Polaroid and photographed the refrigerator, empty except for beer bottles and vodka, and the bathroom, its drains clogged and its toilet unflushed. There were only torn carpet pieces and broken glass for the children to play with. Kendra's favorite doll, in fact, was her little brother. She found a pair of unsoiled jammies for him.

"You can't take my fucking kids! They're *my* fucking kids!" Merl struggled to get out of the low armchair, but couldn't manage it.

"There's baby wipes in there with the diapers," Kendra said in a mature little voice, handing a bag to Hoatlin. The big cop put the bag under his arm.

"Thank you. Are you almost ready to leave?"

"Almost," said Kendra. "I got to get my extra shoes."

"Don't talk to them, Kendra!" her father commanded. "They're going to take you away!"

"It's all right, Daddy," Kendra comforted her father.

"They'll never let you come home!" Merl shrieked at his six-year-old daughter.

"It's all right, Daddy. We'll probably get to go to grandma's again. Mama will be home soon."

"They'll take you away, Honey. You'll never see your Mama again! Don't go with them!"

"It's okay now, Daddy," the six-year-old said to the thirty-year-old. Pridemore and Gibson watched the drunken man's face in amazement. Kendra had managed to calm her father down, while she hurriedly gathered up belongings for herself and her baby brother.

"Fucking pigs!" Merl cried out. He made a futile grab at his daughter, but she was off to find a pair of matching socks.

"You'll want to watch your language, Sir," Carpenter reminded him.

"Fuck you, you cunt cop. Fuck all of ya'll!"

Hoatlin said: "I'm going to have to ask you to stop talking . . ."

"And fuck you, too!" sneered Merl Poleski. He knew his rights. He knew the law. They couldn't do this to him. This was his house! His property! His rights! A man's home was his castle, goddamnit! And no fucking cops could just barge right in, the way these fucking cops had, and take a man's children away from him! This was America, goddamnit! He had rights, goddamnit! He would have all of their badge numbers and all of their jobs! There would be a lawsuit! His bottle was empty. "Honey, go get Daddy another beer, will ya?"

Kendra looked to Hoatlin, who said: "Not now, Kendra. We're leaving."

"We're going now," Kendra said to her drunken father. "It will be all right, Daddy. Mama will be home soon."

Pridemore and Hoatlin situated Kendra and her baby brother into child seats in the back of their cruiser for the trip to the children's shelter. The baby fell asleep after Kendra had sung him a lullaby. Kendra was excited about the trip, seemingly comfortable with the strange police officers. She told them all about first grade and a teacher she liked so much. She was six, going on twenty, thought Pridemore. Her childhood had been short, *real* short. Kendra asked Teddy Hoatlin if he liked music. She wanted to know if the car had a radio that played music. She liked Christmas music, she said. Her mom and dad liked the Grateful Dead, Kendra told them. Andrew liked the Teddy Bears Picnic song. Did Pridemore know that one?

"I'll start it, okay?" said Kendra. She sang the first line, and they soon joined in.

Back at Merl Poleski's house, Becky Carpenter was taunting the drunk. He raged and spat, unable to rise from his dilapidated chair. Carpenter snapped a Polaroid of him, shrieking and cursing, his filthy hair in his unwashed face, his rotting teeth a grimace of hatred and drunkenness. It would make a good photo for the judge on Monday.

"You fucking cops! You can't do this!"

"Sure we can, asshole," Sgt. Gibson reminded him. "We already did. Why don't you get up out of that chair and do something about it?"

"You'd like that, wouldn't you! You fucking cops think you're so tough! You fuckers are nothing without that badge and gun."

"How about me, you cocksucker?" suggested Becky Carpenter. "I'll stuff that beer bottle up your ass."

But Merl Poleski was too smart or too drunk to get up. He wouldn't swing at them or throw his empty bottle, any excuse at all for them to beat the shit out of him and haul his ass off to jail. He just sat and cursed them, and there wasn't much they could do about it. Sgt. Gibson brought a case of beer from the refrigerator that contained no milk and no food. He and Carpenter opened the bottles one by one, slowly pouring the beer into Merl Poleski's lap. It was the best they could do.

"Feel that?" Flex Sinclair asked the kid lying under him on the sidewalk. He pressed his knuckles into the kid's lower back. "That's a nine-millimeter just waiting to smoke your kidneys."
"Okay, okay," the kid begged. "You're hurting me!"
"Not yet I ain't hurt you." Flex caught his breath for a moment.
The kid allowed himself to be handcuffed. Buck Tyler arrived with the cruiser, having been lost in the two-block foot chase. "I found one of the baggies he dropped," Buck told Flex.
"I ain't did nothin," said the kid.
"We know, we know." Flex bent him over the hood. The kid's huge jeans sagged low over his plaid boxer shorts. "You got any sharp objects in them pockets, boy? Knives or needles? You better tell me now."
"All I got's a comb," claimed the kid.
They were parked diagonally in the gas station parking lot at Conklin and Bryden, where scores of drug dealers usually worked. The dealers that had been there had all evaporated into the darkness. The few remaining late night customers pumping gas watched the action. Buck Tyler watched them back. The fat black woman in the bulletproof booth watched them with idle curiosity. The boy had run from them; that was a mistake. Aging, overweight Tyler would never have been able to catch him, but Flex Sinclair could almost go airborne when he poured on the speed. Now, under the watchful eyes of the unfriendly neighborhood, Flex searched the kid's pockets.
There was the comb, of course, condoms, lottery ticket stubs, and coins. The kid had a girl's phone number written on a scrap of paper. Flex slapped it onto the hood of the cruiser, but the breeze carried it away. The kid had a wallet, containing a photograph of a naked black woman looking coy, a grade school photo of a child, a .22 caliber cartridge, and a Polaroid of the kid flashing gang signs with his friends. There was a broken pencil in the right hand pocket, which Flex fished gingerly from the jeans. There was a bundle of cash in the kid's left sock. Some of it spilled out and blew up the street before Flex could trap it.

"Hey!" complained the kid. "My aunt done gave me that for food."

"Your auntie didn't give you jack shit, boy," Flex told him. The money skimmed away across the parking lot.

"She gonna be ang-gry 'bout that."

"This her dope, too?" asked Flex, having found a small bag of rocks in the kid's right sock. He put it on the hood of the cruiser next to the wallet.

"Don't know nothin' 'bout no drugs," said the kid.

"So it's your dope then?" asked Flex.

"Don't know nothin' 'bout nothin'."

"You're a real dumb dude then, Boy," said Flex.

Buck watched the growing crowd as it formed loosely around the parking lot. Some of them had picked up the dollar bills that had blown away. Some simply stood in mute contempt. Flex glanced around, but continued searching the kid.

"Brother, man, can't you lighten up a bit here?" the kid asked.

"I think he means you, Flex," said Buck.

"I ain't your brother, punk-ass," Flex told the kid.

The kid turned to the crowd, pleading for help. "They's just harassing me. Can't you see that? You all are witnesses! The po-lice is just harassing another poor nigger!"

Flex yanked off one of the kid's high-top shoes, and out fell a wad of money. Before either of them could move, the breeze blew the individual bills free. Fives, tens, and twenties scattered across the parking lot. The crowd converged on the blowing money, chasing it across the street.

"Shee-it!" said the kid.

"Shit!" said Flex Sinclair.

"Shit is right," said Buck Tyler.

Flex shook a sack of little bags out of the other shoe. He held up the dope to show the kid.

"This belong to you?" Flex asked.

"Them ain't my shoes," the kid maintained. "But you threw my mama's money away."

"I thought that was your auntie's money," said Buck.

"It shore as shit ain't yours, Officer."

"It ain't nobody's now," said Flex. The crowd whooped and hollered, chasing down the dollars that curled and spun across the lot.

"You sure this isn't your crack cocaine, Son?" asked Buck.

"Don't know nothin' about no drugs," said the kid.

"What do you think, Flex?"

Flex shrugged. "Guess he don't need it."

Buck Tyler ran the kid's name for warrants, while Flex tore the little bags open and emptied them down a storm drain.

"You can't do that," said the kid.

"It's not your dope, right?" said Flex. The kid shook his head. "Then I *can* do it."

"You throwed away all my money," the kid complained.

"What money?" asked Flex. He uncuffed the kid. "Get your shit off my car." The kid scooped up his wallet, shoes, and belongings. He started to say something, but there was no audience any longer. He spat on the pavement as the cop car pulled away.

"I ain't did nothin', I ain't did nothin'," sang out Flex.

"Song of the street, brother," replied Buck, turning the corner.

"I ain't your motherfuckin' brother," said Flex.

"You run like a nigger, you know that?"

"You run your *mouth* like a nigger."

"No, I mean, you ran real good back there."

"It's *well*," said Flex. "You ran really *well*. Illiterate cracker motherfucker."

The room was brilliantly white. Jack Pridemore was dressed in black. The nurse was dressed in white. The doctor was dressed in a somber blue suit. Elaine Christian wore a black mourning dress. Father Price had been there and gone. All that was left was for the doctor to shut off Judd Christian's breathing machine, and it would all be over. The machine sucked and hummed relentlessly.

"Jack," Elaine had said on the telephone, "I want you to be there."

"Okay," Pridemore had replied reluctantly.

"Come for me," she had asked. "Be there for me, won't you?"

"I'll be there," he had promised.

It was a rainy August afternoon. Pridemore had taken a sick day to be there. Elaine had met him in the parking lot, and they had come in together. It was the day to unplug Judd and watch him fade away and die. Once and for all.

It was the end of a long crash. It was the accident with the cruiser and the drunk driver. It was the accident, which Pridemore had felt so guilty about for so long. It was the accident, where Pridemore had been driving eleven miles an hour over the speed limit. It was the accident, which the Department kept reminding him was his fault, his speed, his negligence, his doing. The drunk driver had hit them, sure, but Officer Pridemore had been driving too fast. The drunk was at fault, sure, but Officer Pridemore had to share the blame. The Department and the City were doing him a favor by not firing him. They were doing Judd and Elaine Christian a big favor by not cutting them off completely from the City's insurance plan. They sent notices all the time, in case anyone forgot what a favor they were doing. Every time the Police Union lawyers met with the City's lawyers about the matter, the City's lawyers pointed out that Pridemore's driving had contributed to his partner's condition. It was in the reports. It was in the skidmarks and the sketches. Everyone had seen the lines and the numbers. Eleven miles per hour over. Eleven. Not gross negligence, but negligence just the same. And beyond the rules outlined in the Manual of Procedures. Just look at the numbers.

The numbers were also dollars. There were dollars for doctors and bedpans and I.V. drips. There were the dollars for linen and rubber gloves and tubing. There were dollars for E.C.G. strips and E.K.G. strips. The C.T. Scans and the M.R.I.s cost thousands and thousands. The cranial reconstruction, hopeless as it was, and the neurologists' consultation fees, endless as they seemed, were all measured in dollars. There were dollars for Pridemore's knee and the physical therapy that followed. There were the dollars for the pins and screws that held Pridemore's knee together, which, of course, was really Pridemore's own doing. There were the bandages and drainage tubes and sterile dressings for Judd, which, of course, was really Officer Pridemore's doing, too. The dollars and the numbers, facts and figures, these were what the City lawyers kept bringing up at the conferences with the Police Union's nagging attorneys. When the Union lawyers said "worker's compensation" or "mercy clause," the City's attorneys countered with "eleven miles per hour" and "excessive speed." They threw numbers at each other until they were too bored to continue. The attorneys' efforts went nowhere, but they always agreed to meet again and "explore other possibilities." And both sides always fired off a bill or notice or legal brief to Elaine, telling her how sorry they felt for her, how she could call on them any time, and how unfortunate it was that Pridemore's careless driving had, in fact, robbed her of her husband and her future and her life. And they always sent Officer Pridemore some paperwork, always with a due date, always the deadline, some hearing or motion to be decided somewhere by someone. And, yes, the drunk driver had contributed, but, no, Jack Pridemore had his load to carry, too, which they always reminded him of with their little letters and interrogatories and questionnaires. He had killed his own partner. It was there in black and white. It was he who had brought down all this pain and suffering upon himself and on the soon-to-be widow, Elaine Christian. It was all there in the paperwork. And they were doing the best they could, given the circumstances. But it was really Jack fucking Pridemore's fucking fault, and there was no getting around that.

So when Elaine asked him, he replied: "I'll be there."

He hadn't visited Judd in months, hadn't seen this particular little red brick hospital in the suburbs before. He didn't know his way around at all. Elaine seemed to know everyone in the place, and she managed to smile at each of them, asking about their families and their health. Everyone seemed to know Elaine, all the nurses and doctors, the patients and their visitors, and even the janitor. All of this increased Pridemore's sense of uneasiness when he had first entered Judd's room. He should have gone earlier. He should have sent a card. He should have been there for the move from the intensive care ward to this place. He should have helped Elaine with the car, with the groceries, with something! He should have apologized more often. How often could you say you were sorry for killing a woman's husband? How could you ever make it up again? Pridemore wished he had done more before now.

Earlier, Father Price had held Elaine's hands as the doctors conferred about unplugging her husband's life support. Now, Elaine was holding onto Pridemore's left elbow, a nurse placed strategically to her left in case she fainted. The doctor switched off the white machine, and the room went silent. Elaine all in black, clutched Pridemore all in black, and they waited in the silence of the white, white room. The doctor moved with silent precision, sliding out the nose tube and the throat tube. The nurse spirited away these items and soon reappeared. The doctor waited and listened, as Judd Christian's body gave a little jerk, then sagged, and then gave another little jerk. The body gave out a small snoring sound, which seemed to trouble the doctor. He told the nurse to call a second doctor, who soon arrived and listened to Judd Christian's heart.

But he did not die. They waited and waited and watched Judd sleep. The doctors conferred out in the hall for a while, then came back inside.

It was just a matter of time, they said. The clock inside Judd Christian had not stopped but it would. There was really nothing to keep it going, they told Elaine. It might be minutes or hours; they couldn't be sure. They asked Elaine if she wanted a room to stay in until morning, but she remained at the bedside with Pridemore.

For hours Judd breathed, in and out, up and down, snoring softly as if he was bored with the whole business. They watched and waited. The nurse cranked up the bed a little and swabbed out Judd's mouth where the tubes had chafed the back of his tongue. Elaine sobbed for what seemed like hours and, when she finally stopped, she just gazed at the floor. Pridemore held her shoulders and wished he had been driving eleven miles per hour slower that night long ago. He felt Elaine's body shudder with sobs long after the tears had all dried up. They went out in the hall and took a short walk, but came back for another two hours. At three in the morning, they walked hand-in-hand outside in the night air, she in black, he in black, together in the darkness. When they got back, the doctor met them in the doorway. Judd, he said, was somehow still alive. His vital signs were stable, and there was no telling how long he would stay that way. The doctor suggested that both of them go home and get some rest. They stayed another hour, then left.

They sat in Pridemore's old Plymouth in the dark hospital parking lot. Elaine blew her nose and brushed back her black hair. She daubed at her eyes with a tissue from her black purse. The windows were rolled down to let in some night air.

"I'm sorry, Elaine," Pridemore said finally.

She sighed. "I know. Everybody says that."

"No, I mean, I'm really sorry about all this."

"Everybody says that, too."

"I mean, I'm sorry about the accident," he explained.

"What about the accident?"

"I'm responsible."

"You're responsible? For the accident?" She sounded surprised, as if he had somehow missed the point. "The accident wasn't *your* fault."

"Everybody says that."

"You think Judd's condition today is something *you* did?"

"Yes," Pridemore admitted. He swallowed hard. "I was driving too fast."

She turned to him, her eyes suddenly focused on his face. "That's utter bullshit, Jack."

"No...I..."

"Utter nonsense, and you know it."

"But..."

"Is that what you think I've been thinking all this time? Is that what you're telling me, Jack?"

"No, it's just that..."

"You're telling me that you haven't come out here to visit, because you're feeling guilty? Is that it? Are you saying you haven't answered my phone calls, because you're feeling bad about eleven...measly...fucking...miles per hour? I've read all the reports, you know. Is *that* what you're all about, Jack?"

"I'm just sorry is all." He loved her for saying it, but wasn't sure it was true. He wanted to thank her for forgiving him, for lifting the weight, but he thought it was too soon. Pridemore had lived too long with the nagging suspicion that he had helped murder his partner. It was too much to hope for.

"You really think this is all about you, don't you, Jack," Elaine sighed, shaking her head of dark hair. "Typical big, manly cop attitude. You're the center of the fucking world, and your guilt feelings are all important to you, aren't they?" She saw that his eyes had overflowed with tears. They dripped off his chin onto his black suit coat.

She took his head in her hands and turned his face to look at her.

Her dark eyes and dark hair were a blur through his tears.

"It's not all about you, Jack," she said gently. "It's like lightning struck the car one night, and you happened to be sitting next to Judd at the time. It wasn't your fault. I know that. I think Judd knows that. It just happened is all."

It was awfully nice of her to say it, Pridemore thought, but...

"I know what the City says about the eleven miles an hour," she said, still holding his face in her slender hands. "I know about the paperwork. You know what that's all about. I know what that's all about. Everybody knows what that's all about. It's about money, Honey. It's about...I made a rhyme there, didn't I?"

Pridemore mouth broke into a reluctant smile.

"It's just the City doing their City thing," she continued. "It's the Police Department doing that Department thing. That's all, Jack. I can't believe that you've felt that way all this time."

He shook his head free of her grasp and leaned against the steering wheel, his eyes looking down at his knees.

"You know how Judd used to always say, 'Don't let the bastards get you down,' Jack? Well, that's exactly what you've let them do. It wasn't your fault. You've just let those bastards at the Police Department and the City Hall get you down. That's all. Jack, are you listening?" She leaned down to meet his gaze.

"I just..."

"What, Jack?"

"I just felt...so...fucking...bad..."

"Oh, Honey. I'm sorry you felt that way."

And there it was. They had said, "felt," not "feel." He didn't *feel* that way any longer. He had *felt* that way for a long time, but he didn't *feel* that way now. She had forgiven him for the eleven miles per hour. She had promised him that she had never, ever blamed him for the eleven miles per hour. It seemed such a simple thing now, such a little thing. Elaine had lifted a great burden from him.

He shook his head. "I just felt so fucking guilty about it."

She pulled him to her and kissed his forehead, like a comforting mother. He looked at her with pleading eyes, and she kissed him again, this time on his right cheek. He was comforted, the huge burden decompressing gradually. When she found his mouth in the darkness of the parking lot, he let himself go, like a man diving into a pool of warm water. They held each other and looked at each other, no urgency or tension about it. It occurred to Pridemore that he would have to go out and buy fresh underwear sometime soon. But—Alas!—poor Judd Christian did not die.

Alvin and Trudy Hoskins were in the hospital. The coffee table in their Summit Avenue apartment was broken. Alvin said he had gotten the bump on his face from falling down the stairs. Trudy said she had tripped over the coffee table when she went to help Alvin. Pridemore and Carpenter took the disturbance report.

"Nice fucking job there, Tonto," said Buck Tyler to the out-of-towner.

"I know, I know," groaned Wayne Coleman through his bandages. Wayne had come all the way in from Marion County to the big city to buy some good weed. He had found a couple of crack dealers at

Roxbury and Unger at four-thirty in the morning, and they, of course, had robbed him. They had pistol-whipped him for good measure. Not wanting his ugly old camper, they had taken just his money and his keys. As they were fleeing up Roxbury Avenue, Wayne had gotten his hunting bow out of his camper and fired an arrow at them. Shot from half a block away, Wayne's arrow had missed them completely and had taken out the neon sign over Lucille's Lucky Lady salon on Roxbury. The crack dealers had, of course, returned to kick his ass, burn his camper, and laugh at him. They would have capped his sorry white ass, except that they had no ammunition for their gun.

"Is this William Tell here?" asked Sgt. Lindsey, when he arrived with the Polaroid.

"Robin Hood versus the Hoodies," Pridemore replied, filling out the report on top of a hamper marked "Central Receiving E.R."

"That looks like it hurts," Lindsey said to no one in particular as he snapped a photo of Wayne Coleman's battered face.

"Sure, it hurts," whined Coleman.

"Could be worse, Kemosabe," said Buck. "You're lucky they didn't shoot you."

"I know, I know."

"Next time, son," Lindsey told him, "just buy your dope at the local high school like everybody else. You'll get killed buying dope down here."

"I know, I know."

"Tonto know," said Buck. "Him smart now."

Coleman groaned.

"Natives break-em cheek bone. Smarten him right up."

"Where are you from in Marion County?" asked Sgt. Lindsey, waiting for the Polaroid to come out.

"Monroe City," said Coleman.

"My ex-wife and I used to have a cabin up at Blue Lake. That's nice country up there."

"Blue Lake is north of us."

"Good fishing, too, if I remember."

"Yeah," said Coleman.

"Where the deer and the antelope play, no doubt," said Pridemore.

Lindsey ignored him. "You married, Son?"

"Yes."

"Got kids?"

"Two little boys," replied Coleman. "Two and six."

"Well, Son," said Lindsey, "I would go back home to Monroe City, if I were you, and I would never come back to the City."

"Except for his court dates," added Pridemore.

"Yes," Lindsey reminded Coleman. "You'll have to come down for court dates."

"Court dates?"

"Yes, court dates," said Pridemore. "We've got a robbery here and a felonious assault and an arson and a malicious destruction of property."

"But I'm the *victim* here," complained Coleman through his bandages.

"On the robbery and the arson, you're the victim, yes. On the felonious assault with a bow and arrow, you're the suspect. But that's only good if the so-called 'victims' turn up, which I doubt they will. On the malicious destruction charge, you're the suspect. You'll have to appear in court for that one."

"Destruction of *what*?" Coleman asked.

"Destruction of Miss Lucille's Lucky Lady Salon sign," explained Pridemore.

"I'll have to pay her for that, won't I?"

"Him," said Lindsey.

"Him," echoed Pridemore.

Coleman was confused. "Huh?"

"Miss Lucille of Lucille's Lucy Lady hair salon is a *him*," said Pridemore.

"Oh."

"Him from out-of-town," said Buck. "Him never see Masked Man cross-dressing."

"You'll have to work out some restitution arrangement with the judge," Sgt. Lindsey said. "You'll get subpoenas by mail. Don't fail to show up."

"*Or suffer the penalties that fall thereupon*," quoted Pridemore.

"Okay," said Coleman, nodding in his bandages.

"Go home to Monroe City, Son," Lindsey advised. "Go home and don't ever come back down here. Except for court. They eat people like you for breakfast down here."

Coleman nodded. "I know."

"And stay off the dope." Lindsey handed the Polaroid to Pridemore and left.

"Loco weed heap bad medicine," said Buck.

"You'll have to pay the fee to get your camper out of Impound," Pridemore told the injured man. "It's pretty well burned up, so there's not much you're going to get for it. Insurance usually covers that."

"My fishing tackle was in there, too," said Coleman.

"Tonto's wampum all gone," said Buck. "Gone to great campground in sky."

"Does he have to talk like that?" Coleman asked Pridemore.

"Talk like what?" asked Pridemore. "Him Buck. Him wise man. Him always talk like that."

Coleman groaned.

Out in the hallway, Buck made up an excuse to stop at the nurse's station to talk to a blonde in blue scrubs. She answered his question and looked him up and down briefly before leaving. Buck made a hungry motion with his tongue.

"You know," Buck told Pridemore, studying his face, "you've been in a pretty good mood lately. What are you, getting laid again or something?"

"No," Pridemore replied truthfully. "But I've been sleeping better."

"Sleep, ha! Miles of nurses to go before I sleep."

"What's that, Emily Dickinson?"

"Dr. Kildare, Marcus Welby, Trapper John, M.D., how the fuck would I know?" Buck shrugged. He caught the eye of Nurse Yellow Glasses coming out of Wayne Coleman's room. "Hey, how's my favorite sexy nurse?"

"You're here with Robin Hood and his merry cheek fracture?" she asked Pridemore, ignoring Buck.

"Yes."

"He's got some facial nerve damage, too."

"Permanent?" asked Pridemore.

"Probably," said Nurse Yellow Glasses. "Our reconstructive surgery specialists are away on vacation this week, so he'll have to see his own doctor in Goose Fuck County or wherever he's from."

"I *love* it when you talk dirty," Buck told her.

Yellow Glasses turned to Buck abruptly. "Does that shit ever *really* work?"

"About half the time," replied Buck. "But—oh!—what a memorable time it is."

"This is *not* going to be one of your memorable nights, Officer Tyler," she said, turning to walk away. Buck cocked his head to the side to watch her departing gait.

"She likes you, man," he told Pridemore.

"Does that shit ever work for you?" Pridemore asked him.

"Well, actually, Jacko," admitted Buck, "it only works about ten percent of the time. But, seeing's as how you and I meet about thirty or forty angels of mercy a year on this Watch, that's not so bad, numerically speaking. You know how Lt. Berke likes us to keep our stats up."

Pridemore started to say something, but Buck clutched at his arm.

"Oh, my God! Here she comes."

The Impossibly Beautiful Blonde From X-ray emerged from a doorway at the end of the hall. She swung away from them and walked briskly to the elevator. Even with her speed and distance, they could make out the perfect rump swimming around inside of her green surgical scrubs. The elevator doors opened and swallowed her. Pridemore turned to see Buck standing there with his mouth open.

"What was I saying?" Buck asked, snapping out of his reverie.

"You were telling me about Tonto and the Indian maidens."

"I was?"

"You were," grinned Pridemore. "Ten little Indians. Remember?"

Judith Manley knew a red flag when she saw one. The personnel file on her desk was a "red flag" file, if she'd ever seen one. There were no real flags, of course. There were no so-called "problem employees" that the Department would recognize as such. There was no "Bad Apple" stamp affixed to the corner of a file jacket in Internal Affairs. The thickness of a file might give one an idea of the particular officer's Internal Affairs scrapes it contained, but one incident with several interviews or a lengthy investigation might produce a thick file on an otherwise reputable employee. No, that was not the red flag. The true sign of a "problem officer," Manley knew, was the number of times an officer's Internal Affairs file jacket had been signed out. Every time a particular file was looked at by an Internal Affairs investigator or any time it was reviewed by a member of the Command staff, the name, rank, time, and date were written in little boxes on the back of the file jacket itself. That was the true test of a red flag cop. The last name on the list was Judith Manley's, as she had just signed out Pridemore's file for a follow-up investigation just that morning. Just as the Department refused to acknowledge that there existed unspecified quotas for traffic tickets, the Internal Affairs Unit refused to acknowledge that there was any such thing as a trophy for the headhunters of I.A. But Judith knew that this file was one of those trophies.

There were three files for every police officer who had ever been investigated by Internal Affairs. There was the so-called "public file," which was not really public, but was accessible to the right attorney or the right news organization with the right subpoena. The "public file" was a thin, tidy little folder containing only the dates and outcomes of the officer's various complaints, an Insubordination charge here, an Unfounded Excessive Force complaint there, or maybe an At-Fault accident in a city vehicle. There was the "internal file," which was the Internal Affairs working file and contained all the notes, complaints, and interviews for the past two years. The employee and his Union steward had the right to see the "internal file," given the right subpoena, of course. By contract, the City was only supposed to maintain complaints, founded or unfounded, on any police officer for no longer than two years. After that, according to the contract, the old files were shredded. The third file, which almost no one knew about, was the "administrative file," which was locked in the I.A. Unit supervisor's office. The administrative file contained all the complaints *ever* filed against an officer, his private medical history, including any mental illness or alcohol counseling, notes from supervisors, sick time and on-duty injury reports, allegations from almost anyone, and assorted comments. Judith Manley had not seen Pridemore's administrative file, although she knew one existed, because the name label on his internal file had his last name in capital letters. This was the code that told an insider that there was more information, much more information, in an administrative file locked away from view. To an outsider, the upper case letters meant nothing. To Manley, they were a red flag. She had on her desk Pridemore's internal file. The public file was of no use to an investigator of her caliber. She would look at the administrative file later, as those had to be read inside the supervisor's office and could never be checked out. So, given the numerous times that Pridemore's internal file had been accessed and the fact that his last name appeared in capital letters on the jacket, Judith Manley knew she had a winner. Or loser, depending on one's perspective.

Pridemore's file had been signed out to the Traffic Unit for a "contributing" At-Fault traffic accident, in which his partner had been badly injured. The file had been opened to the City Attorney for an investigation of Pridemore's medical claims. The file jacket had been opened by a clerk, who had inserted an Out of Uniform complaint. Pridemore's file had been seen by a Lieutenant named Berke, who apparently had studied the I.A. jackets of everyone under his command. The I.A. supervisor had gotten into the file to get a copy of the officer's fingerprints and palm prints for the people in Forensics. The file had been opened to an attorney from the Police Union one morning and opened again to the City Attorney's office that same afternoon. The file had been accessed by a clerk, who had inserted a complaint about Unauthorized Use Of A Department Vehicle. The file had been checked out for study by a Captain Maddox of Mercer Heights Precinct. Pridemore's file had been opened so that a clerk could insert a recently filed Littering complaint. And, finally, the file had been signed out to Manley herself, to investigate the Littering charge. This guy, Pridemore, was a liability to the Department, Judith Manley knew.

She telephoned Captain Maddox's office, but got Lt. Berke instead.

"I wanted to touch base with Captain Maddox about his Littering complaint against an officer named Jack Pridemore," she explained.

"I'm familiar with that particular investigation," Berke lied smoothly.

"Well, the Captain brought some trash that he had apparently recovered inside a Department vehicle into the Forensics Unit. Officer Pridemore's fingerprints—excuse me, I mean, palmprints—were lifted from one item of the trash. And, while that's an indicative sort of evidence, you understand, it's not exactly conclusive."

"And why not?"

"Well, Lieutenant," Manley continued, "it means that at some time Office Pridemore touched the item—I think it was a cup of some sort—it doesn't mean he was the one who left the item inside the Department vehicle."

"I understand," said Berke.

Manley wasn't at all sure that he understood.

"You see, Lieutenant, the same Probable Cause issues that come up in criminal cases also apply to Internal Affairs cases against police officers. There are proof issues here. And there are plenty of reasonable doubt problems with it, too. You see what I mean, Lieutenant?"

"So we'll need an eyewitness?" asked Berke.

"No, not at all," Manley assured him. "If I might speak confidentially . . ."

"Go ahead, Ms. Manley."

"Well, it appears to me that this particular individual is giving the Captain problems down in your neck of the woods, so to speak. This same individual has cost the City a lot of money from an automobile accident that he was partially responsible for last year. There's a pretty well documented case of his Unauthorized Use Of A Department Vehicle to transport a female. That's an easy three-day suspension. And the failure to properly report the event, well, that's another four-day suspension. But what we . . ."

"Is the Department separating the Unauthorized Use and the failure to report the Unauthorized Use into two charges?" asked Berke, knowing that three serious charges in a two-year period were grounds for termination.

"Well, see, Lieutenant, that's the problem I wanted to discuss with Captain Maddox. I don't think the traffic case can be tied in with the others, because it's a traffic event, which is handled a little bit differently from disciplinaries. And the Use of Vehicle thing might be seen as a single transaction with the Failure to Report same. There's an Out-of-Uniform complaint which you yourself apparently signed."

"That's correct."

"So the Department only needs one more complaint to seek a Dismissal from the Disciplinary Board for this officer."

"I see."

"And the Littering complaint alone won't do it. As I said, there are Reasonable Doubt problems with the Captain's Littering complaint. The Union will fight that one and win, I'm afraid. And, again, there's the two-part Unauthorized Use of Vehicle, that the Department will argue is two events, counting toward the total of three, and which the Union will argue was a single event."

"And the traffic accident doesn't count?" asked Berke.

"No, not that same way. If a burglar is found to be at fault in a traffic accident, it doesn't make him a worse burglar . . ."

"I am aware of that."

"And, by the same token, if a nice old lady is found to be at fault in a traffic accident, it doesn't make her a burglar," Manley explained.

"Yes, I understand all that, but . . ."

"Pridemore's contributing negligence in that traffic case, by the way, was some little thing about his speed. It was really a drunk driver who caused the thing, it seems. Between you and me, I think the City used that to deflect some insurance liability away from the Department, and that we probably don't want to delve back into all that. Besides, there's a suit in progress on that issue."

"This officer is suing the Department?" asked Berke, incredulously.

"No, the Police Union is suing the City's insurance on behalf of the other injured officer's family, his wife, I think it is. That's all standard operating procedure. It doesn't affect us here with the current problem."

"Okay. So what are we talking about then?"

"Well, Lieutenant, as I was saying about the burglar and the nice old lady, if the nice old lady's fingerprints are found on trash inside a police car, it doesn't make her a burglar. It doesn't even mean she's guilty of Littering."

"But if the burglar's prints are found on it?" asked Berke.

"That doesn't make him guilty of Littering either," Manley explained. She sometimes wondered how Commanders got to be Commanders with their limited skills in logic and law. "We're talking about a person who regularly drives a police vehicle. That person's prints anywhere inside the vehicle or on any item found inside the vehicle doesn't mean much. They *belong* there."

"So the Captain's Littering complaint won't fly? Is that what I'm hearing?"

"Exactly. If you would explain that to Captain Maddox when he comes back, maybe he can develop some other documentation, not for the Littering, but for something else that might count toward the total of three."

"I understand," said Berke.

"Your Out-of-Uniform complaint, by the way, was an excellent example of documentation, Lieutenant."

"Thank you. It pays to be precise, I always say."

"Exactly," Manley assured him.

"I will pass on your input to Captain Maddox."

"Please tell him how sorry I am that the Littering complaint won't do, but tell him I will keep an eye on this particular officer's file from now on."

"Two down and one to go is where we stand?"
"Exactly."
"Thank you for your attention to this matter, Ms. Manley," said Berke.
"Don't mention it. Give my best to Captain Maddox."
They exchanged phone numbers and email addresses. Judith Manley hung up and made some notes for Pridemore's "internal file." Later, she made some notes for his secret "administrative file."

John Doe #86, black male, 15 to 20 years, found dead of stab wound at the rear of The Marble Room, 3260 South Cramer Avenue. No witnesses, no suspects.

Frances Mobley was missing. Her husband, Carl, a retired jazz band drummer, had woken up in the middle of the night and found her gone. Some of her clothes were gone, too. Carl had called 911, because the little sticker on the side of his telephone said, "For EMERGENCIES Call 911." The police officers, Parnell and a new rookie named Glen, had arrived to take the Missing Person report. They stood in the shabby living room of the Mobleys' tiny apartment, while Glen The Rookie broadcast the initial description of the missing woman. Carl Mobley sat at the kitchen table. It was always the kitchen table. Parnell looked at the multitudes of old photographs, ancient nightclub banners, and newspaper clippings that covered the walls of the living room. There was a split in both the carpet and the floorboards between the battered old sofa and the ragged armchair.

"Frances Mobley, black female, 67 years, gray hair, brown eyes, walks with a cane. Last seen wearing a blue dress."

Pridemore and Hoatlin tapped on the screen door and let themselves in. The little living room was suddenly crowded. Glen The Rookie moved out of the way as Pridemore came into the kitchen. Teddy Hoatlin walked straight to the sink and ran some water. He reached up to the cupboard on his right and got out a can of coffee and a coffee filter. While he made coffee, Glen The Rookie looked to him for some sort of explanation. Pridemore meanwhile had adjusted his gun belt and eased into a chair beside Carl Mobley at the table.

"How we doing, Mr. Mobley?" Pridemore asked gently.

"My Frances is missing," replied Mobley. "Do ya'll think you can find her?"

"We'll do our best, Mr. Mobley."

"Is she still using that cane?" Hoatlin asked, searching for some clean coffee cups.

"Ever since her hip operation," answered Carl Mobley. "She don't go nowhere without it."

Parnell was looking at a yellowed poster with frayed corners for a jazz band called "The Limehouse Rounders" on the wall behind the television. There was an old daybill for a nightclub called The Silken Trap and another for a bar called Westley's. A brownish newspaper clipping told of Frances Mobley winning a beauty contest. Parnell looked at the faded picture of a line of black girls, trying to match the names in the captions with the smiling faces.

"Did she take her cane with her, Mr. Mobley?" Pridemore asked.

"No. It's there in the bedroom, right where she keeps it at. That's what I don't understand, how she done gone off and left it here."

"Did she take her clothes this time?"

"Some of 'em. Mostly thought they is still there in the closet."

Hoatlin poured three cups of coffee and sat at the kitchen table on the other side of Carl Mobley.

"Thank you, Officer. You didn't have to do that. I'm so worried."

"Carl, isn't it?" asked Pridemore.

"Yes, sir. Have we met?"

"Yes, Carl, I've been here before. I'm Jack Pridemore. This is Teddy Hoatlin. You might remember Teddy from the last time."

"I'm sorry," said Carl Mobley. "I don't recollect too good."

"Well, it's been a couple months now," said Pridemore.

"Last spring, I think," added Hoatlin.

Carl Mobley stirred two teaspoons of sugar into his coffee. He fished into the pocket of his threadbare bathrobe for his cigarettes and came out with a crumpled package. He offered them a cigarette, although they could see that the pack had no more than two left in it. Pridemore lit a match for the old man.

"Do you think she's run off again, Carl?" asked Hoatlin.

"No, I don't understand it. She run off once before, but that was a long time ago, in Kansas City. She come right back after that. No, I was thinkin more along the lines like she got herself kidnapped."
"Could be," said Pridemore.
"Could be," said Hoatlin.
Glen The Rookie started to interject a question, but Hoatlin waved him away.
"Is Frances still singing at the church there on Trowbridge?" asked Pridemore. He turned to explain to Glen The Rookie. "She used to sing at the Baptist Church down the block."
The rookie nodded, confused.
"Lovely voice, too," said Carl.
"Does she still sing in that choir, Mr. Mobley?" asked Hoatlin.
"No, not so much since she got sick. She had a spell, and the doctors said she might better stay home for a while. You remember that, don't you?"
"Yup," said Hoatlin.
"We remember," Pridemore assured him.
"Then she couldn't get around to take care of the dog," said Carl Mobley, sipping his coffee.
"Jim The Dog," said Hoatlin. "Fattest dog you've ever seen."
He laughed. Pridemore laughed at the memory. Even Carl laughed.
"Good old dog, that Jim," said Carl.
"What ever happened to that old dog anyway?" asked Teddy Hoatlin.
"He run off somewhere after my Frances passed away," Carl Mobley replied.
They sat in silence for a few moments. Pridemore sipped his coffee. Carl gazed through his cigarette smoke. Hoatlin gave Glen The Rookie a sign that it would soon be time to leave.
"What did you feed that old dog to make him so fat, Mr. Mobley?" asked Pridemore, trying to move the conversation along.
"That Jim, he'd eat just 'bout anything me and Frances would feed him. Only dog I ever seen who ate potato chips."
"Potato chips?"
"Yup," said Carl. "He done ate potato chips all the time. Loved them potato chips. Good old dog, Jim."
"Are you going to be all right here, Mr. Mobley?" Pridemore asked gently.

Carl Mobley looked up from his coffee, his wrinkled face wet with tears. He looked to Teddy, then to Jack.

"I'm sorry, Officer," he said. "I forget sometimes."

"That's no problem, Carl," said Pridemore.

"It's always nice just to stop by for a visit," added Hoatlin.

Glen The Rookie closed his report pad.

Mister Alp disappeared at the end of the summer. He slipped out while Pridemore was struggling with the door to 314-B, his arms full of groceries. When he didn't come back for a week, Pridemore threw out his food dish and his litter box. The apartment had gotten neater somehow, what with the airing-out, the window washing, and the floor mopping. Mister Alp had perceived a change in the man who had opened the food cans and had kept him warm at night in the big living room chair. The man, who had before talked at length to Mister Alp every day, had become silent. There were fewer beer cans and frozen dinners around the apartment. Things had changed. Mister Alp was out of there!

Jennifer Pridemore had stopped by before the beginning of the school year. She and her father had gone out to dinner and had a long talk. Jennifer had yet another new earring and told him about another new boyfriend. She was thinking of changing her major again, but to what she wasn't certain. Pridemore noticed that his daughter was starting to look a little like her mother had looked when they were dating, a long time ago, before the weight gain and the arguments. They had even gone out to brunch with Elaine Christian, who was slightly embarrassed by the looks she was getting from Pridemore's daughter. Jennifer was under the distinct impression that things between Pridemore and Elaine were much farther along than they actually were. Pridemore assured his daughter that, while she was a member of the whirlwind romance generation, he and Elaine were just slowly getting to know each other. Jennifer winked at her dad, slyly disbelieving him.

"That's a nice lady friend you have there, Dad," Jennifer had told him at the airport.

"Yes," he had said, "she is."

"You deserve a break, Dad. Go for it."

"I think I deserve a break, too. I'm just not sure this is the break I need. It's complicated."
"Trust me, Dad. She's worth it."
"Trust you?" Pridemore had laughed. "You being the voice of experience?"
"You've just got to come out of your shell is all," she had advised him.
"They're calling your row number, Jen."
"Gotta go. I love you, Dad." She had picked up her backpack.
"I love you, too. Be a good pie."
"I will, Dad." She had kissed him and run for the door to the plane.

Ever since she was a little girl, Jennifer's father had told her to be "a good pie." It was something he always said. She had heard it her whole life. "Be a good pie, because there's nothing better than a good pie."

A few weeks later, Pridemore caught a glimpse of Mister Alp, or a cat that looked a lot like him, peeking through the curtains of an apartment on the first floor. So Jack Pridemore felt a bit more relaxed. His daughter was in good shape. Mister Alp had found a happy home. Apartment 314-B was starting to look less like a drunkard's cave and more like a bachelor's apartment.

Alvin and Trudy Hoskins were in trouble. Their apartment on Summit Avenue was filled with smashed bottles and broken furniture. Trudy said she had gotten a restraining order against Alvin, but had let him move back in the week before. Alvin said that Trudy had broken most of the furniture, including their new television, but that they would try to be quieter in the future. They promised Flex Sinclair and Becky Carpenter they would stop fighting and go to bed.

How Derrick Tremaine Russell got hold of the machete, no one knew. Why he had quit taking those oblong blue pills that the doctors had prescribed for his schizophrenia, no one knew. Even his mother, weary of him playing with himself in public and accusing her of poisoning his food, could not understand how Derrick had come to this. No one could remember having seen him for a week. No one really liked having Derrick around, what with his voices and tantrums and suspicions, but no one had really wanted to see him end up this way either. Before his death, everyone talked about that crazy, tripped-out motherfucker, Derrick, who ate dog shit and huffed paint fumes, until he was so insane that nobody wanted him around. So no one was really surprised when Crazy Derrick reappeared as a walking nightmare, wearing only soiled boxer shorts and a pair of dirty white socks, a halo of silver and orange around his nose and chin from sniffing lacquer out of a plastic bag.

Neal Parnell and rookie Glen Albright were going over some reports in their cruiser. They were parked in a closed restaurant lot at Vanderbilt and South Market, the windows down in the warm night air. Rookie Albright had his elbow on the driver's side window frame, his hand resting on the cruiser's roof. Parnell was looking at a checklist on his clipboard. It went so fast, a blur of reaction, reaction, and reaction, that it seemed to Parnell that the initial action was lost in the shuffle. Parnell would learn the name of Derrick Tremaine Russell that night and would hear that name in his dreams for the remainder of his life. The date would become more firmly entrenched in his memory than his own wedding anniversary or his children's birthdays. Parnell would recall Rookie Albright's face after all the names and faces of all the rookies he ever met had long faded away. The first and last time that Parnell would ever see the living face of Crazy Derrick would be sufficient to engrave that awful image into his brain. It was a thing he would have to learn to live with, that blur and those reactions. But all Parnell would remember later was that he and Glen The Rookie were going over something on a clipboard.

It was a sharp thump. Parnell turned to his left and saw Glen Albright pull his hand in from the open driver's window. There were fingers missing. Parnell caught just a flicker of a shadow behind his partner as the machete hit the roof again. Parnell was clawing at his door handle, while the bleeding Albright tried to scramble away from the driver's seat. The left rear window burst inward. Parnell was rolling out in a half-crouch, a mindless robot of his years of training, reacting helplessly and perfectly to the threat, his gun clearing the holster flawlessly. He came up at the right rear wheelwell of the cruiser, immediately identified his target, which was ducking down by the driver's door, and shifted his stance to the rear of the car. There was screaming as Glen The Rookie tried to get away from the machete and Derrick Tremaine Russell tried to get to him.

It was over in a blur.
Sight picture clearing the roof edge. Bap, bap.
Crazy Derrick's face, looking like a bizarre old man with an orange beard that had spread up around his eyes, was swinging toward him. It was already happening, already gone. There was just Parnell in the tunnel with Crazy Derrick and that machete at the other end. No cruiser, no rookie, no City.
Sight picture of Derrick Tremaine Russell's naked chest. Bap, bap.
Four shots. Two point six seconds. Three in the sternum Ten Ring. One in the shoulder. Parnell's own voice came roaring back to him, screaming orders at the dead man to put out his hands. The dead man wasn't responding. Parnell was screaming himself hoarse. Glen The Rookie squeezed his bloody left hand under his right armpit and emerged from the darkness with his pistol drawn. Parnell eased back on his trigger, surprised at how little slack was left, and re-holstered his weapon. He found his cuffs and hooked up the dead man's wrists. Reaching into the car, Parnell found the mike and wailed something into the radio. He switched on the overhead light bar to make finding them easier. They stared at each other. They stared at the dead man. Two of Glen Albright's fingers were still on the roof of the cruiser.

Hoatlin and Kibelewski got there first. Then came Pridemore and Tyler. Sgt. Lindsey arrived, followed by Nolan and Howard. Becky Carpenter screamed down Market from the north. An ambulance arrived, confirmed that the dead man was indeed dead, and wrapped up Albright's hand. Two cars arrived from South Precinct. A Lieutenant and Sergeant came from Metro and assigned Kibelewski to ride in the ambulance with Albright. A detective rollout from Homicide showed up in three unmarked Fords. The Channel 5 van arrived, but the whole block was taped off by now. The I.A. team pulled up. Forensics arrived and set up an inner perimeter line, inside of which they allowed no one except Homicide. The Detective Sergeant was soon replaced by a Detective Lieutenant. Someone called a second ambulance to the scene, when Parnell started hyperventilating. A half-asleep pair of suits from Community Affairs arrived in a slick-top. The rest of the detective rollout came and began the neighborhood canvas. The Medical Examiner's field crew showed up, but was held back as the Forensic people finished videotaping the scene.

Someone said: "That's Crazy Derrick Russell." The Detective Sergeant headed back downtown to check out the name.

Neal Parnell didn't realize it, but he was surrounded by a sacred fog.

They helped him into the comfortable *front* seat of an unmarked cruiser with a detective and I. A. investigators in the other seats. Someone asked if he was hungry. Father Price brought him a large orange juice. They discretely took his sidearm, gun belt, and accessories and gave him another one, with an empty pistol, for him to wear. The officers dispatched to wake up the Parnell family immediately told his alarmed wife that he was okay. They arranged for a babysitter and transported her downtown. People walked by and touched him. Cops squeezed his shoulder. Someone touched his elbow, handing him a Danish that he couldn't eat. They shielded him from the Channel 5 camera crew and held the crime scene line for a full city block around him. The head of the Forensics team stopped by and asked him some gentle questions about the positions of things and the number of shots fired. He had no idea how many shots he had fired, and no one seemed to mind.

Vanderbilt and South Market looked like a miniature Las Vegas by four in the morning. There were headlights, strobes, camera flashes, and emergency flashers. The air smelled of exhaust from twenty idling cars, trucks, and vans. The traffic flares blocking South Market produced a haze of acrid smoke. A fire truck stood by, its huge engine rumbling and its floodlights pouring over the scene. Parnell's cruiser was a tangle of tape, rulers, probes, tripods, chalk, fingerprint kits, evidence bags, lasers, yellow markers, letters, numbers, protractors, film cassettes, and clipboards. Albright's fingers were gone from the roof. Detectives in suits and supervisors in raincoats walked up and down the parking lot, saying "What?" into their cell phones, some of them not realizing they were calling another investigators at the other side of the lot. Five uniforms crowded into a cruiser and went out slowly through the Market side of the perimeter, giving the news crews something to shoot, while Parnell was spirited away in an unmarked minivan through an alley off of Vanderbilt. The rest of the city was still dark

Parnell was exhausted. He had been up for days, it seemed. It had been weeks since he had shot Derrick Tremaine Russell, he felt, but they went over it again and again. He asked about Glen Albright and was told he was fine. The doctors were optimistic about the reattachment of at least one of his fingers. They took him into a room at Homicide, not a faceless interrogation room with its barren table and three chairs, but a "soft room" with plush sofa, end tables, coffee table, and low wattage floor lamps, usually reserved for the victims of rape or the family of homicide victims. They wheeled in a chalkboard and brought him some soft drinks. They apologized when their cell phones rang and answered them out of the room. Parnell got to spend twenty minutes with his wife during one break in the interview, and they both cried quietly. At nine in the morning, they brought in bags and bags of McDonald's breakfast meals, none of which Parnell could eat. Father Price checked in on him. Once, when the door opened for a moment, he could see Hoatlin and Pridemore giving him a thumbs-up from the outer office. Deputy Chief Forrest stopped by for a minute. Someone from the lab arrived and photographed the bloodstains that had been left on his left sleeve by Albright when he tried to escape the machete and stains that had oozed onto Parnell's pant leg when he had knelt down to handcuff Russell. They all left the room while he changed into a fresh uniform and the old one disappeared into an evidence bag.

There were four interviewers in the room, two from Homicide, one from Internal Affairs, and a Lieutenant Somebody from Community Affairs. They worked on the chalkboard, going over and over the details. They already had prints from digital photographs on a giant corkboard in the corner. Someone changed the audio tapes at regular intervals. It was all a blur to Parnell. He wished he could go to bed. He wished he could wake up and find that it had all been just a horrible dream. He wished he could go back in time and take the night off. He had given up trying to figure out why they were asking the questions that they were asking. It was all so repetitious, the same facts coming back to him in different shapes. Parnell wished he were somewhere else.

Where exactly was Officer Albright when you fired your first shot?
What was he himself doing?
You said Albright was across the front seat when you got your sight picture of Russell. Was he to Russell's right or left?
After you fired your first shot, what did Albright do?
How long was it between your first two shots and your second two?
Had you ever met Derrick Tremaine Russell before?
Did you reload?
How long have you been Trainee Albright's Training Officer?
Why were you parked there?
Are you currently under a doctor's supervision?
What was your last call just before the shooting?
Are you currently taking medication of any kind, including cold medicine?
Russell's older brother, James, was arrested for robbery two years ago. Did you know that at the time of the shooting? Did you have any involvement in the arrest of James Russell?

When was the last time the magazine of your weapon was completely empty, allowing the spring to relax?

What was the approximate distance between the muzzle of your weapon and Mr. Russell?

Was Russell wearing a shirt at the time? What color was the shirt?

In which hand was Russell holding the machete?

Who was the last person you can think of who could verify your whereabouts just prior to the incident?

Do you typically load your magazines with sixteen or seventeen cartridges?

Did your last Use Of Force incident involve a black male subject?

Was the vehicle in Park when the incident started?

When was the last time you field-stripped and cleaned your weapon?

Could you tell that Trainee Albright had been injured when you exited your vehicle?

Russell's mother lives at 2431 South Dudley. Have you ever been to that address?

How many shifts had you previously worked with Trainee Albright?

After you fired your first two shots, what did the subject Russell do?

Did you say anything to Russell before you fired your second shot?

How far were you parked from the nearest light pole?

How many alcoholic drinks do you consume in a week?

Was your window rolled down when the incident started?

Have you ever seen a psychologist or made an appointment to see one?

Russell's sister, Janine, lives at 1905 West Evers. Have you had any contact with her or with that address that you can recall?

What was your last radio transmission from the vehicle prior to the incident?

When was the last time you slept before this shift?

Had you and Trainee Albright taken your meal break prior to the incident?

Have you ever loaded your service weapon with any loads other than the Department-issued ammunition?

Were you parked with your headlights or parking lights on?

What was the last computer transmission you received from Dispatch prior to the incident?

Could you see both of subject Russell's hands at the time of your first double-tap?
What other light sources were there in the vicinity of the vehicle at the time of the incident?
Did either you or Trainee Albright say anything to the responding ambulance personnel?
Did you make any statements to anyone, other than Department personnel, at any time during or after the incident?
When was the last time you consumed an alcoholic beverage prior to the incident?
Did the subject Russell at any time come in physical contact with either you or your holster?
Were your alley lights on?
Did either you or Trainee Albright attempt to unlock the shotgun from its holder?
Are you right- or left-handed?
In your experience with Trainee Albright, would you call him a tense person?
Have you ever heard Trainee Albright make any racist remarks or tell any jokes involving minorities?
Why were you two blocks out of your patrol area?
Did you close the right side door of your vehicle after you exited?
Could you smell alcohol on the breath of Subject Russell?
Did Subject Russell at any time reach into your patrol vehicle?
Was the dome light or MDT keyboard light on at the time of the incident?
Have your ever heard the names of Kenisha Russell, Darren Jamal Russell, or James Talbott Russell?
Did Trainee Albright at any time unholster his weapon?
What was the approximate distance between Subject Russell and Trainee Albright at the time you engaged Subject Russell?
Have you ever made a Worker's Compensation claim against the Department or the City?
How long have you been assigned to Mercer Heights Precinct?
Have you retained an attorney?
Was there any music playing inside your vehicle at the time of the incident?
How much time elapsed between your last shot and your call for the ambulance?

Subject Russell. Trainee Albright. Suspect Russell. Patrol Vehicle. Subject Parnell was beat. It was well past noon when they drove him home. He unplugged the telephone, threw up, and cried.

"You know, it scares me sometimes," Pridemore told her, looking at the candle in the little amber globe on the table between them.

"How so?" asked Elaine. She was watching his face. "Like dating again?"

"Yes, but it's more than that. I'm all nervous like a teenager. I'm over 40 years old, and I'm worried about my complexion and how my breath smells. Does that make any sense at all?"

"Why? You don't have acne or bad breath."

"I just haven't felt this way for a long, long time. So exposed. So immature. Very vulnerable and silly. I'm pouring my heart out here. Stop me if you've heard this one."

"You cops think that holding all the emotional baggage inside you is your strength," Elaine said, "but it's not good for your home life. Judd was like that sometimes. There was just a *wall* there."

"Maybe if we take it slow. Really slow. It takes some getting used to."

"I'm not rushing you, am I?"

"No."

"See there?"

"No. It's me rushing me, I think."

"I'm almost 40, too, you know," she admitted.

"You're not 42."

"I'm almost forty also," she rephrased. "In other words, I'm not some teenage girl you have to be self-conscious around."

"I don't like teenage girls," said Pridemore.

"Well, good."

"Well, you look great for forty-two anyway."

"I'm not 42, damnit," Elaine replied. "I'm 35."

"Well, you look great for 35."

"Thank you for saying so."

"I like your 35-year-old hair," Pridemore admitted quietly. "I like your . . ."

"I color my hair, you realize."

"I like it fine. I like your eyes and your walk. I like the way your voice sounds like you're always purring in my ear. I like the way your hair moves when you turn your head. I like . . ." He paused, looking from the candle to Elaine's deep, dark eyes. "I have liked a lot of things about you for a long time. I liked you back when Linda and Judd and you and I used to go out to dinner."

"That was a long time ago," she said. "Do you know what I liked best about you back then?" Pridemore shook his head, gazing down at the candle. She reached out her long slender hand and lifted his chin. Once he was making eye contact again, she continued. "I liked your hands. Big, rough, strong hands." She placed her hand on his on the tablecloth. "I still do, in fact. You were just a youngster back then, trying so hard to be a big, mean cop. Judd was, too. And I was trying to be a good, clean policeman's wife. Linda was, too, I think."

"Linda wanted to be a good, clean Police *Captain's* wife."

"Yes, she was ambitious that way. Anyway, you two succeeded beyond our wildest dreams at becoming big, mean policemen. But it took something out of the both of you. You stopped having feelings. You stopped—I don't know—being warm, I guess. I want to feel warm again, Jack. I think you want to feel warm again, too."

"That's what I meant about scary. I haven't felt warm in a long, long time."

"I don't mean sexy hot. And I don't mean hot romance. I mean warm and comfortable and protected." She sipped her wine.

"I know," Pridemore said. "That's what I mean about slow. A warming up kind of thing, I guess. I don't know. It's been too long."

"It's not too late."

"I hope not."

"I still like your big, rough hands," she said from behind her wine glass.

"And I still like your walk."

"Do you still like my butt? I work very hard on it."

"I like the whole package," he replied. "I like it a lot."

She ran her tiny fingers up the back of his hand. "It's a good hand."

"Thank you."

"This is where you say, 'I like you, too, Elaine.'"

"I like you a whole lot, Elaine."

"We'll go slow," she told him. "I promise. I know you big, mean guys are not very good at this. I married one, you know."

"You're *still* married to one," said Pridemore, uttering the unspoken for both of them.

"Does that still bother you?" she asked.

"A little, I guess."

"Me, too, a little."

"That's probably healthy."

"What would you like to do tonight, Jack?" she asked after the waitress had come and left their check. "Are you in the mood for a movie?"

"No."

"A drink?"

"No."

"What then?"

Pridemore thought a second. "Do you know what I would most like to do, more than anything else?"

"I give up, Jack."

"I would like someone to scratch my back. I have not had my back scratched in years and years. I would like my shoulders rubbed and my back scratched. It puts me to sleep."

"I could do that," Elaine said, her perfect smile widening.

"When I was little, my mother used to keep me quiet in church by rubbing my head and neck. No one has done that for a long, long time. My ex-wife stopped doing that 20 years ago."

"I could manage that, I think. Do we have to go to church, or will my place do?"

"I could fall in love with a woman who would scratch my back," Pridemore said impulsively, surprising even himself.

"I could do that," Elaine Christian agreed.

They got up to leave. Pridemore helped her on with her coat. She swept her dark hair aside and leaned back into his grasp. He held her delicate shoulders in his big, rough hands.

"Still scared?" she whispered.

"Just a little bit. It's not easy being a 15-year-old again, you know."

Elaine laughed.

Garrett Underwood, black male, 31 years, dead of a single gunshot wound to the face in the south parking lot of The Marble Room, 3260

South Cramer Avenue. Arrested at the scene was Desharn Potter, who had apparently shot himself in the leg and wounded an accomplice, Terry Khalid, while trying to shoot Underwood.

***

"Happy Birthday to you!"

The mental stood right next to Pridemore and Becky Carpenter as they waited for the elevator at 1421 Woodruff. He was singing at the top of his psychotic lungs. There was a mental with a knife wound up on the fifth floor somewhere, stabbed, no doubt, by another mental. The ancient hotel at 1421 Woodruff was a Federally subsidized, eight-story nuthatch with aquamarine painted walls and two elevators that hardly ever worked. The bearded maniac was singing into Pridemore's right ear.

"Happy Birthday to you!"

The elevator still hadn't come. The ambulance crew that had gotten there first had probably locked the elevator open on the fifth floor. Becky Carpenter glanced back warily at the other freaks in the lobby. There was an old nut talking to his shoes. There was a woman making whirly-bird noises as she twirled a milk carton around on the end of a stick. Someone else was retching into the wastepaper basket by the front door. The man watching Congressmen debating a tax proposal on the antique television in the corner was picking his nose furiously.

"Happy Birthday, Mister Police Officer! Happy Birthday to youuuuuuuuuuu!"

Pridemore glared at the singer, who grinned cordially and bowed, apparently the official guest host for the lobby today. The cops were always going to 1421, sometimes two or three times a shift. With a population of manics, depressives, paranoiacs, schizophrenics, and assorted delusional banana-heads, the police were showing up at 1421 all the time. Someone would take a header off the fire escape or tear off all their clothes and run into the street, hollering about God-knows-what, or just up and die crazy and alone in their tiny rooms. The cops would have to come and mediate the ongoing battles between the Cannibal Leopard Men from Persia and the Devil Women of Venus, all the time pretending not to see the talking spiders, dancing mice, and two-headed lizards that freely roamed the halls of 1421 Woodruff. While the CIA, the FBI, and the crew of the Starship Enterprise worked their conspiracies inside the walls and light fixtures of 1421, the cops were always just the cops—bored, irritable, and hoping just to get the fuck out of the place.

"Happy Birthday to you!" The mental had moved around to their left and was singing into Becky Carpenter's face now. The elevator still hadn't arrived. They could start up the narrow stairway to their right, but then the elevator might suddenly arrive, and they would have climbed five flights of steps for nothing. Pridemore wished the other elevator was working. Becky looked over her shoulder at the oblivious throng in the lobby.

"Happy Birth—!"

The butt of Becky's flashlight hit the bearded mental's stomach mid-song, knocking the air out of him. He staggered backward, looking offended and confused.

"Let's take the stairs," Carpenter said. They started up the five floors of aquamarine steps. She was in a hurry and soon got half a flight ahead of Pridemore, who was pacing himself for the long climb. Below them, the madman had started another chorus.

The headline read: "BLACK RESIDENT KILLED BY POLICE."

The Sunday edition titled its story, "ANOTHER BLACK SHOT BY WHITE OFFICERS."

The Channel 5 banner said, "White Rookie involved in police shooting."

The paper's background story said, "Mercer Heights Demands Answers in Shooting."

The Monday edition featured Derrick Tremaine Russell's eighth grade graduation photo. The caption read, "Derrick Russell died in a hail of police bullets."

Several of the stories mentioned his age as 22, although he was 24. Channel 5's most sincere looking anchorwoman said his nickname was "Derrie," but never mentioned "Crazy Derrick."

His mother, Lola, was quoted as saying, "Derrie had his troubles in the past, but he was turning his life around."

His sister, Janine, told Channel 9 that "the cops in Mercer Heights will have to answer for this."

Somebody's neighbor said, "I think the police down here think they can get away with anything."

A South Market resident was shown, pointing at the empty parking lot in broad daylight. "There was a whole lotta cops down here that night."

Reverend Roy Bramble of the Inter-Urban Council was quoted as saying: "It's another example of a pain in the black community and a stain on the police department. We're looking hard for some answers in the killing of this young man."

Familia Urbano leader Encarnacion Ortega told a press reporter that he felt bad for the police officers. "A man cuts off my fingers and I'd shoot him, too." The editor did not use this quote.

Channel 9 mistakenly ran police shooting statistics over a picture of Derrick Russell's brother, James, who phoned them from prison to complain. They showed Derrick's graduation photo the next day.

Surprisingly, it was *Just For Us*, the city's "Only African-American Newspaper," that got many of the facts straight. Being a weekly paper, *Just For Us* was able to develop a perspective on the event that the dailies and the TV newshounds missed. They mentioned that Russell had a history of mental illness, although they didn't mention the "Crazy Derrick" nickname. They were the first to uncover a witness who had actually seen Russell with the machete earlier in the day. *Just For Us* called it a tragedy, but it was a tragedy of a young man who had gone so completely wrong in his life and his mind, not the tragedy of yet another black boy murdered by white police officers. An editorial even urged calm in the Mercer Heights and South Precincts.

By the following Thursday, Channel 5 quit calling it "the crisis of white guns and black sons."

The paper ran a photo of Glen Albright, looking sick and aged, leaving the hospital in a wheelchair, his left arm in bandages. The article said that the surgeons had only been able to re-attach one of his severed fingers.

In an effort at damage control, Deputy Chief Griswold leaked Derrick Tremaine Russell's criminal history to a reporter from Channel 9.

A producer at Channel 5 proudly told a colleague how he had *not* aired Chief Pearson's "transparent efforts at spin control" at a Monday evening news conference where the Chief had mentioned Russell's history of psychosis. By Friday, this was old new, so the news director ran it anyway.

Someone in Community Affairs discretely left a photograph of the two-foot machete, still stained with Albright's blood, on his desk for a reporter to see.

Officer Neal Parnell was reported to be on "a paid leave-of-absence" until the Department's Shooting Board and Internal Affairs Unit had released their findings. The reports had not even reached the Review Boards or interested community groups.

When a reporter called Mercer Heights Precinct for a human-interest update on the involved officers, Lt. Berke blithely told her that Parnell was working a desk assignment inside and that Albright was expected back on the job any day.

What the press didn't find out for another month was that Glen Albright had already quit the Department and moved to Arizona, neither his hand nor his soul ever to fully recover from the nightmare of Crazy Derrick. By then it was all old news.

Elaine Christian scratched Pridemore's back, rubbing out the knotted muscles along his spine with the palms of her hands. She ran her fingers through his hair until he fell asleep. She got up, had a glass of wine, and finished a chapter in the vampire novel she was reading. When she came back to bed, all warm and naked, she woke him up again.

Elaine was soft and yielding. Jack was hard, but uncertain. She was patient with his hesitance. She coaxed and prodded, gently hurrying him, assuring him. She would occasionally stop for no apparent reason, push the dark hair from her face, and gaze down at him. He was working slowly when she wanted to go faster. He picked up the pace, just as she lapsed into a languid phase. For a while, they had tempo problems. When he started to fade, she made adjustments. She was playful, but gentle. He was working too hard at it, thinking too much. She was patient, but tempting. They finally settled into a satisfying rhythm. Near the end, she let out a yelp that surprised both of them. She giggled and covered her mouth like a little girl. His knee was hurting, but he ignored it. He hadn't felt anything like this since he was 18. It was tough being a 15-year-old, like he had told her, but being an 18-year-old again was great. Elaine didn't tell him, but she had never felt like this before. She wondered about the experience, hoping it would go on and on. They both had the feeling it was going to work out all right.

On later nights, they would be sexy or naughty, one or the other of them initiating it. She would try new things she had only read about, and he would go along. It was like trying out new recipes, she thought. Some worked, others didn't. Later they would know each other better, each able to read the other's mood and timing. Pridemore would never again ask to have his back scratched. Sometimes Elaine would ask him if he wanted his back scratched, and other times she would ask him to scratch *her* back. It worked out. But for that first night, they simply ended up holding one another. The first time, with its first night jitters and stage fright, was always the hardest.

Elaine got up early and made coffee. She toyed with the idea of waking him up for a second time, but decided it would keep for now.

Captain Maddox fumbled with his office keys, found the right one, and pushed it into the lock. Stopping halfway, the key would go no further. Maddox checked his key ring. No, this was the right one. He tried it again to no avail, put down his briefcase, palmtop computer, and a stack of mail, and peered into the keyway. He couldn't see very well, because his brow was sweating by now and his glasses kept slipping down his nose. He grunted, trying to see inside the tiny gap. A phone call brought Sgt. Petty running with a flashlight.

"What's the problem, Captain?" asked Lt. Jerry Crawford, who happened to be delivering some paperwork to the third floor.

"I think it's a toothpick," said Sgt. Petty.

"Do you see any scratch marks that might indicate someone was trying to pick my lock?" asked Maddox. He was drinking his stomach-coating liquid straight from the bottle, his supply of plastic spoons being locked inside his office.

"I don't think so, Sir," said Petty, straining to get a better look into the keyhole.

"What's the problem here?" asked Lt. Berke, who had just arrived with a new memo for the Captain to sign.

"Someone tampered with my office door lock," said Maddox. "I have a lot of work to do today."

"I don't think you can pick a metal lock with a wooden toothpick," Crawford advised them helpfully.

"It's a security issue," announced Berke.

"I'm inclined to agree with the Lieutenant, Sir," said Petty, not making it plain which Lieutenant he was refering to. "I think it's more of a malicious mischief thing." He straightened out a paperclip and tried to fish the offending toothpick fragment out of the keyhole.

"Pretty immature, if you ask me," said Maddox.

"It's still a security issue," Berke argued. "I'll call Internal Affairs." He left to find a telephone and start the ball rolling on this investigation.

"Aren't you going to mess up the toolmark evidence or something with that paperclip?" asked Maddox.

"I'm afraid, Captain," said Crawford, "that a soft toothpick can't leave a toolmark on a hard metal lock."

"I think you're right," said Petty.

"Well, what about marks on the toothpick left by the lock?" demanded the Captain.

Crawford explained it gently. "That would prove that the toothpick was inside the lock, which we already know anyway."

"Well, what about, uhhh, tooth marks," Maddox asked irritably.

"Or DNA maybe," suggested Petty.

"Could be, I suppose," Crawford said doubtfully, "assuming that they had it in their mouth beforehand. Have you got any suspects in mind, Captain?"

"Everybody's a suspect," Maddox told him ominously.

"I've almost got it," Petty reported proudly.

"Good," said Lt. Crawford.

"Good," said Captain Maddox.

"Have you got a headache?" Crawford asked, seeing Maddox washing down an ulcer tablet with his stomach-coating medicine.

"Yes," said Maddox. "And I'm getting pretty tired of some of the pranks and poor attitudes around here, too."

Lt. Berke had come back. He had managed to draw a special report number from someone at Internal Affairs, who had impolitely groaned at him over the phone. "I'll get the report started," Berke told the Captain.

"Any luck, Sergeant?" Maddox asked Petty.

"I think I've almost got it, Sir."

The Captain's cell phone buzzed with a call from Deputy Chief Griswold's office. Something about a staffing budget analysis that had not been delivered on time. Maddox stepped out into the hallway for privacy. When he came back, Crawford had gone to find someone from Building Maintenance to help with the lock. Sgt. Petty, it seemed, had broken off a piece of his paperclip inside the keyway, only adding to the problem. Lt. Berke had already begun the Internal Affairs report, when the little Vietnamese man from Maintenance arrived.

Lt. Jerry Crawford was enjoying this immensely. The Captain was supervising two Lieutenants who were supervising a Sergeant who was, in turn, supervising a damn janitor in a joint effort to get the Captain into his own office. Crawford, himself not above the occasional tactless prank, appreciated the simplicity of the thing.

In a jiffy, the Vietnamese guy from Building Maintenance had the knobset out of the door. He banged the lock on a nearby floor vent, freeing both the offending toothpick and Sgt. Petty's paperclip fragment. He opened the door to the Captain's office and re-inserted the lockset, tightening up the screws.

Maddox was livid about the toothpick, but glad to get his office opened. He squeezed past the mess in the doorway just as the telephone on his desk began to ring.

"That was *evidence* you just threw down that vent," Berke scolded the Maintenance man.

"I no know evidence."

"We wanted those little things," Sgt. Petty told him. "They're lost now."

"I thought you wanted door fixed," shrugged the Maintenance man.

Lt. Crawford was in stitches, but he kept his face blank.

"Maybe next time," said Crawford brightly.

"There had better not be a next time," snapped Berke. "This immature nonsense has got to stop!"

"That was our best evidence," Sgt. Petty said, still berating the helplessly confused Maintenance man. The poor workman packed up his tools and left without so much as a Thank-You for his efforts.

"This pattern of disobedience is very disruptive," said Lt. Berke. "I can't understand it."

"Clever devils," said Crawford, shaking his head.

It was a short story. Buck Tyler was telling it.

"So did you have a fatal fire over there on Liberty?" Hoatlin had asked him when he first arrived at the East & West Café.

"Well," replied Buck, "there was this lesbian cooking in the kitchen." He paused for effect.

Teddy Hoatlin glared at him. "Yeah? And?"

"Well, the Fire Department came and put her out." Buck couldn't help but grin, pleased with his summary of the facts. "That's about it. How's your night going?"

June Fothergill had been raped once before. It had been ten days before, in fact, on the night before her eighty-second birthday. The Mexican male had quietly broken her kitchen window without waking her. Her dog, Wilber, had gone to hide in the cellar. The suspect had first appeared to June at the foot of her bed, reeking of beer and fondling his genitals. He had showed her a knife and made her lift up her nightie. He had experienced problems maintaining an erection and had made her touch him. June had barely been able to see him without her glasses and had been unable to give a good description to the police officers. The Mexican man had slapped her and yanked at her white hair, but escaped into the night. Jack Pridemore had called a Canine Unit to attempt a track, but the trail led nowhere. Buck Tyler had driven her to the hospital and had held her hand while she waited for her son-in-law to arrive. Two detectives had arrived at her home the following day and had tried to make a composite picture of the Mexican man. Her son-in-law had pleaded with her to move out of the old neighborhood. But June had stayed in her ramshackle little house on St. Joseph Street.

So, tonight, when the Mexican man broke out the new kitchen window, June crawled out of bed and called 911 from the floor of her closet. The call-taker typed the basic information and sent it to the Area Dispatcher's screen. The call went out over the air as a Home Invasion In Progress. While the Mexican man searched around in her darkened house, June Fothergill told the 911 Operator about the previous rape. Pridemore, Sinclair, Nolan, and Tyler were already flying to the familiar St. Joseph address by the time the Dispatcher changed the call to a Rape In Progress. The 911 call-taker heard the telephone being wrenched out of June's grasp and listened helplessly to the struggle.

They came in dark and fast, Pridemore and Sinclair from the north, Tyler and Nolan in one-man cars from the south. Nolan took the back. Buck found the same window broken as before. They fanned out, guns drawn. They listened and could hear the Mexican swearing inside. Pridemore kicked the front door, and they swarmed inside, flashlights

and pistol sweeping the interior. Tyler already knew the layout of the place and was quickly in the bedroom doorway. Pridemore's flashlight first picked up the suspect straddling the elderly woman on her bed.
"Hands in the air, Motherfucker!"
"Freeze, Motherfucker!"
Pridemore couldn't get a clear shot, because of the woman. Buck had already slammed the knife away and had slashed the suspect's face open with the barrel of his pistol. They dragged him out of the bedroom and into the home's tiny kitchen. Flex Sinclair crashed into the guy and kicked him to the floor. In the dark, the suspect flailed his arms and struggled. Someone shouted. Dishes shattered. There were curses as the kitchen table collapsed. Pridemore punched him hard in the right ear. Buck pistol-whipped him once more before they found the kitchen light switch.
Angelo Fivaro felt the muzzle of Pridemore's pistol pressing firmly into his forehead, as one of them said, "Move, Motherfucker! Just go ahead and move!"
They flipped him over and, with someone's knee on the back of his neck, cuffed him up.
"Fucking spick motherfucker," spat Buck. He ripped open Fivaro's pockets and handed Angelo's wallet to Sinclair. "Fucking wetback sonofabitch!"
Pridemore checked on June Fothergill, who seemed to be unharmed. She was flustered and confused without her glasses, but awfully glad to see them.
"Did you get him?" she asked. "Did you catch him?"
"We got him," Pridemore replied.
"Motherfucker!" Sinclair cried out, and the suspect was back on the kitchen floor.
"Got you, you greasy sonofabitch!" Buck said, still waving his gun.
Nolan came in from the back, found the telephone in June Fothergill's closet, and told the 911 Operator that things were under control.
"You got him okay?" the Operator asked.
"Oh yeah, we got him good," replied Nolan, hanging up.
Pridemore got the knife from the bedroom. Sinclair took a paper napkin and pushed Angelo Fivaro's withered penis back into his pants. The suspect's eye was starting to swell. The gashes in his chin and broken nose bled freely. Sinclair and Tyler yanked him to his feet and ran him into every doorframe from the kitchen to the front door. Sgt.

Gibson, who had hurriedly parked his cruiser on the lawn, met them on the front steps. He shined his flashlight on Fivaro's bloody face.

"You guys are too gentle," said Gibson.

"I'm hurt," cried the suspect.

"Fuck you and your mother, asshole!"

"He's gonna learn the meaning of the word *rape* where he's going," said Flex Sinclair.

"Sorry-ass motherfucker," snarled Buck, shaking the suspect's shoulder violently. "Pick on an old woman like that."

"Nolan's taking the report," said Pridemore, when he had come out to the front yard. "I'll get the Use Of Force reports, and you guys take him in, okay?"

"I don't see any Use Of Force here," said The Sergeant. "Fucker resisted arrest and ran into a fucking door. Piss on him."

"Thanks, Sarge," Flex Sinclair said.

They slammed him onto the hood of a cruiser and ripped out the rest of his pockets. Flex and Buck launched him into the back seat and kicked the door shut.

"Motherfucking greaser," said Buck.

"Motherfucking right," said Flex.

Sometimes—not often, but sometimes—the job was almost worth doing. The rescue of the elderly June Fothergill was one of those times for Pridemore. He was so impressed with the event, that he related it to Judd Christian at the nursing home.

Pridemore had come down with a cold in early September, and Elaine had taken care of him for a week. They had gone to see Judd together several times. When Elaine left for Boston to attend an aunt's funeral, Pridemore took it upon himself to see Judd alone. He sat in the stillness of Judd's pastel blue hospital room and listened to his ex-partner's breathing. The only color on Judd's otherwise lifeless face was a strip of panda bear tape that held the bluish-green feeding tube to his nose. The dead eyes blinked occasionally but saw nothing, never awake enough to listen or alive enough to sleep. Judd Christian looked a hundred years old now, a washed-out shadow of the man Pridemore had known and trusted and even loved like a brother.

Pridemore told Judd the June Fothergill story, updating him on Buck Tyler, whom Judd had known from earlier days on the street. He told him what was new with Flex Sinclair's family and Teddy Hoatlin's kids. Judd had worked Afternoons with both of them in South and Central. Pridemore told Judd that he was in love with Elaine and watched for a reaction. He told him about all the crap from Captain Maddox and about all the silly nonsense that Lt. Berke was pulling. Pridemore related the story of Parnell and Crazy Derrick Russell. He told him about Mercer Heights and news about some of the old heads they both knew from South Precinct. He told Judd that the City and the Police Union will still fighting over who would pay his hospital bills and Judd's nursing home bills. He said Elaine was fine and that she had scratched his back.

There was not a flicker of reaction from Judd Christian, of course, but Pridemore somehow felt better for having said these things aloud. Confession had been good for Pridemore's soul. The light knocking at the door roused him from his reverie. The door opened tentatively before he could respond.

"Mr. Cohen?" asked the perky little voice. The plain looking candy striper stuck her head into the room. Her hair was done up in a silly ribbon, but you could tell she was a bit too old to be playing candy striper. She caught sight of Pridemore, sitting in the chair by the head of Judd's bed. "Oh, I'm sorry. I didn't realize that Mr. Cohen had a visitor."

"You might have the wrong room, Miss," said Pridemore. "This is Mr. Christian."

"I'm sorry," she said again. "Maybe they gave me the wrong room number."

"That's okay," said Pridemore.

"Do you think Mr. Christian would like to come down to the Day Room and visit with some puppies today?"

"I don't think so. Mr. Christian is bed-ridden."

"Oh." She splayed her fingers across her forehead, thinking hard. "I could maybe bring one of the puppies down here, if you like."

"Mr. Christian is in a coma," Pridemore explained to the candy striper. "I don't think he could see or hear any puppies."

"I'm sorry," she said for the third time. "If you change your mind, just ask for Priscilla."

"Thank you," replied Pridemore, not recognizing Lt. Berke's wife.

"It must be fucking Christmas in Internal Affairs this week," grumbled Buck Tyler, tearing open the envelope. He stood by his open locker door, reading the letter. The I.A. notice told him to appear at such-and-such a time on such-and-such a date to answer to a complaint that he had been rude to a woman during a traffic stop some months before. "Me, Rude? Stupid cunt! I'm one of the nicest guys in this shitbox outfit. What'd you get?"

"Well, let's see," said Pridemore. He opened the first envelope. "One Out Of Uniform complaint from Sgt. Petty for not having a tie clip."

"Asshole," interjected Flex Sinclair.

Pridemore opened the next envelope. "A Letter of Recognition from the Board of Awards for saving some lady's teeth."

"Teets?"

"Teeth!"

"Me, I've saved a lot of titties myself," said Buck, "but I never got an award for it."

"That's because you save them all for yourself," Flex told him.

Opening the third envelope, Pridemore read the contents, and then compared them to the Letter of Recognition. "And, lastly, I have an Unauthorized Use Of Vehicle beef from I.A. for driving the woman to the hospital without first getting permission. Jeez!"

"What woman?" asked a confused Flex Sinclair.

"The same woman whose teeth I apparently saved," replied Pridemore. "Can you fucking beat that?"

"You got a Letter and a complaint for the same call? Amazing!"

"Talk about your basically fucked-up, bipolar attention-deficit Police Department," sighed Buck. "We got it covered."

"Some weird shit," agreed Flex.

"I'm rude. He's got no tie clip. Thank you for saving the lady's tits. And fuck you for driving her to the hospital without permission. No wonder we're fucking crazy down here." Buck crumpled up his I.A. notice.

"What did you win?" Pridemore asked Flex.

"An all-expense-paid trip to Internal Affairs for telling some stupid nigger not to act like a stupid nigger," said Flex. "I remember it. I said, 'Man, don't be actin' like some stupid nigger.' And what does this stupid nigger do but call I.A. I knew he was a stupid nigger."

Buck was in stitches. "Tell them you're a stupid nigger, too, and don't know any better."

"I'll tell them I'm related to you, Buck, and they'll believe it," Flex retorted. "I can't even *believe* this fucked-up bullshit."

"I'm just about at the Magic Three," said Pridemore, sourly. "I got these two and then that thing with the fingerprints and the Littering beef." He looked down at the letters in his hand.

"They gotta be three bigger ones than that," Sinclair said. "Tie clips and Littering don't make it. I had five one year. Three were unfounded, and the others were chickenshit, but just the same..."

"Depends who's sitting on The Board that day," said Buck. "It always says '*Up to and including termination*' for the third hit, but it depends who's sitting in on it for you. I remember a fucking guy, worked Afternoons in Central, got three Excessive Force hits and one Insubordination one year and skated on all of it. Another guy on Nights caught a Conduct Unbecoming and two Out Of Uniform charges in a year and a week, and they fucking canned him on the spot. Depends who's sitting in that day."

They heard the sobbing and all stopped talking at once. Flex came around the bank of lockers and saw Neal Parnell sitting on the bench. Pridemore and Buck Tyler put their hands on his shoulders. His head was in his hands, the tears leaking out through his fingers.

"Hey, Buddy," Flex said gently.

"What the matter, Parn?" asked Buck.

"I wanna go home," sobbed Parnell. "I just want to get out of here."

"Well, then *go*," said Pridemore, patting his back.

"Take off, man," said Flex. "We'll tell Petty you got sick."

"I can't," cried Parnell.

"Sure you can, man."

"I mean...I can't get my locker open. I want to go home, but I can't get my clothes."

"What's your combination, Parn?" asked Pridemore. "I'll get it open."

Parnell sobbed. "That's the thing. I can't remember. I can't even remember my own locker combination anymore."

"Oh, Jesus, man," said Flex, shaking his head.

"I've been sitting here for half an hour, trying to remember it." Parnell hung his head.

"Fuck this!" snapped Buck Tyler. He disappeared around the lockers and came back with an old revolver.

"Christ!" cried Flex.

"Wait!" yelled Pridemore, holding up his hand. "Wait! Damnit!" He ran around to his locker. Flex Sinclair moved the sobbing Parnell down the bench a little. Pridemore reappeared with his copy of the Manual Of Procedure. He opened the thick book and held it by its cover, letting the pages fall over the dial on Parnell's locker.

"Where the fuck'd you get that?" Flex whispered, pointing at the old gun.

"Throwaway," Buck replied.

They paused as Jon Howard came into the locker room. He saw what they were up to and stationed himself by the door. He wordlessly nodded an All Clear sign to them. Pridemore held the Manual of Procedures over Parnell's locker dial as Buck pressed the old revolver to its pages.

Ka-Voom! They were all startled by the noise. Pridemore closed the Manual's covers over its shattered pages. Flex kicked the paper pulp and lock fragments under the lockers. Buck wrapped the gun in a towel and took it over to Howard.

"Lose this, will ya?" Buck asked. Jon Howard tucked the package into his kit bag and walked out without a word.

Pridemore opened Parnell's locker. "Now get your shit and go home, Neal."

Flex was liberally spraying deodorant into the air, when Sgt. Gibson came running into the locker room.

"What the fuck was that?" asked Gibson.

"Did you heard that shit, too, Sarge?" asked Flex.

"What *was* that?" asked Buck innocently, his ears still ringing. "Some water pipe upstairs?"

"This place and its fucked up plumbing," groaned Pridemore.

"The whole joint is blowing up, Sarge," said Flex.

"No shit," the Sergeant said. After he left, they checked on Parnell, who seemed to be feeling better now as he changed into his street clothes.

Alvin and Trudy Hoskins were no longer husband and wife. She had stuck him with a steak knife. He had bled to death on the back stairs. Trudy said she was surprised that anyone had that much blood in them. Their neighbors on Summit Avenue were hardly surprised.

Pridemore sat at the kitchen table with the widow Hoskins and wrote down everything she said.

"Watch this," said Buck, having managed to trap another rookie in his snare. He shifted his bulk around in the driver's seat and started typing on the tiny computer keyboard.

"Let me write this down," said Robin The Rookie, searching her enormous uniform for a notepad.

"Don't write it down. Just remember it."

Robin paid strict attention to this new police training.

"Now, if you type INFO: DETECTIVE, you get all the phone numbers in the Detective Unit," Buck explained. "If you type INFO: HOSPITAL, you get all the addresses and numbers for the hospitals in town. Got that?"

"Yes," the rookie nodded, all alert and waiting to have her cup of knowledge filled by the wealth of this senior officer's experience.

"Now pay attention," said Buck. He typed INFO: BATS. There was a pause as the little computer screen flickered, then came to life.

Up popped information on fruit bats, brown bats, and hoary bats. It included their average wing spans, life spans, and mating habits. There was information about the Bat Cave and the Bat Copter. There were baseball bats and batting averages. There were little biographical sketches of Batmen Adam West and Michael Keaton. There was information about one of Babe Ruth's home-run bats and a description of a battering ram. Under "Bats, Vampire," there was stuff about Bela Lugosi, Christopher Lee, Tom Cruise, and all the actors who had ever played Professor Van Helsing. There was an address for a baton twirling organization, along with a list of the winners of last year's national competition. The "Batgirl" section included the heights, weights, and measurements of any actress who had played a batgirl and all the vital statistics of the Catwoman women. There was a small biography of a woman wrestler named Battling Betty. There were "startling facts" about how vampire bats preyed mainly on South American cattle, not human beings. Someone in Technical Services had gone to a lot of effort to type all of this valuable information into the system. It was probably the same playful techie who had put in most of the home telephone numbers of the Command Staff under

INFO: CREAMCHEESE, so that you could hand out a Deputy Chief's number to all the whores along South Bendix Avenue.

"But what is this used for?" asked Robin The Rookie, trying to think of the practical application of Bat Masterson's biography to modern patrol methods.

"It'll keep you from getting bored," Buck answered, slightly disappointed that this rookie was so out-of-touch with modern patrol methods. "Never type in INFO: INDEX though."

"What does that do?"

"That kicks up about two hundred screens worth of alphabetized bullshit that will take you most of the shift to clear off your computer," Buck explained. He knew she would someday try it. Everyone always did. They were always sorry afterward, too. "And never, ever type SYSTEM PROMPT: KILL, because it shuts down the whole network, and they have to reboot the thing, and they'll track which car sent the command and come down here and fire your ass." He always taught rookies this, never brave enough to try it himself, but always hoping that one of them would someday become bored enough or mad enough to fuck up the whole police computer system. Buck wasn't even sure it worked. He was pleased to see that Robin The Rookie was taking notes.

"But why do we need to know all that stuff about bats?" she asked.

Tyler groaned. "Look. This job here is not all fun and games. It's not all just beating down the drunk Mexicans and robbing the nigger drug dealers and planting dope on the butt-plug Puerto Ricans. It's not just some party game. There's real work to be done out here."

"I understand that," said the confused rookie.

"Sometimes you have to feed your head, Kid." He poked at his own temple for emphasis. "Expand your horizons."

Robin The Rookie nodded.

"Grow your mind," Buck commanded.

She nodded again.

"Think proactively!"

Robin nodded energetically.

"We're not here just to grow a huge cruiser butt."

She shook her head, No.

"We need to improve our mental capacities."

She nodded, Yes.

"And we never, ever type SYSTEM PROMPT: KILL from a car that we're logged on to," Buck stated. "Never."

"No," agreed Robin The Rookie.

"Excellent!" he said. "Now let's go to work. There's crime-fighting to be done."

Darryl Suggs, black male, 18 years, dead of a single gunshot wound to the chest, in the same south parking lot of The Marble Room, 3260 South Cramer Avenue where his brother Edwin was killed months earlier. Nobody saw nothing, nobody knows nothing.

Halloween Night at the Black Juju was mass hysteria. The Goth chicks dressed as farm boys or soldiers or kangaroos, and the Metal Tech boys came as mutant rats, Mae West, or giant condoms. The music pulsed, and the colored lights swirled. One enormously fat girl, dressed in nothing but whipped cream, was encouraging people to lick her. The shapely girl in the red cat costume met them at the door.

"How delightful!" she cried, giving Flex a big hug. "You came color-coordinated!"

"Yeah," Pridemore told her, "we thought we'd dress as cops tonight. Where's the restroom?"

The red cat girl took them to Thor, the dyed blonde bartender, who showed them the restroom. The girl playing the part of the passed-out girl on the restroom floor seemed to be breathing okay. The guys playing the ambulance crew came in and took her out, weaving the cart through the dance floor. The guy who had played the part of the thief who had stolen the passed-out girl's purse got away. The men dressed as policemen made their way through the crowd and out the front door.

"Do come again, won't you?" said the red cat girl. She closed the Black Juju's door, and the music faded.

"And you think black kids are fucked up," said Flex.

They sent Pridemore upstairs to do the dirty deed. They had voted on it, and it was decided that Pridemore, who knew Lt. Crawford better, would have the best chance of getting Parnell a new locker. Pridemore told Sgt. Petty that he had to go see the Desk Lieutenant, and Petty let him go, figuring Pridemore was in for a Disciplinary. Pridemore waited outside the Oh-Three office while the Lieutenant finished a phone call. Jerry Crawford waved him inside. Pridemore closed the door behind him, a detail not lost on the old Lieutenant.

"Yes, Sir," Crawford said to someone on the line. "That's sounds like a fine idea. Ummm-huh. Yup. Sure. Ummm-huh. Yes, Sir. Certainly. Goodbye." He hung up the phone. "Assholes." He picked up his peach yogurt cup and beckoned Pridemore to sit down. "What can an old prick like me do for an old prick such as yourself today?"

"You know Neal Parnell?" Pridemore started.

"Ummm-huh."

"The guy from the Officer-Involved Shooting?"

"How's he doing?"

"He's alright. A little slow at bouncing back, but he'll be okay, I think."

The Lieutenant worked his yogurt spoon.

"He had a little problem with his locker the other day," said Pridemore.

"Oh?'

"He had some trouble getting it open."

"I see."

"And he needs a new locker assignment." Pridemore was starting to sweat.

"It broke, did it?" asked Crawford.

"Yes, Sir, it did."

"I see. What is broken on it?"

"It got a hole in it."

"A big hole?" The Lieutenant stirred his yogurt.

"No, just a little one." Pridemore indicated the size of the hole with his fingers.

"I see." Crawford put down his spoon and duplicated the hole size with his own fingers. "About this big?"

"That's about right, yes, Sir."

Crawford shrugged. "That happens." He stifled a belch. "You're sure Parnell's okay?"

"Yes. He's fine."

"I had a partner once," said Crawford, "a Polish guy, if I remember. His locker grew a hole just like that once."

"Yes, Sir, Lieutenant."

"But it was a bigger hole, if I recall." He smiled at the memory.

"And the locker assignment?"

"We should be able to work something out," nodded Crawford. He rolled his chair around to the computer and typed something on his computer. Waiting for a fresh screen to pop up, he took another bit of yogurt. He typed some more and waited a moment. "Neal is E-A-L or E-I-L?"

"N-E-A-L," replied Pridemore.

"Two L's in Parnell?"

"Yes. I really appreciate this, Lieutenant. There's no one else I could go to."

"Not at all." Crawford stabbed at the keyboard a few more times, then wrote down Parnell's new locker number and combination on a napkin. Folding the napkin in half, he slid it across the desk to Pridemore.

"Thanks, Jerry," Pridemore said, standing.

Crawford cleared the computer's screen and picked up his yogurt again. Spooning some peach yogurt into his mouth, he said, "No problem at all. You take care of Parnell. You and I both know how tough that can be."

"I will. Thanks."

Lt. Crawford waved his plastic spoon.

The first call out of the box that night was a Noise Complaint from an old woman on Unger Street. According to the Call Narrative on their screen, Mrs. Wiederhorn had heard some "strange sounds" from the next apartment. She thought the woman upstairs was being murdered. She was afraid for the woman's safety. She had met the burly husband in the basement laundry room, and he looked "all brown and suspicious." Teddy Hoatlin and Flex Sinclair stood in the bathroom of Mrs. Wiederhorn's darkened apartment and listened for the mysterious sounds. Flex could hear Mrs. Wiederhorn's labored breathing but not much else.

"Hear that?" she said, nudging Hoatlin.

"Shhh!" Flex hissed at her. He could just barely hear a creaking sound and a distant voice, filtering down through a ceiling vent.

"That goes on all the time," Mrs. Wiederhorn told them. "But it's worse tonight."

"What's she saying?" Hoatlin whispered to Flex.

"Shhh!"

"It sounds like he's strangling that poor girl," suggested Mrs. Wiederhorn. She picked at a little handkerchief in her hands.

"Shhh," said Flex. He pushed Hoatlin and the old lady out of the cramped little bathroom and closed the door. In the darkness, he could hear the cries from the strangler's apartment above.

"Oh Baby. Oh Jelly. Oh Baby. Oh Jelly."

Flex shook his head. Jelly?

"Oh Jelly. Oh baby. Oh Jelly Baby!"

Flex opened the door. "You check it out. Tell me what you think."

Hoatlin took his turn in Mrs. Wiederhorn's dark bathroom.

"Oh Baby! Oh Jelly! Oh Baby Jelly!" The rhythm increased.

"I don't think you have to worry about that woman," Hoatlin told them when he had come out again.

"You think she's alright?" wondered Mrs. Wiederhorn, worrying her handkerchief.

"I think she's fine," said Flex.

"Don't you think she needs help?"

"No, ma'am," Hoatlin assured her. "She doesn't need any help."

"But she's . . ."

"I think they're making babies up there, Ma'am," Flex told her gently.

"Or jelly," added Hoatlin.

Mrs. Wiederhorn put the handkerchief to her mouth and turned crimson. She was too embarrassed to thank them before they left. They decided not to bother the noisy couple upstairs and headed down to the street.

"Oh Baby?" said Hoatlin. "I understand that. But Oh Jelly?"

"It's a black thing, Theodore," Flex Sinclair replied. "You white motherfuckers don't know a damn thing about pussy."

"Oh Jelly?"

Flex grinned. "You'll never understand."

Pridemore reached in and touched the driver's eyeball. Nothing. The other eye and the rest of the face were somewhere else. The redheaded girl, hanging halfway out the passenger window and wearing only panties, was Dead Right There. From the number of broken bottles inside the car, it looked like they had been having a good time. Until now. The utility pole they had struck hadn't moved much at all.

"You can cancel the ambulance," Pridemore called to Buck. "Better notify a Sergeant."

"Is that a Pontiac?" shouted Buck. "The plate comes back to a Pontiac."

Pridemore looked at the logo on the steering wheel. He thought it was an Oldsmobile. It didn't look like a Pontiac, he thought. But it was hard to tell. The glove box was twisted into the dashboard with the girl's right leg.

"I think it's an Olds!" Pridemore called out. He was surprised to see the pistol on the floor next to the dead guy's boot.

"That's Laurie Compton or Cooper or something," said Sgt. Gibson, who had come up on the passenger side to look at the girl. "Nice ass."

"There's a gun in here, Sarge," Pridemore told him.

"I think she's a pro," said Gibson. He bent down to look up into her fractured face. "*Was* a pro. Wheww!"

Pridemore snapped on a pair of gloves and hunted around for the driver's I.D. He found the Harley-Davidson wallet on a chain connected to a belt loop.

"The VIN comes back as a destroyed vehicle," said Buck.

"Well, it's destroyed now," Gibson observed.

"Shit!" said Pridemore, holding out the wallet with its badge. "This is Ralph Newly from Vice."

"Kilo?"

"Sgt. Newly?"

"Jeez!"

"This is fucked up."

"Oh, man. Look at this fucking guy, will you?"

"Kilo, man, you done fucked yourself up good now."

"*Way* fucked up."

"Jeez!"

"I better call the Lieutenant," said Gibson. "You guys get some tape up. They're gonna have some *weight* coming down here for this shit."

The ambulance arrived nonchalantly, ran strips on both the bodies to confirm what everybody already knew, and gave their names to Gibson. Pridemore put out some flares to block southbound Isabel Avenue and started filling out times, dates, names, and numbers for the Traffic Unit investigators. He duplicated it all on a notepad sheet for the I.A. investigators. Flex Sinclair parked his cruiser diagonally at the intersection to the north and met Tyler, who was stringing CRIME SCENE – DO NOT CROSS tape across the road.

"What's the fuss?" asked Flex.

"It's a company car," Buck told him.

"Oh Shit! Who?"

"Newly from Vice."

"Kilo Newly?"

"Yeah. Dead as fuck. Got a whore in the car, too."

Flex shook his head. "Newly was an asshole, but still . . ."

"Yeah."

"That's fucked up."

"You probably don't want to be here," Buck warned him, wrapping the yellow tape twice around a NO PARKING sign post.

"Yeah," said Flex. But he went in anyway, looked around at the dead Vice cop, the bottles, and the dead prostitute, and loped back to the tape line. He ducked under the tape and back to his car. "I was never here, Buck!"

"Yo," agreed Tyler.

Information from the scene raced and spread along two paths. Sgt. Gibson's cell phone call to the Patrol Lieutenant went from there to Vice, Traffic, and Internal Affairs. The Vice Sergeant, who took the call, dialed his Captain and told three co-workers. The Traffic Unit investigator called his Lieutenant, who ordered out a team to run the accident investigation. The I.A. supervisor rolled a team and dialed the Chief. Chief Pearson's home phone number was busy, because he was talking about the event with Deputy Chief Griswold, who had gotten his information from the Vice Captain. Each supervisor who got the message, fretted about it, called their superior, and engaged in a worried conference about what to do and who else to call.

On the other hand, Flex had typed "V.U. Kilo K in PIA w/ K.P. in co. car S. Isabel HBD" and fired it off to his six best friends in the Department, who send it on to a dozen more, who did the same, and so on and so forth. The message meant that Vice Unit Sgt. Ralph "Kilo" Newly had been Killed in a Personal Injury Accident with a Known Prostitute in a Department vehicle on South Isabel Street and he Had Been Drinking alcohol at the time. The Flex message went from car to car and then to Precinct house to donut shop to cops' home phones to friends and co-workers.

# MAD BADGES

When Deputy Chief Griswold personally telephoned the Records Unit Night Clerk to get a copy of prostitute Laurie Louise Compton's criminal history, he found that the clerk had already heard the story from a janitor. Press photographers at the scene knew the ugly details before the Traffic Unit investigators had arrived. Someone's call woke up Newly's ex-wife, Tanya, in Albuquerque, New Mexico. Tanya laughed out loud and opened a can of beer to toast her ex-husband's rotten memory. Someone else called Newly's ex-wife, Juli, in Southgate, Michigan. Juli was heard to say, "That prick deserves it." Jamie Newly, Kilo's most recent ex-wife in Berwyndale, heard the tale from a girlfriend and began planning a party to celebrate. Literally hundreds of people knew about Kilo's unfortunate end before the Fire Rescue people had even cut his body out of the Oldsmobile.

"That's no way to go," said Pridemore, standing by the unmoved utility pole.

"He was a shit-heel and a drunk," added Buck Tyler.

"That's no way for a shit-heel drunk to go," remarked Sgt. Gibson, looking over the blood, glass, and twisted wreckage.

"You'll notice that his fly is open and his dick is out," said a guy from the Morgue crew. "I'll bet she was blowing him at the time."

"Now *that's* the way to go," said Buck.

Lt. Kenneth Berke did not notice that his wife's hair was getting more and more blonde by the day. Priscilla had told him that the summer sun was lightening her hair, but Kenneth had forgotten that story. The summer was long gone, and she was still getting more blonde. With the help of her friend, Fran, from church, whose sister worked in a salon in Pollard, and with money she saved by secretly saving returnable can and bottle money, Priscilla was changing from mousy dishwater blonde to titillatingly sumptuous blonde, just like it said in the dentist office magazines. Priscilla was also squirreling away some subtle accessories, such as bright scarves and dangly earrings, which she kept hidden away in a shoe box in the laundry cupboard. She liked her new look and was enjoying the looks she was getting, both from men at church and males in the grocery store.

"I'm exercising more," she said, when someone said how much better and younger she was looking. That's what she said to people at church or whenever Kenneth was present. It was true. Kenneth had started to allow her the use of his exercise bike a couple nights a week. But when Kenneth wasn't within earshot, Priscilla would reply, "I'm not getting younger, but my husband's getting older." This was also true. It was either the stress of Command or the late hours spent at home with his paperwork and grant writing or both. She couldn't really tell anymore. She didn't really care anymore. The bright and enthusiastic Kenneth she had married was becoming a petty and ambitious bookworm, who found less and less time for her and more and more time for his silly Police Department drudgery.

There were a lot of things Kenneth Berke was failing to notice about his wife, besides her hair color. The weekly—and sometimes now monthly—sex was not as interesting, at least from her point of view, as she counted spots on the bedroom ceiling. Priscilla was making more visits to her sister's house in the afternoons and evenings. She had talked him into paying for a $30 pottery class, which she had attended religiously every Tuesday evening for months without any additional fees.

"Whose are those?" Berke had asked his wife one night when he found her applying white shoe polish to a pair of tan high heels. Priscilla had never worn heels in her husband's presence, because it made her taller than he. She had come up with one of her first lies to him that evening and had felt a horrible guilt about it for days afterward.

"I'm dyeing these for Frannie," she had said.

"Oh," Kenneth had said. "Why?"

"They go with the nursing home volunteer outfits she made." She silently cursed herself for saying "outfits" instead of "outfit."

"Uh-huh," he had said, failing to notice the slip.

"You can't wear tan shoes with a white outfit, you know."

"Kind of racy, aren't they?" he had asked absently. He got a banana from the kitchen counter and headed back to the statistical sheets waiting in his office.

You wouldn't know racy if it hit you in the head, Priscilla thought.

Michael O'Leary, the Assistant Chief Steward of the Police Union's Day Watch officers, looked troubled as he flipped through the many pages of complaints against Officer Pridemore. The papers trembled in his hands, the result of too little alcohol in his Bloody Mary breakfast.

MAD BADGES

It was getting on to eleven, and O'Leary hadn't had his three-cocktail lunch yet. He was fifty but looked seventy, as he scratched at his heavily veined nose with his shaky, plaster white fingers. His long puffy face formed a frown as he scanned the pages through his bifocals. O'Leary still had a badge somewhere under his suit, but he had been off the street longer than Pridemore had been a cop. Sitting in the waiting room of the Internal Affairs office was one of O'Leary's main activities in life. He knew all the ins and outs, the secrets and the scandals, the skeletons and the backroom politics of the Department. He had known Deputy Chief Griswold when he was a mere patrolman, sucking up to Sergeants and washing the Lieutenant's car. O'Leary had known Captains like Darcy, Maddox, and Davis when they were clueless rookies, eager to please their bosses and always ready to inform on fellow officers. He knew all those guys, even shook their hands at banquets, and hated every last one of the bastards with every fiber of his sodden Irish soul.

When Pridemore came in to the Internal Affairs office for his hearing on the Unauthorized Use of A Department Vehicle, he went to the desk and gave the receptionist his name. The woman checked his name off her list and, with a very bored look, asked him to take a seat. O'Leary was up out of his chair in a flash, surprisingly agile for such a drunken and withered man. He put a finger to his lips as he motioned for Pridemore to follow him outside. Pridemore said nothing. Everybody knew about the microphones in the waiting room. Outside in the hallway, O'Leary pumped Pridemore's hand and led him away from the security camera and the public address speaker, both of which fed sound and picture into the I.A. office. They sat at a bench in the marble-lined corridor that led to the Records Unit.

"We've got a bit of trouble here this morning, Jacko," said O'Leary, flapping the stack of papers. "That Maddox is keeping busy, isn't he? They still call him Captain Maalox down in the Precincts?"

"Yes, we do."

"Always been a rat bastard, that one. Always had it in for the working cop on the street, too. Makes you wonder how they ever got a badge in the first place, don't it?"

Pridemore nodded.

"How's Buck Tyler these days?"

"He's fine. Said to say Hello."

"He still chasing hospital nookie all over the South end?"

Pridemore smiled and nodded.

"How's Judd Christian doing these days?" O'Leary asked, taking off the bifocals and rubbing his bloodshot eyes.

"He's still in a coma," replied Pridemore. "The City's giving him grief about the insurance and the pension."

"They always do. That's their *job*. Screw the working cop and line their pockets. I hear they're giving you the same business with your leg injury. It's the way the bastards work. A damned shame what they're doing with Christian's disability though. Puts his wife in a tough spot. What's her name?"

"Elaine."

"Nice woman, that Elaine. Attractive woman, too."

Pridemore had on his game face as he nodded.

"I hear you're seeing her now and again?"

A look of shock came into Pridemore's eyes.

O'Leary put his hand on his heart. "O'Leary hears things." He made a zipper motion across his thin, pale lips. "O'Leary *tells* no one." He leaned close enough for Pridemore to smell the breakfast vodka. "I think that's nice for the both of you. They tell me you visit him in the nursing home and read to him sometimes. That's a good partner, Jacko."

Pridemore relaxed a little. He was still concerned about where a guy like O'Leary had heard the story and what a guy like O'Leary thought about the story, but he was not worried about a guy like O'Leary *re-telling* the story.

"So this morning's business is a three-parter," began O'Leary, shuffling the forms. "They've got a horseshit Out Of Uniform complaint that won't fly. They've got a Littering complaint, that old Maalox wrote himself, which probably won't fly either. There's this last one that might give us some trouble, this Failure To Report thing."

"It's an Unauthorized Use Of A Department Vehicle," Pridemore corrected him.

"Oh, yes, well there's that one, too. That could go either way. No, I'm talking about this Failure To Report. Some twerp named Berke wrote it."

"What?"

"This here." O'Leary handed him the form. "Looks like something that Maddox had his Lieutenant write up, so that all these complaints would have the same name on them. Haven't you gotten your copy yet?"

Pridemore shook his head. Berke's Failure To Report complaint stated that the above named Officer Pridemore was present at the scene of a police incident in which both abusive language and abusive racial slurs were uttered and that Officer Pridemore failed to report these violations to his superior officer within an appropriate or reasonable time after the incident, in clear violation of the MANUAL OF PROCEDURES, CONDUCT, SECTION 22, PART III, PARAGRAPH 4. To support this charge, Internal Affairs had a certified copy of a 911 tape. Pridemore searched his memory, thinking of at least a dozen such instances.

"I don't understand," he told O'Leary. "What's this all about?"

"What this is about is that the Department is trying to hang a third strike out on you, so that they can get you and your knee insurance problems off their back," replied O'Leary. "But then that's just my personal take on the thing. It's like with the Judd Christian case and the..."

"No," Pridemore interrupted. "I mean, I don't understand *this* charge."

"This? This is some rape case, I guess, where the woman's on the line with the 911 operator. The rapist bursts in and starts to have his way with her, and then you guys burst in and arrest him. Woman's name was, let's see..."

"Fothergill?"

"Yeah," O'Leary said. "Buck Tyler or somebody called the inner-city brown type suspect a 'Spic' or 'Greaser' or something. It's all recorded on the 911 tape, because the telephone was off the hook. You remember any of this?"

"Yeah," said Pridemore, "but *I* didn't call the guy a 'Greaser.'"

"No. *Buck* called him a Greaser. He's probably going to get written for that, too. But he said it in your presence, and Berke says *you* failed to properly report that Buck had violated the M.O.P. by using a racial slur."

"But *I* didn't say it. Buck did."

"I know that. But the M.O.P. states that an officer who fails to report another officer's used of abusive, sexually intimidating, racial, or otherwise insulting language is guilty of a Failure To Report. Buck will get a slip for Conduct Unbecoming A Police Officer, and you get one for Failure To Report *his* Conduct Unbecoming A Police Officer, which occurred in your presence. It's all horseshit, of course, but it's on the tape. A clear violation. Buck, when he gets his, will probably get three days off, unless it's a repeat performance, in which case he'll get more. Buck Tyler has always talked that way. Niggers, spicks, honkies, greasers, groids, white trash, all that stuff. Which is surprising if you know that Buck's first wife was black. Always talked that shit, even when he was married to that woman. I think her name was Delta or Delva or something. Anyway, Buck has always talked like that."

"Buck hates everybody," said Pridemore.

"Exactly," said O'Leary. "Fair, honest, hard-working. Hates everybody. Always has. Great guy, that Buck. But that don't help us here with this problem. This is going to be a three-in-a-row beef with you if we don't play it right. The Littering and the Uniform thing might not fly by themselves, but they'll sure look like a threesome with this thing where you gave some broad a ride to the hospital to get her teeth fixed and this thing with the 911 tape catching Buck yelling at some Mexican suspect. It's trouble, Jacko. That's what I meant."

"This sucks," Pridemore observed wearily. "Jesus, but this sucks."

"Right. What exactly did you do to get Captain Maalox so mad at you? You must have pissed in his Wheaties or something. And who is this Lt. Berke that's got it in for you? What's his deal?"

Pridemore shook his head. "They've got nothing better to do, I guess."

"Well, listen, Jacko. This thing today is a preliminary. The formal will have to be later. You dry clean your uniform and wear all your decorations to that one. Be in a month or two. The Disciplinary Board will have a hearing, conducted by at least a Deputy Chief. Today, we just got to sit there and have them read into the record your Constitutional Rights, your Garrity Rights, your rights under the Contract, and the charges. We'll find out today if they really plan on taking this *Up To And Including Termination*, three-strikes thing to the limit. You ready, Jacko?"

They stood there. Pridemore took a deep breath. They were really after his job this time. Horseshit, O'Leary had said. But the proof was on the horseshit 911 tape and the horseshit thank-you letter from Anita Gonzales with her good-as-new teeth and the horseshit palm print on the plastic cup. They were after his ass this time. Maybe O'Leary was right, that they were trying to shield the City and the Department from his insurance claims and Judd Christian's medical bills. That thought amazed him. It made him angry, very, very angry.

O'Leary thumped him on the shoulder. "Buck up, Jack Boy. We stroll in there and spit in their eye. Piss on them all."

"Yeah," said Pridemore. "Fuck-em if they can't take a joke."

"That's the stuff, Lad," said O'Leary. "A working class hero is something to be." He looked at his wristwatch. Thirty minutes to bar time. He thumped Pridemore on the shoulder again, and they opened the door to Internal Affairs.

Down there, between the spare tire and the jack, just to the left of an empty bleach bottle and an old sock, Pridemore's flashlight picked out the little purple cloth pull-string bag. The car thieves had ripped out the radio, stolen all the wheels, and broken all the windows of the Pontiac, but they had overlooked Kien Thanh's little bag. From the looks of the car, they had tried to burn it, too. It sat, stripped and rusting, behind an abandoned school bus at the railyard off of Cleveland Street. Pridemore carefully felt around inside the bag. The four tiny white and yellow elephant saddles were even smaller than he had imagined them.

"Thirty thousand dollars worth," he said, showing Becky Carpenter the shiny little stones.

"For those? You're kidding."

He explained the story to her, about the Vietnamese guy and his sick sister, the one with the bad cough. Carpenter ran the call history in their cruiser and found the names and address.

Kien Thanh and sister Tuyet, 2944 Scranton Street.

Becky stayed in the car. Pridemore knocked and waited. He could hear the sound of worried voices inside. He knocked again. Nothing. Then he remembered how they had all used the kitchen entry in back last time. He used his flashlight to pick his way through the side yard to the back door. He knocked; it opened almost immediately.

"I am looking for Mr. Thanh," he said to the tiny Asian woman.

She nodded, but said: "No say. No say." Soon there was a second face, then another and another. They look at at him on the dark step in silence. Finally a small boy stuck his head out from behind the Asian woman's skirt.

"Come in, please," said the boy.

They all moved aside as Pridemore stepped into the lighted kitchen. It still smelled of cooking and was still covered with little shoes. An elder male appeared in the far doorway and made a quick bobbing motion with his head. The old man spoke to the boy.

"My grandfather says Welcome," the boy told Pridemore. "What can we do for the police?"

"I am looking for Mr. Thanh. His car was stolen, and we found it."

The boy translated for the old man. The name didn't sound the same when the boy repeated it. The old man shook his head and replied.

"My grandfather knows of no Thanh."

"Maybe he moved. He used to live here."

The boy spoke to the old man, who kept shaking his head.

Pridemore took them back to the bedroom near the end of the hall, where he remembered the little man with his shoebox and his Polaroid of the jade stones. The room was completely different now, half a dozen sleepy faces gazing back at him. The boy asked some of the others if the name meant anything to them, but they all shook their heads. They headed back up the hallway to the kitchen. A skinny boy coughed in the bathroom.

"Mr. Thanh had a sister who coughed," Pridemore told the boy. He showed the boy Kien Thanh's name on his notepad.

The boy translated for the old man. To Pridemore's relief, the old man started nodding and explained something at length to the boy.

"Well?" asked Pridemore.

"Kien moved."

"Where?"

"My grandfather say he doesn't know."

The little Asian woman said something from across the kitchen. The old man replied, then said something to the boy.

"They do not know of this man. They only know he moved away. Where, they do not know."

"Did he leave his job?" Pridemore was asking, but the woman was speaking again, and the boy was listening to both her and his grandfather.

"They say this man move away after his sister die," said the boy.

"I see," said Pridemore. "Okay. Thanks." He backed up through the sea of shoes to the kitchen door. Several of them bowed to him. He forced a warm smile and left. Tuyet had been her name, according to the report. Pridemore could remember her useless coughing.

"How'd it go with the Chinese?" asked Carpenter, once he was back in the car.

"Vietnamese. They're gone. Disappeared. The guy's sister died, and he vanished."

"Inscrutable little pan faces," said Carpenter. "What are we going to spend the loot on, Jack old buddy?" The look he gave her, caused her to explain. "I'm kidding. Christ! You look like someone just ran over your mother with a truck."

"I just wanted it to work out better," he said, pulling away from the curb. "Fuck it. Let's go get a cup."

There were no other cruisers in the back lot when Pridemore parked behind the East & West Café. They went in through the kitchen, past Mister Chi and the Korean bakers. Becky stopped at the restroom. Pridemore went out to the front counter, where Magda poured him a fresh cup of coffee. The homely girl showed him her crooked smile.

"You look mightily pissed off tonight," Magda said.

It broke him up. His laughing made her laugh.

"Look what I found tonight," he said, gently pouring the tiny elephant saddles onto the glass display case. The light from the donut display came up through the carved stones, making their edges seem to glow. When he looked up from the little yellow and white saddles, Magda was gone. When she reappeared in the kitchen doorway, both her prettier sister, Lia, and Mister Chi were with her. Mister Chi approached Pridemore's find slowly, almost as if it frightened him. He smiled and nodded at Pridemore.

"May he touch them?" Magda asked Pridemore.

"By all means, help yourself." Pridemore stepped back from the counter and sipped his coffee.

Lia's pretty eyes shown in the light as she touched a stone with her fingertips. Mister Chi picked them up one at a time and marveled at them. He said something to Lia.

"You sell these?" Lia asked.

"No," said Pridemore.

"You steal these then?"

"No. I found them. You like them?"

"Yes," said Mister Chi.

Becky Carpenter came in, saw what they were doing, and got herself a donut, unimpressed. Magda started a new pot of coffee.

"How's this?" said Pridemore, leaning on the counter. "You take one, and you take one, and you take one, and I'll keep the fourth one." He pushed an elephant saddle toward each of them. There was a huge Korean discussion about buying or selling or trading. Lia and Mister Chi politely refused Pridemore gesture but, when he insisted, they gladly accepted his gifts. Magda added her profuse thanks. "Think nothing of it."

"Thank you, Officer Jack," said Lia. She smiled. It was the first time Pridemore had ever seen her smile, and he noticed that her teeth were as pretty as the rest of her.

"Remember. Tell no one where you got them."

They all agreed. When the bowing and thank-yous were over, Mister Chi and his prettier daughter went back into the kitchen. Ugly sister Magda put her hand on Pridemore's forearm and squeezed. He took her hand, turned it over, and placed the fourth stone in her palm. Magda squealed with delight.

"It's yours for one of these toothpicks," Pridemore said, plucking one from the little pink bowl on the counter beside the cash register. "But tell no one. Understand?"

Magda promised.

"What exactly was that all about?" Becky Carpenter asked, when Pridemore had settled into the chair across from him.

"What exactly was *what* all about?"

"You gave that shit away?"

"Just trinkets," said Pridemore. "You didn't believe all that bullshit about $30,000, did you?"

"I thought they looked kind of small," said Carpenter. "I guess they have some sort of cultural value, huh?"

"I suppose," replied Pridemore, sipping his coffee. "Inscrutable Koreans, you know."

"I thought they were Vietnamese."

"Whatever." He waved away the discussion.

When Magda brought the coffee pot around again, she filled Becky's cup first, then Pridemore's. The ugly girl paused beside Pridemore.

"My father says your coffee is free for eternity."

Becky Carpenter choked and blew coffee out of her nose.

The stop was just a routine traffic stop at first. The night before Thanksgiving Day was miserably short-staffed, and Pridemore was working alone. Neither he nor Elaine had made any big plans for Thanksgiving dinner. She said she was going to the nursing home to sit with Judd. The day before, Pridemore had visited the lifeless Judd Christian and had told him the Mystery of the Missing Jade Elephant Saddles story and related his latest troubles with Internal Affairs. Judd had only yawned reflexively at the I.A. tale, probably as bored as anybody with the latest Departmental shenanigans. Pridemore's old Plymouth had been in the shop, so he had gotten a ride with Buck Tyler, who lived not too far from the nursing home. Buck had hung around for a while, too, not so much to visit Judd Christian, whom he had never known very well, but more just to hit on the nurses, a few of whom were passably attractive.

So the traffic stop started out as an uneventful blip on Pridemore's activity log, something to do to pass the time. The Chevy had been southbound on Merritt Avenue, doing 50 in a 35, taillight out, muzzler hanging half off the back end. There were two black males in it, shifting and jumping around in the front seat. Pridemore picked them up on Boston, ran their expired plate, and followed them down to Chapman before lighting them up. When he first hit the overheads, he noticed that their tailpipe spouted a burst of smoke. While the Chevy didn't move any faster, that smoke told Pridemore that the driver had briefly hit that gas. When they finally pulled over in a restaurant parking lot at Merritt and Kendall, Pridemore saw the passenger stick both of his empty hands out the window into the cold night air. At least one of them had been through a good felony stop before. Pridemore called for back-up and played his spotlight over the car. He reached across and flicked on his passenger side spot, just to make them think he was a two-man car. Eventually, the driver put his hands out the window, too.

Hoatlin and Carpenter came from the south, passed the Chevy warily, and flipped around beside Pridemore's cruiser. Pridemore got out, watching the Chevy cautiously. He could see the two men with their hands out the windows, but wasn't sure if there was someone else crouched down in the back seat. Becky Carpenter took the curbside, shining her flashlight at the back of the passenger's head. Neal Parnell, knowing how rarely Pridemore actually made traffic stops and knowing how even more rare it was for Pridemore to call for back-up, slid up from behind and added his strobes to the already lit-up street. Pridemore checked the empty rear seat on the Chevy as he approached the driver's window. So far, so good.

"May I see your license and registration, please?" Pridemore said to the driver's from slightly behind the driver's side door.

"I left it at home, Officer," said the driver. "My insurance papers is gone, too. Somebody stoled them."

Pridemore was about to ask the driver to step out, when he heard the pounding and shouting from inside the Chevy's trunk. His sudden rearward movement alerted the others that this was no longer a routine stop. Pridemore drew his weapon and backed up quickly behind his own spotlight, where he met the shotgun-toting Parnell. Teddy Hoatlin covered from his cruiser on the left. Becky had backed up to a spot in the darkness on the right. Using his speaker, Pridemore talked the driver out, backing him up, proning him out, and cuffing him. Pridemore patted him down and deposited him in the back of Teddy's cruiser. The passenger came out the same, knowing the step-by-step procedure and not wanting to die. Once the vehicle was clear, Pridemore got the keys and carefully popped the trunk open. The third black male in the trunk had been beaten and bound up with electrical cords. He said his name was Leonard Bramble and that he owed the other guys some money for some weed, a lot of weed. They had kicked his ass and burned him with cigarettes, but he hadn't been able to come up with the money. Leonard apologized for having pissed his pants. Pridemore struggled to free him from the electrical cords, while Becky Carpenter called for an ambulance.

"I knew we shouldn't have stopped," the Chevy's driver said from the back seat of Hoatlin's cruiser.

"You'd be one dead sonofabitch now if you hadn't, Pal," Teddy told him.

The ambulance arrived and took Leonard Bramble to Central Receiving Hospital. Pridemore checked the Chevy, finding a .380 with no magazine, several blunts, and a hammer with blood on it. He called for a wrecker.

"I told him we should have taken my sister's car," said the Chevy's passenger from the back of Parnell's cruiser.

"Sure," agreed Parnell. "Friends don't let friends drive Chevies."

Sgt. Gibson arrived and had the arrests explained to him. He put in a call to the Detective Unit to roll an investigator to the hospital.

"See what you get for making one fucking traffic stop?" Gibson said to Pridemore.

"Yeah. I'll have to try this more often."

"It was a nice quiet evening," Hoatlin chimed in, "until you had to go stir up the septic tank."

After the Chevy had been transported to the South Precinct Impound Lot, Pridemore drove by the hospital to check on his victim. Central Receiving was busy as hell. Nurse Yellow Glasses told him that Leonard had a broken eardrum, but otherwise was okay. The Impossibly Beautiful Blonde From X-Ray came by with Bramble's films and stuck them on a light box on the wall. Leonard's mother arrived and thanked Pridemore for the routine traffic stop. Pridemore wished her a Happy Thanksgiving and headed back to Mercer Heights Precinct for the paperwork.

"Your third-quarter overtime stats are late," Deputy Chief Griswold barked into his telephone, irritated that almost half of his Captains had failed to provide their required reports on time. He told Captain Maddox in no uncertain terms exactly how pissed off Chief Pearson was about it, although the Chief was out of town for the week at a Community Policing Symposium in Las Vegas. Griswold lied to Maddox that, of all the Captains in the Department, only the Mercer Heights third-quarter overtime reports were late. Griswold was actually upset about not being invited to the winter conference of the Law Enforcement Professional Leadership Association being held in Miami Beach. He chewed Maddox out for a solid five minutes, then hung up on him.

"I don't see your bid specs for the Community Coordination Officers grant on my desk yet," Captain Maddox growled at Berke. "It's this sort of thing that has held up the project for so long. I can't have a right-hand man who can't pull his weight around here with the details, if you get my drift." Maddox, his guts still in flames from the Griswold scolding, was unloading on Berke in person. Maddox had told Berke to take a seat and then had towered over the Lieutenant, berrating him mercilessly. It was Berke's fault that the grant was late. It was Berke's fault that the troops were unmotivated. It was Berke's fault that the lock to Maddox's office door had grown yet another toothpick. It was actually Berke's fault that the cruisers they had were way beyond their useful life spans. It was all Berke's fault. "Do you understand what I'm saying, Lieutenant?"

"I'm not getting the field interrogation numbers or the moving violation numbers or any of the arrests-per-officer numbers that I ask you people for *weeks* ago," Lieutenant Berke reminded Sgt. Petty, Sgt. Gibson, and Sgt. Lindsey. He made them stand, while he sat at his desk, going over the reports. "I cannot tolerate this continually unresponsive attitude among my street-level supervisors. This is an organizational effort here, and you people don't seem to understand your contributions and—dare I say?—*obligations* to the overall effort.

You're falling behind on your productivity. All of you are falling behind on your employee motivational plans. The Chief and the Captain and I expect responsiveness, responsiveness, responsiveness, and not just excuses and poor attitudes from you people. If we can't count on you people to turn this thing around, we'll have to find some Sergeants who will. Am I making myself clear?" Sgt. Lindsey glanced at Gibson, who gave him a grimace. Sgt. Petty stared straight ahead, ready to be responsive.

At line-up that night, Sgt. Petty reprimanded Parnell's new rookie for not wearing his necktie. The rookie was embarrassed. Next, Sgt. Petty started in on Parnell about the lack of shine on his shoes.

"I'm sorry, Sergeant," said Parnell, "I wasn't listening. Were you talking to me?" This made Petty repeat the whole shoe polish and necktie tirade. Anything to waste Management's time, bleed their energy, and shorten their lives was okay with the cops in the back row. When it was over, Parnell just said, "Yes, Sergeant," and they all left. Pridemore thumped Parnell on the back. Buck Tyler and Becky Carpenter welcomed the rookie to Hell.

"You're coming right along, Neal," Hoatlin told Parnell.

"I'm learning," replied Parnell.

"We're going to have to teach him the secret handshake," Flex Sinclair said.

Rosella Ayala's grandson was hanging in the closet next to his parrot shit green hostess gown. Alberto had been mixed up his whole life, a cross-dresser since his teens. He had left a stack of neatly lettered farewell cards on white orchid stationary atop the bedside table. Rosella had been unable to cut through the television coaxial cable that he had used. She had phoned her neice, who had dialed the 911 operator, who had sent Buck Tyler, Jack Pridemore, and an ambulance. Before everyone had arrived, Rosella spread out a dozen or more crucifixes and rosaries around the door to Alberto's closet. Then she had washed his feet with her long gray hair. She was just finishing up, when the cops burst in. They swept aside the crosses and the old woman. With Pridemore holding the knees and Tyler grappling with the shoulders, the ambulance guy sliced the coaoxial cable. Dead

MAD BADGES

Alberto and the cops fell to the floor. The ambulance guy unknotted the cords around Alberto's throat and banged Alberto hard in the chest. The dead Albert surprised them all when he farted and kicked Pridemore in the head. Tyler looked down as Alberto started to gasp. Amazing! Even the ambulance crew was impressed. Rosella fell to her knees in prayer. They packed Alberto aboard the ambulance to Mount Mercy.

"Can you beat that?" said Buck. "Kicked in the head by a dead faggot. What other job in the world could you have where you'd get kicked in the head by a dead faggot? I ask you."

"Don't repeat that," said Pridemore, rubbing the side of this head.

"You okay?"

"Yes. Just don't repeat that, alright?"

"Okay," Buck lied.

"He's going to be a really retarded dead faggot, too, if we don't get him to Mercy E.R. in a hurry," said one of the ambulance guys.

"Go!" shouted Pridemore. "We'll bring the family."

"Go!" said Buck. "I'll bring him a spare dress."

The ambulance howled up Bendix Avenue.

Rosella Ayala's priest and neice arrived. When she told them that dead Alberto was alive, they comforted her, thinking it was only the ramblings of an old woman. It took Pridemore a few moments to convince them that Alberto had actually breathed and that he was on his way to the hospital. They all packed into the cruiser, Pridemore driving and Rosella mumbling prayers, and headed north. Rosella's neice said it was not meant to be. Alberto was not meant to die before Christmas, which was his birthday. The priest said it was a divine intervention. Rosella prayed all the way to the Emergency Entrace behind Mount Mercy. Buck jumped out and opened the back door for them. Rosella, her neice, and the padre went inside.

The ambulance guy stopped by the cruiser and told them Alberto would probably live. There did not appear to be much brain damage. Buck thanked him and got started on the report.

Rosella's priest came back out to the cruiser and spoke to Pridemore.

"Mrs. Ayala wanted me to tell you how sorry she is that her grandson kicked you," the priest told him. "Does that make any sense?"

"Yes," Pridemore replied. "But tell her it's no problem at all. Tell her, good luck."

"Luck has nothing to do with it, Officer."

"Whatever," Pridemore replied. "You know what I mean."

"I know what you mean," said the priest. "Thanks again." He went back inside.

"Kicked by a dead faggot," Buck remarked. "That's some weird shit."

"Yup," said Pridemore, chewing his toothpick thoughtfully. "It's been a weird shit week this week."

It *had* been a weird shit week. The City had suddenly agreed to the terms of the Police Union's suit, awarding him work comp pay, giving him back his lost vacation time, and compensating him for all his medical bills for the knee surgery and rehab. The City had also taken care of Judd Christian's medical expenses, six figures worth, and had surprised Elaine with a hand-delivered check. Elaine, like Rosella's priest, thought it was divine intervention. Jack thought it was more likely the devil's hand. Either way, the shadow of debt and fret and worry had lifted. Suddenly Jack and Elaine were golden, and they didn't know why.

"Why? You want to know WHY?" Deputy Chief Griswold's fist came down hard on the stack of papers on his desk.

"But I thought they were very reasonable complaints, Sir," Captain Maddox said, picking up the Internal Affairs reports where Griswold had thrown them on the gray carpet.

"They're nothing, Captain! They're bullshit!"

"But I . . ."

"The Chief sent me a copy of a goddamned three-page letter he got from Reverend Roy Bramble." Griswold waved the letter in the Captain's face. "Do you know who Reverend Roy Bramble is, Captain?"

"I understand he's with the Urban . . ."

"The Right Reverend Roy Bramble," interrupted Griswold, "is the goddamned *Chairman* of the goddamned Inter-Urban Council, Captain. The *Chairman*, mind you! He's the goddamned voice of the goddamned minority community in this city, and he's thanking the Police Chief. On paper! In a letter! With a copy to the goddamned *newspaper*! Do you know why, Captain?"

Maddox opened his mouth but never got out a word.

"Why?" continued the Deputy Chief. "Because this officer of yours somehow found Bramble's son, Leonard, in the trunk of a goddamned car and saved him from a kidnapping and probably a goddamned murder. That's why! You can't buy that kind of public relations with a million dollars, Captain. You can't work that kind of hat trick with the minority community with all the grant money in the world. You also can't have a hero in the Department whose goddamned Captain keeps writing him up for chickenshit Littering complaints and chickenshit uniform violations. It's bullshit."

"Pridemore made a routine traffic stop," Maddox tried to explain.

"And it turned into a gold mine for the Chief's office!" snapped Griswold. "You can't have a hero in your Department who had to sue the City for medical payments. You can't have a hero in your Department who is getting written up for helping a Mexican woman to the hospital in his cruiser. You can't have a hero in your Department whose ex-partner is lying in a coma while his wife fights the City for insurance bills."

"But..."

"But *you're* not getting the big picture here, Captain. The big picture is this. The Chief and I think that you somehow just pulled these complaints OUT OF YOUR ASS! And the Chief and I would be very pleased if you would just put them back up your ass where they belong."

"But," stammered Maddox, "I just..."

"Is that goddamned clear, Captain?"

"Yes, Sir."

"I don't need to draw you a goddamned map, do I, Captain?"

"No, Sir."

"And you'll need to write him up for a citation," added Griswold.

"Who?" asked Maddox, his stomach turning into a volcano.

"Your officer there. Uhhh? Pridemont."

"Pridemore."

"Pridemore, yes. You write a nice, professional, first-rate letter for the man, and have it on my desk Monday morning?"

"Monday is New Year's, Sir," said Maddox.

"Tuesday then," said the Deputy Chief. "First thing Tuesday morning."

"Yes, Sir."

"A really professional letter, something the Chief could read at a press conference, if he needs to. Understand?"

"Yes, Sir."

"And, Pat?"

"Yes?" Maddox asked hopefully.

"You look like shit, Pat. You really ought to see a doctor or take a vacation or something."

"Yes, Sir. And thank you."

"That is all, Captain," said Deputy Chief Griswold.

And Patrick Maddox knew that it was time to get out.

Buck Tyler stood by the drinking fountain and watched the approaching blonde skirt. You didn't see that much anymore, he thought. She was in her thirties, he judged, but petite as a colt and healthy as a horse. When she stretched or bent, he could just glimpse the hem of a lace slip under the little dress. He sucked in his gut as she got nearer and smoothed his reddish gray moustache with his great left paw. She was carrying a green plastic watering can, tending to all the potted plants and flowers in the lobby. She had a tendency to open her eyes wide and make an "O" with her lips as she concentrated on the watering. Her tiny fingertips balanced the nozzle of the watering can as she tried to give every thirsty plant the right amount of attention. She also had a tendency, Buck noticed, to place her little white high heels and her little white pantyhosed knees together as she arrived at each plant. She bent at the knees, always making that charmingly modest sweep of her skirt with her free hand, tucking her skirt beneath her. It was a delicate process, that graceful hand across the narrow buttocks and down the backs of her thighs. Buck would have loved to help her with that. When she got to the Chinese Elm closest to him, he mustered up the courage to speak.

"Excuse me, but have you got the time?"

Her eyes came up to meet his. On the way up, they caught sight of the watch on Buck's hairy left wrist. A very slight smile crossed her lips as she looked first at his face and then at his wrist and then at his face again. To him, it seemed as if she was giving his groin the once-over. This could go either way, he thought. Good or bad. He was encouraged by that hint of a smile. He tried a smile in return.

"Your watch says four-thirty," she told him without the merest flicker of recognition that he was coming on to her. Her eyes strayed upward from the hairy wrist to the thickly muscled forearm to the broad shoulder. He brought his large, rough hand up to his rough, weathered face and smoothed his thick moustache again. She liked that hand.

"Are you a nurse?" Buck Tyler asked, his tone one of earnest innocence.

"No," she replied, surprising him. "I'm a volunteer."

"Oh, I see." He *prayed* that she was a volunteer at heart.

"May I help you?" She absently played with the collar of her candy-striper's dress, inadvertently exposing some freckles and a tiny mole on her neck. He imagined that the freckles went all the way down in a warm and meandering path to her pantyhose. It was making Buck crazy.

"I'm waiting for my friend," was all he could think to say. Normally not at a loss for words, Buck was finding himself tongue-tied with this little blonde doll.

"You're a police officer, too?" she asked.

"Why yes, I am. How'd you know that?"

"I've seen you here before with Officer Pridemore." She watered the Chinese Elm generously. "Too bad about his partner."

"Yes," scrambled Buck, trying to think fast. "He was a good cop."

"Do you work with Officer Pridemore?" she asked.

"Yup. Just about every night."

"Then maybe you know my husband, Lieutenant Berke." As soon as she said it, she could see the clouds of disappointment crossing his face. She had seen it before, the pain and disappointment that came with the mention of Kenneth's name. She wished she could have taken it back. Things had been going so well up to that point. "You don't look very pleased."

"Well, Mrs. Berke," Buck stammered, "I didn't realize. I was going to ask you where I could get a cup of coffee around here." He felt dumb. He felt betrayed by those strong little thighs and those pretty knees. He wanted to become invisible.

"There's coffee in the nurses' lounge," she said. She lowered her head, but raised her large eyes to his, giving him her best up-from-under look and trying to repair the damage she had done by the mention of Kenneth's name. She put down the green watering can.

"Am I allowed in there?" Buck asked, hoping against hope.

"Sure," Priscilla said, "*if* you go with me."

And then it happened. To his surprise, she put out her fragile little hand into the huge rough palm of his left hand and turned to lead him to the nurses' lounge. To her surprise, his giant hand enclosed hers with the utmost gentleness and even the hint of a squeeze. She pulled, but he didn't budge. Priscilla turned back to him.

"You're sure this is okay?" Buck Tyler asked, still not quite certain he was touching her.

"*Sure* I'm sure," she replied and smiled. She squeezed Buck's hand, letting him know she was pulling him along and not pulling away from him.

"My name's Jim." He could smell the fragrance of her hair. He realized that from this height he could probably peek down the front of her dress, but he didn't.

"I'm Priscilla," she said. "Do you like this outfit, Jim?"

"I love that outfit," he gulped, quickly adding, "if you don't mind me saying so."

"I don't mind at all," she replied.

She pulled him toward the nurses' lounge, and he followed eagerly, neither of them quite sure where all of this was leading. At the end of the hallway, they turned. He let go of the little hand to open the door for her and saw that no one was inside the lounge. She stopped in the doorway, under his arm, and looked up at him.

"So you work the *Night* Shift?" she asked.

New Year's Eve Night Shift was the usual madhouse of drunks hitting their wives and drunks hitting their husbands, while other drunks shot each other, and still more drunks drove into fire hydrants, parked cars, and other drunk drivers. The emergency rooms of both Mount Mercy and Central Receiving were jammed and busy. A South Precinct cop got shot at, but the cops there caught the gunman and kicked his ass. A drunk in Metro crashed into one of their cruisers, and they kicked his ass, too. The downtown lock-up was filled to capacity, and the Jail personnel were suggesting a Beat & Release policy for the street cops. The easiest way to deal with drunk drivers in between your gun calls, stabbing calls, and domestics, was to whip their car keys into the snow and call them a cab.

The East & West Café was closed for the night, so Pridemore couldn't even stop by for a cup of eternally free coffee. Becky Carpenter got bit by a psycho in the stairwell of 1421 Woodruff. Flex

Sinclair managed to completely and permanently blow out the transmission of old 1710 on a short chase up Summit Avenue. Gunderson came out to photograph the scene of a double shooting behind The Marble Room as Buck Tyler and Teddy Hoatlin guarded the tape. By sunrise, the exhausted city fell quiet, its bottles and bodies covered with a light snowfall. The ragtag Third Watch of Mercer Heights dragged themselves into the locker room and turned the whole miserable shitstorm over to the fresh cops from Day Shift.

Pridemore made it home in time for Elaine to make him a bowl of hot soup. She asked about his night and massaged his aching shoulders. He talked again about possibly switching to Day Watch. She kissed him and playfully mussed his hair.

"You always say that, Jack."

"I'm getting too old for Nights," he replied.

Captain Patrick Maddox looked like a poster boy for Irritable Bowel Syndrome when he arrived at the Mercer Heights Precinct parking lot. The pain and itch of hemorrhoidal tissues were jockeying with his acid reflex and enlarged prostate gland to see which of them would dominate his life that day. You couldn't have a decent bowel movement if you couldn't stand to eat anything more than oatmeal, and you couldn't eat anything if nothing was coming out the other end. Maddox was stuck, plugged, and ornery. He had fallen on the ice in his driveway that morning, but somehow had managed not to fracture his spine or blow out a knee. He had managed to rip his pants, which necessitated him going back inside to change his suit again, from the integrity blue with the muted stripes to the gray wool blend. His son, coming in from a two-day drunk, had once again told his dad how much he despised him, and Sandra Maddox had picked this morning, of all mornings, to announce that she was taking a three-week trip to Europe. So Patrick Maddox was in *no mood* that morning.

Among the bundle of administrative paperwork in his briefcase that morning was the letter Deputy Chief Griswold had told him to write about Officer Pridemore. It had almost killed him to write it, made him sick just thinking about it. Here was this worthless, lazy street cop, a virtual nobody in the Department, making a very routine traffic stop, when he hardly ever bothered to make traffic stops before, and by doing so he had managed to sidestep all of the perfectly legitimate

Internal Affairs complaints about his poor performance, had managed to endear himself to both the Chief's office and the minority community, and had put Maddox's career and digestive tract in a bind. It was simply not fair. More than that, it was criminal. For the length of his professional life, Maddox had battled guys like that, guys who always cut the corners, guys who bent the rules and didn't give a damn about The Book. You had to have The Book or you'd have chaos. You had to have procedures, or you'd find yourself running an army of layabouts and barbarians. If not for the Manual of Procedures, you'd have yourself a gang of mad badges stampeding all over the City, stirring up problems for Internal Affairs, the Chief's office, and the Community Affairs Unit. No, you couldn't run a professional law enforcement operation that way. Couldn't be done. There had to be The Book. Without The Book, there was nothing. And Maddox hated those uniformed guys who couldn't understand such simple logic.

Someone had left a cruiser in his parking spot, which he hated but had gotten used to. He stepped out onto the slush-covered parking lot, the cold gray slop oozing into the seams of his shoes, and opened the back door to his Precinct. He would have to put that twirp, Berke, on the trail of whatever prick left the cruiser in his spot, Maddox thought. Stamping the snow off his shoes, he encountered that blatant suck-up, Sgt. Petty, in the first floor hallway.

"Good morning, Captain," Petty said brightly.

"Morning, Sergeant," said Maddox. "Move that car out of my parking spot, will you? One of the troops apparently can't read the sign."

"Right away, Sir," replied Petty smartly.

Idiots everywhere. Nothing but idiots, thought Maddox. The elevator was on the blink again, naturally, so he took the stairs, hardly glancing at the uniforms that passed him. He paused to rest at the top of the steps, angry with the elevator, angry with his lungs, and angry with the arrogant Griswolds of the world. By the time he had reached the third floor, having mercifully avoided Lt. Berke and any of the other building toadies, Maddox was out of breath. His chest heaved; his butt ached. What else could go wrong? He fished his keys out of his pants and pushed the office key into his door. Halfway into the lock, it stopped dead.

All of the helpless rage boiled over. Without even taking his key from the door, he dropped his briefcase, drew his service weapon, and fired at the offending lock. In the silence and smoke following the explosion, Maddox heard himself saying, "Nooooo!"

The guts. The guts. The guts. He dropped the gun and staggered back against a file cabinet. Oh, *not* the guts. The bullet hole was just about at his belt. He could already feel something going terribly wrong in his intestines. The report from the Medical Examiner would later explain that the damage done by the ricocheting bullet was not in itself a fatal wound, but that the deceased had died of a heart attack as a result of the shock. He clutched at the gray wool blend cloth around the wound. He plucked at the tie that was choking his breath. He didn't fail to notice that the dented lock on his door still held, toothpick and all, barring him from his own office. Reeling about, he looked like a madman who was simultaneously trying to rip all the clothes off of his chest and stuff them into his stomach. The guts. The guts. *Not* the guts. When it was all over, Captain Patrick Maddox went down like a tree, sprawling onto the briefcase full of administrative paperwork.

Lt. Berke came out into the third-floor corridor, a stapler still in his hand. He would later tell Internal Affairs that he first thought someone had left a pile of dirty laundry outside the Captain's door.

Jack Pridemore was pouring himself a glass of ice water from the little blue plastic pitcher that the nursing home staff kept filled at Judd's bedside, while he related the story of Captain Maddox. Judd's blank eyes had opened and shut, opened and shut, mindlessly ignoring the tale. Pridemore had told him about all the Internal Affairs complaints suddenly going away and about Neal Parnell making Sergeant's stripes. But when he got to the part about Maddox shooting himself in the stomach, Judd Christian's mouth opened, and he made a sputtering sound. There was a wheeze, almost like the sound of some weird laughter, and then the whole face went slack. The nurse, who first got there and checked Judd's pulse, put her hand on Pridemore's arm and said, "It's for the best."

"I know," Pridemore replied, but he was crying. Elaine, who had just stepped out to stretch her legs, knew exactly what was wrong when she opened the door. They held each other until the doctor arrived to make it official.

"He's gone," the doctor told them. "It's all for the best."

Elaine nodded. She had cried out her supply of tears a long time ago. Pridemore tried, but could think of nothing to say.

It's all for the best," the doctor said again. "The pain is over."

Lt. Jerry Crawford was typing away at his home computer, chatting with a teenage hacker in Denmark. Together they were designing a worm virus that would invade a third party network firewall and work its way into secured text files. The kid in Denmark thought it would be cool if the virus changed whatever text files it attacked into lines of lyrics from the Sex Pistols. Crawford, who wanted his last day on The Job to be more memorable, opted instead for a virus that changed *all* the words in any text file with the phrase "*up to and including suspension*" to the words "*everything not prohibited is compulsory.*" They worked late into the night.

At the Department's Annual Awards Banquet, Chief Pearson stood up in his ill-fitting dress uniform and thanked everyone for being there. Deputy Chief s Griswold and Forrest sported tailored dress blues with their hat bills clear of fingerprints or unsightly smudges. Rona Buckley, the bony cunt from City Hall, sat at the Chief's table, ignoring the fact that no one was talking to her. Professor Lindstrum was in Tulsa, Oklahoma, giving a speech called "Community Policing and Metropolitan Entropy," and had not been able to attend. Captains Davis, Brandt, Nettleton, Jasper, Zane, Taylor, and Torres all sat at their own tables, gossiping with their various underlings and applauding loudly whenever one of the people under their command received an award. Deputy Chief Griswold stood and delivered a short heartfelt speech about the late Captain Maddox and his many and various contributions to the Department. Sgt. Ralph "Kilo" Newly was mentioned for his on-duty death "during an undercover Vice operation."

The press photographer got a picture of Griswold giving the Civilian Employee of the Year award to a Record Units clerk who no one had ever heard of. The Channel 5 cameraman caught Chief Pearson handing the Police Officer of the Year Award to a Detective who had actually *solved* one of The Marble Room parking lot murders. Channel 9 interviewed the Chief and Captain Darcy. Darcy was trying to say that the patrol cop was the backbone of the Department, but stumbled on the words and said "back side" instead.

Sgt. Petty swelled with pride as he stepped up to the stage, accepting Neal Parnell's Combat Cross, apologizing that, "Neal is on vacation." When he accepted Pridemore's Honorable Mention Award for the traffic stop and subsequent arrest of Leonard Bramble's kidnappers, Petty lied and said Pridemore was on vacation, too. It was all over with for another year, what with the drinks and desserts and back-slapping, only the most ambitious Lieutenants staying to the bitter end. Petty sat looking at the awards on the linen tablecloth and ordered another drink from the black waiter, who discretely spit in the glass first before pouring it.

Sgt. Parnell was sitting with Flex Sinclair, Teddy Hoatlin, Becky Carpenter, and Carpenter's new rookie in the East & West Café. The homely Magda served their coffee and listened to Becky tell the one about the time Pridemore drove the Hot Rod Kid in the Buick into a dumpster on South Sloan. Magda was wearing her newest "I Go For Guys in Chevy pickups" T-shirt, still hoping Teddy would notice her. When Carpenter's war story was over, the rookie asked a stupid question about Department policy, and everybody just stared at him wearily.

Pridemore was getting his back scratched. Elaine was talking about their future. Pridemore said he was seriously thinking about going to Day Watch for his final year on The Job.

The desk clerk at the Berwyndale Motor Inn looked at the apparently healthy "James Tyler" as he checked in, wondering exactly why he needed the little blonde nurse.

Acting-Captain Kenneth Berke's office looked nothing like it had when the late Patrick Maddox had occupied it. The old photographs from the policeman's ball had been replaced by softer, gentler images of icy waterfalls, autumn landscapes, and a large, graceful photograph of a white tulip that Priscilla had bought for him. He had sent the curtains out for dry cleaning and had replaced the ragged Old Glory and the worn-out City banner with newer flags. Gone were the glass-topped desk and the wood-grained accessories, all of it replaced with clean wheat-colored metal furniture. The Placards of Merit and the Certificates of Attendance were arranged in orderly rows along the left wall. The closet held his dress blues and three white Commander's shirts, which he knew he would only wear for press conferences or police funerals. The door lock had been replaced with a card key system. The new Captain kept the card in a little clip next to the new pagers on his belt. The extra pager, with its direct connection to Chief Pearson's office, had made it necessary for Berke to slide his new gold badge further to the right and transfer the holster all the way around to the left side, an arrangement that balanced better under his new suits.

The engraved pen and pencil set, presented to him by Deputy Chief Forrest, sat on his desk, neatly aligned with the calendar blotter and the new 18-button telephone. Deputy Chief Griswold had sent him a gold pencil box with the City logo on it, along with a gracious card of congratulations from Griswold and his wife. The newer, faster computer they had given him rested on its own brushed metal stand next to his desk. The brand new high-speed laser printer, which sat on a separate little brushed metal stand, was not working yet, because the City hadn't sent over the proper connecting cables. Kenneth, Jr. had drawn him a picture of a cowboy on a frightened horse shooting a rattlesnake and was proud that his dad had found a place for it on his desk. The clean metal credenza between his chair and the window held an artificial flower arrangement, a family portrait, and a photograph of Berke standing between Deputy Chief Griswold and Captain Darcy at the last Chief's conference.

Berke had ordered new copies of Wainright's "Management Strategies in the Modern Police Environment," "Non-Linear Modeling in Police Theory and Organization" by Siegel and Jennsen, which Kenneth felt he understood now, and the latest edition of "Conscientious Discipline in Public Administration" by Dr. J. K. Fletcher. They sat on the brushed metal shelf next to a leatherbound Commander's Copy of the Department's Manual of Procedure. He had moved all of his back issues of the American Law and Law Enforcement Association's Journal from his home office to Mercer Heights and had put a new stair-stepper exercise machine in their place. His latest argument with Priscilla had been about the stair-stepper and how she had used it without putting the climb-rate dial back to his strength setting.

The new Acting-Captain had started out the day, addressing the troops down in the basement Squad Room, telling them about his plans for an employee empowerment program, a suggestion box protocol, and his open-door policy. They seemed at least a little more enthusiastic, Berke felt. He was excited about the motivational opportunities that had opened up to him. Things would be different now that the "old boss" methodologies of Captain Maddox were gone. Berke had arranged individual meetings with all of the Sergeants of Mercer Heights, including Sgt. Petty, whom Berke considered management material, and new Sgt. Parnell, whom Berke did not trust. He told them about his carrot & stick discipline plan and his open-door policy, then he had closed his office door with its new card key lock. All in all, Berke felt the transition to his style of multi-faceted management was going well.

The telephone buzzed. Acting-Captain Berke slipped a mint into his mouth and answered the call.

Officer Jack Pridemore peeled out of the Mercer Heights Precinct lot in the filthy Ford cruiser. He swung west on Maynard, which had already been plowed, and then south on Trowbridge, down through the projects, the barrio, and the hood. Down into The Depths of Nights in The Heights. Teddy Hoatlin was squirming around in the passenger seat, trying to get used to his new vest. They turned west again onto the slush of Perez Street.

"Did you hear about the Captain's new dress code policy?" asked Hoatlin. "He wants us to start wearing our whistles."

"The gold little ones?"

"Yeah, those little toy whistle things."

"I don't know if I even still have mine," said Pridemore, reaching down to check the car radio's volume. He crossed Filmore, Liberty, Bendix, and Racine.

"Where does Command find the time to think up bullshit like that?" Hoatlin wondered aloud.

"I guess they've got nothing better to do," replied Pridemore.

At the corner of Perez Street and Denton Avenue, Pridemore spotted Cynthia Jester out working her corner again in the cold night. Her purple parka and red boots really didn't go with the black fishnet stockings. The old cop waved. The old whore waved back.

* * *